Risk

ANN CHRISTOPHER

Kensington Publishing Corp.

http://www.kensingtonbooks.com

DAFINA BOOKS are published by

Kensington Publishing Corp.
850 Third Avenue
New York, NY 10022

All Kensington Titles, Imprints, and Distributed Lines are available at special quantity discounts for bulk purchases for sales promotions, premiums, fund-raising, and educational or institutional use. Special book excerpts or customized printings can also be created to fit specific needs. For details, write or phone the office of the Kensington special sales manager: Kensington Publishing Corp., 850 Third Avenue, New York, NY 10022, attn: Special Sales Department, Phone: 1-800-221-2647.

Dafina and the Dafina logo Reg. U.S. Pat. & TM Off.

ISBN-13: 978-0-7582-1434-8
ISBN-10: 0-7582-1434-0

First Dafina mass market printing: February 2007
10 9 8 7 6 5 4 3 2 1

Printed in the United States of America

To Richard

Acknowledgments

I can't thank the following people enough:

My agent, Sha-Shana Crichton, who has a seemingly endless supply of tenacity and supportive words at the right time;

My editor, Sulay Hernandez, who graciously helped me whip the book into shape at the last minute;

Magistrate Rogena Stargel of the Hamilton County, Ohio Probate Court, who patiently answered my many questions about the guardianship process;

Gupreet "Rosie" Thind, M.D., the pediatrician extraordinaire who answered my medical questions; and

Eric Bertelsen, R.Ph., who answered my drug questions.

Ann Christopher

Intimacy requires courage because risk is inescapable.

—Rollo May

Prologue

Ten Years Ago

He had to find her, and soon.

A quick glance at his watch told him what his knotted gut already knew: his precious little bit of remaining time continued to sprint past like Carl Lewis at the Olympics. The wedding reception hummed along at full speed and Justus Robinson had survived enough of these gigs in his seventeen years to know how they worked: dinner, then cake and dancing, then the throwing of various silly items, then everyone split. The chattering, overdressed crowd had already swilled their gourmet dinner like starving pigs at a trough, so he figured they'd slice the cake any second. His frustration grew. With each tick of his watch he felt chances slipping away, opportunities evaporating; magic vibrated in the air tonight and he meant to take full advantage of it. If only he could find her.

"Nice party, man."

Justus turned to see Brian Henderson saunter up, his tan face flush with excitement. Justus grunted, unbuttoned his tuxedo jacket, shoved his hands in his pants pockets, and leaned against the nearest marble pillar. "I guess."

The place did look beautiful, he thought grudgingly. Glittering crystal chandeliers lit the gilded, ornate art deco carvings on the walls and ceiling. Tall candles on taller candlesticks flickered on the tables, so that pruned Aunt Martha over at table five—for tonight, at least—glowed like Halle Berry. In the middle of every white-clothed table sat a bowl or urn or some such glorified dish crammed with enough pink and white flowers—fragrant roses and lilies—to stock a florist shop for a month. Justus couldn't get over the waste. By morning every one of those flowers would droop, and by tomorrow evening this time they'd be nothing but a distant, expensive memory.

Brian leaned against the other side of Justus's pillar and tugged at his bow tie. "Your dad sure can spend some money," he said, raising his voice over the sound of the Mozart-playing string quartet ten feet away in an alcove.

Justus's jaw tightened. "You have no idea."

He knew, even if Brian didn't, that his father engineered this whole blowout to demonstrate to Cincinnati's elite—black, white, and otherwise—that he'd arrived and planned to stay for a good long while. The old man should have just handed out copies of his bank statement and been done with it. Then he could have donated the $75K he reportedly spent on this overblown party to the Boys & Girls Club or something else worthwhile. He scanned the crowd and saw his beaming brother, holding his new wife's hand, accepting congratulations from an elderly man at a table across the room. V.J. looked happier than he'd ever seen him, and he was glad for that. But his father's corresponding smugness pissed him off.

"Anything for V.J. Nothing's too good for the crown prince."

Brian rolled his eyes. "Don't start."

Justus sulked for a moment in silence. Predictably, his

father had spared no expense in his ongoing efforts to impress his "friends." Tuxedoed men and perfumed and primped women strutted past like peacocks on parade; if he lived to be a thousand he would never understand his father's obsession with all things expensive and ostentatious. Cincinnati's finest—including the mayor, two federal judges, and a local TV anchor—had bellied up to their tables and chowed down on lamb chops, rare beef tenderloin, and rarer yellowfin tuna as if it'd been their last meal for the week.

Several of the guests now hovered around the cake table where a seven-tiered monster teetered under still more roses and lilies. Bartenders at the three open bars poured alcohol like they meant to empty every bottle in the place; every fifteen seconds on the clock another waiter marched past with a tray full of fizzing champagne flutes. The scent of coffee flavored with chicory filled the air. On the tables good-sized boxes of Godiva truffles waited for the guests to claim on their way home, not that anyone would think of leaving before the liquor ran out. It was, Justus decided, the most ridiculous display of conspicuous consumption he'd ever seen his father stage, and he'd seen plenty.

"Where's Carla?" Brian asked.

"She went to the bathroom. No telling when she'll be back." Justus focused for the first time on Brian's blond hair, which stuck up all over his head like a rooster's comb. "What the hell's wrong with your hair?"

Brian grinned and swiped his hand through it. "It's the style. Carla liked it."

"Carla ain't got no sense."

Truer words were never spoken. Carla had her uses—Justus patted his back pocket to make sure he'd remembered his jimmies—but they were pretty much limited to looking good and being eager and available. The woman he wanted so badly to find, on the other hand, intrigued him infinitely more than his date. His gaze swept the room again.

Brian's eyes narrowed suspiciously. "Who do you keep looking—" He trailed off suddenly, his body jerking to attention. Only one person in the room commanded this reaction; Justus turned to see his father approach and hold out his hand to Brian.

"Hello, Brian," Vincent Robinson said. "Welcome."

"Hello, Mr. Robinson." Brian took his hand. "Great reception."

When he saw his father's chest puff up, Justus scowled. Why didn't people ever see through his father? Was he the only person on earth who saw the old man as the frustrated, egomaniacal dictator he really was? Oh, sure, at first glance he looked perfectly normal: tall, slim, salt-and-pepper hair trimmed short and neat, dark brown skin clear and unlined, sharp eyes framed by frameless glasses, fancy silk tuxedo, and gleaming patent leather shoes. He looked exactly like what he was: a very successful civil rights attorney with his own practice.

But when he opened his mouth, well, that was where all the problems began.

"Thanks, Brian." Vincent's perfect white teeth gleamed in a wide smile. "Glad you could come." His smile faded away as he turned to Justus; his gaze flickered disapprovingly to his ears, then back to his eyes. "Hello, Justus."

Automatically Justus slouched a little more deeply against the pillar and crossed his hands over his chest. Maybe Brian didn't see the man's animosity oozing from his pores like sweat, but he sure did. "What's up, Vincent?" he said coolly.

As expected, his father's temples began to throb. It was childish, sure, to get such pleasure from something as easy as calling his father by his name, but why pass up a sure thing?

Vincent looked back at Justus's ears. "I see you wore those earrings."

While Brian stared fixedly at the cake table and pretended he'd suffered a catastrophic hearing loss, Justus fingered the two-carat round cubic zirconium studs he wore in his earlobes. He'd planned to take them out before the ceremony, but forgot in the pre-wedding excitement. Now he was glad he still wore them.

He widened his eyes into his best innocent expression. "They're not too much, are they?"

Vincent's lips thinned into invisibility. Abruptly he turned back to Brian and clapped him on the back. Brian look startled. "When do you leave for New Haven?"

Brian darted a glance at Justus. "We'll, uh, . . . you know, go on vacation first, then get there a few days before school starts."

"Some of the best days of my life were at Yale," Vincent said thoughtfully. "Vincent Junior's, too. It's where he met his wife, of course." He shot a fond smile in the direction of the newlyweds, who had moved to a nearby table. Justus saw V.J.'s worried gaze flicker briefly between him and Vincent; Justus made a show of studying his fingernails, waiting for the inevitable criticism. "I'd hoped both of my boys would go to Yale and join me at the firm, but, well . . ." Vincent shook his head ruefully.

Justus yawned hugely, refusing to take the bait.

Brian apparently couldn't let Justus go undefended. "Well, you know," he said nervously. "Xavier's a great school, and—"

Justus couldn't stand by and let Brian waste his breath. "Don't bother, man. Some people would be glad their kid got a full ride at a good school, but not Vince, here." He jerked his thumb at his father.

Vincent's head whipped back around to Justus, his face purpling. "I did *not* pay for all those years of private school for you to play basketball at Xavier University! I can't believe any son of mine has these ridiculous hoop dreams!"

Poor Brian cringed and melted away into the crowd. Justus tried to stay calm although his heart pounded with anger. He had no hoop dreams beyond college—he was nowhere near good enough for the NBA, and he knew it; he wanted to become a personal trainer with his own gym after he graduated. One day he'd tell Vincent the real deal. But not today.

"Don't worry, Old Man." On a sudden inspiration he grabbed a champagne flute from a passing waiter's tray, raised it in a mock cheer to his father, and sipped appreciatively. He rarely drank; his friends called him D.D. for designated driver. But tonight he quite enjoyed the tart, crisp taste. "When I move out in August you won't ever have to spend another dime on my butt. And when I'm drafted and get my signing bonus I'll write you a check for the $100K you've spent on my education up till now. How's that?"

Check and mate. Vincent went rigid with speechless fury; Justus wondered idly whether he'd actually lunge for him right here in front of God and everybody.

But then V.J. materialized at Vincent's elbow. "Dad? Hey, Dad?"

Vincent grunted, still staring at Justus and vibrating with righteous anger.

V.J. moved until he stood directly in front of Justus, shielding him. "Judge Meyers just asked for you. He's over there at table twelve."

Vincent blinked once or twice, as if waking from a trance. "Fine." He gave the bottom of his jacket an efficient tug, as if to brush off Justus—and any lingering after-effects of their conversation. Justus shrugged and raised the flute to his lips again. Vincent's arm lashed out and jerked the glass away, catching Justus by surprise. "No seventeen-year-old son of mine drinks alcohol in public," he snarled, then spun on his polished heel and stalked off, the champagne sloshing out of the glass and spilling over his fingers.

Without missing a beat Justus snatched a fresh glass off the tray of the same beleaguered server as he hurried by again, and took a sip.

V.J. turned to him, raising his hands palms up. "Why?" he cried. "Why do you always let him think the worst about you?"

Justus scowled. "Because he's a jerk, that's why."

"He's our father."

"He's still a jerk."

V.J. laughed suddenly and threw his arm around Justus's shoulders. "He's not so bad."

"To *you*."

"Come on." V.J. nodded toward the dance floor, where several servers wheeled the cake table. "It's time to cut the cake."

"Wait, man." Justus caught his brother's arm; this was the first second they'd had alone since the wedding, and the occasion seemed to call for a few words. He cleared away the unexpected lump in his throat. "You did good. Carolyn's great. I'm happy for you."

V.J. beamed, as light and happy as a helium balloon floating in the clouds. "Thanks. Thanks for being my best man." He pulled Justus into a bear hug so tight Justus expected to hear his ribs split with a loud crack. "I love you, man."

Justus pushed him away, perilously close to tears. "Let's not get carried away."

V.J. laughed again. "Let's go."

V.J. rocketed back to his wife's side with Justus trailing behind. A little chocolate cake would taste pretty good right now, Justus thought. He watched, bemused, as V.J. and Carolyn cut the cake and then fed each other as the guests cheered. Carolyn laughed, then turned to say something to her smiling sister Angela, the maid of honor.

And Justus froze.

There she was! His stomach tightened the way it some-times did before a big game. Recovering a little, he took his place with the jostling, laughing members of the wedding party, making sure he could still see her. While everyone else all day had gushed about the bride who, as far as he was con-cerned, resembled the meringue on top of a pie in her fluffy, lacy dress, he'd been unable to stop staring at the bride's sister.

Like all the other bridesmaids Angela wore a pale pink dress that reminded him of the dress Marilyn Monroe wore in that old movie where she stood on the subway grate so her skirt could blow up. It had a halter top and some sort of pleated knee-length skirt that left too much—way too much— of her gorgeous flesh visible. Her skin was perfectly smooth, a deep, reddish brown he desperately longed to touch and taste; he wanted to run his hands and lips all over her bare back, shoulders and arms, to have her wrap her long, shapely legs around his waist. He wanted other things, too: to bury his face between the breasts that filled the front of her dress and threatened to overflow; to squeeze the rounded butt; to clamp his hands on those curvy hips and anchor her while they made love with her on top. The gnawing ache in his gut grew.

He watched while Angela chatted and laughed with V.J, re-laxed with his brother in a way she clearly wasn't with him. His fascination with her, which grabbed him by the throat when they met yesterday at the rehearsal, made absolutely no sense. When V.J. introduced them at the church and he saw her—the heart-shaped face framed by a widow's peak, the long, gleaming, dark brown hair, the wide brown eyes tipped up slightly at the outer edges, the straight nose, the lush, bow-shaped lips—he felt like he'd been whammed in the ribs with a baseball bat.

Why couldn't he escape her gravitational pull? She was

beautiful, sure, but he'd dated—slept with—lots of beautiful girls in his short life. Her age—twenty-four—and the fact that she already had a political science degree and a year of law school under her belt intrigued him, but he didn't think that accounted for her appeal, either. The only other thing he could think of was her primness. It drew him just as surely as if she'd used a giant shepherd's hook to catch him around the waist and pull him to her. It made him want to ruffle her feathers and make her laugh.

Even though, as best man and maid of honor, they'd spent a lot of time together in the last twenty-four hours, he hadn't really had a chance to talk to her. Worse, when the reception ended later he had no idea when he'd ever see her again. So when he saw her take a piece of cake and wander back to her seat at the head table, Justus, plagued by a nagging curiosity that refused to let him go, followed her.

Angela Dennis impulsively pulled her sister in for a hug, carefully balancing her cake plate well away from Carolyn's pristine white gown. She felt absurdly pleased they'd navigated the last week without any major blowups, as if they'd jointly summited Everest and now stared down into Tibet.

"I'm so happy for you," she whispered.

Carolyn smiled beatifically. "This will be you one day. I'll be matron of honor at your wedding when you find someone as wonderful as V.J."

I doubt it, Angela thought as she let her sister go and turned away. Of course Carolyn couldn't imagine any fate more glorious for her baby sister than for Angela to follow along the path she'd blazed. But she'd had enough of following in Carolyn's footsteps for a while—she couldn't think of anything she'd ever done that Carolyn hadn't done first and better, so it was time she found her own path. If Carolyn's greatest ambition was to be a wife and mother, well, fine. Angela would be the career woman in the family. At least for the foreseeable future.

Teetering dangerously on the four-inch stiletto sandals Carolyn had picked for her attendants to wear, Angela found her place at the table, sank gratefully into the high-backed, white slip cloth-covered chair and looked self-consciously around. For the moment the long table was empty and she felt a little awkward sitting by herself, but others would join her soon. No signs of Justus, thank goodness. For reasons she didn't care to examine, Justus agitated her, and she'd decided to avoid him for the rest of the night. Angling her hips a little to the left to accommodate the table, she stretched out her tired legs, crossed them, and arranged her skirts. Hopefully the back of her dress wasn't getting too wrinkled, not that it mattered after tonight.

A movement caught her eye. Justus, with an arrested expression on his face, loomed over her like the Empire State Building. She stiffened. As she watched, his gaze traveled slowly up her legs and the rest of her body before it settled on her face. Their gazes locked and paralysis set in. Heat crept up her neck and over her cheeks, then shivered down her body. What could he want? He wasn't going to sit *here*, was he? With her?

"Hey," he said, his deep voice easily slicing through the babbling crowd and music.

"Hi," she managed weakly.

Was he raised by wolves? Without any invitation at all, he ignored all the other empty spots at the table, pulled out the chair right next to her, and sat down, putting his champagne glass on the table in front of him. His long arms and legs shrunk the table as if he'd cut it in half with a saw, and immediately her body went into heightened alert. One of his knees lightly brushed her thigh as he settled himself, and she drew up a little, resisting the urge to pick up her chair and move away.

He was very tall. If she had to guess she'd say he was at least six-four. She'd thought she'd gotten used to his size by now; after all they'd walked, arms linked, together down the aisle today. But she hadn't adjusted to his height, or the broad shoulders, or the long, long legs, any more than she could adjust if a lion moved into her apartment. She stared, her cake forgotten.

Amusement appeared in his eyes after a lengthy silence. "So . . . how's the cake?"

"Cake?"

One dark, heavy eyebrow went skyward; he laughed. "Yeah, cake. Or whatever you're calling that stuff on your plate."

Oh! Her cake! Relieved to have something else to look at besides his wide, boyish grin, she looked at her plate.

The problem with Justus, which she'd avoided diagnosing until this very second, was that he was way too attractive, especially for a teenager. His velvety chestnut skin was perfectly smooth; apparently he'd never gotten the memo about teens having acne. His short black hair grew in a straight hairline across his forehead. But his skin and hair, nice as they were, weren't the problem. No, the problem began with his hooded black eyes and climaxed with his full, sensual mouth. His straight nose she could live with. But the mischief in his eyes, the delight in his gleaming white smile, the energy he exuded like a pheromone, well, those things made it impossible for her to look him in the face for more than half a second at a time. Worse, they made her want to squirm in her seat.

Sheepishly, she picked up her fork and cut a corner of cake. "I haven't tried it yet." She shoveled it in her mouth, smearing icing on the outer corner of her lips. "Oh." The dense lemony cake dissolved on her tongue, sending a delightful rush of sugar to her head and veins. "Ummm." She smiled a little; with the tip of her tongue she licked the edge of her mouth. "It's wonderful." She took another bite.

"Because—" Justus's voice sounded a little hoarse; his face seemed strained, his eyes brighter all of the sudden, his skin flushed, but of course all these bodies moving around heated the ballroom like a furnace. He cleared his throat. "I was thinking of the chocolate."

"No," she told him. "I definitely recommend the lemon crème."

After a minute he lounged in his chair, throwing his arm over the back. "How's law school?"

She dabbed her mouth with her napkin. "I like it. And you! Playing ball at XU in the fall—you must be so excited!"

Smiling broadly, he dropped his head as if embarrassed. "Yeah."

"You're still going to get your degree, though, aren't you? Because if you get injured—"

"Absolutely." He nodded firmly. "That's the point of college, isn't it?"

"Absolutely." A flash of mutual understanding pulsed between them; they smiled. "So what do you want to do when you graduate? Do you think you'll be drafted?"

He shuddered as if being drafted into the NBA was the single worst thing that could happen to him. "No way. I want to open my own gym. Be a personal trainer."

Something told her he would be very good at it. His relaxed manner, his way with people, his athletic experience. "Yeah." She nodded her head with approval. "I think that's the perfect job for you."

"You think so?" he asked excitedly, as if she'd told him he'd make an excellent president. "Because my father wants me to be a lawyer, like him and V.J."

Angela snorted indelicately. This boy had about as much business being a lawyer as she had being an Olympic bob-sledder—anyone with two eyes could see that. "What's the world need with another lawyer?"

A slow, wide smile dawned across his face and her answering smile felt as natural as taking her next breath. His gaze strayed back to her mouth; his smile faded. "There's a little"—his hand came down from the back of his chair and, cupping her chin with his fingers, he gently brushed the corner of her lips with his thumb—"icing."

Angela jumped as if he'd pitched a kettle of boiling water at her face. Unthinkably, her skin heated with pleasure. She jerked away and wiped her mouth again. "Thanks."

Justus watched her, a terrible, speculative gleam in his eye, but said nothing.

The lights dimmed, creating a halo around the flickering candles throughout the room. Suddenly Angela felt be-witched; the food, champagne, wine, and music—the excite-ment in the air converged and crystallized into an enchanted world where anything seemed possible. She sighed breath-lessly, a half-smile on her lips. Over on the dance floor, V.J. and Carolyn took their places under the spotlight, and the jazz combo started playing "When I Fall in Love." Angela stared at them, acutely aware of Justus's gaze riveted to her face. Something deep in her belly fluttered to life. This wasn't the first time he'd stared at her. A couple of other times she'd caught his eye and he'd hastily looked away as if she'd caught him playing with himself in public. If she didn't know better she'd almost think he was attracted to her. Ridiculous.

Anyway, he had a girlfriend. Her stomach clenched, inex-plicably protesting the idea. "Where's Carla?" she asked, turning back to him at last. "I haven't seen her tonight."

Uncrossing her legs, she scooted forward a little in her seat and picked up her fork again.

"Dunno." Justus leaned closer and planted his elbows on the table, staring openly at her.

She couldn't shake the idea he'd done it just to unsettle her and see what kind of reaction he could provoke. She felt crowded again—almost trapped. Worse, she felt the heat radiating off his powerful arm and onto her bare skin. Her flesh—not just her left arm but every inch of her skin— tingled into awareness. With an awkward, jerky movement she smoothed her hair just to get her goose-bumped arm away from him; she shivered.

"Cold?" he asked, that awful, speculative look in his eyes again.

"No." She looked away, studying the far side of the room but seeing nothing. Still he stared at her. She fidgeted, thoroughly flustered now. "You don't sound like you care where your girlfriend is." She carefully refolded her napkin in her lap. "What if she's decided you weren't paying her enough attention and left with someone else?"

He laughed, shrugging those endless shoulders. "Maybe I'd care more if she was really my girlfriend instead of just some girl I have sex with."

Scandalized, Angela gaped at him. "Wha—?"

"Yes?" He leaned in closer, gleefully enjoying her discomfort.

She looked wildly around, half wondering whether she wasn't the unfortunate victim of a prank on some TV show. Obviously he wanted to shock her and had done an outstanding job of it; still, as his elder, she felt some obligation to be the voice of reason. "I don't even know where to start! Does she *know* she's just the girl you're sleeping with?"

"She should," he said, his level gaze never wavering.

A horrible thought entered her head. "There . . . there aren't any others are there?"

A bark of laughter answered her. "Do I look like a monk to you?"

No, he most certainly did not. With his earrings he actually looked like some sort of modern pirate. Nothing about his looks suggested how young he was; he clearly had street smarts far beyond his years. If she hadn't known otherwise she would have thought he was at least twenty-five. More troublesome than his looks was his charisma, which his body couldn't contain any more than a wire basket can contain a cumulous cloud.

"Well," she said, huffing, "I guess I don't need to have the safe sex talk with you, do I?"

Without a word he reached under his jacket and withdrew something from his back pants pocket. Flicking his wrist he unfurled a string of foil-wrapped condoms like a grandfather flipping open his wallet to show pictures of his grandkids. "Guess not."

Excruciatingly conscious of the fact that they were sitting at the head table, the focal point of the entire ballroom, Angela grabbed his hand and shoved it down into his lap. "What are you doing?" she snarled, horrified.

The hateful boy just laughed, relishing her embarrassment. A couple of people from a nearby table eyed them curiously; Angela resisted the urge to crawl under the table and hide. "Come on, Duchess." He nudged her good-naturedly with his arm before he put the condoms away. "You can go ahead and laugh. That was funny. Admit it."

Angela crossed her arms and legs and pursed her lips. She'd never considered herself a prude, but next to Justus she felt like a cloistered nun visiting Vegas for the first time. What was wrong with youth today? Why were they so anxious to grow up? Had this child never been in the Boy Scouts? The church choir?

"It wasn't funny, and why are you calling me *Duchess*?"

"Because you're sitting like someone shoved a metal rod up your spine, like a duchess waiting for her maid to bring in the tea. You should lighten up a little, Angie."

"Angela."

"See?"

She could hear the laughter in his voice even though she was determined never to look him in the face again. "Well," she said coolly, "I'm glad to see that even though you're rude, annoying, and promiscuous, you're smart enough to protect yourself from becoming a teenage father."

Justus threw back his head and laughed heartily; despite herself Angela laughed, too. "I don't smoke or do drugs or drink—"

Angela looked pointedly at his champagne glass. "What's that? Sparkling apple juice?"

"Oh, that." He waved a hand. "I just grabbed it to piss off my father. I can't drink if I want to stay in shape, now can I? Anyway, the point is if I didn't have that one little vice, I'd be damn near perfect." He shot a glance at V.J., still twirling Carolyn on the dance floor; his smile faded, then disappeared. "Like my brother."

Angela felt an unexpected twinge of sympathy for him; she certainly knew what it meant to live in a sibling's shadow. Impulsively she squeezed his arm. "And what fun would that be?"

Justus's intent gaze flew to her face again, and they stared at each other for a long, charged moment during which neither of them seemed to breathe. "Well," she said finally, her voice unaccountably throaty, "one day you'll fall in love and get your comeuppance for all these girls you're just using for sex. And I hope I'm around to see it."

He blinked furiously. "Love?" His upper lip twisted

into a sneer. "That's something that'll never happen to me. Or marriage."

Her heart squeezed as if someone had run it through a meat press while she wasn't looking. She didn't know why his feelings mattered so much to her, but they did. How could someone so young be so jaded? Who had ruined this poor boy at such a tender age?

"Why not, Justus? You make it sound like syphilis."

His jaw flexed and tightened. Glaring off in the distance, he said, "My mother fell in love with my father and married him. He made her life hell until she died two years ago." He turned to look at her then, and the vast bitterness in his eyes and, underneath that, the sadness, made her wince. "So if you ask me, love and marriage don't do anybody a damn bit of good."

"Angela!" boomed a voice behind them, sparing her beleaguered brain from having to think of any response. Startled, she swung around in her chair to see Vincent Robinson standing next to a distinguished looking older gentleman with white hair. Out of the corner of her eye she thought she saw Justus scowl. "This is Judge Meyers from federal district court. I told him you were starting your second year of law school, and he wanted to meet you."

Angela leapt to her feet and shook the man's hand. "So nice to meet you."

Mr. Robinson edged in front of Justus who, strangely, remained seated. "Angela has a poli-sci background."

Angela darted an uncomfortable glance at Justus. Though his head was slightly bowed as he stared down at his clenched hands resting on the table, she could see he'd taken on a ruddy flush. "I, uh—" she began, distracted. "I hope to be a litigator."

"Wonderful." Judge Meyers fished around in his inside jacket pocket. "Here's my card. You call me, and I'll put you in touch with a couple of people you ought to talk to."

"Thank you." Angela realized Mr. Robinson had completely blocked Justus from view and clearly had no intention of introducing him to the judge. A red haze of anger suddenly clouded her vision. Her opinion of Mr. Robinson, whom she'd heretofore considered merely pompous, dropped exponentially. What kind of man was this? Why would he be so rude to his own son? She leveled her most frigid glare at him; he flinched, his eyes widening slightly. Stepping deliberately around him, she smiled down at Justus, caught his elbow, and tugged it until he had no choice but to reluctantly stand up.

"Judge Meyers, have you met my friend—"

Mr. Robinson smiled broadly, stepped forward, and clapped Justus on the back as if he'd intended all along to introduce him. "My youngest son, Justus."

Justus smiled bravely, but his strained face and drooping shoulders broke her heart. More unbearable was the fact that the mischievous glint had left his eyes, which were now dark and flat. He was obviously deeply wounded by his father's treatment and in that moment Angela hated Mr. Robinson.

Justus took the judge's hand. "How are you?" he asked politely.

"Well," Mr. Robinson said, steering the judge toward another table, "let's go over here and say hello." The two men moved away.

Justus shoved his hands deep in his pockets and stared fixedly at the tips of his shiny black shoes. Angela's chest constricted painfully and she discovered, much to her surprise, she infinitely preferred the brash, cocky Justus to this wounded, brooding one. "You and your father don't get along, do you?" she asked quietly.

Still looking down at the floor, he shook his head. "Nope."

She stepped closer. "Well, that's his loss, isn't it?"

Justus's head jerked up; their gazes locked and held for a long, heated moment.

Spellbound, Angela wondered what, exactly, this young man had done to her. She wanted both to throw herself into the moment with him and see where it would take them, and also to run away and never see him again. She wanted—

Across the ballroom, a singer in a gleaming, white satin bias-cut gown with a gardenia in her hair joined the jazz trio and reached for the microphone, heightening Angela's sense of enchantment. Was it Billie Holiday? If so, she wasn't surprised. It wasn't, of course, but the husky alto voice singing one of her favorite Louis Armstrong songs, "A Kiss to Build a Dream On," sent chills up and down Angela's spine just the same.

"Dance with me, Duchess." He caught her hand and an excruciating jolt of awareness shot up her arm, pooled in her belly and throat, and became an ache. Against all her better judgment she let Justus, his intense black gaze still locked with hers, tug her as he backed up to the dance floor. Once there, he reeled her in and slid his big hand, fingers splayed, slowly down her bare back to her waist.

Shivering with desire, she stared up at him and tried to fight her terrible attraction. There was no point in pretending it was anything else. Her head knew he was underage, but her body—her throbbing breasts, her soaking wet sex, her pounding heart—refused to believe it.

His gaze flickered to her mouth and she felt his desperate longing as strongly as she felt her own; she imagined the sweet pressure of his full lips on hers and the taste of the champagne in his mouth until her loins tightened painfully. As if the small distance between them had become too great, he pulled her closer until they stood thigh to thigh, chest to chest. She went willingly. Every inch of him was hard and powerful, as if an oak tree had leaned down to wrap her in its branches—except no oak tree had ever felt so warm and vibrant, so *right*. Bending his head a little, he pressed one warm cheek to her forehead. He smelled delicious—spicy, citrusy, sophisticated. She breathed deeply; if nothing else, she would take his scent into her body.

When he spoke his voice was so soft she thought at first she'd only imagined it. "You're so beautiful," he said, exhaling slowly, "it hurts to look at you." She sighed helplessly, swaying into him, wishing—desperately *wishing*—she could ask him to come home and make love to her.

Before her eyes drifted closed she saw that the couples surrounding them were all engrossed with their own partners and paid them no attention. Had a more romantic setting ever existed? What had ever happened to his girlfriend? She didn't know and didn't care, as long as Carla didn't interrupt this moment. One distant corner of her mind warned she had gone too far, dancing with a minor like this, but she couldn't make herself care; she was just grateful she'd somehow resisted the strong urge to press her hips against his.

It was over much too soon. When the song ended she stepped out of his resisting arms and looked up into his stunned, strained, and ravenous face. He wanted her, too. She had the uncomfortable certainty this boy knew far more about making love than she did and, worse, he would be an exceptional teacher.

"Justus?"

The plaintive voice announced the reappearance of his long-lost girlfriend, Carla, in her skin tight, slinky, slitted red dress. Carla would have Justus moving inside her tonight, not her. Never her. Angela's fingers itched to curl into claws and scratch the girl's pretty doe eyes out. Determined to forget this terrible night when she'd felt such a powerful sexual attraction to a minor, Angela turned and, without a word, burrowed into the crowd to put as much distance between them as possible.

Justus, ignoring Carla, stared after Angela until she disappeared, grateful his buttoned jacket hid his violent arousal. *Angela*. He wanted her—more than he wanted Carla or anyone else, more than he wanted to leave home, more, even, than he wanted to tell his father to stay out of his life. He wanted her back in his arms so he could feel her ample breasts against his chest again; so he could touch her bare back and wonder where the silk of her dress ended and that of her skin began.

As he walked off the dance floor with Carla, he swore to himself that one day—he had no idea where or when—he and Angela would finish what they'd started tonight.

Chapter 1

Present Day

Angela's life fell apart with a one-two punch at the end of November.

The first blow fell halfway through dinner at her favorite Italian restaurant.

It started out the same as any other Friday night. They arrived right at six-thirty, the perfect time for dinner; the early hour allowed time for their food to digest and gave them the option of going to a movie around eight, if the mood struck. The server seated them at a very nice booth near the huge picture window overlooking the duck pond. Someone had decorated the dining room for the holidays, and tiny white lights framed the window and swooped in and out of the limbs of strategically placed ficus trees. Jazzy Christmas tunes played over the speakers. As soon as they sat she began to relax and feel the week's pressures slip away.

Her icy Riesling tasted tart and crisp, the sourdough rolls, appropriately crunchy on the outside and spongy on the inside, melted in her mouth, and her Caesar salad—once she sent it to the kitchen for more lemon in her dressing—was delicious. Tonight promised to be perfect.

"I can't marry you," said Ronald White IV, her boyfriend of three years, the man she'd thought would give her a diamond ring for Christmas. "I—I don't want to get married. It's not you—it's me."

Angela very carefully swallowed her mouthful of wine and put her glass on the table. She stared at Ronnie, positive she'd misheard. Her first reaction was to snort with laughter, but he seemed serious. He looked the same as ever: fair skin, curly black hair, and mustache that were the products of his mixed parentage, earnest brown eyes behind his wireless glasses, pin-striped charcoal-gray suit, her favorite yellow bow tie. Nothing about him indicated he was about to pull the rug out from under her life.

"What did you say?"

"I know we've talked about it," he continued, planting his elbows on the table and steepling his fingers in that nervous habit she hated, "but I'm not ready. I just—I'm sorry."

Angela's heart fell through her stomach; she threw her hand over her belly as if to protect it from any further revelations. "You—you don't love me anymore?"

"Of *course* I do," Ronnie cried in his squeaky voice, a slight sheen of perspiration appearing on his forehead. He was clearly nervous but determined to dispatch her in as professional and upbeat a manner as possible. "I just need some time to, you know, concentrate on my career right now. It's not you. It's *me*. I'm not even sure I'll ever get married."

Too shaken to speak, Angela just sat there, gaping and digesting his words. She knew what the platitudes meant; she'd watched Oprah and Dr. Phil and read Dear Abby long enough to know what Ronnie didn't have the guts to tell her to her face: while he may care about her, he wasn't in love with her and would never marry her. Since most men got married eventually, he would likely marry someone else, probably sooner rather than later. Her mind flashed to all the times in the past three months he'd worked really late—maybe he had her replacement lined up already. Was that it? Ronnie hated being alone; he would never cut her loose unless he had something in the pipeline.

Horrified, she cried, "Is there someone—"

A figure stepped up to their table. "Angela? Is that you?"

Frowning at the interruption, Angela looked up and gasped. Justus smiled with surprise and delight; she recognized him immediately even though she hadn't seen him since her sister's wedding. Dressed in a black turtleneck sweater and gray wool slacks, he was as tall and handsome as ever, although he seemed to have filled out a little and was no longer so wiry; he'd replaced his flashy ear studs with one small hoop in his left ear.

He stood with a tall, thin but shapely woman who kept her arm linked possessively with his, as if she feared he'd run away if she let go. Upset as she was, Angela still noticed that the beautiful woman's sleeveless black sheath with square neckline perfectly complemented her perfect hair, nails, and makeup. One glance at the woman's bosom, which was crammed into the low-cut dress and shoved somewhere up near her throat, told her what Justus would be doing later tonight. In her functional but decidedly untrendy black silk wrap dress, Angela felt like she'd just stepped out of the pages of *Working Woman* next to this *Essence* cover girl.

Angela managed a crooked smile and tried to swallow the huge lump in her throat. "Justus! How are you?"

Justus's searching gaze met hers and skimmed over her features so thoroughly she lost all hope of hiding her upset from him. His grin faded and his brows lowered; he darted an accusatory look at Ronnie. "I think I'm doing better than you. Are you okay?"

Thoroughly embarrassed now, she gave him a dazzling why-would-you-ask-such-a-question-I've-never-been-better smile. "Of course!" She indicated Ronnie. "This is my good friend Ronald White. Ron, this is Justus Robinson, my sister's husband's brother."

Ron stood and shook Justus's hand; he was shorter than Justus, of course—everyone was. She thought she saw Justus's jaw tighten slightly as he discreetly looked Ron over, but of course she must be mistaken. Justus turned to his girlfriend. "Janet Walker, this is Angela Dennis and Ron White." They all murmured pleasantries while Angela desperately wished Justus would take his arm candy and leave so she and Ronnie could talk. Any other time she'd have been glad to see him and eager to hear about what he'd been up to, but not tonight.

After a moment of awkward silence, Justus took the hint. "Well." He pressed his hand to Janelle's? Jane's? Janet's? back. "Good to see you," he told Angela, then steered the woman toward their server who stood, menus in hand, waiting patiently at a booth catty-corner to theirs.

She immediately turned back to Ron, who squared his shoulders and regarded her warily. "Is there someone else, Ronnie? Is that what this is about?"

"Of course not!" He managed to sound outraged, as if she'd accused him of cannibalism, but his gaze darted away from hers. "But . . . I need some time to get my head together."

Angela made a strangled sound. Oh, God, he was lying. Right to her face.

Random thoughts churned uselessly in her brain. Everything he'd said tonight was a lie—except for the part about not wanting to marry her. *That* was true. He didn't love her, even though he'd told her for years that he did. So he'd either fallen out of love with her, or he'd never loved her in the first place, both options equally appalling.

Hysteria bubbled up from her chest, with anger close behind; she cried out with outrage and people nearby looked at her curiously. "So that's it?" she demanded, her voice louder than she'd intended. Ronnie cringed. Justus, now sitting facing them, stared openly, not even bothering to pretend he wasn't listening to their conversation.

Embarrassed—she must never, *never* make a scene in public, no matter how upset she was—she planted her elbows on the table and rubbed her forehead with shaking hands. "After three years and telling me you wanted to get married when the time was right and stringing me along—that's it?"

"No, Angela." Ronnie reached over the table and tried to stroke her hand soothingly, but she snatched it away, sending her glass of Riesling crashing to the tile floor with a loud, wet crash. The attention of every single person in the room now riveted on them. A worried looking server scurried over to sop up the mess.

Angela barely noticed. How could this happen to her? She and Ronnie were the perfect couple—everyone always said so. She was a lawyer, he was a doctor. They both loved Martha's Vineyard in August and the opera and movies. They were both staunch Democrats and worked at the homeless shelter every Thanksgiving. Sure, they'd never been able to spend as much time together as they would have liked, but that was only because they both worked so hard on their careers. They'd always been on the same page . . . until now. Now Ronnie, the man she loved, her best friend, the man whose children she'd thought she'd bear, had thrown a stick of lit dynamite into the middle of their relationship and blown it up.

Her breath came in gasps—she couldn't seem to expand her lungs all the way—and she wondered if she would have the first panic attack of her life. She clutched the edges of the table and tried to get a grip on herself. Ronnie shifted uncomfortably in his seat; Justus stared. Twenty feet away the kitchen door swung open and their server marched through it. Three lifetimes ago, before her known world ended, she'd ordered the veal Marsala. The server strode purposefully toward them balancing their food high on a tray, as if the advent of some protein and a nice pasta would stop her from making any more of a scene.

Ronnie cleared his throat. "So I was hoping we could still . . . be friends."

The final insult. With a sob, Angela jumped to her feet, snatched her purse and coat from the back of her chair and, ignoring Ron's voice calling after her, ran from the dining room. Only when she passed the hostess station did it occur to her she had no way to get home—Ronnie drove tonight. Angela whirled left and right, desperately looking for someplace to hide. Her choices were limited: the standing-room-only bar or the ladies' room. Jerking open the heavy ladies' room door, Angela looked over her shoulder to the hostess. The poor woman's eyes widened into baseballs and Angela could see she wished she could crouch behind her stand and disappear.

"Please call me a cab," Angela managed before she ducked inside.

The restroom was a fancy deal that had probably required its own decorator: the outer room featured a loveseat and overstuffed chairs arranged around a heavy coffee table on a rug. Over on the granite countertop framed by a large mirror with elegant light fixtures sat enough toiletries and feminine products to stock a day spa. Two well-dressed women of a certain age primped and chattered in front of the mirror. When they saw Angela they froze. Immediately Angela felt worse—as much on display here in the lousy john as she'd been out there. A crying mess did not belong in this lovely sanctuary.

One woman's hand went to her throat. "Are—are you okay, miss?"

Embarrassed, Angela snatched a tissue from the counter and sank onto the loveseat. Crossing her legs, as if crying in the bathroom was the most normal thing in the world, she said, "I'm fine, thanks. I just need a minute."

The women, obviously relieved not to be called into some sort of uncomfortable service, nodded, shoveled their makeup back into their designer handbags, and hurried out before Angela changed her mind. When the door swung silently shut behind them, Angela collapsed back against the cushions and reviewed the wreckage of her so-called life.

It was all over now; at thirty-four she was no spring chicken and had probably just missed the last train out of spinsterhood. She'd never find someone else now! And even if she met someone tomorrow, it'd be years until they'd dated, gotten to know each other, and married. Her eggs didn't have years! And even if they did, she didn't want to be a forty-five-year-old first-time mother! And she didn't want to be a single mother! And she didn't want to adopt; she could never love another woman's child like her own.

Groaning, she threw her hand over her face. How would she spend the holidays? Who would she kiss on New Year's Eve? When would she ever get flowers and candy again for Valentine's Day? She thought of the impending loneliness and embarrassment when she told her friends and colleagues of her split with Ronnie. They'd feel sorry for her and immediately start to fix her up on blind dates with their loser single friends because all the good men were taken! People said it wasn't true, but it was! The men she'd consider dating—the good men, the ones worth having, the ones with advanced degrees, like her, the professionals, the doctors, lawyers, architects, accountants, executives—had been snatched up years ago! They were on their second or third child by now!

Suddenly waves of nausea overwhelmed her and she sat up and gagged; by sheer force of will she stopped herself from retching. Angry now, she swiped her wet face with her hands and took several deep breaths. She would not let Ronald White do this to her. No, she certainly would *not*. If only the cab would come! She just needed to get home so she—

"Angela!"

She twisted in her seat and saw Justus poke his head in the door. Oh, God—not Justus. Not now. She really wasn't in the mood to talk and she must look a fright; she quickly ran her fingertips under her eyes and wiped off the black mascara she knew must be trailing down her cheeks. "I'm fine." She smiled a bright, false smile. "I'm going home in a minute."

Justus stared disbelievingly at her for a long moment as if trying to decide exactly how big a liar she was. Finally his mouth twisted down and he came inside, ignoring her surprised splutter. She braced herself for his invasion.

Chapter 2

All broad shoulders, long legs, hard planes and angles, Justus looked ridiculous in this bastion of femininity—like a stallion in Victoria's Secret. He regarded her gravely, clearly worried. After a minute some of his tension eased, as if he felt satisfied she wasn't contemplating homicide or suicide. A smile softened the corners of his mouth. "I kicked his ass for you."

For one stunned second Angela just stared at him, then she burst into hysterical laughter. She laughed until tears streamed down her face again. He grinned, but she could still see the concern in his eyes and the rigidity in his shoulders. Finally she collected herself a little and wiped her face. "Did you make him cry?"

"Squealed like a girl."

Abruptly her mood swung back to despair; instead of laughing she made an embarrassing little choked sound. "Good." She dropped her head, unable to stop her tears and unwilling to let him see her cry. The soggy, bedraggled mess in her hand was now useless, and she gave up all hope of repairing her face. If only she had a fresh tissue.

Justus sank onto the loveseat next to her and his hand,

clutching a blindingly white handkerchief, came into her field of vision. He'd surprised her again. She jerked her head up, hesitated, then took the fine linen and wiped her nose with it. The hankie smelled like him. She remembered his spicy scent very clearly from that long-ago night.

"What's this?"

His lips twisted with amusement. "It's a hankie, you ignorant girl."

Laughing again, she blotted her eyes. "I really wish you'd stop making me laugh when I'm trying to cry here."

"I really wish you'd stop trying to cry." As he stared at her, a flush crept over his cheeks. "He's a fool, Angela," he said vehemently. "You know that, don't you?"

She quickly looked away; sympathy always had the unfortunate effect of making her cry harder, and that was the last thing she needed to do right now. "I wouldn't take you for the handkerchief type, Justus."

This time he laughed. "I'm quirky."

It occurred to her that he'd interrupted his date—and dinner—to come in here and check on her. "You should go. I'm sure your girlfriend—"

He rolled his eyes. "There you go assuming again."

Angela sighed harshly. She should have known; some things apparently never changed. "I'm sure the woman you're having sex with later is wondering what happened to you."

He laughed and opened his mouth to say something, but the door swung open again to admit another well-dressed woman and a brief burst of music and chatter from the crowded outer hallway. When she saw Justus she started, then huffed.

"This is the *ladies'* room," she informed him.

Justus's gaze remained riveted on Angela's face. "I know," he said irritably. "I read the sign on the door when I came in."

The woman drew herself up, preparing for an outraged rant,

but Justus seemed to realize he'd been rude. He swiveled around in his seat and, focusing his hooded gaze on the woman, smiled a wide, charming, dimpled smile like the sun dawning the morning after a hurricane. "I hope you don't mind, but we need to talk for a minute."

The poor woman never had a chance—she melted like a Hershey's chocolate bar left on the dashboard in August. Blushing furiously, she smiled and simpered. "Of course." She had a difficult time peeling her gaze away from Justus as she backed out, shutting the door behind her.

Angela grunted with disbelief. "You really ought to stop."

Still smiling, he leaned back against the cushions and studied the ceiling as if he considered it perfectly normal to spend a Friday night in a ladies' bathroom. "Do you need a ride home?"

"I asked the hostess to call me a cab."

"Okay," he said reluctantly.

She felt an unexpected surge of fondness for him. "What are you—my knight in shining armor tonight?"

"Just a friend. Do you want to talk about it?"

"No."

"I don't know why you were with that jerk anyway. I didn't like him."

In the past if she'd ever heard someone make a comment like that about Ronnie she would have come out swinging. But under the circumstances, defending Ronnie was a colossal waste of time. Was there some other term for a man who broke up with his long-term girlfriend at a restaurant? She smiled tiredly. "And here it took me three years to realize he's a jerk."

The door swung open again, and the hostess cautiously peered inside. "Your cab is here."

They both stood and turned to go, but Angela put her hand on his arm. She meant to thank him for looking out for her tonight, but words, suddenly, seemed inadequate. Impulsively she stood on her tiptoes and kissed his smooth, hard cheek, then wrapped her arms around his waist for a hug. She'd surprised him; she felt him stiffen, but immediately his arms went tightly around her and he held on for several seconds past the point when she would have moved away.

Finally he let her go and opened the door, his expression somber but otherwise unreadable. He didn't look at her. She started to walk through, then paused. "Thank you, Justus. I hope your dinner isn't cold." He stared intently without responding and she wondered if he'd heard what she'd said. "Well." She moved away. "Good night."

"Angela!" He stepped closer, his face strained, and hesitated. "It's . . . good to see you," he murmured gruffly, but she knew that wasn't at all what he'd wanted to say.

"You're telling me Ronnie dumped you over drinks?"

Angela balanced the cordless phone against her shoulder, squinted against the glaring morning sun streaming through the kitchen window, and rubbed her tired, gritty eyes. *Exhausted* didn't seem like a big enough word to describe how she felt. When the cab dropped her off last night she'd cried bitter, angry tears for so long she half expected she'd need to go to the hospital for a hydrating saline drip. Sleep was out of the question, so she didn't even bother. Instead, knowing nothing cleared her head like a little cleaning and the orange scent of her favorite disinfectants, she'd set to work.

She'd cleaned her two bathrooms and scrubbed the grout. Then she'd changed the linens on the bed, dusted the living room from top to bottom, shaken the rugs over the edge of the balcony, and lined her kitchen drawers with the blue-and-yellow-striped shelf paper she'd bought the other day. Only the lateness of the hour had stopped her from also vacuuming—but she didn't think her neighbors would appreciate the noise at two in the morning.

Finally, having worn herself out a little, she'd fallen into her black wrought-iron four-poster bed—the bed where she would never again make love to Ronnie—burrowed under her crisp white hotel sheets and brick floral duvet, and lain awake until five. Then she'd gotten up, run her four miles on the treadmill in the second bedroom that served as both office and exercise room, and done two hours of paperwork so she wouldn't have to go into the office today.

Finally, at eight, she'd called Carolyn, knowing she'd be up with Maya.

"Technically, it was over salad," Angela told her. She stopped rubbing her lids, realizing she'd succeeded only in making her eyes tired *and* irritated. Blearily, she focused on the sage-taupe-and-black-speckled countertop, sprayed it liberally with cleaner and began to wipe even though it was already spotless. "He said he needed time, didn't want to get married now, wanted to work on his career, blah, blah, blah."

Carolyn murmured sympathetically. "So do you think it'll all work out, or . . ."

"I don't think so. I don't know." Angela dropped the sponge and scowled; for the first time she could remember, cleaning— her favorite mindless, repetitive task—did nothing to settle her nerves. She was, in fact, getting more and more agitated. Throwing the sponge in the soapy dishwater, she squeezed her eyes shut and leaned against the counter. "I'm so angry right now. I just don't know what happened."

"Well," Carolyn said, then stopped.

The ominous weight of the silence fell over Angela like a lead blanket; she braced herself.

"I don't think he wants to ever marry you, Sweetie." The words spewed forth, as if Carolyn thought they would be less toxic if she said them quickly. "V.J. and I have talked about it for years—"

"Great," Angela muttered.

"—and we just don't think it would take him this long to propose if he was really serious about you. For God's sake, you're both in your mid-thirties—"

Angela made an odd, strangled sound.

"—so what could he be waiting for? V.J. says if Ronnie had been serious he wouldn't have let so much grass grow under his feet."

A fresh batch of furious tears welled in Angela's throat. She choked them back, launched herself away from the counter, picked up her broom, and jabbed at a thin spider web laced between the arms of the brass chandelier over the kitchen table. This was just great. Everyone, including Ronnie, had known for years that Ronnie would never marry her—everyone except her. The chandelier swung dangerously with an ominous tinkling noise, and she hastily dropped the broom and reached up to steady it.

"Well, why didn't you ever say anything?" she snapped. "This whole time I've been—"

"Put it down, honey," Carolyn said, her voice now muffled as if she'd put her hand over the receiver. "Put it down."

Angela knew what that muffled phone voice meant and resisted the urge to stomp her foot in frustration. The little monster Carolyn liked to call her daughter had entered the room and the adult part of this conversation was, therefore, now over.

"Would you like to say hello to Aunt Angela?" Carolyn murmured, now speaking in that annoying squeal—*Hiii-iii! How aaaaare youuuuuu!*—suitable only for small children and pets. "Come here, Sweetie."

Angela cringed and wondered how rude it would be if she hung up then called back at Maya's naptime giving the excuse that her phone's battery had suddenly died. Why did parents always think it was cute to put their little kids on the phone? What was the point? It wasn't as if a preschooler was a witty conversationalist. Why didn't they ever realize the rest of the world was never as in love with their children as they were? And why couldn't she have the briefest conversation with her sister without Maya interrupting?

"Carolyn," she cried quickly, "Don't put her on the phone! I really don't have time for this now, and—oh, hello, Maya."

"Hi, Aunt Ang-la," Maya said in her high-pitched singsong.

A long silence, punctuated by Maya's heavy breathing, followed.

Angela studied her fingernails and impatiently cast around for something to say. "So . . . how is school?"

"Good."

"Wonderful." Her obligation to speak to the child now fully discharged, it was time to move on to more important matters. "Put your mom back on the phone, please. And don't hang up on me this time, okay?"

Carolyn's irritated, sarcastic voice came back on the line. "Hoo-boy, Angela. Such enthusiasm. I'm going to nominate you for the aunt of the year award."

Angela had picked up the broom and started sweeping the floor, but now she stiffened in surprise. "What's that supposed to mean?"

Carolyn huffed in her ear; Angela braced herself for a rant. "Can you at least *try* to be nice to her, Angela? Maybe pretend— just for once—you have some interest in my child? You're the only aunt Maya has! You and she are the only family *I* have! Do you have any idea how much it would mean to me if my sister actually liked my daughter? Can't you do it for *me*?"

Furious, Angela threw the broom to the tiled floor, where it clattered. "Are you kidding me? Maya couldn't ask for a better aunt! I've never missed a birthday or Christmas, and let me remind you that the American Girl doll I got her last year was *not* cheap! And what about the—"

"I'm not talking about spending money on her!" Carolyn's voice rose several octaves. "I'm talking about spending time with her, getting to know her, and—"

Angela had had enough. As far as she was concerned, this whole stupid conversation had strayed way too far afield from the topic at hand, which was her ruined love life. She clutched the phone hard to her ear, ignoring the ache in her protesting fingers. In the background she heard muffled noises and Carolyn murmuring to Maya again, but she ignored that too.

"My life has been ripped to shreds and you want to talk about your *daughter*?" she yelled. "I don't have time for that! I need to know why you let me spend three years—"

Carolyn made an abrupt, aborted sound, as if she wanted to scream but was determined not to make a scene in front of her daughter. Then she exploded anyway, shrieking in Angela's ear. "When are you going to stop being so selfish? When are you going to wake up and realize it's not all about *you* and *your* career and *your* romance? What will it take for you to stop being so self-centered?"

A red haze of fury clouded Angela's vision; she resisted the urge to hurl the phone against her cheerful butter-colored wall. "Well forgive me for wanting to talk about what's going on in my life! Forgive me for being a little upset about being dumped! How could I be such a bitch?"

A long silence followed until finally Angela wondered if Carolyn had hung up on her. "Hello?" she snarled. "*Hello*?"

"What did you say, Angela?" Carolyn sounded harried now. "I didn't hear you."

Disgusted, Angela jerked open the cabinet under the sink, fished the window cleaner out, sprayed some on a fresh cloth and attacked the window. This was the way it always went with Carolyn and her: they talked, one or the other got angry, they shouted invectives at each other, and then they moved on. If Carolyn's attack just now had seemed a little more personal than usual, or had hit a little closer to home, Angela did not particularly want to explore the reasons why. Some dogs were best left quietly asleep.

"I want to know why you let me spend three years of my life—"

"PUT IT DOWN, MAYA!" Carolyn screeched.

Angela jerked the phone away from her ear but was still able to hear a huge, wet, crashing sound, then Carolyn yelling and Maya crying. Angela cursed; this phone call was over and she was no closer to getting any answers than . . .

"I've got to go," Carolyn barked. "Maya just knocked the flowers off the table."

Of course she did. That little tyrant had more arms than an octopus family reunion and a reach to make George Foreman weep with envy. For God's sake, why couldn't Carolyn put her foot down with Maya every now and then and whip her into shape? The child was three and a half years old, and she ran their whole household. Everyone always cooed about Maya as if she were the cutest child to ever walk the face of the earth, but Angela knew better.

"Well, I need you, too! I'm having a personal crisis here, and I need a little of your time!"

"I'm doing the best I can, Angela!" In the background Maya's crying increased ten points in volume. "I can't do everything!"

It really was a shame, Angela reflected sadly, the way motherhood had reduced Carolyn to this high-strung, shrieking mess. Angela remembered a time, not so long ago, when Carolyn had been a wildly successful bond trader. She'd worn power suits and talked in complete sentences and read the newspaper. What had happened to that sophisticated human being? When *she* became a mother, Angela vowed, she'd do it much better than *this*.

Carolyn spoke calmly now, her tone conciliatory. "Look. My car's still in the shop, but maybe V.J. can drop me off over there after dinner and we can talk for a while. He can take Maya to the mall or something. Okay?"

"Fine," Angela said, slightly mollified. "By the way, before I forget to mention it, I saw Justus last night. What's he been up to?"

"Oh, he just opened his gym," Carolyn said, clearly distracted. "He's pretty excited about that. Still screwing every woman in sight. Same as always."

Angela laughed. "That's what I figured. I'll see you later."

But Angela never spoke to her sister again.

Chapter 3

"Uh-oh!" Flapping her arms in an effort to keep her balance, the half-naked, doe-eyed young woman "stumbled" dramatically off the BOSU ball. Justus reflexively caught her, which gave her the opening he knew she'd been looking for the whole session: she threw her hands onto his biceps, squeezing hard, and thrust her ample, scientifically enhanced chest against his. The hard little points of her nipples were unmistakable, as was the invitation in her hot eyes and the seductive smile on her dewy lips.

"Sorry," she said huskily, stepping closer.

Justus tried not to snort.

He firmly and efficiently extracted himself from her arms, set her to rights, and stepped away. "No problem." He smiled coolly and checked his watch; it was almost time for his next appointment. "I think we're done for today."

"Oh." The beautiful face fell with obvious disappointment. She caught her lower lip between her teeth and he could see the wheels trying to turn in her vacant little mind. "What about Monday?" she asked hopefully.

Justus stooped to pick up the ball, then walked across the blue exercise mat and put it with its mates over in front of the huge floor-to-ceiling windows. Turning back, he picked up his water bottle from the weight bench, opened it, and took a long sip while he dredged up a diplomatic answer. "The beginning of the week's pretty tight. But if you check at the desk, I think I have a cancellation on Thursday afternoon."

"Oh," she said again. "If you think that's soon enough . . ."

"More than enough," he said crisply, holding his hand wide to indicate she should follow him to the door. "I'll walk you down."

He watched as she dejectedly gathered her expensive but obviously rarely used gym bag and hiked up her skintight black knit capris until they almost reached her belly button. Her teeny tiny bra top left nothing to the imagination. Obviously, this girl did not believe in subtlety. Her whole committed-exerciser routine would be much more convincing if only she'd actually exercised while she was here; she'd lifted only the smallest weights but heaved and huffed like a railway worker laying tracks. Breaking a sweat did not appear to be one of her goals, but then she was only twenty-one and time was on her side, at least for now. Little did she know that in a few years she'd really have to work to keep her sleek body. The thought of her drenched with sweat after an hour on a treadmill was strangely cheering.

He was sick and tired of clients like this one—and a lot of them seemed to be just like this one—who saw coming to the gym as a chance to see their friends, show off their new hundred dollar outfits, and seduce him. He wouldn't be surprised if some of these little babies—he always thought of younger women as babies because they all seemed so frivolous and giggly—had made a bet among themselves to see who would seduce him first. They were wasting their time; besides being bad for business, the idea of sleeping with one of these girls was as appetizing as a peanut butter-and-squid sandwich.

But he had to be nice. They paid their membership dues and put food on his table.

Justus trailed behind her down the steps to the second floor, performing a silent inventory as he went. On the plus side, the gym was in full Saturday morning swing, thank God; exercisers occupied all the treadmills, ellipticals, and bikes. The mirror along the main wall sparkled, fingerprint free, as did the tall windows, where the bright sunlight streamed in, creating a cheerful, upbeat effect. The powerful beat of some hip-hop song or other kept the energy level high. In the hallway the hardwood floors gleamed with polish; across the way in the converted parlor spinners groaned and struggled to keep up with the instructor, who barked out orders like Lou Gossett Jr. in *An Officer and a Gentleman.*

On the minus side, and much to Justus's dismay, the stairs still creaked a little beneath him. That was the thing about this old Victorian house. Sure, it had been a steal, and it made an interesting place for an exercise studio. But even though they'd finished the major renovations already, there was always another creak, leak, or break that demanded his attention—and money. Luckily Brian, his silent partner, had deeper pockets than he did.

He'd just turned to go down the second flight to the first floor lobby area, when he saw V.J. barreling up the steps toward him, shoulders squared, his mouth compressed into a tight line. At the top of the landing he looked around, caught Justus's eye, and glowered.

Justus's jaw tightened, but he said nothing. Great. This was just *great.* He knew why his brother had come and he didn't feel like hearing it. Not today, not ever. Crossing his arms, he scowled at V.J.

His client stared, wide-eyed, at them. "Well . . . bye, Justus," she said uncertainly.

Justus grunted and she scurried down the steps.

V.J. came closer. "Got a minute?" he asked sharply.

"Not really." Justus spun away and trotted down the steps to the lobby, where the receptionist sat her post answering phones. To the right clients occupied every table in the smoothie bar, and a steady stream of people came and went out of the locker rooms. "I've got a client."

"Make some," V.J. said, hot on his heels.

Cursing, Justus strode into his office, leaned a hip on the side of his desk, and watched while V.J. slammed the door. "What's the problem, man?"

"Where were you last night?" V.J. barked.

Justus picked up a file from his desk and rifled through it, seeing nothing. "Eating dinner. Why?"

"We were counting on you to come for Pop's birthday dinner."

Justus spared him a quick glance. "Why would you do that? I told Carolyn I wouldn't be there." He lowered his head again.

Without warning, V.J. snatched the file away and tossed it to the desk. "How long are you gonna keep up this wounded son routine? How many more birthdays do you think he's got left? His heart's—"

Furious, Justus shot to his feet and wheeled around his desk. "Don't give me that bull," he cried. "The old man's heart's been acting up for years, and he's still the same as—"

"He's not! He's sick!" V.J. roared.

Justus started. He couldn't ever remember seeing V.J. so angry before.

"No one lives forever!" A vein throbbed in V.J.'s temple; he threw his arms wide, palms up. "How many chances do you think you're gonna get?"

Justus snorted. Planting his hands on the desk, he hung his head for a moment, collecting his thoughts. He had no intention of falling for his brother's little guilt trip, although the temptation was there. "Cut the drama. He enjoyed his birthday more without me. Trust me."

V.J. looked to the ceiling, as if he hoped to see instructions for dealing with Justus scrawled on the white paint. "If Mama were here—"

As usual, a sharp bolt of pain sliced through his chest at the mention of his mother; his jaw tightened until he felt his temples throb. "Don't bring her into this," he warned softly.

V.J. seemed to realize he'd gone too far. He ran a hand through his hair, practically vibrating with frustration. "I don't want you to regret this one day. That's all."

The beseeching note in his brother's voice was hard to resist, as was the faint glimmer of hope in V.J.'s expression. Justus sighed harshly, then looked away. For long moments, neither of them said anything.

Finally V.J. cleared his throat. "Maya's been asking about you."

Justus's heart swelled and instantly all his anger evaporated; the little angel was the love of his life. "Tell her I'll be by tomorrow to take her for lunch at the mall. She liked that the last time." Relaxing, he dropped into his high-backed leather chair and swung his feet onto the desk.

V.J. rolled his eyes and settled onto the edge of the desk. "Just don't let her talk you into buying her another one of those stupid makeup kits. Those things make a big mess."

"Okay." Now that the storm had passed, Justus's mind veered back to Angela, where it had been since he saw her last night. His heart rate kicked up several notches. Fingering his cup of pens, he strove for a detached, clinical tone. "I saw your sister-in-law with some guy last night at dinner. She seemed pretty upset."

V.J.'s expression turned grim. "You must have seen the fireworks. Her jackass boyfriend dumped her. I think she thought he'd give her a ring at Christmas."

"Hmmm," he said, his mind spinning. So that was what happened. He'd known whatever it was had been pretty bad, or else Angela would never have been so upset. "Who is this jerk?"

"An internist over at University. We never knew what Angela saw in him."

"Oh."

He'd planned to drop it, but something in his tone or on his face must have alerted V.J. because his eyes narrowed suspiciously. "Why do you ask?"

Justus didn't meet his brother's gaze. He shrugged, then sprang to his feet and went to the window, which overlooked the crowded parking lot and tree-lined street. "No reason."

V.J., who had a sixth sense bordering on omniscience where Justus was concerned, twisted around on the desk and stared, open-mouthed at him. "Oh, no you don't." He stood up and jabbed a finger in Justus's face. "Don't even think about it. She's just been dumped and she doesn't need *you* trying to get in her pants."

Justus scowled and felt his blood start another slow boil. V.J. acted like he was the Marquis de Sade. Squaring his shoulders, he faced off with his brother. "I don't see what the problem is. We're both grown-ups."

V.J. roared with outrage. "Angela isn't one of your little hoochies, Justus! She's a great woman and she's vulnerable right now! What the hell am I gonna tell my wife if you try to screw around with her sister?"

Justus seethed in silence, unable to think of a single thing to say in his own defense. V.J. was right, of course—his intentions weren't exactly honorable. He'd never believed in fate, but fate or something like it had dropped Angela back into his life, and he planned to take full advantage of this opportunity.

Because he wanted her. *Still* wanted her. He'd thought about her a lot over the years, wondering what she was doing and whether he hadn't imagined how beautiful and sexy she was. Well, now he knew; she was, if anything, more stunning than he'd remembered. And she still felt *right* in his arms—her little gratitude hug and kiss last night had proved that.

So even though he felt bad she'd had her heart broken, he planned to make the most of the situation. He would be gentle and patient, and he would woo her if she wanted. Or he could be her rebound fling. But either way he planned to get Angela Dennis into his bed and keep her there for a while. Because ten years ago he'd promised himself one day he would make love to her, and it was time to collect.

V.J. stared thoughtfully at him, then smiled a smug little smile that made Justus want to slug him across the face. "On second thought," V.J. said, "I'm not going to worry about it. You know why? Because you're not her type. In fact, I have a better chance of marrying Rosie O'Donnell than you do of seducing Angela."

Justus clenched his fists into tight balls at his sides. "We'll just see about that," he snarled.

Laughing, V.J. opened the door and walked out. "I can't wait."

Furious, Justus looked wildly around for something to hit him with. He grabbed a fluffy white towel from the top of his file cabinet and hurled it. "Punk!"

The towel caught V.J. squarely on the back of the head. Still laughing, V.J. kicked it aside and disappeared down the hall, leaving Justus to fume.

It's not true. There's been a mistake. God would never do this.

The mantra ran through Angela's head in an endless loop as she shuffled, exhausted, back into her darkened apartment that evening. She flicked on a light and saw that nothing there had changed in the two hours since she'd been at the hospital. Since she'd answered the phone. Why had she answered the phone? Maybe if she hadn't, none of this would have happened.

Ms. Dennis? I'm so sorry . . . There's been an accident . . .

Two hours had passed, and life as she'd known it was over. In that time she'd aged a thousand years and lost the only person she had left. Two hours.

Her throat and chest tightened, reminding her of all she'd lost. She'd become nothing more than a mass of skin, bones, and tissue in agonizing, screaming emotional pain. Would she pass out from her broken heart? God, she hoped so. Then she wouldn't have to deal with the pain, at least for a few minutes.

But then she felt a movement beside her, and she remembered. God hadn't taken everything after all. She wasn't alone, and she wasn't the only one who suffered right now. Someone else had lost far more than she had tonight.

"Come on, Sweetie."

Angela took her niece's tiny soft hand and led her to the sofa, praying for strength with each step she took. She could do this. She would do this. She had to. For Carolyn. She would not cry, and she would not shout at God. There was plenty of time for falling apart later. Right now she had to break her three-and-a-half-year-old niece's heart and tell her that both of her parents were dead.

Maya looked so tiny—so lost and forlorn in her puffy pink jacket with dangling purple mittens. In her other hand she clutched a floppy stuffed animal. A dog, Angela thought. Thank goodness the poor child had one small bit of comfort to hold onto.

As they sat on the sofa, Angela's guilt took over, shoving her grief aside. When had she last seen Maya? When was the last time she'd spent more than three minutes talking to Maya when she did see her? She couldn't remember. They got along so much better in small doses, or so she'd always thought. She'd been busy with work and figured there was plenty of time for getting together with her family next weekend, or the weekend after that.

What a joke.

Angela's frantic brain ran in endless circles, trying to think of a way she could explain the inexplicable to a child. Did Maya know about death? Did she believe in heaven? How much should Angela tell her?

Maya stared at her, waiting, her huge brown eyes wise and wide in the little chipmunk face that looked so much like Carolyn's. A single ray of sunshine dawned in Angela's heart. No, God hadn't taken everything, after all. She still had Maya.

She really was adorable. Carolyn had braided her long, wavy black hair in two ponytails on each side of her head, with colorful, beaded rubber bands at the top and bottom of each braid. Another wave of sorrow washed over Angela. Carolyn was gone forever and tomorrow *she* would have to braid all that hair.

Angela felt her lips begin to quiver again. Pressing them tightly together, she tried to smile. "You've had a very busy night, haven't you?"

Tears shone in Maya's eyes. "That deer ran into the car. It hurt Mommy and Daddy."

Nodding, Angela dipped her head and surreptitiously swiped a tear. "I know."

Miracles did happen, didn't they? How else could Maya have survived, unscathed, in the back seat of Carolyn and V.J.'s minivan, when a ten-point buck had mangled the vehicle's front end beyond recognition?

Maya's pouty little mouth twisted and her brow furrowed as she tried to understand the incomprehensible. She raised her dog and, hugging him, pressed him to her lips, clearly struggling not to cry. "Are they in heaven?"

Angela's neck and chest tightened to the point of agony, choking the word off in her throat. God, she didn't want to be the one to tell this child her parents were dead. She would give anything if the earth would just open up and swallow her whole so she didn't have to deliver this news. Buying herself a little time, she cupped the side of Maya's face, rubbing her thumb over a satiny, chubby cheek. Then she caught one of her long braids and smoothed it.

"Yes."

Maya whimpered softly and tears ran down her face behind the dog. She lifted him a little and used his furry brown head to wipe her eyes. "Are they with Grandma and Grandpa?"

The question was Angela's undoing. She took a fresh tissue out of her pocket and, covering her mouth with it, wept quietly. She should have known Carolyn would tell Maya about her grandparents, even though they'd died long before she was born. And of course Carolyn would have also told her about heaven.

Recovering, she smiled a little at Maya. "Yes. They're all together now, and I think they're happy. And I think they're watching over us. And they'll always be in our hearts. We'll never forget them, will we?"

But Maya just blinked at her, looking vaguely reproachful, as if she was offended Angela expected her to buy such a load of bull. "I want to go to bed now."

"Oh," Angela said, a little surprised. "Okay. Let's get you a bath first. How would that be?"

Maya didn't answer, but she obligingly stood and walked with Angela down the hall to the bathroom. Angela turned on the taps, then opened the medicine cabinet to see if she had an extra toothbrush for Maya.

The sight of Ronnie's red toothbrush in its cup froze Angela in her tracks. The blind fury she'd repressed until now surged back, tightening every muscle in her body and making her face and ears burn.

She'd seen the bastard tonight outside the hospital.

As she'd walked to her car with her orphaned niece, as she'd tried to absorb the knowledge that her sister and brother-in-law had been killed in their prime of life, as she'd wondered what the hell she was going to do, she'd looked up and seen him—the man she'd thought she'd marry—standing fifty feet away. Seen *them*.

Ronnie and the woman he'd dumped Angela for, kissing by Ronnie's car, twined around each other like the strands of a rope.

Cursing silently, Angela hurled Ronnie's toothbrush into the trash can.

After a quick bath and a glass of milk, Maya went willingly to bed with her dog snuggled under her arm. Angela made up the double bed in the guest bedroom/office/exercise room for her and she fell asleep before Angela flipped the wall light switch. She left a small lamp burning on her desk in case Maya was afraid of the dark. The soft, even sound of the girl's breathing provided an odd sort of comfort; it reminded Angela she wasn't entirely alone in the universe—one other member of her family was still alive. Shutting the door behind her, Angela shuffled, exhausted, back out to the living room, wishing she could as easily put this nightmarish day behind her. She glanced at her watch: ten-fifteen. There was no way she would sleep tonight.

She wandered into her walk-in closet and took off her shoes, lining them up in their slot at the end of the row on the floor, and tried to decide what to do next. Should she take her shower now, or wait a little while? She didn't know how light a sleeper Maya was, or if she'd have bad dreams tonight, and she wanted to be able to hear—

A knocking sound, so faint she thought at first she'd imagined it, startled her. Retracing her footsteps, she crept to the front door and checked the peephole.

Justus.

Someone from the hospital had called him for her, thank goodness. She opened the door and stared at him for a long, charged, moment. He looked awful: tight, strained face, bloodshot eyes, red nose, flaring nostrils. He seemed to have aged twenty years since she saw him last night. At the sight of her, the edges of his lips turned up in what might have been the beginnings of a rueful smile, and he opened his arms. With a cry she threw herself at him, grateful to be with someone who could share her pain and help her through this long, dark night. His heavy, muscular arms clamped around her like shackles and his hands sifted through her hair, then rubbed roughly over her shoulders and back as if he needed to make sure she, at least, was still in one piece.

She clawed her way closer to him, fingers digging into his back and shoulders, reveling in his warmth and unyielding strength. "Justus," she said, sobbing. "What are we going to do?"

His grip tightened to the point of brutality. "Shhh. It'll be okay," he said hoarsely. "Everything'll be okay."

Still holding her, he backed her inside the door and shut it behind them. Angela pulled free, but he held onto her hands, his grip somehow strengthening her. "Where is she?" he whispered.

"Asleep. In the guest bedroom."

"Show me."

It was on the tip of her tongue to say he'd have to see Maya tomorrow because she didn't want to risk waking her up, but one look at his determined face told her that would be a waste of time. She led him down the dark hall—she'd have to remember to get a night light in case Maya had to go to the bathroom in the middle of the night—and cracked open the door.

Justus hovered on the threshold, then strode past and sat on the enormous bed, which seemed like a soccer field compared to Maya's tiny form. At first he just stroked her cheek, but then he made a strangled sound from deep in his throat and picked her up, pulling her out from under the blankets and into his lap. The white T-shirt Angela had given her to sleep in rode up over her short, sturdy legs. Her head fell limply back over his arm, but she didn't stir and seemed not to breathe. Justus pressed his lips to her forehead, kissing her over and over, rocking back and forth, and murmuring unintelligibly. Angela wondered if she shouldn't leave and give him a little privacy, but her feet were suddenly rooted to the floor. She watched as he kissed Maya one last time.

"I'll take care of you, baby girl." Very gently he laid her back down and arranged the blankets and the dog around her. "Don't you worry. I'll take care of you."

He rose and, swiping his hand under his eyes and nose, brushed by Angela again and went back to the foyer; she trailed after him, too moved to speak. At the front door he paused, and when he took her hands again it felt natural and right.

It killed her to admit to a weakness, even tonight, but she couldn't stand the thought of being alone. "Don't go," she whispered, squeezing his hands. "You can sleep on the couch. And Maya will want to see you when she wakes up."

Regret filled his dark eyes. "I have to go tell my father. I didn't want to do it over the phone."

She didn't envy him that awful task. Very reluctantly she let go of his strong hands. "Okay."

"I'll be back first thing in the morning. I guess we've got a lot of arrangements to make."

Nodding, she dabbed her eyes with the ever-present tissue.

Abruptly he wrapped his arm around her waist, pulled her to him and pressed a warm, hard kiss to her forehead. "We'll get through this, Angela."

She nodded even though she didn't believe him for a second.

At eleven o'clock, Justus pulled past the tall English ivy-covered brick wall and into the driveway of his father's house, turned off the engine and headlights, and stared. He'd never thought of the place as home any more than a person could consider the Louvre or a mausoleum home. Brian's childhood house, half as big as this one and nowhere near as grand, with its slightly rumpled great room, where hockey sticks leaned in the corners, floor pillows invited people to settle in and stay for a while, and children could accidentally leave occasional smudges on the walls without threat of immediate and severe sanctions, now *that* was home. *This* was just a building—a place he avoided like a Congolese village during an Ebola outbreak.

When had he last come back here? Was it Christmas two years ago? He couldn't remember. He'd pretty much kept his promise to himself not to return once he went to college, and he could count on one hand the number of times he'd been here in the last ten years. Why bother to come? He'd disliked the ostentatious shrine to his father's ego, so unlike all the other kids' houses, even when Mama was alive, and after she'd died when he was fifteen he'd hated it.

As usual, stepping into the shadow of this citadel made him feel small and insignificant, and, worse, trapped. The style, he knew from his father's many lectures, was English Tudor, but he'd always thought of the imposing crème brick structure as a castle or fortress. The shape was essentially rectangular with a sloping blue-slate roof, but a rounded portion in front with a pointed center gave the effect of a tower. Tasteful spotlights lit the immaculate landscaping and rolling emerald grounds, and a huge wreath decorated with fall reds and oranges dominated the top half of the massive front door. The overall effect of this million-dollar piece of real estate was to awe and impress, which was, of course, his father's whole reason for existing.

That and being V.J.'s father.

Justus heaved himself out of the car and made his way up the long cobblestone path to the door; unfortunately, no matter how slowly he walked, he got there eventually. He sighed harshly and rang the fancy bell, which sounded like the carillon at St. Paul's in London. He still had a key on his keychain, but he hadn't used it in years and didn't plan to start now.

Footsteps inside alerted him to his father's approach and he braced himself. Behind the beveled glass he saw a light come on, then the heavy mahogany door swung open and Vincent stared, open-mouthed, clearly astonished to see him. The old man had aged, and not very well. His short hair was almost entirely white now, and deep grooves framed his disapproving mouth. He'd lost weight, probably a good twenty pounds or so. A paisley silk robe covered his dark pajamas, and slippers protected his feet from the cold hardwood floors.

"Justus," he said coolly, "what are you doing here?"

Justus waited for an invitation to come inside; none was forthcoming. "Can I come in?"

"Uh, yeah . . . sure," Vincent said with all the enthusiasm of a rancher letting a wolf into his cattle pen. He stepped aside and let Justus pass through, shutting the door behind him.

Justus surveyed the foyer, which was inside the tower portion of the house and therefore circular. Nothing had changed, not that he expected it would; the staircase curved gracefully upstairs, the same ornate round table sat on the same round

Persian rug. A huge cornucopia overflowing with silk flowers and miscellaneous fruit perched on top of the table. Vincent stared at him, waiting.

Justus cleared his throat. "I . . . have some bad news, Pop."

Vincent stiffened; one clawlike hand—had they always been so thin and wrinkled?—reached out to clutch the edge of the table for support. "What is it?" he whispered hoarsely.

Justus faltered, not at all certain he could get the words out. "V.J. and Carolyn ran into a deer tonight with the car. They . . . were killed."

Vincent, still clinging to the table, made a strangled, broken sound, and doubled over at the waist. Before he could fall all the way to the floor, Justus leapt to his side, grabbed his thin elbow, and steered him into an intricately carved, high-backed mahogany chair he and V.J. used to call the "throne." Vincent collapsed heavily. His chest heaved frantically; he sounded as if he was having an asthma attack, although Justus was certain he didn't have any breathing problems. For the first time in a thousand years he felt an emotion for his father other than anger, disgust, or contempt: he felt pity.

"Breathe, man." He stooped over Vincent and rubbed his back. "You've gotta *breathe*."

Vincent's lips opened and closed uselessly; he looked like a flounder out of water gasping for air. "Lena," he finally managed. "Get Lena."

Justus had forgotten all about Vincent's long-term girlfriend. Of course she'd be here, spending the night, even though she and Vincent maintained the pretense of living in separate homes. "Lena!" Galvanized, he sprinted up the stairs, made a sharp left at the top, and ran a few more feet before he nearly ran into Lena belting her silky pink robe around her. Her short white hair was mussed, but otherwise she looked as cool and elegant as ever. Justus was glad to see her. He liked Lena a lot and had never quite figured out what such a great woman saw in his father.

"What is it?" Her eyes wide with alarm, she clutched his forearms.

"It's V.J.," he told her gently. "And Vincent's having trouble breathing."

"Oh, God." She spun around and ran back down the dark hall to the open door of the lighted master suite. She ran right back out, a dark bottle of prescription medication in her hand. Justus followed her down the stairs, half afraid of what they'd find when they got to the bottom. Despite the low lighting from a small table lamp next to the throne, Justus could see Vincent's skin had turned an odd gray color; his breathing was, if possible, even harsher than before. Very efficiently Lena opened the bottle, shook out a tablet, and put it into Vincent's mouth.

"Just relax." She crouched by the chair and pressed her palm to his cheek. "Relax."

Vincent stared at her with stricken eyes; his tongue worked the tablet inside his cheek. After a minute his breathing evened out and he slumped, his head falling back against the chair. Tears streamed from beneath his closed lids. "Vincent Jr. is dead," he whimpered. "My son is *dead*."

Justus stared, paralyzed, at his father. Here was an old man with heart problems who'd just lost his favorite child and law partner. Wasn't this the worst pain a human being could endure—the loss of a child? His own pain, as bad as it was, was nothing compared to what his father must be feeling right now. No one, not even Vincent, deserved such anguish. A desperate need to do something—anything—to help blossomed in his heart.

Lena stood up, murmuring to Vincent as she took his arm. "Let's go upstairs. You'll feel better in bed." Vincent scooted weakly to the edge of the chair.

Justus raced around the chair and caught Vincent's other arm. He could help him get upstairs and make sure he settled in a little before—

Vincent's head whipped around and he stared at Justus with unwavering, accusatory wet eyes. Justus flinched, and for a long, charged moment they stared at each other while Justus absorbed the animosity radiating from his father like fumes from a skunk's tail.

Finally Vincent's lip turned up in a sneer. "I don't need *your* help."

Stunned, Justus dropped his arm and backed away, recoiling from the message that was as clear as any neon sign: Vincent didn't understand why, as long as he had to lose a son, it couldn't have been Justus. Pain knifed through Justus's own chest, much to his surprise. He'd thought he'd long ago made himself invulnerable to this kind of attack, but he'd been wrong. Tears squeezed his throat; when his nostrils began to flare he turned away, unwilling to let his father see how much he'd hurt him.

"Vincent!" Lena hissed, shooting an embarrassed, apologetic look at Justus. Vincent ignored her, snatching his arm away and turning toward the stairs on his own steam. Lena looked worriedly back and forth between the two of them. Finally she reached up and kissed Justus on the cheek. "I'm sorry," she whispered.

He nodded numbly.

Aloud she said, "We'll talk first thing, Justus. Okay?"

But Justus had already turned and opened the door to leave, determined never to reach out to his father again. Ever.

Chapter 4

Angela woke slowly, her forehead shrieking with pain even before she cracked open her swollen eyes and saw the bright morning sun streaming through the closed blinds. For one second she couldn't remember what was so terribly wrong and looked around in bewilderment. Her English country bedroom certainly felt as cheerful as ever. Every embroidered pillow sat in its place on the overstuffed brick red floral chintz chairs in the little seating area by the window. The twin night-stands holding tall hand-painted reading lamps and ornately framed black-and-white family photos sparkled from the dusting she'd given them yesterday; the lemony smell of the furniture polish she'd used competed with the soft fragrance of the yellow tea roses she habitually kept in round glass bowls throughout the room. The huge wrought-iron four-poster bed with crisp white hotel sheets and floral duvet seemed the same even though Ronnie wasn't in it. So why did she feel so—

It all came flooding back. The accident, the hospital, Maya. She groaned. The ache in her forehead and temples throbbed anew; struggling not to cry again—not again—she threw her hands over her eyes and sat up gingerly, trying to give her forehead time to adjust to the altitude change. A spell of light-headedness disappeared as quickly as it had come.

She'd sobbed and sobbed after Justus left, loud, wracking sobs so violent they seemed to rip her skin from her flesh, her flesh from her bones. She'd cried until finally she'd vomited, the bile irritating her already raw throat. Every few minutes she'd think she'd gotten a little control, but then a fresh image—Carolyn holding Maya in the hospital just after she was born, Carolyn and V.J. crushed in their car by some stupid deer, Maya getting married with no one to walk her down the aisle—would flash through her mind and the endless tears would start again. She didn't think she'd ever—

A faint rustling sound by her open door jarred her out of her thoughts and she dropped her hands. Maya stood in the doorway, her braided hair mussed, her eyes still droopy with sleep. Tiny bare feet peeked out from under the oversized white T-shirt she'd slept in. Again she held her floppy-eared brown dog to her mouth and stared at Angela with solemn wide eyes.

"Hi, Sweetie," Angela said, her voice froggy with sleep and tears.

"Hi," Maya said, her voice muffled by the dog.

Angela wracked her brain for an available, age-appropriate topic to discuss with her—something that wouldn't trigger immediate questions or memories about her parents. "What—" she cleared her throat. "How did you sleep?"

"Good."

"Good."

The silence lengthened as they stared at each other. For the life of her Angela couldn't think of anything to say. What on earth did people talk to three-and-a-half-year-olds about? "How did your doggie sleep?"

"Aunt Ang-la." Maya rolled her eyes. "He's a *toy*. He doesn't sleep."

"Oh." Angela nodded. "Right. I should have known that."

Maya's eyes blinked at her from over the top of the dog's head.

Angela chewed the inside of her cheek nervously. Why did Maya keep staring at her like that? They'd never had very much to say to each other before, but she couldn't ever recall her just standing there *staring*. Was this normal? Or was it some symptom of posttraumatic stress disorder she should be worried about? Did other kids stare like this?

She decided to give conversation another try. "What's your doggie's name?"

Maya shrugged.

At a complete loss, Angela fell silent again. "Scooby?" she suggested hopefully. "Marmaduke? Lassie?—"

Silence.

"—Rex? Max? Fido? Are you telling me this dog doesn't have a name?"

Silence.

Angela gave up. Sighing, she threw the covers back and climbed out of bed; they might as well face the inevitable and begin what was sure to be a horrible day. "Well, we'll have to work on a name for him, okay?"

"Okay."

Angela took Maya's warm hand and led her down the hall to the kitchen. "Let's see what we have to eat. Are you hungry?"

Maya nodded.

Angela swung open the refrigerator and stooped down to look inside. "Yogurt?"

"Eeeeew!" Maya's face wrinkled up like a Shar-Pei.

"Ri-iight," Angela said. "Well, how about some cereal and milk?"

"Okay."

Relieved, Angela turned to the pantry and opened the door.

"Have a seat at the counter," she said, waving at one of the stools. Maya regarded the high-backed stools dubiously for a moment, then swung one plump leg onto the bottom rung and heaved herself into her seat. Angela pulled the box of Mueslix from the shelf, then turned to find a bowl.

"What's that?" Maya asked warily, as if she suspected Angela of trying to sneak her a plate of liver, onions, and spinach.

"Mueslix."

"Eeeeew!"

Angela felt the first stirrings of impatience. She put the box back and surveyed her other choices. "What about Raisin Bran?" She looked over her shoulder in time to catch the look of horror cross Maya's face. "Alrighty, then," she muttered. "No yogurt, no Mueslix, no Raisin Bran. I suppose Special K is out, too?"

Maya's little face scrunched into an obstinate expression Angela figured didn't bode well. "I want Count Chocu-laaa," she said in a high-pitched whine only slightly less annoying than a guinea pig's squeal.

"Maya," she said crisply, trying to channel "The Look" her mother used to give her and Carolyn when trouble was pending, "we do not whine in this house."

Maya glared impotently at her, but wisely kept quiet.

Immediately Angela felt terrible. Surely she could tolerate a little whininess from a preschooler who'd just lost both parents. "Okay," she said gently, deciding to give diplomacy one last chance, "the only other choice you have is a peanut butter and jelly sandwich on wheat bread. That's the best I can do."

Maya's lower lip slowly poked out until finally she looked like someone had taken a baseball bat to her mouth. "I want Wonder Bread."

Angela repressed a shudder. That fluffy, sugary concoction of white flour and empty calories? Oh, no. Not in this house.

Crossing her arms over her chest, she planted her feet wide. Enough was enough. By the time they finished breakfast negotiations it would be time for lunch. "Peanut butter and jelly on *wheat* bread. *With* crust."

Maya's withering gaze faltered, then fell. Still, she wouldn't let Angela have the last word. "Cut it in four pieces."

Angela cupped her hand to her ear. "Do I hear a nice word?"

Maya's lips thinned and disappeared. "*Please*," she said nastily, as if what she really wanted to tell Angela was to go to hell.

Relieved they'd reached a truce, Angela quickly made the sandwich, poured a glass of skim milk and plunked them down in front of Maya. One look at the white milk had Maya's lower lip ballooning again.

"I want choc-late syrup."

The uneasy peace, such as it was, collapsed within the hour. Angela cleaned Maya up, slathered her with lotion, and dressed her in her clothes from yesterday, grateful she'd had the foresight, as tired as she was, to throw them into the wash before she went to bed last night. Maya, who seemed as determined not to mention her parents as Angela was, settled onto the sofa with her dog and asked to watch TV.

"Well, . . . sure." As a general rule, Angela believed children under the age of, oh, say, eight should never watch TV. When *she* had children, she would have them look at picture books and play with blocks and quiet toys in their rooms to develop their imaginations and creativity. Parents who relied on TV to baby-sit their children were lazy at best and neglectful at worst. But this one time it wouldn't hurt anything if Maya watched half an hour's worth of educational shows while Angela got dressed.

She quickly found the remote. Standing at the corner of the coffee table, she turned the TV on and flipped through the usual Sunday morning news shows looking for something kid-friendly.

Maya watched with interest. "Turn it to Nick," she suggested helpfully.

Angela paused to look at her. "Nick? What's Nick?"

Maya's mouth fell open with dismay. Clearly the poor child could not fathom an adult who did not know what "Nick" was. "The *kid's* channel. Push two-eight."

Angela gaped at her. Did she know how to work the remote? How much TV did she watch, anyway? "Is that cable? I don't have cable."

Before the explosion came—and judging by the way Maya went rigid, flung herself onto her back and balled up her fists, it was going to be a biggie—the doorbell rang. Nicely diverted, Maya leapt to her feet and ran into the foyer, jumping up and down.

Angela glanced hopelessly down at her tank top and boxer shorts; normally she got up at six or six-thirty, ran on the treadmill for an hour or so, and was showered and fresh by eight. Today she counted herself lucky she'd been able to steal thirty seconds to brush her teeth while Maya ate. She had no idea when she'd have the chance to make calls and start the arrangements. On her way past the hall table and mirror she swiped at the edges of her hair around her face, which were falling out of her ponytail. Sighing, she followed Maya to the door and opened it.

"Uncle Justus!" Maya streaked past in a flash of flying legs and pigtails and launched herself at Justus, who stooped down in time to scoop her up and swing her in the air before he held her to his chest, her legs dangling.

"Hi, Baby Girl!" His eyes closed as he hugged Maya. Angela saw him breathe deeply as if to absorb something invisible but essential—as if he gathered strength from holding his niece. Opening his eyes, he looked for Angela. When he saw her, his gaze flickered discreetly over her from head to bare feet, and his jaw tightened. "Hi. Hope I'm not too early."

"Hi," she said, excruciatingly aware of this strange man in her apartment while she wore nothing but her pajamas. Why hadn't she at least put her robe on before she opened the door?

But Justus's attention shifted immediately back to Maya, and if he thought Angela looked bad he tactfully kept his opinion to himself. "How are you, Little Girl?" he asked Maya, whose arms wrapped around his neck. "What's wrong with your face?"

"It scratches," Maya told him, raking her short nails over her cheek.

Angela took a good look at Maya and realized she had several red welts, all larger than peas, dotting her face. Had they been there all morning? She didn't think so, but then again she hadn't really taken a good look at her face. Justus shot her a quizzical glance.

"I don't know," she said, shrugging. "I washed her clothes last night. Maybe she's sensitive to the detergent I used. Or it could be the lotion I just put on her."

Justus stared at Maya, frowning thoughtfully. "Well, should we call the doctor?"

"No-ooo!" Maya shook her head so violently she threatened to give herself whiplash. "I don't want any shots!"

"I don't think we need to do that." Angela tried to sound confident, as if she'd had vast experience with children and rashes. "It's just a rash. I have some calamine we can put on it. We'll watch her and see how she does."

Justus nodded, looking relieved. He seemed perfectly willing to defer to Angela's decision, as if, simply by virtue of her sex, she somehow knew more about kids than he did. Turning back to Maya, he nuzzled her ear. "Did you sleep here last night?"

"Yeah." Her head bobbed eagerly. "In the big bed."

Justus's eyes widened. "The big bed! Did you fall out?"

"No." Her smile faded. "Uncle Justus, when can I go home?"

Angela froze and Justus stiffened, his stricken gaze holding Maya's innocent, trusting one. He shot Angela a look over Maya's shoulder, and she tried to smile encouragingly but her mouth wouldn't cooperate.

"Well, Little Girl," he said softly, smoothing her braid, "you know Mommy and Daddy—"

"Are in heaven," she said dully. "But when will they come back?"

Strain flashed across his face; he swallowed convulsively. "They're going to stay in heaven with God, Little Girl," he told her. Maya's lips quivered for a second, but then she pressed them together and raised her chin, clearly determined not to cry. "But they're watching out for us, all the time. So you have to listen and clean up your room and go to school and work on your letters and do all the things you always do, okay?"

Maya squirmed, pulled her arms away from his neck and pushed on his chest. Justus swung her down. Maya went back to the sofa, climbed up and reached for her dog. "Aunt Angla doesn't even have Nick," she said sourly.

Justus straightened and caught Angela's eye and she smiled gratefully at him. He was wonderful with Maya, so much more at ease with her than she was. "Good job," she whispered.

"Thanks." He shoved his hands in his jeans pockets and studied the floor.

"I'm bo-ored." Maya went rigid again and flopped unto her back, stomping her shoeless feet into Angela's hundred-dollar embroidered pillows. Instinctively Angela opened her mouth to stop her—children these days clearly had no respect for nice furniture or other people's belongings—but it occurred to her they all had more important things to worry about.

Justus sprang into action and marched into the kitchen. Curious, Angela watched as he filled the sink with water, then added some dish soap for bubbles. He turned over his shoulder to look at her. "Measuring cups?" he said. "Turkey baster?"

"Second drawer."

Justus jerked the drawer open, found the items, and dumped them into the water. Over in the living room Maya stopped stomping the pillows long enough to sit up and stare. "What's that?" she demanded.

"What, this?" Justus's eyes widened innocently. "Oh, nothing. Just some water play."

"Water play!" she squealed, jumping off the sofa and running into the kitchen. Angela watched, astonished, as Maya grabbed one of the heavy kitchen chairs and shoved it across the tiled floor to the sink, climbed up, and happily splashed in the water.

Justus, a wide, satisfied smile on his face, sauntered over to Angela. "She'll be there for hours."

She put her hands on her hips, frowning. "Well, aren't you the cock-of-the-walk?"

His smile brightened even further. "I like to think so."

They laughed together, but then Maya's arms dove into the water, generating a wave that soaked the front of her clothes, the countertops and the rug underneath her stool. Angela turned on Justus and waved a hand at Maya. "Who's going to clean this mess up?"

"Last time I checked, water didn't leave a stain."

Angela snorted indelicately, but he seemed not to notice. His gaze slipped over her body before he looked away to watch Maya squirt water down the drain with the turkey baster. "Do you, ah, want to get a shower? We've got a lot of stuff to do."

Self-conscious again, Angela crossed her arms over her chest. "I didn't have time—"

The wall phone rang, startling them. Angela snatched it up. "Hello?"

"Angela," said a deep, gravelly voice. "It's Vincent Robinson."

"Oh, Mr. Robinson," she began, "I'm so sorry—"

"So am I," he said simply. "How is Maya?"

Angela looked back at the sink. Maya raised a wet arm and poured frothy water from the stainless steel measuring cup back into the sink. "Fine. She was really happy to see Just—"

"We need to make some arrangements," he interrupted. "If you can come over here Lena will watch Maya while we talk. Say, in an hour?"

His tone was perfectly pleasant, yet he somehow managed to convey that this was a command, not a request, and that no excuses would be acceptable. Normally Angela would have bristled and said no just to establish some boundaries, but of course Mr. Robinson was right. They did need to get things started. "That's fine. We'll be there."

"See you then."

Angela hung up and turned to Justus, whose intent gaze had been on her the whole time. "Let me guess," he said through his clenched jaw. "Command performance?"

"Yeah," she said, remembering the tension she'd seen between Justus and his father years ago at the wedding reception. "In an hour, if that's okay."

He shrugged, his face dark and moody now. "An hour, two hours. It doesn't really matter, does it? They'll still be dead."

"Justus." For some unfathomable reason she put her hand on his rigid arm. Normally she wasn't a touchy-feely person but she desperately needed to pull Justus back from whatever dark place he'd gone to. "I didn't have the chance to ask how things went with your father last night."

Clearly she'd asked exactly the wrong question. He snorted, his face twisting into a crooked, ugly smile. "How do you think it went? The crown prince and heir is dead."

He wheeled around and stalked over to Maya, exclaiming over her bubbles. Troubled, Angela left.

Chapter 5

Justus took Maya in his SUV and Angela trailed behind in her own car as they drove to the Robinson . . . estate? Mansion? House was much too modest a word for this dwelling, Angela thought as she pulled past the gated brick wall and into the long, cobbled drive. She'd grown up hearing Vincent Robinson's name, of course. He was one of Cincinnati's most prominent civil rights attorneys and had also written several commercially popular books about the law. But she'd had no idea he'd done so well. Normally she was pretty low-key about such things, but as she climbed out and started up the walk past Justus's car she felt her mouth fall open into a gape. Justus watched her, his lips stretched thin, as he unbuckled Maya.

"You grew up here?" Angela asked, awed.

"It's just a house," he snapped.

Startled by his vehemence, she decided to just keep her big mouth shut.

Maya bounded out of the car and rang the doorbell and Angela and Justus followed. Immediately the door swung open and Vincent appeared. "Gran' pa!" she shrieked, throwing her arms around his legs. He stooped down to hug her, then said, "Miss Lena's in the kitchen waiting for you. She's got some chocolate chip muffins." Angela watched Maya run off down some long hallway.

Vincent straightened and turned to her, his expression somber. She was startled to see how much he'd aged in the ten years since she'd seen him, and how poorly. His hair was entirely white now, deep hollows rimmed his eyes, top and bottom, and his skin looked pasty. Was this how he looked two days ago, or had he aged this much since he'd heard the news? "Angela, dear." He held his arms open, and Angela hesitated then stepped into them for a hug. Tragedy created the strangest intimacies, apparently. She put her hands on his shoulders, surprised by how frail they were, and tilted her head to accept his kiss.

"It's good to see you," she murmured.

"How did she do last night?" He pulled away, holding her hands in his thin firm grip.

"Very well. She doesn't ask many questions. I think she's trying not to cry."

Vincent nodded thoughtfully. Finally—and belatedly, Angela thought—his cool gaze went to Justus, who stiffened perceptibly. "Son."

"Pops."

Vincent took their coats, then, extending an arm to direct her, steered them into a stunning living room of some sort. Or was it a sitting room or library? Her first ridiculous thought was that she'd underdressed in her black slacks and sweater. Her second ridiculous thought was about where the live-in servants were hiding. A house like this surely had some. Slowly she looked around. A huge bay window with mullioned panes in a diamond pattern dominated one wall; the rich, pale blue raw silk of the drapes was repeated in the overstuffed chairs and pillows on the seven-foot sofa. Intricately carved mahogany tables loaded with antique Oriental ginger jar lamps, jade bowls, black-and-white family photos in heavy sterling frames, and other bric-a-brac dotted the room. In another corner a nine-foot black Steinway gleamed, its lid soaring toward the heavy wood beams visible against the white ceiling. On the floor sat a beautiful Persian rug at least a hundred years old.

This time Angela managed to stop her gape before it began, but it wasn't easy. She was here to plan her sister's funeral as best she could, according to what she thought Carolyn would want—not to admire beautiful antiques. In the last hour or so, since she'd cried again in the shower, numbness had come over her and she hoped it would last long enough for them to get through most of the planning without her bawling like a baby.

"Sit down," Vincent told her as he chose a carved chair for himself.

Angela perched on the edge of the sofa—this room required perfect posture. Justus sat next to her. In some distant room a phone rang and was quickly answered. "We've been making a lot of calls." Vincent reached for the ornate silver tea service—*tea service?*—on the coffee table and poured a cup of tea into gold-rimmed bone china so fine she could see Vincent's fingers through it. Also on the heavy silver tray sat a plate of raspberry scones and the promised chocolate chip muffins. "The phone's been ringing off the hook." He passed the teacup and saucer to her, along with a heavy linen napkin. She hastily took them and draped her napkin over her lap. Beside her Justus flung his arm over the back of the sofa and slouched deeper into the cushions. Vincent did not bother asking him if he wanted tea. "They'll start arriving soon."

"Of course," Angela murmured, adding her own cream and sugar.

"To my knowledge neither of them had a will—"

"Right."

"—even though I told him when Maya was born they

needed to get their affairs in order in case—" his voice cracked. Pressing his lips together he poured a second cup of tea with unsteady hands, then hastily took a sip. Angela studied the fragrant, steaming amber tea in her cup—English breakfast, probably—and waited for Vincent to compose himself. She did not look at Justus, who kept quiet.

"A-hem." Taking a deep breath, Vincent flipped open a manila file on the coffee table and slid a pair of bifocals onto his nose. "Is First Methodist okay with you for the service on Tuesday?" he asked, peering at her over the rims of his glasses. "That's where they were married."

"That's fine," Angela said, nodding.

He picked up an expensive black fountain pen and checked something off his list. "The minister will be by this afternoon." Another check. "Lena's ordered some flowers and the limousines." Check.

He kept talking and Angela watched him with a sort of fascinated horror. The man was so coolly efficient—so detached—one would think he lost a son every day. Did he have this all on the computer, for God's sake? Studying his face she saw no sign of grief or anger or anything other than brisk efficiency. From the corner of her eye she saw Justus's jaw flex, but he remained silent.

Vincent flipped to the next page in the file. "Now, for the interment, we have a family plot at Spring Grove and—"

"No!" Angela cried. Vincent's head snapped up and a slight frown creased his forehead as his brows came together. "Carolyn always said she didn't want to be put in the ground." Angela choked up and had to pause a minute to collect herself. How often had she and Carolyn had that same offhand conversation? For as long as she could remember, Carolyn had always said the same thing. "She said it was a waste of money to buy an expensive casket and bury someone in it. She said she wanted to be cremated."

"I see." Vincent rested his elbows on the arms of his chair and steepled his fingers. "But you do agree Carolyn and Vincent Jr. need to remain together?"

"Of course."

"Well, my wife is buried in a very nice spot on a hill under a flowering crabapple tree," he said quietly, the soul of logic and reason. "I will have the plot next to her, and we bought plots for the boys and their spouses a long time ago. We always thought we'd be together."

Angela stared, aghast, at Vincent; Justus's alert gaze remained on her but he kept quiet.

"Angela, dear, how long has it been since you spoke with Carolyn about it? Isn't it possible she'd changed her mind—"

"No."

"Well," Vincent said, smiling ruefully, "I'm sure if you think about it you'll realize the reasonable thing—"

The renewed throbbing in her temples told Angela she'd had enough. Maybe this manipulative, albeit somewhat charming, little diplomatic routine worked with other people, but it wasn't going to work with her. Very deliberately she replaced her teacup and saucer on the silver tray, folded her napkin, and placed it on the table.

"Mr. Robinson," she said pleasantly, "I don't care where we have the service. I don't care what kind of flowers you order or what kind of limousines you get. I don't care if the service is Tuesday or Wednesday or Friday." She set her jaw. "But I am telling you we will not bury my sister in the ground. She wanted to be cremated and have her ashes scattered, and *that's* what we're going to do."

Their gazes, equally unyielding, collided and held for what felt like years. Gradually it seemed to occur to him she wasn't about to back down. Clearly angry, Vincent huffed, snatched the bifocals off the end of his nose, and opened his mouth to respond.

"Let it go, Vincent."

Surprised to hear his voice, Angela looked to Justus. He sat up straight and fixed his father in his unblinking gaze. Very slightly he leaned closer to her and she felt the feather-light touch of his fingers on her back. Immediately she felt comforted and, even better, shielded, physically and emotionally, from Vincent.

"We can cremate them both," Justus continued. "V.J. wouldn't want you arguing with Angela over something like this. *Just let it go.*"

Vincent shot Justus a look designed to cause him a lingering, painful death, then slid his bifocals on again. Lowering his head, he flipped to another page in the file. "I think we'll just have them both cremated," he said as if it had been his idea in the first place. "That makes the most sense. Now, about the donations—"

"Mr. Robinson." Angela, feeling drained and deflated, pressed her fingers to her temples. She really didn't care about the donations or the service—she was sure Vincent would do a lovely, classy job—and she wanted to conserve her limited emotional resources. "I wonder if we could handle some of this later. I still need to call the office and Maya's preschool for tomorrow, and I'd like to go to the house and pick up some of Maya's toys and clothes. I thought maybe she could stay here while I did that."

That slight frown passed over his forehead again. Obviously Vincent did not appreciate being interrupted mid-way through his Funeral List. Did everyone automatically do everything he wanted them to do? Was she the only one who ever told this man no? "That's fine, Angela," he said with relative grace, replacing the cap on his pen. "Will you be back in an hour or so?"

"Yes." She stood up.

Justus trailed her to the foyer, putting a hand to the small of her back. "I'll help you."

As always, she bristled at the suggestion she couldn't handle something alone. "Oh, you don't need to come. I've got it under control—"

"I'm coming."

"Really, Justus, I can—"

She glanced over her shoulder at him and the glower on his face stopped her cold. "I know you're Wonder Woman and all," he said softly, "but your sister just died. We need to help each other, and if you think I'm going to let you go there by yourself, you damn well better think again." He smiled a grim, tight smile that told her there'd be hell to pay if she argued. "Okay?"

Caught completely off guard, Angela spluttered uselessly. He stared her down, crossing his hands over his chest like a bouncer blocking her entrance to a club. "Fine," she said ungraciously. "If you're going to act like a caveman."

It was the wrong thing to say. His shoulders squared and their gazes locked for a long, challenging moment. "This ain't nothing, Duchess."

It was a warning if ever she'd heard one. She held his intent, angry gaze for as long as she could, but then her face began to burn and she had to look away. Infuriated, she whirled and snatched her purse and jacket from the chair.

"Let's go," she barked.

Justus gave her a mocking little bow and opened the door for her. As she swept through it she caught a glimpse of Vincent's astonished face staring after them.

Justus trailed Angela into the oppressive emptiness of his brother's house, keeping a close eye on her as she flicked on lights in the foyer and living room. She hadn't said two words in the car on the short drive over, and he was worried. Why was she so quiet? Was she okay? This had to be the worst week of her life, bar none: first her punk of a boyfriend dumped her in public and now this. How much more could she take?

Angela aroused some heretofore dormant protective instinct in him that he didn't like but couldn't ignore. At a time when his attention should be focused on his orphaned niece, he found himself nearly as concerned about Angela, a woman who was, for all intents and purposes, a complete stranger. Sure, she was strong; the way she'd firmly dispatched his father and his ridiculous burial plans this morning proved that. But she was fragile, too, vulnerable. And he planned to stay close and make sure nothing—not her boyfriend's defection, her sister's death, or his father the dictator—broke her.

She marched into the huge kitchen, her face set in tight, grim lines. Fascinated, he watched as she walked around the island with its speckled granite countertop and stopped to look in the sink. Peering over her shoulder he saw bowls—white with blue and pink flowers—soaking in water with a few limp bubbles of dish liquid left, dried oatmeal coating their rims. He tried not to think about the fact that V.J. and Carolyn would never need these bowls again.

Angela's lips turned up in a sorry imitation of a smile. "Carolyn never could keep house."

Unthinking, Justus ran his hand over her back and squeezed her shoulder. Blinking furiously, she raised her head to look at him with shimmering eyes. "Are they really gone, Justus?" she whispered, her voice strangely hopeful, as if she thought he had secret resurrection powers he might use for just such an occasion.

"Yes."

She nodded, a lone tear trailing down her cheek. Turning, she walked down the hall to the steps and he followed along. Maya's pretty room at the top of the staircase, to the left, looked exactly the same. He'd half expected the rooms to darken automatically out of respect for the dead, but that apparently wasn't the case. Bright sunlight shone through the white curtains, which were made out of the same wispy material as a ballet dancer's skirts. The pale pink walls and white wicker headboard and rocker screamed that a young girl lived here. Stuffed animals competed for space on every available surface, especially the pastel quilt covering the bed. On the dresser sat several family photos in silver frames: Maya as a newborn in the obligatory shot from the hospital nursery; Maya, V.J., and Carolyn smiling at the beach with Maya wearing silly, white-framed sunglasses; Maya and V.J. asleep together on the sofa.

Justus's chest tightened as he watched Angela stare at the pictures, her long, delicate fingers lightly touching her sister's smiling, one-dimensional face. From behind he saw her shoulders heave and, fearing she was about to cry again, he touched her arm. Startled, she stared up at him, waiting.

"Don't do this to yourself, Angela. Not today."

To his complete surprise she smiled—a full smile that wrung his heart in a way nothing else ever had. "I was just remembering how happy they were. The day Carolyn met V.J.— I think it was at freshman orientation—she called to tell me she'd met the man she was going to marry. I laughed my head off and told her she was crazy, but she was right." Her smile widened. "And I was thinking how glad I am they had each other, even if it was just for a little while."

She turned to another picture, one he hadn't noticed: him at about age four, in shorts and a T-shirt, his skinny legs ending in sandaled feet that looked only slightly smaller than his feet were now, with V.J., laughing at the bottom of the slide in the back yard of their first, smaller, house. With their mother.

Mama. She was laughing, her head thrown back, her long

hair blowing to the right of her face in the wind. He remembered the day very well. Vincent—in a rare good mood—had just finished setting up their new jungle gym. After they'd run around like maniacs for a couple of hours, they'd grilled burgers and, his personal favorite, smoked sausages, and Mama had topped the evening with her homemade vanilla ice cream. After tossing a coin to decide the matter, V.J. had won the right to lick the dasher, the one tense moment in an otherwise perfect summer day.

Seeing Mama now, and realizing that half—the good half, frankly—of his nuclear family was gone felt like a sword slashing through his heart, cleaving him in two and threatening to make him collapse on the floor and unman himself in front of Angela. He breathed deeply, struggling for control.

Fortunately, Angela didn't seem to notice his turmoil. She smiled again, still looking at the picture. "Ahh, look at you, Justus," she murmured, almost to herself. "I should have known you were an adorable child. Your children will be so beautiful." Something about her wistful tone distracted him from his sudden loneliness and he stared, mesmerized, at her. "And look at your mother." Her gaze shot to his, her eyes teary now, as if she felt sorry for him.

Normally he hated pity of any sort, but Angela's concern, and her complete understanding of his feelings felt like the most precious gift he'd ever received. His heart swelled.

"You must miss her so much," she told him. "But V.J. and your mom are together now."

God, he hoped so. That was the only thought holding him together. Despite all his determination not to, he choked up, his face crumpling, a few stray tears refusing to be denied. He hated crying. V.J. had always said there was no point to it, and he was right. Embarrassed, he swiped at his eyes.

Angela stepped closer. "Shhh." She covered his cheek with her soft palm. "It's okay."

With a cry he jerked her into his arms and clung, hard, having already discovered he always felt better whenever he touched Angela.

Chapter 6

Her cell phone rang as Angela hurried into the sleek glass and chrome lobby of her office building at nine the next morning. Having missed the morning rush because she'd taken Maya to preschool first, Angela was surprised to see how quiet the soaring, sunny atrium was; only on very rare occasions was she not at her desk by eight at the latest. Slowing slightly, she fished the phone out of the side pocket of her purse and flipped it open without bothering to see who it was. She stopped at the second bank of elevators and pushed the UP button.

"Hello?"

"Hey," Justus said. "Did you get Maya dropped off okay?"

The bell dinged and the elevator doors slid open. She stepped into the empty mirrored car and pressed nineteen. She should have known he'd call because he seemed determined to be an active part of Maya's life. "She did really well. I think she was glad to be back with her friends."

"Did they ask her a lot of questions, or—"

"Well, the teacher did, but I'm not sure the other little kids even know what's going on."

He heaved a relieved sigh. "Thank God for small favors."

"Amen." The doors slid open and she stepped into the hushed, elegant reception area of her firm. Several clients sat, some reading the paper, others talking quietly, in the plush, modern chairs near floor-to-ceiling windows. "Are you at the gym?" she asked, automatically lowering her voice as she waved at the receptionist behind her granite-topped station and started down the hall to her office.

"For a while. You gonna be there all day?"

"Probably not. I don't have much going on, and I won't be able to concentrate very well. And I don't want Maya's first day back to be too long." She turned into her office and flipped the light switch.

"Well, I thought I'd come have dinner with you later. I'll bring a pizza or something."

Angela froze in the act of taking off her jacket, surprised he'd suggest something so attentive. She had little to no experience with thoughtful men; in her three years with Ronnie he'd picked up dinner once or twice. He'd always seemed to think it was her responsibility to plan the meals even though she worked as long and hard as he did.

"Bless your heart," she said, thinking of how tired she'd be by dinnertime. "Aren't you a sweetheart?"

He snorted. "Yeah, I get accused of that a lot."

"I need to go," she said, laughing. "I'll see you later."

"Later."

Angela hung up, sat in her tall, navy leather chair and booted up her computer. She fully intended to review the large stack of mail in her inbox, the same as she did any other Monday morning of her life, but the huge knot that suddenly formed in her gut stopped her. Carolyn was dead and Maya was an orphan. Why read the mail?

How could everything look the same in this one little part of her world, when the rest of her world had been shattered? The sun still shone through her floor-to-ceiling windows, the same as always, and her carved cherry desk was still neat and clean, the family pictures nicely framed and arranged. Over on the bookshelves a violet orchid bloomed; on top of the walnut file cabinet a fern stretched its fronds to the light. Her cheerful impressionist prints, Monet and Renoir, hung on the wall, mocking her.

She planted her elbows on the desk, buried her head in her hands, and struggled not to cry.

"Angela!"

Angela jerked her head up in time to see her good friend— actually she'd been promoted to best friend now that Carolyn was dead—and colleague, Carmen Rodriguez, rush in. Carmen looked exactly the same, too: milky white skin, wavy raven hair falling around her shoulders, almond-shaped mahogany eyes. Carmen rushed around the desk, stooped and gathered Angela into her arms.

"Oh, God, are you okay? Why haven't you called me back? I've been so worried. How's Maya? Is she doing okay? Is she back in school?"

Angela extricated herself, no easy process. The last thing she needed right now was a soft shoulder to cry on. Once she got started with the bawling these days there was no stopping. "We're okay," she said, sniffling. "Maya's in school. I'm sorry I didn't call. I've been so busy."

Carmen nodded sympathetically, pulled Angela to her feet and towed her to the navy-striped loveseat in the corner. "When's the funeral?"

"Tomorrow."

Carmen pressed her hands. "What can I do?"

A sob surged from Angela's tight throat. She clapped her hand over her mouth but, to her horror, she still made a pitiful choking sound. "Pray for us."

Carmen pulled her into another bear hug, shushing her, and this time Angela was too upset to resist. Finally Carmen leaned away, handed Angela a tissue from the end table, and took one to dab her own eyes. "What about Maya? What'll happen to her? What do their wills say?"

"They didn't have wills."

Carmen gaped. "V.J. was a lawyer! For God's sake, how could he not have a will?"

Angela could only shake her head. "I wish I knew."

Carmen stared off in the distance, as if she needed a minute to absorb the magnitude of the problem. "So what will you do with her?"

This was the question Angela had been avoiding asking, even to herself. But the funeral was tomorrow and it was time to make some plans. Maya needed permanency in her life.

Do you have any idea how much it would mean to me if my sister actually liked my daughter? Can't you do it for me?

Besides, she owed it to Carolyn. "I've got to take her."

"*You*?" Carmen stared at her as if she'd suggested Maya live with a convicted child molester. "But you're not ready to be a mother! You're a single woman living in an apartment and you work seventy hours a week!"

"Carolyn would do it for me."

"Well . . ." Carmen cocked her head thoughtfully. "Maybe after you get engaged—"

Angela recoiled, then gave a hoarse bark of laughter tinged with hysteria. "That's right! I haven't told you my other big news! Ronnie dumped me Friday night."

"No!" Carmen shrieked.

"He said he wasn't ready to commit, blah, blah, blah. But when I went to the hospital to get Maya, I saw him in the parking lot with his lips all over some nurse or something."

"That son-of-a-bitch!"

Angela nodded grimly. Carmen's outraged horror on her behalf was deeply satisfying, and any other time she'd like to wallow in it for a good long while. But right now she needed to focus on Maya. "So I'll have to be a single parent. I can manage."

"Oh, but, Angela," Carmen said, "it's such a big responsibility. Are you sure you're ready?"

Agitated now, Angela jumped up to pace back and forth in front of the windows. "Of course I'm not ready! I'm not married, I don't know anything about kids. I don't think I have any maternal instincts." She snorted. "Maya doesn't even like me."

Oppressive guilt, her other new best friend, reared its ugly head again. If she and Maya didn't like each other, it was because she'd never made the slightest effort to get to know her niece. Why? Because she'd been selfish.

When are you going to stop being so selfish? When are you going to wake up and realize it's not all about you and your career and your romance? What will it take for you to stop being so self-centered?

Tears—how could she even have any bodily fluids left after all this crying?—prickled the backs of her eyes again and she furiously blinked them back. It was time for her to grow up. This one time in her life she would put someone else's needs first. Maya needed her and she would be there for her. Period.

"Will you draw up the guardianship application for me?" Angela asked. "And represent me at the hearing? It shouldn't be that big a deal, right?"

"Yeah, sure. It's just a formality, really." Carmen hesitated, then plowed ahead. "But maybe her grandfather could take her. Did you ever think of that?"

Angela shook her head. "Vincent's getting old, and he didn't look any too healthy to me yesterday. I'm thinking he might even be sick. There's no way he's got the energy to run around after a three-and-a-half-year-old."

"Why couldn't Justus take her?"

Angela's jaw dropped. Surely no one had suggested an idea

this bad since New Coke. "Are you insane? Justus is living the single life on top of just starting his gym. He doesn't want to be saddled to a kid any more than Hugh Heffner does. Trust me."

"Really?" Carmen tilted her head thoughtfully.

"Well, sure he's been great with her so far." Angela flapped her arms impatiently. "This is all fresh and new. But in a couple weeks he'll be back to life as usual and he won't want to bother with a kid. You mark my words. Anyway, Maya needs a mother."

Carmen looked dubious. "Did Justus *say* he didn't want her?"

"Of course he doesn't want her," Angela cried, thoroughly exasperated now. "What twenty-something man wants to be a single parent?" She took a deep breath and tried to get used to the awesome responsibility she'd just assumed. "I don't have any choice." Trying to ignore the panic roiling in her gut, she set her chin. "And one day I'll adopt her."

Justus knocked eagerly on Angela's apartment door, the pizza balanced on his hip. He was ten minutes early, but so what? He wanted to make sure both of his girls—he preferred not to think too closely about when he'd started to regard Angela as his girl—were okay. Immediately the six-panel door, which had a harvest wreath covered with small pumpkins and squash—he'd bet his last dime Angela had a wreath for every holiday and season, including Arbor Day—swung open. He felt ridiculously happy to be there, as if St. Peter had just opened the gates of heaven for him.

Angela smiled, obviously glad to see him. "Come in," she said, standing aside.

Grinning, he went to the kitchen and put the pizza on the counter, taking a minute to really look at the place. The kitchen walls were a warm, buttery yellow, and a pretty glass-topped table sat in the breakfast area, but the kitchen was too clean, almost sterile. Appliances marched up and down the counters, but there were no crumbs, no piles of mail, no signs that a human being actually lived here. The living room, on the other side of the granite countertop, was the same: beautiful hardwood floors with sofa, chairs, and rugs in rust, tan and blue. Beautiful but way too neat. Angela obviously liked to keep things in their place and she obviously liked to be in control all the time.

He'd have to change that.

He turned to look at her more closely. To his relief she looked a little better today. Her eyes weren't puffy, so maybe she'd stopped crying so much. She'd leashed her gleaming brown hair back into a long, low pony tail, a shame since he much preferred it hanging loose around her face. She must have changed out of her work clothes already because she wore a plain white T-shirt and black yoga pants that unfortunately clung to her curvy hips and butt and showed a crescent-shaped sliver of her taut brown belly. While this outfit was not quite as revealing as the shorts she'd worn yesterday morning, it still disturbed his equilibrium.

Quite a bit.

"Oooh, LaRosa's." She lifted the lid of the pizza box, inhaled deeply, and smiled delightedly at him, as if he'd brought her a sable coat. "You read my mind. Thank you."

His mouth went dry. Surely there wasn't another woman this beautiful anywhere on earth. Longing shot through him like a bolt of lightning, but he managed to shrug nonchalantly. "How was your day?"

She turned away and opened a cabinet. "Okay." Reaching up to grab a stack of paper plates, she flashed a generous portion of her smooth lower back. Worse, her tight butt flexed as she rose on her tiptoes. "I didn't get much work done, though.

Everyone stopped by to give me their condolences, and I made some more calls and worked on the arrangements. I think I talked to your father about ten times." She turned back around to face him from across the island. "How was yours?"

Somehow he managed to jerk his gaze back to hers before she caught him ogling her. He pulled one of the tall chairs out from under the countertop and sat down. "Pretty much the sa—"

"Uncle Justus!" shrieked Maya, her bare feet pounding the floor as she raced into the kitchen. Without breaking stride she launched herself at him, hugging him around the legs. "What're you doing here?"

"What am I doing here?" He swung her up into his lap and smacked a loud kiss on her soft little chipmunk cheek before he dropped her back to the floor. "I brought you a delicious LaRosa's pizza to eat."

"Yay!"

"Oh, but I forgot." He stopped smiling, drawing his face into a thoughtful frown. "You don't eat pizza."

"Yes, I do!" She hopped up and down on one foot, her braids, now half unraveled, flapping around her face. "I love pizza!"

"No," he said, standing up and reaching for his keys on the counter. "I'll just go back out and get you some broccoli and cabbage."

Maya froze and her stricken gaze narrowed suspiciously. "Uncle Justus!" she said, stomping one foot, "you stop joking me!"

"I would never joke you."

Maya resumed hopping happily, and Justus looked up to see Angela smile broadly at him, a sweet, warm, addicting smile; he had the feeling she thought he was as good with children as Bill Cosby in a Jell-O commercial.

His heart turned over, hard, filled with emotions he was determined not to explore.

After dinner Justus insisted on giving Maya her bath, forgetting all about her unfortunate tendency to splash like a pod of dolphins. When it was over and she bounced off to the bedroom to find her jammies, he surveyed the damage to the normally pristine bathroom. The bottom of the heavy green-and-blue-floral shower curtain—it reminded him of some of the expensive curtains over at Casa Vincent—dripped water all over the nubbly little matching area rug. A large puddle glistened on top of the taupe ceramic floor tiles. Water splattered the ornate gold gilt mirror over the sink.

Angela wouldn't like this. In her world water belonged in pricey blue bottles in the fridge, not on the floor. Sighing, he snatched the hand towels off the rack—she had them artfully arranged and folded, the crème towels on top of the green ones—and threw them on the puddle.

The good news was he'd had the foresight to at least take off his sweatshirt. One of the great benefits of running a gym for a living was he got to wear comfortable clothes and shoes every day, so only his white T-shirt and the tops of his sweat pants got wet. The bad news was he'd used all the towels. Chilly now, he took the T-shirt off and threw it on the floor.

"Angela!" He stepped into the hallway but saw no sign of her. "Angela!"

Brisk footsteps came up behind him. Angela marched around the corner from the kitchen, folding Maya's little pink flannel Barbie nightgown as she came. "Here I am." When she got within four feet of him she finally looked up, saw him, and froze. Her gaze flickered over his bare chest and arms, shot back to his face, then down to the floor. "Wha—" She cleared her throat. "What is it?"

Bemused, he watched her shift restlessly, then toss her ponytail over her shoulder with a shaky hand. If he didn't know better he'd almost think she'd never seen a man's naked chest before. Experimentally he stepped closer; without looking at him she took a hasty step back. He felt a huge surge of satisfaction.

"Where do you keep the towels?" The huskiness in his own voice surprised him. "I'm a little wet."

"In the linen closet. Right there."

"Oh," he said, fascinated. "Thanks." He purposefully didn't move.

After a minute it seemed to dawn on her that she'd have to edge past him if she wanted to get down the hall. Her flustered gaze darted up from the floor, met his, then jackrabbited away. "Well." She smoothed her hair again, clutched the nightgown to her chest in a death grip and squeezed by, practically hugging the wall. Obviously she'd dive into a vat of nuclear waste before she'd let one part of her body touch his now, which was strange because they'd gotten used to touching each other constantly since the accident.

Safely beyond him now, she paused, then hesitantly gave him a sidelong look over her shoulder. When she realized she'd been caught doing it, her head jerked back around and she practically ran the rest of the way to the bedroom.

"Say your prayers, Sweet Girl." Justus, fully clothed again, sat on the side of the bed. Maya, tucked under the covers, her dog nestled in the crook of her arm, obediently put the palms of her hands together and closed her eyes.

> *"Now I lay me down to sleep*
> *I pray the Lord my soul to keep.*
> *If I should—"*

Justus had bowed his own head and closed his eyes, but when her voice trailed off he looked up. Maya stared at him, frowning, a wrinkle between her fine eyebrows. Her bottom lip quivered and Justus braced himself for a crying jag, which was, as far as he was concerned, long overdue. God knew she'd been brave and strong these last few days, but she wasn't even four yet. Her young life had imploded and if she wanted to cry she was certainly entitled.

"What's wrong, Maya? Don't you want to finish your prayer?"

Maya pulled the covers up higher and turned to face the wall. "I don't like this prayer." Her voice sounded very small and fragile.

"Okay," he said softly, at a complete loss. He leaned forward to kiss her, but she stiffened and pulled farther away. He rubbed her cheek instead. "Good night."

Maya didn't answer.

Troubled, Justus turned out the light, shut the door, and went back to the kitchen. Angela stood behind the counter, spraying some orange cleaning stuff all over everything. He watched while, with absolute concentration, she wiped the counter with her sponge, working in methodical circles. Her face tightened and she scrubbed, grunting, as if someone had smeared the counter with dung, even though he couldn't see a speck of dirt anywhere. Finally satisfied, she put the sponge in the dishwasher—the dishwasher?—and started it. Only then did she look up and start when she noticed him.

"What did that counter ever do to you?"

She shook her head, as if awakening from some altered state, then grinned sheepishly. "I don't like dirt."

He grunted as he pulled out a stool and sat. "I will try to remember that."

The wall phone rang before she could reply. "Sorry," she

told him, turning away to pick it up. "Hello?" She listened and her whole body stiffened.

Justus went into heightened alert and strained to hear whoever was on the line. Was it Vincent again, calling to bother her with some minute funeral detail, like whether they should serve smoked rather than maple turkey tomorrow after the service? If so he would happily snatch the phone from her and deal with his father himself. The last thing he wanted was someone—anyone—upsetting, or even bothering, Angela the night before her sister's funeral.

But then Angela, her face strained and flushed, said, "What do you want, Ronnie?"

Justus cursed silently, his blood doing a slow boil.

Chapter 7

"For God's sake, Angela!" Ronnie's voice quavered with righteous indignation. "Your sister died and you didn't even call me! I had to hear about it from one of the other docs. Did you think I wouldn't want to know?"

Angela leaned back against the counter, her heart pounding in her throat. "I didn't think about you at all," she said truthfully. Her gaze caught Justus's and he stared intently, his body rigid despite the negligent way he sprawled on the stool. His disapproving frown told her he was deeply interested in Ronnie's call, although she couldn't imagine why. Normally she'd take the call in the other room, or at least turn her back to show her displeasure at someone listening so obviously to a private conversation, but something about Justus's concern was oddly comforting.

Ronnie sighed harshly in her ear. "I still care about you, Angela. I want to do what I can to help. That hasn't changed."

Remembering the way he'd had his hands—and lips—all over that woman at the hospital, Angela longed to scream at him for being a liar and, worse, a coward. But she'd die a thousand gruesome deaths before she'd let Ronnie know how badly he'd humiliated her. And she certainly didn't want

Justus to know how she'd been dumped for a younger, sexier woman—exactly the type of woman Justus liked.

"I don't need your help." Her hand began to throb and she loosened her grip on the phone. "So if there's nothing else?"

"Angela—" Ronnie began.

"Good night, then," she said, quickly hanging up. Agitated, her heart thundering, she pressed her hand to her forehead, unwilling to meet Justus's gaze. After a minute, unable to think of anything else to do, she jerked the cabinet under the sink open, snatched up her cleaning spray, drenched the counter with it and scrubbed ruthlessly. Had she wiped the counters already? She couldn't remember. Why would Ronnie call her? Hadn't he already hurt her enough? Why go through the pretense of caring about her when he'd hooked up with someone—

"Angela." Justus reached out and covered her sponge hand with his large, warm, palm. She stilled, slowly lifting her gaze to look at him. "The counter can't take any more scrubbing." A hint of amusement glimmered in his eyes. "Look. The color's starting to fade."

The edges of her mouth tried to turn up in a smile, but the maneuver seemed strange, as if she'd never smiled before and didn't know how it should feel. "I feel better when I clean."

Justus's hand tightened over hers. "Maybe you'd feel better if you talked about it."

She shook her head in a violent *no*. "I can't. I don't—"

He scowled. "Drop the sponge, Angela. Or we're going to have a serious problem."

This time she had to laugh. Justus laughed, too, clearly relieved. Tugging her hand, he pulled her behind him to the sofa, where they both sat. Very deliberately Justus put his feet on the coffee table, watching her.

With an outraged cry, Angela smacked his thigh; his heavily muscled leg felt like it was made of concrete encased in granite. "What do you think you're doing?" she demanded, scooting a bowl of flowers and a couple of framed pictures out of the way before he knocked them over with his size nineteens.

One heavy brow winged upward. "I'm loosening you up. You need it, Duchess."

"Don't call me *Duchess*," she hissed.

To her further consternation, he leaned back against the cushions in what could only be called an insolent pose and put a hand to his ear. "Wait! What's that?" She listened but didn't hear anything. "I think—yes, I think it's the sound of the earth still turning on its axis even though I have my feet on your coffee table! What do you know?"

Angela spluttered speechlessly for a second before she reached around, grabbed one of her hundred-dollar pillows, and smashed him in the face with it. Laughing, he snatched it away.

"You drive me crazy," she huffed. "You're like an annoying little brother or something!"

His smile immediately disappeared and his eyes glittered dangerously. "I'm not your brother. Don't ever forget it."

The new, vaguely threatening note in his soft voice caught her completely by surprise. Stunned, she stared at him for a long, charged moment. Finally he looked away, his jaw flexing. He sprang to his feet, stalked back into the kitchen as if he owned the place, and poured himself another glass of the dark, rich Burgundy they'd had with dinner. Taking a sip, he watched her over the top of the goblet. He seemed troubled.

"What's going on with you and Ron?"

She shrugged irritably and sank back against the cushions. She wanted to tell him it was none of his business, but she had the feeling all conversation would grind to a screeching halt until she answered his question. And for some reason she wanted him to stay. "He dumped me the other night. I guess you figured that much out, huh?"

"Why?"

Sulking, she crossed her arms over her chest. "He doesn't want to get married."

He cocked his head to one side, eyes narrowed suspiciously, as if she'd just tried to sell him some real estate on the Ohio River. "What's the real reason? Is there someone else?"

God, he was infuriating. Marching around in her kitchen, drinking her wine and interrogating her about her own personal business. What right did he have to demand explanations and force her to share her worst humiliations? And why did she feel like she needed to answer?

"Yeah," she cried shrilly. "She's beautiful. Big breasts, big butt, younger—you'd love her. She's exactly your type."

His mouth twisted nastily. "You don't know anything about my type, Angela. Trust me."

There was a story there, but now wasn't the time to pursue it. Better to wallow in her humiliation for a minute. "So now you know my embarrassing secret," she snarled. "Happy?"

He sauntered back and resumed his seat on the other end of the sofa, putting his wine on the end table next to the lamp. Unsmiling, he faced her. "Am I happy to see you with your heart broken? No. Am I happy you're not wasting any more of your life with that punk? Hell, yeah."

"How can you judge him?" she said irrationally, flapping her arms. Maybe she felt the need to stick up for the person in whom she'd invested so much of her life; otherwise she was left with the unavoidable conclusion that she was a horrible judge of character. "You don't even know him!"

He gaped at her, incredulous. "You're *defending* him?"

God, what other nonsense would she spout before the night ended? "No! Of course not! It's just that you don't know Ron and you barely know me. How can you call him names?"

Shrugging, he said, "Fine. Maybe he isn't a jerk. Maybe he's the finest human being ever to walk the face of the planet. But he's still wrong for *you*."

Unwillingly intrigued, her anger fading, Angela turned to face him completely, tucking her foot under her. She propped her elbow on the back of the sofa and rested her head on her hand. "Why do you say that?"

Amusement glimmered in his eyes again. "Because I took one look at him and knew he'd let you walk all over him with your pretty little spiked heels. What you need is someone to stand up to you and tell you to knock it off when you get too bossy."

Outraged into speechlessness, Angela glared impotently. "I . . . you . . ." One corner of his mouth lifted in a smirk and she balled her hands into fists so she wouldn't hit him right in his smart mouth. "I do *not* walk all over people, and I am *not* bossy!"

"Whatever you say, Duchess." His eyes widened innocently. "So life with Ronnie was never boring, huh?"

That shut her up. Immediately her mind shifted to the routine she and Ronnie had established so easily. The routine that, looking back, now seemed . . . dull. The Friday nights with dinner and a movie. The Saturday mornings with pancakes and scrambled eggs. The droning conversations about politics and the failure of the health care system. The tame sex. Yes, she may as well go ahead and admit it now. Making love with Ronnie had been exactly as exciting as . . . well, as. . . . Cringing inwardly, she realized what the problem had been: anything was more exciting than sex with Ronnie; buying a fabulous new pair of shoes, discovering a new restaurant, even the new bath foam she'd discovered at Bath & Body Works.

Her gaze flew back to Justus's. Underneath his deliberately bland expression she could sense his intense interest in her answer. "Of course life with Ronnie was never boring!" she cried with the little bit of enthusiasm she could muster. She nervously adjusted the pillow behind her back. "And this topic of conversation is off limits."

Satisfaction gleamed in his eyes, although he tried to hide it. "Fine," he said disinterestedly. "What do you want to talk about?"

"Well," she huffed. "Let's examine *your* personal life in minute detail for a while."

"Fine," he said again, leaning back against the cushions and stretching his endless legs, which were back on the floor now, in front of him in a gesture of supreme relaxation. "Go ahead."

Angela watched him dubiously, although she strongly suspected he would answer whatever personal question she was rude enough to ask. The question was, how rude was she willing to be? Very, she decided. "So who was your little friend the other night?"

He didn't look very surprised by her choice of topic. Still, he seemed determined not to make things easy for her. One side of his mouth turned up in a smirk. "A friend. Janet Walker."

"A *friend*," she said sourly.

His smile widened and he raised that stupid eyebrow at her. "What exactly do you want to know, Angela? Whether she's a friend who grants me . . . privileges?"

Her mind veered back to the sight of Justus bare-chested and she felt her face burning. She'd never believed in the concept of a perfect body any more than she'd believed in Sasquatch or the Loch Ness Monster—until, that is, she'd laid eyes on him tonight. He *was* physically perfect, or at least as close to perfect as she'd ever get: long legs, tight butt, gleaming skin that had to feel like satin—and that was just the beginning. His long arms were heavily muscled without being bulky. His chest and belly consisted of slab upon slab of well defined, rippling sinew. He was startlingly, brutally masculine—as potently male as a stallion put out to stud. Thank God he'd put his sweatshirt back on.

Surely any woman even remotely interested in Justus would happily grant him privileges at the earliest possible opportunity. No doubt Janet and countless others of her ilk were only too anxious to warm Justus's bed. His private life—and she was sure he had a varied and exciting one—was none of her business. Still, she couldn't squelch her overwhelming curiosity.

"Oh, I'm sure she grants you privileges," she said, and he laughed. "The question is whether any of the hundreds of women who probably grant you privileges is any more special that the others."

His smile faded and she felt a strange surge of satisfaction. Maybe this once she'd touched a nerve, the way he liked to do to her. Had some woman broken his heart? Was that it?

He blinked once. "No."

"Doesn't *that* get a little boring?"

A cocky, mischievous smile crept back across his face. "Having sex with beautiful women never gets boring."

She didn't bother answering, instead leveling her most disbelieving glare on him. He met it for a moment, but then his own, defiant gaze wavered and fell. He looked away, shrugging one shoulder. "Sometimes," he said begrudgingly. They sat quietly for a minute, but then he turned back to her and grinned smugly, the way a poker player does when he lays down his hand to reveal a royal flush. "But not as boring as I'll bet it got with you and Ron."

Before she could blast him, Carolyn's image, laughing and happy, flashed through her mind and she immediately felt the blinding pain of her loss, along with guilt that she'd been enjoying herself—just for a second—with Justus. He instantly sensed her mood change and leaned forward to catch her hand between his.

"What's wrong, Angela?"

For what seemed like the millionth time that day, she started to cry. "I don't think Carolyn and V.J. were ever bored. Do you?"

His face darkened, but then he smiled ruefully. "No."

Sitting here, sparring with Justus, she'd avoided thinking about it, but the fact was in the morning she'd have to say good-bye to her sister forever. "I don't know how I'm going to get through tomorrow, Justus." She sniffled, wiping her nose. "Or the holidays. I don't know what I'm going to do without my sister."

"I know, Duchess." He let go of her hand, opening his arms. She gratefully scooted closer to him and laid her head on his broad, hard chest. His hand came up to cup her head, soothing her. "Maybe we can help each other through. And Maya."

"Maybe," she said, oddly comforted.

"Here." He handed her a tissue from the box on the end table.

She dabbed her eyes, then sat far enough back to look up into his face. His hand remained on the back of her head, his fingers curled in her nape. "I'm really sick of crying. You probably won't believe this, but I usually never cry. I'm going to stop after tomorrow. I swear."

His fingers gently stroked the back of her neck. "You cry as much as you need to. I won't tell."

"You haven't cried that much."

He looked away, nostrils flaring. "Yeah, I have."

She laid her head down again, tightening her arms around his waist just in case he had any thoughts of moving away. That same sexy chest also made a very fine refuge. Listening to the strong, reassuring thump of his heart under her ear, Angela wept silently, making a wet patch on his sweatshirt.

Justus rested his chin on top of her head and once or twice she thought she felt one of his tears fall into her hair.

A scream! Who's screaming?

Angela jerked awake. Flinging back the covers, she sat straight up and threw her legs over the edge of the bed, her heart racing. Disoriented, she looked wildly around her silent, dark bedroom, wondering where she thought she was going. The only light came from the glowing red numbers on the clock radio on the nightstand: four-twenty. After Justus left at about eleven, she'd gone to bed, tossing and turning for hours before she fell asleep sometime after three. What had woken her? Had she had a nightmare? She couldn't remember now. Sighing, she stood and turned toward the bathroom. She may as well go before she tried to go back to sleep—

A tortured wail, muffled only slightly by the wall, pierced the quiet. *Maya!* Angela sprinted down the hall almost before the sound registered with her brain. She threw open Maya's door, expecting to see, at the very least, a masked intruder trying to kill the girl. She did not expect to see the night light illuminate Maya lying quietly on her back, eyes closed, with her blankets rumpled around her bare legs and feet. Angela stood in the doorway, frozen with indecision. Was it normal for a three-and-a-half-year-old to cry out like that in her sleep? Was she having a nightmare? Should she wake her up, or was that a bad idea?

She'd just decided to leave—whatever may have been going on, Maya seemed fine now. But when the girl cried out again. Angela hurried to the bed, put her hand on Maya's shoulder, and shook her gently. "Maya. Wake up, Sweetie. *Maya.*"

Maya's lids flew open and she looked at Angela with unfocused eyes for several seconds. Then her little face twisted. "Mommy," she said, whimpering. "I want Mommy."

Angela sat on the side of the bed and gathered Maya into her arms, squeezing her tight. Her braided hair, mussed by the pillow, smelled sweetly of coconut hair oil and her Barbie nightgown smelled like the powder-fresh dryer sheets Angela used earlier. "I know Sweetie." She kissed the top of her head. "Did you have a bad dream?"

Maya tried to twist away, becoming more agitated by the second. "I want Mommy," she howled, crying now with loud, wracking sobs. "Mommy! Mooommmy! *Mooommmy*!"

Never before in her life had Angela felt so useless. An instinct, dark, primal, and overwhelming, roared to life in her gut: she must protect this child. No matter what. *Protect her.* "Shhh," she said soothingly, holding her tight, rocking her. "It's okay, Sweetie. It's okay."

After a while Maya quieted a little, her sobs tapering off to shuddering whimpers. "I want to go ho-ome."

Angela took a deep breath and wondered, again, what to do. She'd never intended to spring the news on her like this, in the middle of the night, but the time had obviously come. "You are home, Sweetie," she said gently. "You're going to live with me now."

Maya stilled, then pulled away to look up at her. "I am?"

"Yes." Angela felt suddenly calm, peaceful. Carolyn wanted this. She felt it as surely as she felt Maya's soft, springy hair under her fingers. She wiped the girl's wet cheeks with the edge of the sheet. "You and I are going to be a family now. You're going to live with me and this will be your bedroom."

Silence. Maya looked dubiously around the room.

"I know it's not as nice as your bedroom at your old house," Angela said quickly, surveying the treadmill and her desk; she'd have to clear that stuff out so Maya could have a space that was more—much more—child friendly. "But over the weekend we can move some of my things out. And we can paint the room a new color, maybe pink—"

"I hate pink."

"Oh, okay—maybe purple, then, and we can get you some new sheets—"

"Jenny has Dora the Explorer sheets."

Angela had no idea who Jenny was, or Dora the Explorer, for that matter, and she didn't really care right now. "Cool! We can go to the mall and get you some Dora sheets and—"

"Dora's for babies."

Angela laughed. She eased Maya's head back down to her pillow, found her floppy dog, and covered her with the blanket. Maya watched her through half-closed eyes. "So do you think that would be okay, Maya? You living here with me?"

Maya nodded slowly, her huge eyes unblinking. "Yeah."

Angela laughed again, leaning over her. "Can I have an extra good night kiss? I need it."

Maya puckered her lips and planted a sloppy wet kiss on Angela's cheek. Angela squeezed her, stood up, rearranged the covers, and went to the door. "Good night, Sweetie." She turned to go, yawning.

"Aunt Ang-la?"

Angela turned back. "Yes, Maya?"

Maya stared, taking an unaccountably long time to speak. "Can you sleep with me?"

The sight of Maya, a tiny figure alone in an adult's room without so much as a Dr. Suess poster on the wall, wrung her heart. Even so, Angela was no dummy. She knew very well that sleeping with a child—even once—was a recipe for disaster. She'd heard horror stories of friends who'd foolishly let their child sleep in their bed, only to have the child remain there—hogging the blankets, flailing and snoring—until the age of seven or eight. Sharing a bed with a child was always—*always*—a mistake, and she had never knowingly made a mistake in her life.

"Sure, Sweetie."

Angela stepped back to the bed and climbed in beside Maya, who obligingly slid over for her. Angela laid her head on the pillow, pulled the warm covers up over both of them, and wrapped her arm around Maya. Maya scooted back until they lay spooned together, her warm little body cranking out BTUs faster than a furnace, and immediately fell asleep. Angela listened to her even breathing until the sun came up, feeling connected to her niece for the first time since the tragedy. No, for the first time—ever.

"I think the funeral went pretty well, man, don't you?"

Justus put his empty plate down and turned away from the luncheon buffet table to face Brian. Casa Vincent overflowed with people talking in hushed, respectful tones. Early afternoon sunlight streamed gaily through Vincent's spotless mullioned windows, an obscene contrast to this dark gathering. The mourners all wore black—to Justus they looked like a flock of crows—and spilled from the dining room into the adjoining living room, library and solarium. On easels on either side of the roaring fireplace in the living room stood several poster-sized pictures of Carolyn and V.J. in happier times: on the beach, laughing, Carolyn's hair blowing in the wind; the couple at V.J.'s hooding ceremony when he graduated from law school; endless wedding pictures. Justus supposed staring at the pictures was easier than staring at them in open caskets would have been, but not much. He couldn't make himself believe their vitality was gone forever.

Iced shrimp, beef tenderloin sandwiches, lamb chops, and other assorted delicacies, along with an endless spread of cookies, pies, and cupcakes all looked delicious, but Justus's appetite still hadn't bounced back. He shrugged dispassionately; this nightmare day couldn't possibly end soon enough. "Yeah. I guess so."

They moved away from the table and, standing side by side in front of the French double doors to the walled courtyard, watched the crowd in silence for a moment. Finally Brian sighed harshly and swiped his hand through his hair, making it stand up in the usual blond spikes. "I still can't believe he's gone. Remember that time he kicked my ass when I knocked over those model cars in his room?" He shook his head, a rueful smile on his lips. "I didn't think I was going to come out of that alive."

Justus laughed. He hadn't thought about that incident in years.

Brian's chin trembled, and he dropped his head. "I still owe him thirty dollars he loaned me when I was fifteen," he said, his voice cracking.

Justus snorted. "Yeah. Veej always talked about how he could have retired early and moved to the Riviera but for that thirty bucks you shorted him."

Brian jerked his head up in surprise and laughed. "*Asshole*," he muttered.

"I keep thinking he's going to come in and ask what the hell's going on."

"Yeah." Brian hung his head again, sadly studying his shoes. After a minute he looked around the crowd and jerked his head in Vincent's direction. Vincent, in one of his fancy dark suits, stood by the bar in the corner, hugging and kissing some woman Justus didn't know. "How's your dad holding up? He doesn't look so good to me."

It was true. Deep hollows had sprung up around Vincent's eyes and his cheeks had a thin, gaunt look Justus didn't remember from the other day. "He always holds up," Justus told him, watching his father disappear into the crowd. "But I don't think his heart's too good."

Brian frowned disbelievingly. "You don't *think*? Why don't you ask and find out? He's your *father*, man. Just about the only family you've got left."

Justus bristled. "Yeah, and he's not Ward Cleaver like your father, so just drop it."

Brian, nostrils flaring, muttered something R-rated under his breath. Justus ignored him. He scanned the room for Angela, and saw her on one of the sofas with some woman from her office. She had her hair in that sleek ponytail he hated, her widow's peak emphasizing her heart-shaped face. She was wearing some terrible black suit with white blouse that was fine for a funeral but did nothing for her. Today she seemed a little better even though she still had dark circles under her eyes. Hopefully she was making good on her promise to stop crying—he hadn't seen her cry today, even during the service when the choir sang *How Great Thou Art*.

Brian followed the path of his gaze. "She taking good care of Maya?"

"Yeah."

"But you're going to take her, aren't you? She belongs with you."

"Yeah."

It'd taken him two seconds to decide he wanted Maya, even though he was a twenty-seven-year-old, single man. So what? He loved her and had spent more time with her than anyone else had, other than her parents. Ever since she could toddle he'd taken her one weekend day nearly every week. They'd gone to just about every park and mall in the city, and to the zoo and children's museum more times than he could count. He'd given Maya her first basketball and her first tricycle. He'd taken her to her first movie, some Disney cartoon they'd had to leave after about five minutes because she'd been freaked out. Well, Maya had a lot more firsts coming—first soccer game, first bra, first date, first day of college—and he planned to be there for all of them.

"You told anyone yet?" Brian asked.

"No."

"Does Angela want her?"

"I doubt it." Angela had had very little to do with Maya, up until now, at least. He couldn't think of one time in three and a half years that he'd heard of Angela taking Maya for an afternoon, or a play date, or even visiting her. "She might make a few noises in that direction just to make it look good, but I don't think she really wants her."

Brian turned to look at him again, his gaze speculative. "What's going on with you two, anyway? And don't say nothing because I've seen the way you've been staring at her."

Justus thought about denying it, but what was the point? "I want her," he said simply.

Brian rolled his eyes. "You *want* everybody."

"Not like this."

"I don't know," Brian said dubiously, studying Angela as if she were a specimen on a slide under a microscope. "Women like that tend to go for professional types."

"I—*we*—are professionals. We own our own gym."

"Yeah, but you're not a doctor, lawyer, architect, or accountant."

Justus's gut knotted. Leave it to Brian to put his finger right on his biggest fear. Besides the age issue—Angela was still seven years older than he, even though he was an adult now—he worried she'd never give him the time of day because he didn't have a white collar. "Your whole little supportive best friend routine needs some work."

Brian grinned. "Yeah, well, I hope you work fast. I bet my last dollar she wants Maya too. And if you try to take her away she's not going to have anything to do with you."

Shoving his fists deep into his pants pockets, Justus fought the urge to tell him to go to hell. Brian was right, of course. Still, there was nothing he loved better than a challenge. He looked back at Angela and remembered his oldest, strongest desire: to get Angela hot, sweaty, naked, and moaning, to thrash around with her under the tangled sheets of his bed, to endlessly love every inch of her. His resolve hardened exponentially. He glared at Brian, silently daring him to contradict him, and told him the same thing he'd told V.J.

"We'll see about that."

"I know this is probably the last thing on your mind right now, but the partners were planning to meet this afternoon," Carmen told Angela.

Angela settled more deeply into the sofa and tore her gaze away from Justus, where it seemed determined to wander every chance it got. They'd developed some sort of strange but comforting system where they looked across rooms for each other, just to exchange glances and make sure the other person was okay. Today, though, if she were honest with herself—a practice she avoided whenever possible—she'd admit she kept staring at him because he looked unbelievable in his pin-striped charcoal suit with white shirt and burgundy tie. Every time she saw him, in fact, she felt a jolt of appreciative surprise: look how broad his shoulders were! Look how his torso tapered to his slim waist! Look how velvety his brown skin was against the stark white of the shirt! Seeing him today reminded her very much—too much—of how he'd looked the night of Carolyn and V.J.'s wedding.

She turned to Carmen, put her arm across the back of the sofa, and tried to focus on the conversation. "The partners? What are they meeting for?"

"Well, I assume it's about us." Carmen crossed her legs and

smoothed her skirt. "They're probably going to start our evaluations and look at our hours for the year."

"Great," Angela muttered. "My hours this month are going to be through the floor, what with planning the funeral and Maya and everything. I've wanted to become a partner for so long, but now it seems really unimportant—"

"I know."

"—and I can't really say I'd care if I didn't make it."

Carmen raised an eyebrow. "Get real, Angela. You're the most ambitious person I know. You'd care, trust me."

Angela picked up her wine glass from the side table and took a sip of the dry chardonnay. "Before I forget to ask, did you get those guardianship papers drawn up for me yet?"

"Yeah. They're ready to file whenever you want."

"Good." Angela scanned the room and saw Vincent, ever the charming host, even at his own son's funeral, pour coffee from a gleaming silver pot into some woman's raised cup. "I'll mention it to Vincent first, but I don't think he'll object. He's too old and sick to take her."

"Fine. Is Maya in school today?"

"Yeah. I didn't think it was a good idea to have her here and—"

"Uh-oh." Carmen's gaze flew to the archway between the dining and living rooms.

Bemused, Angela put her glass on the side table and twisted around. To her horror, Ronnie, wearing the requisite dark suit and tie, stepped into the room and scanned the crowd, obviously looking for her.

Angela gasped. "What's he doing here?"

"Well, obviously he's come to pay his respects," Carmen hissed out of the side of her mouth. "If you'd followed my advice at church and just spoken to him instead of ignoring him like a two-year-old, he wouldn't have had to follow you here."

"Respects?" cried Angela, whirling back around and trying to shrink lower against the cushions. "Why do I want respects from the man who just dumped me for some other woman?"

"Shhh!" Carmen cried, grabbing her arm to silence her. "Here he comes."

Sure enough, Ronnie had spotted them and his thin lips widened into a sad, strained smile as he approached. Angela frowned. "Hello, Carmen," he said, stopping in front of them.

"Ron," Carmen said coolly, smoothing her skirt again.

Finally his gaze settled on her face. "Hello, Angela," he said softly. "Do you have a couple of minutes? I'd like to talk to you." Angela huffed once, then stood. Squaring her shoulders, she marched stiffly into the solarium, where it was less crowded. Justus glowered after them in a way that made her glad there were no sharp knives nearby.

Chapter 8

The solarium was a beautiful, sunny, open, octagonal room filled with expensive rattan chairs and settees, as well as a jungle's worth of enormous palms, ferns, and other tropical plants. Twenty or thirty people—even the smallest room in this mausoleum could easily absorb dozens, she'd discovered—sat or stood here and there, buffet plates and drinks in hand, murmuring amongst themselves. Angela navigated through the various seating areas and walked to a relatively quiet spot near a twelve-foot ficus tree, her high heels clicking on the yellow tiles.

She turned to face Ronnie, already regretting her earlier rudeness. There was no excuse for bad behavior, and it wouldn't kill her to be gracious. Ronnie was not a monster, after all, even if he was a lying, cheating dog, and he would want to personally tell her how sorry he was. Over the years she and Ronnie had spent a fair amount of time with Carolyn and V.J., and Ronnie had always seemed very fond of them both.

"You really didn't have to come, but thanks."

Ronnie gaped as if she'd told him he really didn't need to brush his teeth every day. "You know how much I care about you! Why would you think I wouldn't come?" he cried.

Whatever momentary good will she'd felt toward Ronnie imploded like a skyscraper being demolished. A red haze of rage clouded her vision. She stepped forward, her chin jutting up, and crossed her arms over her chest to keep from slugging him in his earnest face. "What would make me think? Hmmm, let me see. Maybe it was when you dumped me at a restaurant the other night. Or—"

Ronnie sighed harshly, dropping his head and rubbing the back of his neck.

"—maybe it was when you lied and told me there was no one else."

Ronnie's head shot up; his panicked gaze met hers.

Strangely satisfied, Angela nodded thoughtfully, tapping her index finger to her lips. "No, wait. I know what it was. It was leaving the hospital with my orphaned niece and stumbling on you kissing some other woman in a way I can't remember you ever kissing me!"

Her voice rose at the end until, embarrassed, she realized several people were staring at her for disturbing the somber tranquility. Worse, Justus, his glittering black gaze still pinned to her and Ronnie, sauntered over and leaned against the doorframe ten feet away. Staring openly, he raised his glass and took a generous swallow of red wine. He'd obviously come to monitor the situation more closely, and if she so much as broke a whisper or gave him any other sign Ronnie had upset her again, would probably kick Ronnie's butt—funeral or not.

Well, this was just wonderful. For the second time in less than a week she'd allowed Ronnie to upset her to the point of making a scene in public and in front of Justus. She snapped her mouth shut before she really lost it and fervently wished she could just leave.

Ronnie had the decency to look stricken. "I—I'm sorry, Angela," he whispered. "I didn't mean for you to find out about Brianna and me like that—"

"*Brianna*," she said faintly, the name like a karate chop directly to her gut; she pressed a hand to her forehead, wondering if she wouldn't faint. So it was already "Brianna and me," was it? Last week it would have been "Angela and me," but look how neatly she'd been replaced. If anyone had ever asked her, she would have sworn both that Ronnie would never dump her and that if he did he would at least wait until her side of his bed was cold before he replaced her. Well, she'd been wrong on both counts, hadn't she? He'd probably been sleeping with his little Brianna for a while; she felt suddenly grateful that they'd religiously used condoms when they'd made love and she therefore would not have to take an HIV test. Funny, though. She couldn't recall the last time she and Ronnie had made love.

"Brianna . . . and you?"

"I'm handling this all wrong," Ronnie told her, stepping closer and putting a light hand on her arm. "I didn't mean—"

"Don't touch me!" She snatched her arm away, earning more curious looks from the bystanders. One woman sitting on a settee to her right said, "My goodness," with exaggerated concern, to Angela's further embarrassment.

Ronnie jerked his hands away from her, as he feared he'd lose them both if he touched her again. "I didn't mean—"

"Is there a problem?" asked a soft, menacing voice.

Angela and Ronnie turned together and saw Justus arrive at Angela's side. His gaze, worried and intent, quickly scanned her face. Apparently he did not like what he saw because his frown deepened. He took Angela's elbow firmly in his hand, gently pulled her back and away from Ronnie, then stretched up to his full height, a sight as impressive and intimidating as a cobra unfurling its hood and spitting.

Ronnie cringed.

* * *

Angela wasn't surprised to see Justus come to her defense; the only surprises were that he'd held off this long and that he hadn't managed to commandeer a white stallion for the occasion. She'd have to be deaf and blind not to realize that sometime in the last several days Justus had appointed himself her protector. Actually, she was very glad to see him; she'd had about as much of Ronnie as she could take for the moment.

Ronnie recovered his composure and stuck out his hand, apparently determined to remain pleasant. "Justus," he said, adopting the crisp, professional doctor's voice Angela had heard him use countless times before. "I was so sorry to hear about your brother."

Justus looked at Ronnie's hand with utter disgust and ignored it, as if he were Howard Hughes noticing an overflowing can of garbage. "You're upsetting Angela." He managed to make *upsetting* sound like *raping* or *murdering*. Ronnie dropped his hand and shrank inside his skin like a startled turtle hiding in his shell. "It's time for you to go," Justus told him.

Ronnie's expression darkened impotently. Obviously he didn't like Justus's edict, but was smart enough not to argue with someone six inches taller and a good forty pounds heavier. His accusatory gaze shot to Angela instead. "What's *this* about, Angela?" He nodded in Justus's direction. "Maybe you've been keeping a few secrets yourself."

Angela winced and prepared to run for cover, certain Justus would rip Ronnie's throat out for making innuendos. How could Ronnie have the nerve—the *gall!*—to throw nasty little stones when he lived in a glass house? Exactly how big a hypocrite was he? But Justus, strangely, kept quiet. Instead, he watched her, obviously as interested in her response as Ronnie was.

Bewildered by Justus's lack of a reaction, she rounded on Ronnie. "How dare you?" Ronnie's jaw tightened; he crossed his arms over his chest. "Justus"—she grabbed Justus's arm for emphasis—"is a good *friend*. He's practically *family*. He's been like a *brother* to me since this whole thing happened." Justus's arm tensed under her hand, but she didn't pause to wonder why. "I don't know how I would have gotten through the last few days without him." She raised her chin in the stubborn gesture she knew drove Ronnie insane. "Please leave."

"Angela . . ." Ronnie began beseechingly.

She raised a hand to stop him. "We don't have anything else to talk about."

Ronnie's face twisted, but then he took a deep breath and seemed to collect himself. "Have it your way, Angela," he told her, looking suddenly sad and drawn. Lobbying one last glare at Justus, he wheeled around and stalked out.

"Asshole," Justus muttered to Ronnie's departing back.

Angela smoothed her ponytail with a shaky hand, feeling thoroughly unnerved. "Yeah, well," she said briskly, trying to recover some control, "even though you interrupted a private conversation, and even though I'm perfectly capable of taking care of myself, I'd like to thank you for—"

Justus leveled his flashing black gaze on her. She shut up immediately and alarm skittered up her spine. "You wanted to marry that guy?"

Angela bristled. He made it sound like she'd planned to marry Saddam Hussein. "Excuse me, but I—"

"Because he's a *jerk*, just in case you still hadn't realized it."

He obviously thought she was a horrible judge of character, and it stung. She felt the irrational need to defend herself and, by extension, Ronnie. "Yeah, well, he wasn't all bad." She held up her hand, ticking off his accomplishments on her fingers. "He was chief resident, and he's got a great job now, and he's active in his church—"

Justus snorted incredulously. "I don't want his *resume*," he cried, scowling down in her face. "I know he looks good on paper! But did you ever look beyond that and see he doesn't give a damn about you and what you need? He only came to keep up appearances! Why else would he show up here, today, when he knew you didn't want him to come? Huh? I'll bet your whole little relationship was like that, wasn't it?"

Stunned, she couldn't answer. Justus had really hit the nail on the head this time, and she didn't like it one bit. Her mind veered off onto the times she'd asked Ronnie if they could vacation somewhere else besides Martha's Vineyard, only to be shot down. And the times she'd wanted to try a new restaurant or play or DVD, only to have Ronnie talk her out of it. And the times—way too numerous to count—she'd tried to talk with him about her day or her clients or her work pressures, only to have him roll his eyes and say she didn't know anything about pressures because *she* didn't have people's lives in her hands like he did.

To her horror Justus stared at her, his expression sympathetic now rather than angry. He felt sorry for her, obviously. She crossed her arms over her chest; pity was one thing she didn't want and wouldn't tolerate. "You don't know anything about it."

He went rigid and looked away, muttering unintelligibly. Finally he looked back, his gaze shuttered. "He's no good for you, Duchess," he said gently. "Don't let him hurt you again."

"I won't," she said irritably. "What do you think I'm going to do—elope with him? All I did was talk to him for five minutes."

"He *upset* you."

The way Justus said *upset* made it sound like a hanging offense. Justus's obvious concern for her feelings, especially when juxtaposed with Ronnie's lack of the same, touched a chord deep within her and her anger evaporated. "You're really something, Justus." She smiled slightly and a new, intense light appeared in his eyes. "The one good thing about all of this," she told him, "is I've gotten to know you better—"

He stepped closer, the light in his eyes growing brighter. "Angela," he said, his voice unaccountably hoarse.

"—and you've been such a good friend to me. I don't know how I ever would have gotten through the last few days without you."

The light disappeared, and his lips thinned slightly before he blinked once and resumed a neutral expression. Too late, she remembered he didn't seem to like when she labeled him. He hadn't liked it when she'd said he was like a brother, either. Why was he so moody?

"Justus—" She put a mollifying hand on his arm.

"Here you are!" cried a syrupy voice behind them.

Angela dropped her hand and turned to see Justus's girlfriend, or sex partner, or whatever she was, sweep into the solarium.

An inexplicable wave of irritation swept through Angela, and Janet did not seem particularly happy to see her, either. Her back to Justus, she watched Angela coolly, her eyes slightly narrowed, before she threw herself into Justus's arms and kissed him on the cheek. "Hi, Baby," she crooned in what was supposed to be, Angela felt sure, a Toni Braxton-ish sultry voice but in reality sounded like RuPaul. "How are you doing?"

"Uh . . . hi." Clearly startled, Justus recovered enough to press his hands to her back for an unenthusiastic hug, then stepped away. "Thanks for coming." His lips twisted up into a strained, brief smile before his gaze darted back to Angela.

Janet kept a proprietary hand on Justus's arm. "Where else would I be?"

Angela couldn't help but stare at Janet's black ensemble. She wore a clingy knit wrap dress with a belt, along with her stiletto boots. Her ample cleavage was on display, although she'd apparently decided that for a funeral it was only appropriate to show half of her breasts instead of the three-fourths she'd flaunted the other night at the restaurant.

Justus, whose face now seemed oddly flushed, cleared his throat and extended a hand toward Angela. "Janet, you remember Angela."

"Hi-iii," said Janet, as if she and Angela were old friends who'd stumbled across each other at Target. Now that Justus was watching, Janet oozed warmth and sympathy. She pressed Angela's arm. "I was so sorry to hear about your sister."

"Thank you."

Janet made a show of looking back and forth around the room. "Where's your handsome boyfriend? Is he in the other room? We don't want to monopolize you."

Beneath the exaggerated concern, Angela saw a predatory light in Janet's eyes, for which there was only one possible interpretation: Janet wanted to know if Angela was a contestant in the Snare Justus Robinson Sweepstakes. Janet apparently thought Justus was her own personal property and wouldn't hesitate to take Angela off at the knees if she ever thought she was a direct threat.

Angela looked at Justus to gauge his reaction to this little performance; as she should have expected, the edges of his lips turned up in an unmistakable, amused smirk. Of course he would enjoy seeing his little groupie's thinly disguised jealousy.

Angela decided to have a little fun with Janet. "He's not here," she said sweetly, sidling up to Justus and putting her hand on his other arm. Janet froze, her lips stuck in a sickly smile. "And I'm really glad because it's given me more time to spend with Justus." Angela smiled beatifically at him; after a surprised moment he grinned back, apparently deciding to play along. She lowered her voice into bedroom range. "I'll see you later, okay?" She pulled on his arm and, bemused, he leaned down for her lingering kiss on his warm, slightly scratchy cheek.

Before she turned and swept away, Angela had a glimpse of a speechless Janet, her face turning purple. That image was the one bright spot in the horrible day.

Janet whirled on him as soon as Angela was out of earshot. "What's going on with you and that woman?" she demanded, her body shaking with anger.

Frowning, Justus said, "Nothing." Technically it was the truth; he didn't see any need to do a Jimmy Carter and confess he was lusting in his heart after Angela.

Janet drew herself up and crossed her hands over her chest. "What did she mean by that—'I'll see you later'?" Her voice rose an octave and her head bobbed. "What's *that* mean?"

Justus stared at her, his temper simmering. He didn't like being interrogated, especially by a woman with whom he was having, at best, a casual sexual relationship. Very deliberately he kept his voice low. "I suppose it means she'll see me later."

Janet snorted, one hand finding a hip. "You're screwing her, aren't you?"

Justus had had enough. What had started out as a perfectly pleasant seduction between him and Janet had lately begun to irritate him. Well, actually, *Janet* irritated him, and had for a while. As soon as they'd started sleeping together a few weeks ago she'd turned into a spider web, clinging, refusing to let go. She called constantly, always wanting to know where he'd been, and with whom. She was suspicious of every female client at the gym and, worse, every female he spoke to. She wanted to know when they would go out again and why he didn't call and why he didn't spend the night after they'd had sex.

All this when they'd agreed up front that all they wanted

from each other was sex. And now here she was grilling him about his nonexistent extracurricular activities at his brother's *funeral*. "I just told you nothing's going on," he said testily, determined to be polite no matter how she acted. "She's my brother's sister-in-law and we'll be spending time together." He glanced at his watch, then around the room. The crowd had thinned a little and he'd hardly mingled at all. He turned to go. "And I really need to talk to some of the guests, so if you're through with your little inquisition—"

"Justus—wait." She put her hand on his arm and stepped close enough for him to see the hurt in her eyes. "Should I come over later?"

Justus sighed harshly, weighed down by guilt. Now was not the time or place to give her the boot, but he didn't want to string Janet along or give her any false hopes. He hated loose ends. As far as he was concerned, their relationship, such as it was, was over, and it was time for them both to move on.

"I don't think so," he said gently.

The silence grew, eventually becoming awkward.

Tears shimmered in her eyes. "I'll call you then."

Justus dropped his head, his jaw flexing. Why did she have to push so hard? Why couldn't she just let him end things gracefully? Why did he have to be the bad guy when *she'd* tried to change the rules mid-game? They'd agreed up front what the deal was. So why was she acting like he'd broken her heart when he was only behaving the way he'd told her he would? He thought of sugarcoating things, of saying 'Yeah, great, call me,' then just ignoring her when she did. But that was the coward's way out and he wasn't a coward.

"I'll . . . understand if you're too busy to call, Janet."

Painful comprehension finally appeared in her eyes. "Fine," she snapped, looking away.

"Take care of yourself." Cupping her face, he pressed a

quick kiss to her cheek, then walked off, involuntarily scanning the room for Angela even as he mingled with the guests.

While Vincent ushered the last of the guests to the door at three-fifteen, Angela, feeling tired but strangely peaceful, and craving a little fresh air, wandered out the back door into the elaborate courtyard. English ivy climbed the six-foot wall, creating the illusion she'd entered a secret haven. Wrought-iron benches and tables sat invitingly next to bare branches that would, she knew, turn into a glorious rose garden by June. In one corner, water splashed down large flat stones that had been stair-stepped into the wall, and filled a kidney-shaped koi pond. Overhead the sun shone and the sky was a vibrant, unreasonable blue. Angela ignored the cold in the air, breathed deeply, and sank onto one of the benches, crossing her legs and closing her eyes.

As she'd somehow known he would, Justus materialized within seconds and settled next to her. "You okay?" he asked softly, apparently not wanting to disturb her peace.

"Umm-hmmm." She didn't bother opening her eyes. The funeral, oddly, had been just what she needed. She'd received a powerful comfort from being surrounded by distant relatives and others—mothers from the playgroup at school, church members, and neighbors—who'd known and loved Carolyn. All of them insisted—repeatedly—that she call for help with Maya, who seemed to be universally well liked. "You okay?"

"Yeah."

Taking another deep breath, she opened her eyes to discover Justus staring at her, his dark eyes intense and mysterious. He blinked once and whatever thoughts he'd had disappeared from view, not that she'd have ever read them anyway. His lips turned up slightly at the edges, softening his expression. "I think we did pretty good, don't you?"

"Yeah." She smiled. "I think it's a beautiful day for them to be remembered. Carolyn would have liked it."

He nodded thoughtfully. "Yeah. V.J. too."

The cold air finally penetrated her clothes and she shivered, running her hands up and down her arms. "Here." Justus whipped off his jacket and threw it around her shoulders, where it hung like some huge tent. Grateful, she slid her arms in the sleeves and absorbed the raging heat from his body. Almost immediately she began to feel warm—very warm—and she couldn't quite figure out why. Of course, it had nothing to do with the inherent intimacy of sharing someone's—Justus's— clothes. Nor did it have anything to do with Justus's subtle, sophisticated scent, which clung to the fine wool. The delicious fragrance he wore was a tiny bit citrusy and had a spicy note that reminded her of the exotic smells in a boutique she knew that sold sculptures, incense, and other items from the Caribbean.

She shivered again.

Justus noticed, of course. His hooded, speculative gaze skimmed over the jacket, then down her thighs, ending on her crossed legs. Finally it shot back to her face and she felt the strangest jolt. "Still cold?"

The awful man had to know she wasn't; a ridiculous, burning flush crept up her neck and across her face the way spilled water spreads over the floor. She looked away. "No."

"Good."

She heard the amusement in his voice even though she refused to look at him again. Her face grew hotter and her hips felt restless, as if she suddenly needed to squirm. She was on the verge of making up some excuse to go inside when the door creaked and Vincent came out. He still looked awful. Not that she expected anyone to look good at a funeral, and certainly not at the funeral of his or her firstborn.

"Well, that's everyone," he said, sitting catty-corner from them on the walled edge of the koi pond. "The caterers are cleaning up."

"Mr. Robinson, I can't begin to thank you enough for all you've done. Carolyn would have loved the service."

"V.J. too," Justus murmured.

Vincent spared her a tired smile, but did not look at Justus. "I'm glad." He paused, and then gave her his let's-get-down-to-business look. "Angela, dear, we've got a lot to discuss: Maya, the finances, the house—"

"I know." Of course he and Justus would want to make sure they'd have visitation rights when she adopted Maya. She'd be only too happy to work out some reasonable schedule; Carolyn would want Maya to have frequent contact with what little family she had left. Still, Angela was way too tired for this talk right now. "I thought maybe I could come back to-morrow and we could discuss everything. I've had about enough for today, haven't you?"

Vincent waved a hand. "Fine, fine. Why don't you come by around four."

"That's fine with me." She turned to Justus, who looked grim. "Can you make that?"

Before Justus could answer, Vincent said, "Oh, I'm sure we can fill Justus in later—"

"I'll be there," Justus said flatly.

"Fine," Vincent said sharply, as if he'd just received word Hannibal Lecter intended to crash his party. He managed a sickly smile that came nowhere near his eyes.

"Mr. Robinson?" One of the white-jacketed caterers stuck his head out the door. "What did you want us to do about the lamb chops?"

Sighing, Vincent rose heavily to his feet. "I'll be right

there." He turned to wink at Angela. "I don't think this day will ever be over with, do you?" He disappeared inside.

"I better go." Angela stood up and smoothed her skirt. "I want to pick Maya up before it gets too much later." She moved away.

"Wait!" Justus jumped up and touched her arm, stopping her. "I thought maybe . . ." He hesitated, smiling sheepishly. "I'm a pretty good cook. I thought maybe you and Maya might want to have dinner at my place tonight. Just so you don't have to cook, I mean."

She stared at him. Uncertainty, an expression she'd never before seen on his face, crossed over his features as he shifted on his feet. The dinner with Justus sounded wonderful, and not because she was tired and hungry. "Uh, yeah . . . sure," she stammered. "If it's not too much trouble."

He grinned, looking relieved. "No trouble. Come at six."

Chapter 9

"Uncle Justus!" Maya streaked past the second he opened the door, pausing only long enough to kick her shoes into the hall basket and give him a quick hug around the knees. She raced into his bedroom, shedding hat, mittens, scarf, and jacket to form a trail they could follow if they needed to find her. The door slammed shut behind her.

"What just happened?" Angela asked, wide-eyed, as she slowly stepped over the threshold and into the small foyer. She stared down the hall at his bedroom door. "What've you got in there? Disneyland?"

"Better," he said, laughing. "Cable, a king-sized bed, and a big-screen, high-def TV."

"Oh, I see."

He stepped behind her to help with her buttery-soft black leather jacket, unable to stop himself from skimming his fingers along the bottom of the gleaming heavy satin of her hair as he did. He figured the movement of the jacket over her shoulders would disguise his touch, and if it didn't, well, it was about time she realized what his intentions were anyway.

Unfortunately, the brief contact was only enough to torture him a little and make him want her more, if that was even possible. She stepped away, smiling her thanks, and he took the opportunity to stare at her as she did a slow turn around the foyer and then crept into the living room. God, she was beautiful. For once she'd freed her hair from that awful perpetual ponytail, letting it fall softly around her face and shoulders, her long bangs off to one side emphasizing her dramatic dark eyes. The vee of her black sweater drew his gaze down to the amazing breasts he longed to explore. Her faded jeans were a mixed blessing: while they unfortunately covered those long, smooth, shapely legs she'd taunted him with after the funeral, they compensated nicely by clinging to her lush butt.

He watched as she lightly ran her fingertips over the simple but heavy walnut foyer table, pausing for half a second to smooth her bangs in the round mirror above it. He trailed after her into the living room, seeing it through her eyes. When she'd said yes to dinner, he'd raced home to clean the already neat place up a little, and now he was glad he had. She smiled approvingly as she looked around his apartment. A collection of oversized black-and-white photos—nature scenes, mostly forests and waterfalls—hung on the bare brick wall behind the overstuffed Navajo print sofa; it was an unusual combination, of course, but it seemed to work. Floor lamps glowed invitingly and side tables framed both ends of the sofa. In front of the sofa a low, square coffee table sat on a Navajo rug; a huge fern dropped its fronds over the top of the table. On each end of the table sat comfortable navy chairs with pillows. Ficus trees stood in the corners. To the far end of the room sat his simple Shaker dining table and chairs. Past that was the kitchen.

"Oh, Justus." Her voice turned into a croon he'd never heard before but quite liked. "I *love* your apartment."

Trying to stop his pleased, ridiculous grin was impossible. People—well, women—tended to like his apartment and comment on it the first time they came. But he couldn't recall when a compliment meant quite as much as this one. "Thanks." He pointed. "Note the coffee table. Feel free to put your feet on it any time."

She laughed and then, to his astonishment, reached up and patted his cheek with her warm, soft hand. His breath caught. "Poor Justus," she said condescendingly. "You're so tragically misguided." Too soon she moved away and sat on one of the chairs. "This apartment is the opposite of your father's house. It feels like a *home*."

Arrested, he stared at her. She was sharp, this girl. Way too sharp. How could she know that making this apartment warm and inviting—unlike Casa Vincent—had been his guiding principle? "Damn straight."

He sat on the corner of the sofa nearest her and they smiled at each other for a minute in complete understanding, until he felt that same tightening in his chest he always seemed to feel around Angela. Turning away, he tried to fight off whatever it was she did to him. "How'd our girl do at school today?" he asked casually.

"Pretty good. I was thinking I'd call a child psychologist— Dr. Brenner. Maya's preschool teacher recommended him. He specializes in grief counseling for children. I thought it couldn't hurt." She watched him, the question in her eyes.

He nodded. "I agree. Good idea."

She smiled, then looked to the closed bedroom door, where no sound escaped. "She's not in there watching the Playboy Channel or something, is she? I've never heard her so quiet."

"Don't worry. I've got all her little kiddie channels programmed. She likes to surf."

Her mouth twisted with disapproval. "A surfing three-year-old. Wonderful." She lifted her chin in the air, sniffing. "Something smells fantastic. What's for dinner?"

He waved a hand. "Just spaghetti."

"I don't think so." She shot to her feet and made a beeline

for the kitchen and the stove, which sat in the middle of the island. He watched, amused, as she lifted the lid on one of the steaming pots and breathed deeply, her eyes drifting closed. "Ummm." Opening her eyes, she grabbed the wooden spoon from the counter and stirred. "See? I knew it; I could smell the fennel. There's fresh sausage in here." She looked back and forth around the kitchen. "Wha—? No empty spaghetti sauce jars anywhere? This is *homemade*!" Her teasing gaze shot to his. "You can really cook!"

"I know."

She replaced the lid and spoon, then turned to the Burgundy, which he'd opened and left to breathe. "My favorite! You remembered."

Yeah, he remembered, all right. He remembered the type of wine she liked, how many slices of pizza she'd eaten the other night, where she kept her plates, how she smelled, and how she felt in his arms. "Oh, is that the kind you like?"

His little nonchalant routine was lost on her. She picked up the bottle, pursing her lips. "I have to serve myself, huh?"

"Can you pour me a glass while you're at it?"

She shot him a death glare, then obligingly poured two glasses, handing his off to him. Taking a sip from her own, she roamed over to the table, where he'd laid out the salads—crisp romaine lettuce covered with grated purple cabbage, carrots, and grape tomatoes. "And look at these beautiful, healthy salads!"

His lips twisted. "Try not to sound so surprised. I'm a personal trainer. I know a little bit about nutrition."

"Ah, but not enough to keep the sausage out of the spaghetti."

"Touché," he said, laughing.

She wandered back to her chair and sat. "So tell me about your exercise studio. I'd heard about it opening." She propped one elbow on the armrest, put her chin in her hand and waited, wide-eyed, as if he was about to divulge the final resting place of the Ark of the Covenant.

He lapped up her attention, excited to tell her about his baby. "Well, it's got all the basic classes—you know, aerobics, spinning, yoga, Pilates." She smiled encouragingly, which only fired him up more. "In the main room we have treadmills, ellipticals, bikes, and weights. I do personal training, and we'd like to add another trainer and maybe a massage therapist."

"So is this the royal 'we' you're using, or do you have a partner?"

He laughed sheepishly. "Brian's my partner—you remember him. Luckily he's got deep pockets, what with his trust fund and all."

"It pays to know people."

"You got that right." His sipped his wine, staring at her over the rim of his glass, happier than he could recall being since . . . well, since . . . he couldn't recall. "You should check it out."

"Will you give me a free thirty-day membership?" she asked hopefully.

At the moment he couldn't think of anything he wouldn't give her if she kept smiling at him like that. Still, he didn't want her to think he was a pushover. "We'll see."

She huffed, then glanced toward the bedroom door again. "Maybe I should just check—"

"She's fine," he said, a little more sharply than he'd intended. He'd spend more time with Maya later, of course, but right now he wanted Angela all to himself. "In a minute she'll come out, wanting to know about dinner. Tell me about your job. Are you a partner yet?"

"No." She pulled a face. "I'm up this year, though. In fact, my friend Carmen—you met her at the funeral—said they're starting the evaluation process." She tried to smile. "Just in case I needed one more stressful thing to deal with right now."

"So what kinds of things do they look at to see if they want you to be a partner?"

"What kinds of things?" she cried. "And you call yourself a lawyer's son?"

He grimaced. "You oughta know by now I ignore everything my father says to me."

"I noticed." She looked down, picking at lint on the arm of her chair. "I also noticed he's not exactly Cliff Huxtable in the father department, is he?"

She said it softly, without a hint of reproach, but he had the feeling she perfectly understood his fractured relationship with his father and didn't blame him for it. He remembered some other comment she'd made at the wedding reception, about it being his father's loss for the distance in their relationship. Her understanding felt as powerful and addictive as crack.

"No," he said faintly, a tight coil of longing for her twisting deep inside his belly.

For a charged second she stared intently at him, then seemed to sense his turmoil and looked away. "I noticed Janet didn't stay very long today," she said after a minute. "Did she need to go home and try to find the rest of her dress?"

He gawked at her for a surprised second, then threw back his head and laughed. Angela had never shown the slightest tendency toward cattiness, but the steely glint in her eyes intrigued him. "You didn't like Janet?"

Her eyes narrowed a hair. "I liked her fine." She took a delicate sip from her wine. And then, as if she couldn't help herself, she muttered, "I just wondered if she owned a whole dress."

This time he roared with laughter. She'd pegged Janet so neatly; he couldn't think of an occasion when Janet had managed to cover both of her breasts, not that her exhibitionism had ever been anything other than a plus in his book.

Angela replaced her wine on the table. "She didn't like me, though. Did you tell her Maya and I were coming tonight?"

Something about her unconcerned tone did not jibe with her rigid shoulders and tight jaw. Why? Deeply curious, he shook his head. "I don't need to check in with Janet."

"*Really*?" she said sourly, her fine brows inching toward her hairline.

It crossed his mind to string her along a little to see if he could get a jealous reaction from her, but that would be a pretty bad strategy. His goal—his only goal—was to lure Angela to his bed, sooner rather than later, and he certainly couldn't do that if she thought he was in some other relationship. There couldn't be any ambiguities or gray areas. He shrugged and gave her his blandest expression.

"Since you're so interested—"

He ignored her outraged hiss.

"—I might as well go ahead and tell you Janet and I, such as we were, are over."

She stared suspiciously at him. "*Over*?"

"Yeah."

Her brows snapped together. "You fired her at the funeral?"

"'Fire' is such an ugly word." He took a long sip of wine.

"I can't believe you." She spluttered wordlessly, obviously struggling to decide where to begin her attack.

He could see her preparing to defend Janet, a woman she didn't even like, and working up an outraged rant on behalf of all womankind, so he raised a hand to stop her. "Look. Janet and I are both adults and we both knew what we were getting—and not getting. She tried to change the rules midgame when she knew up front I'd never get serious with her."

This perfectly reasonable explanation only seemed to make Angela more upset. She glared as if she'd just seen him kick a puppy. "Yeah, well, you'll have to forgive me if I'm a little touchy these days about men dumping women in public."

His blood began a slow boil. She wasn't putting him in the same category as the jerk who'd broken her heart, was she? If so, this nonsense needed to stop right now. "Yeah, well, at least I didn't lead her on for three years, tell her I loved her, and *then* dump her."

Her eyes widened. He couldn't tell if she was mostly surprised or mostly mad, and he didn't really care. Angela needed to start getting used to the idea that the only thing he, the next man in her life, and Ron, the former man in her life, had in common was excellent taste in women.

"I'm not anything like Ron," he said angrily. "The sooner you realize that, the better."

Her mouth fell open in a gape, but she didn't answer.

"Besides." He softened his tone and stared pointedly at her full, dewy lips, "Janet isn't the one I want." He looked back up into her shocked eyes and saw the comprehension dawn. Close behind it was alarm, as if she'd seen him light a match near a gas pump. She tensed but held his gaze, and he stared defiantly, letting her see his absolute determination.

A deep flush spread over her face; her breathing turned harsh. Suddenly she looked away. "Well," she said lightly, a slight catch in her voice, "I'm sure your next target will be thrilled to hear she's been selected for your flavor-of-the-month club, along with every other woman under forty in the tri-state area." Leaping to her feet as if she'd been fired from a cannon, she snatched her wine from the table and practically ran back to the kitchen. She quickly refilled her still-full goblet, then gulped audibly from it, her hand trembling slightly. Finally she lowered the glass and looked at him. "More wine?"

Justus cursed silently, wondering what, exactly, it was about this sharp-tongued witch that wouldn't let him go. Other than the way she'd checked out his chest the other day, he had absolutely no indication she had any romantic thoughts about him whatsoever, and it didn't look like he'd get one any time soon. Any other woman would be throwing herself at his feet by now, but no, not the one woman he wanted. Not Angela. For all he knew she really believed the nonsense she'd been spouting about his being a great friend and brother to her. He stared sullenly at her, frustration churning away at his gut.

Before he could say anything the bedroom door slammed open and Maya raced out, the black remote gripped in her chubby little hand. "I'm hungry."

"Check, Uncle Justus! Look! You're in check!"

Justus stared down at the blue-and-white chessboard on the kitchen table and acted surprised. "What?" Captured pieces— flying monkeys and Munchkins, among others—stood idly on the sidelines. As he'd planned, Maya's Wicked Witch of the West queen had trapped his Cowardly Lion king in the corner. There were a couple of ways he could escape, of course—for one thing, his Scarecrow bishops were still in play, but she'd stuck to it for fifteen minutes this time—a record— and he wanted her to win. He looked back at her and grinned hugely.

She waited breathlessly for his pronouncement, her braids quivering with excitement.

He surveyed the board again, just to make it look good, then smiled again, soberly now. "Congratulations on a fine game, Maya," he solemnly told her, extending his hand. "You win."

Maya shrieked and leapt from her chair, performing a victory dance consisting mainly of shaking her bottom in the air. Watching her, he almost wondered whether she hadn't secretly flipped to BET and watched a few hip-hop videos earlier. "I won! I won! I wo-on!" She whirled to face Angela, who watched absently from her perch on the sofa. "I won, Aunt Ang-la!"

Angela stirred, making sure she didn't look Justus directly in the face, something she'd avoided doing all through dinner. He'd thrown her completely off-kilter with his veiled revelation, and he was glad. Plus, she seemed never to have recovered from the shock of learning he'd taught Maya to play chess with a set of Wizard of Oz pieces. Still, she smiled gamely and clapped her hands.

"Wonderful! High-five!" She held her hand out, high enough that Maya had to jump up to smack it. She let Maya dance around for another minute or two, then checked her watch. "Time to go, Sweetie."

After the usual protests, Angela quickly bundled Maya, who had started to yawn, back into her coat, mittens, and hat, then slipped into her own coat. They all walked to the foyer and Angela reluctantly faced Justus, keeping Maya in front of her. He had the feeling Angela needed some sort of barrier, no matter how small, between herself and Justus.

"Thank you for dinner." She smiled uncomfortably. "I think that was the best spaghetti I've ever had."

"I didn't think you liked it," he said softly. "You hardly ate any."

She quickly looked away, shifting restlessly on her feet. "Oh, you know. Long day and all." She looked down at Maya and frowned. "Where's your scarf, Sweetie?"

Justus knew how to seize an opportunity when one appeared. "Maybe it's in the bedroom, Maya." He steered her in the right direction; Angela had no choice but to unclamp her hands from the girl's shoulders and let her go. They both watched Maya scurry off.

The second he looked back at Angela she lowered her head, reaching into her pocket for her black leather gloves. "You're so good with her, Justus. I can't believe you taught her to play chess." Clutching the gloves in one hand, she raised her eyes and he saw her sincerity. "You're a wonderful uncle. She's lucky to have you."

His heart contracted, hard. Unable to stop himself, he stepped closer. "And you."

The air vibrated with energy while she stared fixedly, her wide eyes riveted to his face as if she'd been hypnotized. She blinked finally, looking away and compulsively adjusting the purse strap on her shoulder. Again he stepped closer.

"You okay, Angela?" His voice's sudden hoarseness surprised him.

Her gaze shot back to his, her eyes unusually bright now. She shrugged. "Rough day."

"It wasn't all bad."

The edges of her mouth softened slightly, as if she wanted to smile but didn't dare. It didn't matter; he knew she'd enjoyed being with him tonight, even if she wouldn't say it.

"Here it is!" Maya ran back into view, ruining the moment, her purple scarf streaming behind her like a banner.

Angela used the distraction to take a hasty step back and away from him; he cursed his niece's horrible timing. "Say good-bye to Uncle Justus, Sweetie," Angela said, taking the scarf and wrapping it around Maya's neck. "It's time to go." She reached behind her to open the door.

"Bye!" Maya quickly hugged his knees, then darted out the door and down the hall.

Flushing, Angela stared after her. "I don't think that girl walks anywhere." She pulled a set of keys out of her purse. "Well. Goodnight." She moved away.

"*Angela.*" Justus caught her arm. Stiffening, she stopped but didn't look at him. To his great relief she also didn't step out of his light grip. Over the last several days they'd hugged, kissed, and touched each other constantly—for comfort, of course. Those days were over now. They both knew it. But he couldn't just let her go. He needed—*needed*—to touch her and didn't care how shameless he had to be to do it. "Don't go."

She finally took a deep breath and looked back over her shoulder at him. Seeing the raw panic in her eyes, he smiled a little to lessen the intensity of his expression. "No hug to thank the cook?"

Chapter 10

When she hesitated he tugged, very gently, on her arm. After a moment's indecision she came the rest of the way on her own, her arms going around his waist, surprising him. He hugged her, hard, to him, one hand around her waist, the other cupping her nape so he could feel the glorious silk of her hair and smell the fragrance of lilies on her skin. She shuddered. Her soft, full breasts heaved against his chest, telling him she was having as much difficulty breathing as he was. He felt her softening, opening to him against her will, and he hardened completely in response.

Too soon, she went rigid and pulled away, keeping her face down. It didn't matter. He knew it had to be hot and flushed with passion, just like his. Letting her go was one of the hardest things he'd ever done. When she whirled and ran off down the hall, he realized just how much his touch disturbed her. He felt a tremendous surge of satisfaction.

Angela. *Angela*.

He stared after her, painfully aroused and deeply frustrated, smart enough to know just because she'd let him touch her tonight didn't mean she'd let him do it again anytime soon.

* * *

Vincent stared across his desk at Angela, who unflinchingly stared back. She'd apparently come straight from work, and looked very pretty in a navy silk dress. She seemed right at home here in his library: professional, businesslike. Unlike some other people he knew. His gaze flickered disapprovingly to Justus, who sat in the chair next to hers. As usual Justus watched him sullenly, and as usual he wore casual clothes: warm-ups and athletic shoes. Most likely he'd come directly from his little gym.

"I assume you'd like to adopt Maya," Vincent told Angela. "Yes."

Leaning back in his tall black leather chair, Vincent ran his hands along the edge of his massive desk, enjoying, as always, the smoothness of the fine mahogany. The library was probably his favorite room in the house. The hunter green walls and floor-to-ceiling bookshelves on three of the walls were formal without being cold. He'd found the Turkish rug on a trip to Istanbul a few years ago. The massive antique globe came from the nicest little London shop. On the bookshelves stood row after row of his exquisite, leather-bound first editions; he didn't much care what a book was about when he bought it—just that it was a first edition and in beautiful condition. Behind Angela and Justus, the tall windows let him look out into the rose garden, not that there was much to see this time of year. On the walls hung prints of the hunt in the English countryside.

In a place of honor on one bookshelf sat one of his most prized possessions, the hand-carved oak chess set he'd found in St. Petersburg: Napoleon and Josephine faced off against Alexander I. Once upon a time, a million years ago, he and Justus had played chess together. He doubted Justus even remembered. Now his fondest wish was to teach Maya to play, although it seemed unlikely. His health got worse every day and of course she was much too young now to play a game as tricky as chess.

He started, realizing he'd let his mind wander; Angela and Justus stared curiously at him.

"I . . . think that would be for the best," Vincent told Angela, clearing his throat. A small frown creased her forehead, as if she'd expected him to put up a fight. "I would insist on taking her myself, but . . . my health isn't . . . what it should be."

That was easily the most outrageous understatement he'd ever made. In the last couple of years his body, which he'd taken such good care of all his life—eating right, walking, no alcohol—had betrayed him and basically told him to go to hell. Heart failure. What a kick in the teeth. Only sixty-four years old and his heart was ready to call it a day, even if he wasn't. He had no idea how much time he had left, but he knew he couldn't spend it chasing a preschooler around the house.

"I understand," Angela said sympathetically. "But I know how much Maya needs you. Maybe we can work out a schedule—she could spend every other weekend with you, or maybe one night a week. Whatever works for you."

Justus, who'd been listening with his typical surly expression, made a strangled sound.

Angela shot him a surprised look, but said nothing, which Vincent thought was a little strange. The last few days they'd been glued to each other's sides, touching and hugging, shooting each other all kinds of supportive looks. That was also strange because he didn't think they knew each other well, and he didn't think Justus had ever really been friends with a woman, or had an honest-to-goodness girlfriend, not that he'd be in a position to know. But today they acted stiff and formal, as if they'd just met and didn't particularly like each other.

Angela shifted nervously, uncrossing and crossing her legs, then looked back to Vincent. "You'd probably like to think about it and get back to me—"

"If you two have finished carving up the Maya pie," Justus drawled in that hateful tone he always used with Vincent, "I have something to say."

"What is it?" Angela, looking vaguely alarmed, twisted sideways to look at Justus.

"*I* want to adopt Maya."

Horror lanced through Vincent. He and Angela exchanged flabbergasted looks, as if neither of them thought they'd heard properly. It was out of the question. As far as he was concerned, he'd sooner let Michael Jackson adopt Maya, and from the shocked look on Angela's face, she felt the same way.

"What . . . did you say?"

Justus stared him down. "You heard me."

"But, Justus." Angela, perhaps sensing a blowup, smiled a little and put a conciliatory hand on Justus's arm; Justus tensed. "You need to have lots of time with Maya, too. We weren't excluding you from the discussion. You and Vincent can alternate weekends, and I know you'll be involved in all her activities." She warmed up to the topic, growing more enthusiastic. "And there's summer vacation, and—"

Justus pulled his arm away, his face hardening. "You don't get it, Angela. I don't want her for a night here and there. I want to *adopt* her. And I'm a better choice than you." He leveled his challenging gaze on Vincent. "Or you. God knows I've been way more involved with her life than either of you ever has."

Vincent was too shocked to speak. The ornate silver frame on the edge of his desk caught his eye suddenly, and he stared at the lovely black-and-white photo of Sharon the year before she died; she was smiling in the rose garden, the wind ruffling her shoulder-length hair. Wouldn't she be spinning in her grave if she knew the lengths her favorite son would go to just to spite him? He held his hand out to the picture, glaring up at Justus.

"Absolutely not. If your mother—"

Justus shot up, knocking his chair to the carpeted floor with a muffled thunk. "Don't you dare ever mention her to me!" he roared.

Angela flinched; her hand flew to her throat.

Enraged, Vincent leapt to his feet and slammed both palms on his desk. Through the red haze of his rage he heard Angela cry out. "Do you think I'd ever let Maya live with *you*? When you have no respect for anything or anyone and no sense of duty and no ambition other than wondering where your next piece of ass is going to come from?" he shouted, spittle flying from his mouth. That same invisible fist, always with him these days, tightened in his chest, squeezing his heart painfully. Only by sheer force of will did he stay upright and not press his hand to his chest. "Are you *crazy*?"

Justus's face twisted into a sneer of fury; Angela jumped up and caught his arm, holding it, as if to stop him from lunging for his father. Vincent raised his hand and pointed across the desk at Justus. "You'll raise my only grandchild over *my dead body*!"

An endless, excruciating silence, broken only by everyone's harsh breathing, followed. Finally Justus shrugged. Veins throbbed visibly in his temple and jaw, and his nostrils flared. A nasty, crooked smile twisted his lips. "Suit yourself." Turning abruptly, he stalked out.

Angela took a hasty step after him, her arm outstretched, as if she meant to physically drag him back. "Justus, wait!"

"Oh, let him go!" Vincent shouted. "*Let him go*! I never wanted him here anyway!"

Angela had reached the library door, but she stopped

and turned, shaking with righteous fury. At her sides her fists clenched and unclenched, as if she could barely control the urge to punch him. "What kind of a man are you?" she shrieked, arms waving. "Don't you see what you're doing to your son? Your only child? Don't you care?"

"No."

Her eyes widened with horror. Well, fine. He couldn't possibly expect this woman—this *stranger*—to understand his and Justus's mutual contempt. Son? Justus was no son of his even though his unwitting sperm had spawned him. When had Justus ever acted like a son to him? From birth Justus had hated him—crying when he touched him, howling when he held him. When had Justus ever wanted to read a book with him, or play tennis with him, or just sit and watch TV with him? When had Justus ever done anything other than scorn his career and his wealth and his house and his work ethic, all the while dining on the fruits of his labor?

Calling Justus a son, in the same category as Vincent Jr., God rest his precious soul, was like calling a kitten a tiger. Sure, they were both cats, but all similarities ended there. Vincent Jr., now he was a *son*. *Vincent Jr.* had played tennis with him, and gone to Yale like he had, and practiced law with him.

"I don't expect you to understand, Angela." Tired now, he sank heavily back into his chair, too drained to hide his despised weakness. Leaning his elbows on the desk he lowered his head into his hands.

Angela didn't seem to notice his infirmity. She marched right up to the edge of his desk, eyes glittering with animosity. "Well *I* care about Justus. He's a good man," she snarled, leaning over him, jabbing her thumb at her chest for emphasis. "So I am telling you right now I will *not* stand silently by while you rip his guts out. And I will *not* let you contaminate Maya's life."

Slowly he raised his head from his hands and watched her. He'd gotten rather fond of Angela over the last few days, although he'd already discovered she wasn't as . . . malleable as he would have liked, most notably over the burial issue. Still, he'd admired her courage and her sense. Until now.

"Are you threatening me?" he asked, incredulous.

Her furious, unwavering gaze held his for a long, tense moment. "Yes," she said through her locked jaw. She whirled and swept out, her high heels drumming loud, angry steps as she retreated down the hall.

Vincent pressed a hand to his head, not surprised he'd broken out in a clammy sweat. He shrugged out of his jacket to discover that his fine, heavily starched cotton dress shirt and undershirt were sopping wet. With a shaky hand he pulled open a desk drawer, pulled out a bottle of nitroglycerin, shook several tablets out onto his blotter, took one, and immediately felt the familiar bitter sting under his tongue. Breathing deeply, he waited for the pressure in his chest to ease enough to go upstairs and lie down.

"This isn't a good time, Angela."

Justus, arms crossed, perfectly framed in the doorway to his apartment, watched her with moody, dangerous eyes. For the first time ever he wasn't thrilled to see her, and she was surprised how much it hurt. After her little scene with Vincent, she'd come directly here, equally determined to make sure Justus was okay after his father's attack and to work out a compromise about Maya. But he didn't look okay, and his tight, hard jaw told her he probably wasn't in a compromising mood.

"It'll have to be." She ignored her heart's jackhammering and marched right up to him, thinking he would step aside and let her in. He didn't. His glittering, angry gaze locked with hers and she felt a powerful burst of adrenalin. Was this the flight response? She sure wanted to turn and run for her life. Instead, she narrowed her eyes. "Excuse me," she said coldly.

His heavy brows crashed over his eyes, forming a forbidding unibrow. Very slowly he angled his body the minimum amount to let her squeeze through. Angry now, she nudged his massive, granite body with her shoulder as she passed, to no visible effect. Thank God he'd decided to let her in. If he'd wanted to block her she'd have had more luck pushing an elephant out of the way.

She went to the living room, where she took off her long wool coat and gloves and threw them on a chair. The door slammed shut and then Justus appeared from the foyer, his face still dark with tension. She tried to think of something conciliatory to say.

"I won't keep you, Justus. I need to pick Maya up from preschool in a few minutes, so this is the only time I'll have today to talk. And I wanted to do this in person."

He said nothing.

Her unease grew. His living room, so warm and cozy only last night, felt dark and dangerous now, as if she was trapped in a cave with a bear she could hear but not yet see. He hadn't bothered turning on any of the lights. Weak afternoon sunlight filtered through the blinds, creating harsh shadows on the walls. On the mantle a clock ticked, the sound thunderous in the oppressive silence.

Angela tried unsuccessfully to swallow the huge lump in her throat. "Can't we work things out with Maya?" She wrung her hands, realized she was doing it, and clenched them together at her waist. "You know I'd let you have as much time with her as you wanted. We can put together a schedule, and—"

"You won't *let* me do anything."

If she hadn't seen his lips move, she never would have recognized the low, ugly tone as his voice. Recoiling, she took an involuntary step back.

He stalked toward her, but she stood her ground. "If I was a woman, we wouldn't even be having this conversation. You don't even want her—"

She sputtered impotently.

"—and you're only taking her because you know I'm the only other choice."

"No. *No,*" she began weakly, "that's not true! I do want her! And I told her the other night she'd be living with me! I told her she could have the guest bedroom! I promised we'd paint it this weekend!"

He said nothing.

"I promised her! I can't go back on my word! I promised her we'd be a *family!*"

His glittering gaze caught hers and held, as immovable as Mount Everest. Suddenly she knew there was not the slightest possibility of compromise. "You shouldn't have done that," he told her quietly. "You know how I know you don't really want her? Do you?"

"No!"

He circled, his gaze sweeping relentlessly up and down her body, a panther stalking his prey before the kill. "Because you never gave a damn about her until her parents got killed."

She froze and made a humiliating little whimpering sound.

"Isn't that right, Angela?" He leaned right into her face so the only things she could see were the gold-and-black sparks in his gleaming dark eyes. The physical impact of his closeness, anger, and masculinity was like an uppercut to her jaw. "Huh? Before last week, when did *you* ever voluntarily spend ten minutes with her? When did *you* ever take her to the zoo? When did *you* ever take her to McDonald's for a Happy Meal?"

Oh, God, how his jeering hurt, especially when he spoke the truth. Unable to answer, unshed tears of shame and guilt blurring her vision, she turned away from the smug satisfaction in his eyes. Her refusal to look at him only seemed to enrage him further. He pinched her chin between his thumb and forefinger and, ignoring her surprised cry, jerked her head back around.

"And now *you* want her? And *you'll* let *me* take her when I want her? I don't think so."

Finally Angela found her spine. Maybe she'd been a negligent aunt in the past, but those days were over. She'd opened her heart—and her home—to Maya and she would *not* let him bully her like this. Violently she jerked her head away, blinking back her tears. "You don't know what kind of aunt I've been, you arrogant jerk!"

Justus's eyes widened in surprise.

Righteous indignation took over, and she welcomed it. "You have the nerve to talk about what kind of parent *I'd* make? Well, what about *you*?"

"Don't you dare—"

She marched up to his face, until they were nose to nose, and jutted her chin. "She's a three-and-a-half-year-old *girl*, Justus," she taunted. "Who are you going to use for a mother figure for her? Janet and the other twelve-year-olds you date?"

A hateful, knowing smirk curled his lips. "Jealous?"

Paralysis rooted Angela in her spot. The air in the room had just shifted dangerously, and she knew it. For a long time she stared at him, her chest heaving, unable to catch her breath. Finally she forced a laugh. "Don't flatter yourself."

His entire body went rigid.

Desperate to take control of the conversation and steer it back into safer waters, Angela latched onto the first hurtful thing she could think of to say. "You know what? Your father was right! How do you think you can be a good parent when you spend all your time at the gym or with your little—"

His eyes bulged with fury and she knew she'd hit her mark. "Don't even try it," he roared, sweeping his arms wide. "I heard you. *I heard you*!"

"Wha—?"

He wheeled away, pacing back and forth in front of the sliding glass doors. "Earlier! In the library with my father! I went back to tell him to go to hell, and I heard you defending me. You don't believe anything he said about me! *I heard you*!"

Angela floundered. She'd had no idea he'd heard and, worse, no idea she was capable of something as despicable as throwing his father's words in his face. "It doesn't matter what I said then," she began, backpedaling. "The point is, with your lifestyle—"

"My . . . *lifestyle*?"

A new, dangerous quality threaded his low voice, and if he'd hit her then she wouldn't have been that surprised. How had it come to this between them? Weren't they friends? Hadn't they cared about each other when the day began? She took a calming breath and chose her words very carefully.

"I'm sure you'll agree if you think about it that Maya shouldn't be exposed to all your little girlfrie—"

"My God." He eyed her incredulously, a hot, disturbing light shining in his face. "You're a hypocrite to the bone, aren't you?"

Her heart lurched crazily. What could she say? That he was right? That no matter how much she tried to pretend otherwise, the thought of him and Janet—or any other woman, for that matter—made her sick to her stomach? This was a topic she would never explore—not with herself and certainly not with him. She kept quiet, but her silence only seemed to make things worse.

"Aren't you?" He strode purposefully toward her.

Suddenly she realized he had no intentions of letting it go. Not this time. The room collapsed around her, leaving no air to breathe. The panic she'd managed to control so far finally exploded, turning her belly to lead and her legs to Jell-O. *Run! Now!* The voice inside her head screamed. Justus on a good day was a wild card. This new, angry Justus was brutally honest and determined to strip her bare. The time had come to abort her whole misguided peacekeeping mission. She'd failed miserably in reaching a compromise, and now she needed to get out of here before anything else happened— before either of them rang a bell that couldn't be un-rung.

A surge of adrenalin energized her. "It's late." She whirled away as if a rabid dog had caught her scent, desperate not to hear what she knew was coming. "I have to go." Snatching her purse and coat from the sofa she took two steps toward the door before he caught her arm and swung her back, up against the hard, thrilling warmth of his body.

A long, breathless moment passed.

"I don't think so," he told her softly, his glittering gaze slipping to her lips. "We have one other thing we need to talk about, and it's waited long enough."

Chapter 11

The second he touched her, she knew she was lost. Hadn't this moment been ten years in the making? Hadn't she wanted it—yearned for it—since the second she saw him again the night Ronnie dumped her? Even so, her instinct for self-preservation would not let her surrender.

"No," she whispered.

Ignoring her, he tightened his brutal grip on her upper arms and pulled her closer, until their bodies were fused together from shoulder to knees. Her nipples throbbed painfully against the iron slabs of his chest; her loins, long since filled to overflowing, pulsed urgently against his insistent arousal. Unable to summon the strength or will to pull away, dizzy with lust, Angela dropped her purse and coat, clutched his trembling forearms and prayed her knees would hold out. Staring into his intent, strained face, she felt his anger go up in smoke, only to be replaced by a passion every bit as intense.

With a strangled cry, he quickly backed her up against a wall—she no longer had any idea where they were or what they'd been talking about—wedged one of his unyielding thighs between her legs, and buried his face between her neck and shoulder. She whimpered with need; he shook with it. Her eyes fluttered shut and her head fell back.

"Ahhh, Angela," he murmured, nuzzling her cheek and the sensitive hollow below her ear until his hot breath singed her skin. "What have you done to me?"

Never before in her life had she felt such unbearable pleasure as Justus's lips on her body. She leaned her head to the side, giving him greater access to her neck. "Don't do this," she said ridiculously.

"I can't help it." Raising his head, he filtered his hands through her hair, kissing her forehead, temples, and eyes. "I need you." The agonized longing in his voice was excruciating. His hands slid up her sides, the heels pressing her breasts, and she writhed beneath him. Just as quickly his hands slipped over her shoulders and down her back until finally he cupped her butt, kneading and grinding her against him.

Sensations tumbled through her, faster and faster now—undeniable. She teetered on a razor's edge, wondering if he wouldn't make her come right here, up against a wall, without ever even removing a stitch of her clothing—

He raised his head again, staring at her with hot, vulnerable eyes, running his restless hands all over her too-willing body. "At night, when I should be thinking about my dead brother, I can't sleep because I keep wondering about your beautiful body even though you try to hide it from me under these awful dresses—"

"Don't."

"—and I wonder what it would feel like to make love to you, to come inside you."

"Oh, God."

Planting his hands on either side of her head, he smoothed her hair away from her face. He stared, as if hypnotized, at her mouth. She parted her lips, waiting, waiting—

"I've always wanted you, Angela," he whispered. "God, I *want* you."

Angela stiffened and the world rushed back. That one word was ice water in her veins. Janet's pouty face flashed before her eyes, breaking his spell over her. With a cry she jerked away, wrenching out of his arms before he could kiss her. He *wanted* her? Was that supposed to mean something?

"You get away from me!"

He froze, his stunned wide gaze holding hers. Obviously bewildered, he reached for her again and she furiously slapped his hand away. His face darkened and his shoulders squared off, preparing to fight. "How—how dare you do this?" she shrieked. "How dare you sexualize our friendship and ruin everything? How can we go back to where we were after *this*?"

"We can't. We both know it. And we both know we're more than friends even if you won't admit it. We've been more than friends since we laid eyes on each other."

Truer words were never spoken, but she couldn't think about that now. "We *were* friends! I trusted you! Oh, wait—my mistake!"

His eyes narrowed and he turned away.

She smacked her forehead. "How stupid of me! What would make me think *you* could be friends with any woman? Coming on to women is like the sneezing reflex to you—isn't it, Justus? Every now and then you just need to do it—isn't that how it works?" Her voice rose with hysteria. "And now I'm supposed to feel *special* because you *want* me? Coming from you that means nothing! *Nothing*!"

"Angela—"

"That's like me feeling special every year when I get the new Yellow Pages—why should I get excited when everyone else gets one, too?"

He refused to take the bait. "No," he said, unsmiling, reaching for her again. "I've never wanted anyone else the way I want you. Not even close."

God, she wanted to believe him. She felt herself melting, weakening. "Don't!" She threw her hands up and backed away, knowing even if thirty feet separated them she would still feel the heat pulsing from his body to hers. "Don't do this to me when you know Ronnie just dumped me. *Don't do this*!"

"I'm sorry he hurt you, but I'm glad he's out of your life because it's time for you and me now." His voice dropped, becoming a seductive whisper, enticing her, luring her to a place she could never go. "I knew the second I saw you at the restaurant, and I didn't care about Ronnie, and I didn't care about Janet. And even if Ronnie hadn't dumped you, and even if the accident hadn't happened, I would have found you and come for you." His jaw hardened. "Nothing would have stopped me."

She wanted to clap her hands over her ears so she wouldn't have to hear another word.

"I've wanted you since I was seventeen. And I'm not a boy anymore."

Angela cried out, her panic finally breaking free and surging, full-blown, from her throat. God, she knew he wasn't a boy—as if anyone could mistake his tall, muscular frame for anything other than a man overflowing with testosterone and virility. As if any woman could look into those dark, hooded eyes and do anything other than wonder what such a man would feel like between her legs. Even ten years ago, when he'd danced with her at the wedding reception, she'd known he wasn't a boy—not really. A desperate longing—for him to touch her with his hands, his lips, and his tongue—twisted inside her gut.

He smiled then, a mesmerizing, seductive smile full of promise. "It's going to be so good between us, Angela. We both know it."

Yes. *Yes.* "No."

Again he stepped closer, blocking out her ability to see anything other than his smoldering eyes, erotic mouth, and wide shoulders. "I want us to finish what we started the night we danced together. Do you remember?"

Oh, yes, she remembered, even though she'd tried, over and over again, not to. Remembered the exquisite pleasure of being wrapped in those hard arms, the thrill of his warm hands sliding down her bare back, the torture of his broad chest pressed against her throbbing breasts, and the excitement of feeling his smooth cheek pressed to her forehead. Angela swayed on her feet, her eyes closing; her body strained for him, and only sheer willpower kept her from reaching for him.

She was in terrible trouble. In another minute she'd be in his arms, and once she was she knew she wouldn't care about any consequences. She floundered for a moment and then made what she hoped was a bewildered, annoyed face.

"*Dance?*" she said coolly. "You're making a big deal out of that one little dance we had?"

His face darkened, contracting, and she knew she'd hit a nerve.

She laughed. "You *were* young, weren't you? Why would you think there was anything special about some dance ten years ago? Is *that* what this is all about?"

Justus's face twisted with hurt and fury and her stomach lurched sickeningly. Somehow, in trying to hurt him, she'd hurt herself worse. "'Some dance?'" he said in a mangled voice.

"Get over yourself, Justus," she said, turning away.

He stalked around her, blocking her. Their gazes collided

for an endless, challenging moment. "Are you telling me," he said, his jaw clenched so tightly he could barely get the words out, "that there was nothing special about dancing with me that night?"

"Yes," she said, in the worst act of cowardice of her life.

He roared with anger. "You little liar!"

Alarmed, her nerves stretched beyond the breaking point, she turned to run away. Once again his arm lashed out, hauling her roughly back against him. He clamped his hands on her butt, his fingers sliding over the silk of her dress, and pressed his hips to hers. She cried out. She'd foolishly thought her body had cooled down a little since he let her go, but she was wrong. His rigid arousal burned and crazed her; of their own free will her hips shifted against his. The ache deep between her thighs grew until ecstasy shimmered on the horizon.

"Let me tell you something, Duchess," he said, his voice low and seductive, his eyes glinting mercilessly. Again she sensed his immovability, his absolute determination. "You and I are going to make love very soon. It's inevitable. It's been inevitable since I first laid eyes on you ten years ago. Get used to it." His hands stroked her once more, as if he couldn't help himself, before he shoved her rudely away.

Angela gaped at him, her frustrated body crying a silent, desperate protest at being deprived. Her thoughts swirled like a vortex. What had happened here tonight?

"How can you do this?" she cried. "Tell me you're taking Maya away from me, then turn around and tell me you want me? I don't understand you!"

"One thing has nothing to do with the other."

"My God! You're insane! And you won't be getting anything you want, I can promise you that!"

"A judge will have to decide about Maya." He stared her down, his gaze unwavering and unconcerned. "And as for you

and me, we both know the truth." His lips turned up in the beginnings of a chilling, ruthless smile that sent jolts of electricity shooting from her belly to her aching loins. Stepping
toward her, his voice again dropped to that husky murmur
that made her want to leap out of her skin. "And before I
make love to you, I'm going to punish you for telling such a
ridiculous lie. That's a promise."

Cringing inwardly, she somehow managed to defiantly
hold his gaze for a moment, until finally she couldn't take it
anymore. To the depths of her soul she knew he would never
change his mind or give up on either of the things he wanted.
Worse, she knew Maya probably did belong with him. And
she knew making love with him would be a hot, wild, sublime
experience that would obliterate the memory of years of tepid
sex with Ronnie and forever destroy her chances of finding
sexual fulfillment with any other man.

And she knew she could never let it happen.

The coward in her won out. She turned, snatched up her
coat and purse and, for the second time in as many days, ran
from his apartment.

"Magistrate Brooks is very fair and she goes out of her way
not to favor women over men, so I think we were really lucky
she got assigned to the case. Now, when our case is called,
we'll go to her office and—" The voice trailed off. "Justus?
Justus? Are you listening to me?"

He wasn't; he shifted impatiently in his uncomfortable blue
pleather-and-pressed-wood chair and tried to focus on his
lawyer. County probate court was nothing like the grandiose
and intimidating federal courtroom Vincent had dragged him
to years ago in one of his misguided attempts to recruit him
into the family business. Probate court, in a utilitarian brick

building a few blocks from the justice center and the main courthouse, looked like any other office: a reception area, a waiting area, glass-enclosed offices with nameplates by the doors. Still, court was court, and the seriousness of the occasion weighed heavy on his shoulders. In this building, on this issue, on this day, he and Angela were enemies who'd hired lawyers to protect themselves from each other. His stomach churned. "Sorry," he muttered.

Mollified, his lawyer nodded curtly and resumed his lecture. "When we go in, you'll—"

After ten seconds of the man's droning, Justus gave up trying to listen. Angela also sat in the waiting area—not twenty feet away—and, as usual, when Angela was nearby he couldn't focus on anything else. Especially when she ignored him, like right now. Well, she hadn't completely ignored him. She'd given him an offhand, distant, "Hello, Justus," when she first arrived for the hearing. Just like that, "Hello, Justus," as if they were acquaintances—and not even friendly acquaintances, at that—who'd run into each other in the produce section at the supermarket. Not as if they were two people teetering on the brink of an inevitable and passionate affair, which they were.

As he'd expected, she'd shown him no signs of warmth or affection in the ten minutes they'd been waiting, much less any signs of the explosively passionate woman he now knew lurked beneath her stern navy suit and white blouse. After she'd deigned to speak to him, she'd primly assumed her remote post in a chair as far away from him as she could get while still remaining in the building. Tossing her head as if she didn't have a care in the world and couldn't be bothered any more with him, she'd crossed those long, long legs with a swish of nylon that fogged his brain, apparently determined never again to look him in the eye.

He stared hungrily at her. The two days he hadn't seen her felt like twenty years. She'd very cleverly avoided any contact with him at all by dialing the phone for Maya at bedtime each night, then letting the girl speak to him, thereby circumventing the one legitimate reason he had to talk to Angela. Obviously he'd thrown her completely off-kilter the other night, and he should have been pleased. Instead he missed her so much he felt like he'd entered one of the seven rings of hell. Of course he'd missed Maya, too, but this was different. The court would help him get Maya. If he wanted Angela, though, he had to get her himself, a mission impossible if ever he'd seen one. But he couldn't—would never—give up. He wanted her too much.

Justus jerked his gaze away from her face and tried to focus on his attorney who was, after all, charging him two hundred dollars an hour for the advice he spouted, whether Justus listened to it or not. "What did you say, Tom?"

Tom Wilson, whose carroty hair streaked with strands of silver made him look about forty or so, sighed reproachfully, as if he couldn't quite conceive of a world where his clients didn't hang breathlessly on his every word. "I said I've had a lot of experience with this magistrate and I think she'll be fair. And quick."

"Good."

Just then a petite, willowy blonde in a nondescript gray dress and sensible black shoes marched through the rectangle of chairs, tables, and fake ficus trees, pausing in the glass-enclosed doorway of a small office. Justus barely registered her presence until he realized Tom had straightened in his chair and was now staring expectantly at her.

She smiled at Tom. "I'm ready for you now." She gestured to Angela and her attorney, then continued into the office.

Tom shot to his feet. "Let's go."

"That's her?" Justus asked. Somehow he'd expected an imposing middle-aged man with black robes—someone, frankly, like his father. Trailing Tom inside, he waited for the magistrate to sit, then sat in the last of the four chairs in front of her nondescript desk. Angela sat on the other end; between them sat Tom and Carmen, Angela's friend from the funeral, who was apparently also her attorney.

"Magistrate Brooks, this is my client, Justus Robinson," Tom said.

Justus stood, leaned across the desk and took the woman's hand. Her grip was surprisingly strong, her gaze direct. Justus liked her. Carmen introduced Angela, then they all sat and watched while the magistrate flipped open the file and frowned over it. Finally she looked up.

"So we have competing petitions for guardianship?" she asked no one in particular.

"That's right," Carmen said.

"Well." Magistrate Brooks pursed her lips sadly, looking at first Angela, then Justus. "I'm very sorry for both of you. I'm sure this is a very difficult time."

"Thank you," Justus said; Angela just nodded.

Magistrate Brooks slid her chair closer to her desk, then clasped her hands on top of the file. "Are you two the closest next of kin?"

Justus started. He'd thought the magistrate would talk only to the lawyers, but apparently she wanted to hear directly from him. "Uh . . . not quite. My father is still alive, but his health isn't that good anymore and—"

"I see," Magistrate Brooks said briskly, apparently having heard all she needed to know on that particular topic. She turned to Angela. "And Maya has been living with you?"

"Yes."

Concern wrinkled the magistrate's forehead. "How is she doing so far?"

"Fine," Angela said quickly. "She's been going to pre-school and—"

"Have you considered a grief counselor for her?"

"Yes, actually," Angela told her, darting a glance down the row at Justus. "Justus and I talked and we thought it would be a good idea, and so—"

"Good." Magistrate Brooks picked up a pen and started writing on a blank form of some sort. "I'm glad to see you two are able to talk about things. That's good for Maya."

Angela held Justus's gaze for a moment, a question in her eyes, but then she turned away. For the three millionth time he cursed his temper and impulsivity the other day. He'd rocked the boat and now had to pay a steep price—she wouldn't even look at him.

Magistrate Brooks finished writing and looked up. "I'm putting on a temporary order. I want Maya to stay where she is, for now." Tom put a restraining hand on his arm, as if he thought Justus might spring to his feet and curse the magistrate, but Justus had expected as much. Staying with Angela probably was the best thing for Maya—for now—and he didn't want to uproot her unnecessarily.

She continued, "And I would like Mr. Robinson to see her regularly during the pendency of the case." Her eyebrows inched toward her hairline. "You can work out a schedule?"

Her look needed no translation: she expected Justus and Angela to work expediently and cooperatively if they hoped for a favorable ruling from her. "Of course," Justus quickly told her. "But I would like Maya to spend some nights with me like we've always done."

Magistrate Brooks looked at Angela. "Ms. Dennis?"

Angela blinked several times, nostrils flaring slightly, as

if she'd been forced to pretend she hadn't just caught a whiff of rotten fish. Finally she smiled a tight smile that may have fooled the magistrate but didn't fool Justus. She was annoyed. "That's fine."

"Good." Magistrate Brooks wrote on her white paper. "I'm scheduling the final hearing on your applications for three months from now. And I'm also going to order a home study for both of you. We really need it in this case since you're both single and you're both siblings of the decedents. As far as the court is concerned, right now you're in exactly the same legal position—either one of you could be Maya's guardian."

Satisfied, Justus relaxed a little, his mind back on Angela while the magistrate turned to the lawyers and dithered over legalese for a few minutes. He shouldn't have pushed her the other night, of course, but she'd infuriated him with her hypocrisy—about Maya, his father's comments and her feelings for him—until he'd lost all control over what he said, something that happened only very rarely with him. She pushed him beyond all his limits. He'd exploded, and now he'd have to pay the piper. If he knew anything about Angela, she'd avoid him for a good long time if she thought he still wanted a physical relationship with her.

If.

In his desperation to simultaneously get back in her good graces and get her into bed, a plan had come to him. Well, not a *plan*, really—*plan* was such a devious word. A *thought* had come to him. What if he apologized and renounced his sexual interest in her? What if he told her he was sorry he'd come on so strong—that was certainly true, since it had cost him so dearly—and that he should have been more sensitive to her recent breakup, also true, and that her friendship was vitally important to him, still true, and that therefore he could put aside his attraction to her and just remain friends?

Not true. But she didn't need to know that. Not right now, anyway.

If he apologized and behaved himself for the time being Angela's innate kindness, along with her overwhelming attraction to him, would force her to accept him, to be nice to him, to spend time with him. And if he was with her he could wear down her resistance until finally she caved.

It was only a matter of time.

He hazarded a glance at her while the lawyers had their heads bent over the magistrate's order, and caught her staring at him, her face deeply troubled. The second his gaze met hers she looked away, as if she feared she'd turn into a pillar of salt if she watched him for too long.

Sighing, frustrated, he looked down at his hands clenched in his lap. Why did she bother fighting him? Why did they have to play these games? Because he knew—they *both* knew—how attracted she was to him. He'd seen her longing glances. He'd felt her shiver when he touched her. He'd sensed her barely controlled passion for him. If he'd pressed the issue a little the other day he could have made love to her right then; she'd wanted to and it wouldn't have been that hard. And once he had her in his bed, she'd want to stay there. He knew it.

But it wasn't that simple at all because afterwards she'd hate him for it. She wasn't ready, and he didn't want to have to keep fighting the same battle when he could have her willingly if he only waited. He wanted her begging him to make love to her. Panting for him. Crying for him. And he would make her beg, too—as punishment for claiming, with a straight face, that they were just friends and their dance at the wedding was meaningless. What a liar she was. She needed to learn—*immediately*—that while she could lie to herself she couldn't lie to him.

Oh, yes. He would pretend all day if it got him Angela in the end. He'd already waited ten years for her. What did a few more weeks matter?

When the hearing ended a few minutes later and they all wandered back to the waiting area, he caught her elbow. She started and turned to look at him, her eyes wary and filled with dread, as if she knew, as well she should, that any efforts to resist him were futile.

"Angela," he said softly, keeping his tone and expression bland. "Can I talk to you for a minute?"

Chapter 12

Angela stared at him in a panic, her heart racing uncontrollably. Again he'd worn that wicked dark suit, the one that made him look so commanding, so irresistibly handsome. His light grip on her arm made her warm and agitated, as if he'd rubbed his hands all over her body. What should she do? She'd planned to avoid him at all costs and she'd almost made a clean getaway. Now what? She wanted to throw him off, scream *no*, tell him to leave her alone and she'd see him in court. In the end she felt too paralyzed to say anything.

Justus watched her, waiting.

Carmen seemed not to notice her turmoil. Hitching the strap of her briefcase onto her shoulder, she said, "I'm going to talk to Tom. I'll just see you back at the office, Angela."

Angela swallowed convulsively, her gaze still locked with Justus's. "Okay."

Tom clapped Justus on the back. "I'll call you later."

Justus looked away, turning to shake Tom's hand. "Great. Thanks."

Angela watched the lawyers walk off together, chattering animatedly about the case. She felt doomed, like a just-surfaced scuba diver watching the boat return to shore without her. Justus was, of course, the shark.

Except he didn't look like a shark today. He smiled a little, his eyes empty of amusement, sarcasm, smugness, heat, longing, or any of the other emotions that had become so familiar to her in the last week. "Can we sit down?" He steered her toward the chairs.

Without answering, unable to think of a reasonable excuse to refuse him, she marched stiffly to a row of chairs in a corner—the area was deserted—and sat, her purse and coat clutched in her lap as if they could somehow shield her from this man's overwhelming masculinity. Justus sat right next to her, which was, of course, much, much too close. He made no move to do so but she knew he could easily throw out his long arms and trap her, engulf her. When he leaned down to rest his elbows on his powerful thighs, his face was right at eye level with hers. She wished she could blindfold herself so she did not have to see those sexy brown eyes, or the smooth skin, or the tender lips up close. She waited miserably for him to speak, trying to keep her breath shallow so she wouldn't have to smell his delicious cologne too deeply.

He clutched his hands together, dropping his head as if to gather his thoughts. Finally he looked up at her, his expression troubled. He took a deep breath. "I'm . . . sorry about the other night, Angela," he murmured in a husky bedroom voice that made her think of her limbs tangled with his as they slid around together on satin sheets. "I got carried away. I think I was . . . seeing things that weren't there and projecting my feelings onto you." His jaw tightened as if he was anguished by the magnitude of his own misbehavior. "I hope you can forgive me. And that we can still be friends."

Angela stared, too flabbergasted to speak. She'd expected— had braced for—another attempt at seduction, or maybe wheedling or negotiation. Never in a million years had she expected him to back off entirely; quitting didn't seem to be part of his character.

"You're apologizing?"

He nodded earnestly, his eyes wide and innocent. "Can we get past this? It'll never happen again."

"Never happen again?" she echoed faintly, unable to believe her ears. She frowned, watching him suspiciously. Was this some sort of terrible joke? Where was the wolf from the other night—the one with the hot, wicked eyes and the steely, unwavering determination to have sex with her? What had happened to him? And who was this other, respectful, nonthreatening Justus? "Are you serious?"

"Yes."

She felt curiously deflated, almost disappointed, although of course she would never feel disappointed if Justus decided he didn't want her after all. Still, this abrupt about-face made no sense. Was he really that fickle? Or had he gone back to Janet? For some unfathomable reason her stomach lurched sickeningly at *that* thought. "I . . . don't understand."

He shrugged, a rueful smile tugging at his lips. "Well, I mean, I had the chance to think about it and you were right. I blew some silly dance ten years ago way out of proportion."

Angela flinched. How could he trivialize one of her most precious memories like that? Because despite what she'd claimed, the time she'd spent with him at the wedding reception *had* been special—more than special. The awful truth was that dancing with Justus, and the connection she'd felt with him, had, sadly, been the most romantic thing that ever happened to her. She remembered every second she'd spent with him, every look they'd shared, every touch. Worse, she remembered how she'd felt like a statutory rapist for entertaining sexual thoughts—even for one second—about a boy barely out of high school. She wished she didn't remember, but she did. Even so, she didn't wish the night had never happened. Did he?

Chuckling now, he said, "I was just a young kid and you were an older woman. I guess that was exciting to me at the time. But I've grown up. And I'm too old for little romantic fantasies." He laughed, rubbing the back of his neck as if embarrassed by his own foolishness. "You probably think I'm an idiot."

Somehow she managed to smile brightly even though she suddenly had the inexplicable but strong urge to cry. She'd die a thousand gruesome deaths before she'd let Justus think she cared whether he wanted her or not. "Of course not," she said, looking away so he couldn't see how upset she was. "I understand."

"There's so much going on right now with Maya, anyway. We don't need more complications."

"Right."

"And we both know you're not really my type."

He said the words with no particular inflection, but she thought she heard a vague challenge in his silky tone. Angela winced as she absorbed this invisible knife through her heart. If he'd been trying he couldn't have possibly picked a more hurtful thing to say to her because lately it seemed she wasn't really anyone's type. She jerked her head back around to stare, stricken, at him, but again his face looked bland, his eyes wide and innocent. So he hadn't meant to slice her feelings to shreds, then. It hardly mattered; the damage was done. Why would she have ever seriously believed a man like Justus would be interested in a woman like her?

Bravely she kept her chin up and smiled. "We're not each other's type at all."

He studied her for a minute, eyes slightly narrowed, before he reached into his inside jacket pocket to pull out what looked like a blue credit card. He held it out to her. "Here. I

brought you a peace offering—a free membership to the club.
I want you to come and bring Maya. There's babysitting, so
she can go there while you exercise."

For some reason she felt irritated now, almost angry, although
she couldn't imagine why. What did she care if Justus rejected
her? Better men than him had rejected her before and probably
would again. She took the card, resisting the urge to throw it in
his stupid earnest face. Hell would freeze over—twice—before
she set foot in his rotten little club. "Great. Thanks."

"And I thought maybe I could take Maya to dinner
tonight."

"Great."

He beamed at her then, his boyish smile so wide and beautiful just looking at him actually made her heart ache. Before
she knew what he was doing, he reached out and caught both
of her hands, clasping them in his warm, strong fingers, rubbing his thumbs over her knuckles. Jolts of alarming sensa-
tion shot from her belly to her groin. "Thanks for being so
understanding, Duchess." Leaping to his feet he leaned down
and, ignoring her slight noise of protest, kissed her. Except
he seemed to miss her cheek and instead hit the sensitive spot
where her ear joined her cheek, his lips and breath hot on
her ear. Immediately her insides turned to pudding, and only
with great difficulty could she stifle a gasp.

He straightened and let her go, still smiling as if he'd discovered a diamond mine in his back yard. "I'll see you tonight."
He wheeled around and strode toward the elevators.

Angela stared after him and waited a long time for her legs
to collect enough strength to let her get up and walk back to
the office.

"What did Justus want?" Carmen asked.

Angela and Carmen sat alone in the firm's large conference room waiting for their meeting to begin. A glittering Waterford crystal chandelier hung over the tennis court-sized mahogany table; a colorful Oriental bowl from some dynasty or other, filled with silk hydrangeas, peonies, and hollyhocks of varying shades of crème, pink, and red graced the center. One wall consisted entirely of floor-to-ceiling windows and had a breathtaking view of the river and the green hills of Kentucky, dotted with expensive houses and condominiums on the other side. To the right both Great American Ball Park and Paul Brown Stadium—which looked like a space-aged disk that had escaped from an episode of the Jetson's—were visible.

Angela flushed uncomfortably, ambivalent about telling Carmen the whole story. Still, her thoughts were in such turmoil, and Carmen always gave such good, hardheaded advice, that it might be worthwhile to talk things over with her.

"He, uh, wants to take Maya tonight." Very casually she twisted in her seat, reached for the silver water tray on the sideboard behind them and poured herself a tall glass of ice water. "And he apologized for coming on to me the other night."

Carmen gasped, looking appropriately scandalized. "Justus came on to you?"

Angela nodded.

Carmen's jaw remained on the floor for an interminable second. Recovering, she whooped with laughter. "Oh, my God, you lucky witch!"

"Wha—?"

"Honey, if Justus came on to me, we'd be in bed before he even finished asking. He's about the sexiest man I've ever seen."

A tight knot of irritation, something she rarely felt with Carmen, wedged in Angela's throat. Apparently the woman immune to Justus's fatal charm had yet to be born. "Well, of course *you* would." Carmen, for as long as she could remember, had had a lack of inhibition about sex that intrigued and annoyed Angela. She always seemed able to blithely enter into relationships with men, thoroughly enjoy sex, then not have her heart smashed when the relationships ended, which they always did. She never had expectations beyond a few weeks or months of enjoying the man's company, and if the man suddenly stopped returning her calls, Carmen's attitude was that there were always more fish in the sea.

"When are you going to stop being such a Puritan?" Carmen asked, laughing.

Angela clenched her jaw, unable to stop thinking that if Justus were here, he would agree wholeheartedly with Carmen's assessment. "I'm not a Puritan. But in case you haven't noticed, I just got out of a relationship last week. I'm not ready. Plus, Justus is Maya's uncle. Plus, he's much younger than me. Plus, he's promiscuous. Plus, we have nothing in common. Okay?"

"What the hell is wrong with you?" Carmen flung her arms wide, flapping them in obvious frustration, as if she was speaking Chinese to someone who only understood Russian. "I'm not saying you should marry him! And I'm not nominating him for sainthood! All I'm saying is why don't you have a little affair and enjoy yourself? I would!"

Shocked, Angela threw her hand over her heart, unable to recall when she'd ever heard such a foolish idea. "I can't have sex just for *fun!*"

"That's your problem."

Angela snatched up her water and drank deeply, her blood simmering. Why on earth had she thought she could rationally discuss this with Carmen, a woman whose advice generally consisted of "leap now and ask questions later"? After a few minutes of silent seething, another question came to mind. She smoothed her hair nervously, not certain her ego could take whatever painfully frank answer Carmen would give her.

"How do I look to you?"

Carmen's eyes widened in surprise as she paused in the act of pouring her own glass of water to stare at her. "You're beautiful, of course!" she said vehemently.

Slightly mollified, Angela smiled. "What about my clothes—and my hair?"

Carmen dropped her eyes and froze, lips pursed, her glass suspended halfway to her lips. "Why do you ask?"

Alarmed, Angela touched her arm and steeled herself. "What is it? I can take it."

"Well, honey . . ." Carmen said uncertainly, her gaze flickering to Angela's hair, then back to her face. "You know, that ponytail." Angela reached back to grab her low ponytail, as if to shield it from the forthcoming criticism. "It's a little . . . severe."

Angela's jaw dropped.

Carmen apparently found the courage to speak freely and plowed ahead. "And your clothes could be a little . . . sexier."

Angela defensively smoothed the fine wool of her suit. "I've been working my butt off for the last ten years! I don't have time to be sexy!"

"Make time," Carmen muttered quickly, raising her glass to her lips.

"*Et, tu*, Carmen?"

"Sorry."

Oh, how the truth hurt. Justus's mocking face flashed before her eyes, telling her again she wasn't his type—not that she wanted to be his type!—and she knew why, didn't she? She'd known without asking Carmen. She may be passably pretty, but she wasn't sexy. Sure, she was smart, funny, successful and, well, functional, but she hadn't been sexy enough to hold Ronnie who, on the sexiness scale, rated a five or six out of ten on a good night.

Justus was a twenty. Why on earth would he ever be interested in her?

Sulking now, Angela jerked open her black leather portfolio and flipped her legal pad open to a fresh page. She'd had enough of this stupid conversation, and anyway it was now two-thirty; Larry should be here any minute. Sure enough, the door opened just then and the firm's managing partner, a tall, lean figure, marched in. Angela and Carmen snapped to attention.

Lawrence Whittington sat at the head of the table, as was his right as the oldest—seventy—and most senior member of the partnership; he'd been with the firm for forty-five years. Angela always thought Larry looked like he'd been sent over from Central Casting. His silvery blond hair, patrician nose, sharp cheekbones, and expensive suits, always with heavily starched cotton shirts and French cuffs that showcased his vast and varied collection of cuff links, made it impossible for Angela to imagine him as anything other than a senior attorney, except for, maybe, U.S. senator.

"Angela, I know it's hard to talk about professional matters at a time like this, but it can't be helped," he said after greeting them.

"I understand, Larry," Angela replied. "Life goes on."

He nodded sadly. "Life goes on, and it's time for us to start evaluations. You know we like to get this done by the first of the year or so." He flipped open a file and rifled through some pages. "I think both your chances are excellent at this point. You've both been here ten years. Your hours have always been very good and this past year they've been outstanding." He slid a pair of bifocals up his long, straight nose and examined a spreadsheet of some sort. "Angela, it looks like you're on track to bill twenty-two hundred hours this year, which is superb."

"Thank you," Angela murmured. She allowed herself a moment's pleasure at this praise, which was about all an associate ever got in a firm this size. In return for her handsome— well, borderline obscene—salary, the partners expected her to put her nose to the grindstone, work her butt off, never complain, and only come up for air long enough to troll for new clients. Angela had never complained or minded, but now she wondered what the seventy-hour weeks had cost her. If she'd been home more, could she have saved her relationship with Ronnie? If she hadn't canceled so many dates with him at the last minute to work on some case, would he still have hopped into some other woman's bed? Had focusing on her career doomed her chances of getting married before she turned forty?

"Of course, your performance on the Golden Valley case will be very important."

"I know." Angela had been defending the Golden Valley Snack Company against a charge of age discrimination for the last two-and-a-half years and could hardly recall a time when GV hadn't dominated her professional life. The jury trial was set to begin after the first of the year. If GV lost the case, which it well might because some of the evidence against it was pretty damning, it would have to pay damages of up to two million dollars. Worse, if it lost the case GV would likely reevaluate its relationship with the firm. The unspoken long and short of it was if Angela lost the case and GV consequently fired the firm and took its business with it, Angela would not only not make partner, she'd be out on her butt.

"When is the final pretrial conference?" Larry asked.

"In about a month."

"I'm sure you've got everything under control. Let me know if you need any help." Larry leaned back in his chair and removed his glasses. "Well," he said crisply, smiling. "Do you have any questions for me?"

Angela cleared her throat nervously. "I do, actually." She ignored Carmen's alarmed warning glare and plowed ahead. "You know I have my niece now—"

"Yes, I understand Carmen, here, is representing you for the guardianship."

"Right. And this is going to be a transition period for Maya, and I—"

Larry made a slight tutting sound. One tufted white brow lifted slightly, managing to convey exactly the sort of disapproval Angela had feared. She shut up immediately, before she committed career suicide. "Angela, you know we encourage family commitments—"

Angela tried not to snort. Last year two of the senior partners had divorced their wives for younger women. Larry, here, probably hadn't been home for dinner in the last thirty years.

"—but I'm going to be honest with you." His piercing blue gaze caught hers, pinning her to the chair. "Now is not the time for you to slack off."

Angela's heart sank. She couldn't possibly raise Maya while continuing to work the hours she'd worked for the last ten years. It simply wasn't possible. How on earth could she eat dinner with Maya, help her with her eventual homework, and tuck her into bed every night when she normally didn't get home from work until eight-thirty or nine?

Realizing Larry's questioning gaze was still on her she smiled brightly and said the only thing she could say. "I understand."

Larry cleared his throat. "May I suggest a nanny . . . ?" he said delicately.

Suddenly Angela saw Carolyn's horrified face, as clearly as if she were sitting right across the table from her. Let a nanny raise her dead sister's only child while she slaved at the office? Never. She'd let Justus have her first. But it wouldn't come to that. She would think of something. She had to.

"I'll think about it," she told Larry.

He smiled, clearly relieved that difficult topic had been resolved, never to be discussed again. "Good." Glancing at his watch he said, "I have another meeting. Thank you, ladies."

Angela and Carmen murmured their good-byes and Larry left. The French door had barely closed behind him when Carmen hissed, "What the hell are you doing? If you're trying to blow up your career why don't you just go ahead and bring a loaded shotgun to work? You didn't really expect him to say, 'Go ahead and take all the family time you need,' did you?"

"Of course not," Angela snapped. "But I'd hoped he'd be a little more supportive than *that*." She propped her elbows on the table and pressed her face into her hands. "God, what am I going to do? There's no way I can take care of Maya and come home late every night."

"I know, honey." Carmen smoothed Angela's hair, and Angela relaxed a little. "But you need to do something. You don't want to wind up like Michele Avery."

Angela tensed and her heart rate took off again. Carmen had, in her unerring way, put her finger directly on Angela's worst, though unspoken, fear. Michele Avery was a name, usually spoken only in hushed whispers in dark corners of the hallowed halls here at Grant & Delamere, LLC, that struck terror in the hearts of every ambitious associate while vividly illustrating the firm's culture: move up through the ranks or get the hell out. The unfortunate Ms. Avery, whom Angela vaguely remembered from her early days with the firm, didn't make partner the year she was eligible—allegedly because her billable hours were low. Even though the partners murmured supportive platitudes and professed their continued faith in her, they very quickly reassigned her biggest cases and began to oversee her work to a degree no self-respecting lawyer with ten years' experience could tolerate for long. The writing on the wall, Ms. Avery resigned within three months. The last anyone heard of her, she'd set up her own practice in a shabby office somewhere on the unfashionable outskirts of downtown, put her name on the public defender's list for appointments, and been making less than half of what she'd made at the firm.

"I know that," Angela, snarled. "Do you have anything even remotely helpful to say? Because I've got to tell you—so far you're batting about zero."

"Well . . . why don't you go ahead and hire a nanny?"

Angela jerked her head out of her hands. "I can't do that! First of all, Carolyn gave up her career to stay home and be a full-time mother. She'd haunt me for the rest of my life if I handed Maya over to some stranger to raise." Agitated, she leapt from her chair and strode to the window, staring out. "And I'm sure the court won't let me have Maya if I can't spend any more time with her than that."

Carmen waved a hand. "You don't have to have a full-time nanny. Just someone who can help out a little after school."

"No way." Angela shook her head vehemently. "I can handle it myself. I can leave the office early and work after she goes to bed." The more she thought about it, the more that seemed to be the perfect solution to all her problems. "Yeah, I think that's what I'll do."

"I don't know," Carmen said dubiously. "What about your social life?"

"Get real," Angela told her. "Anyway, Maya goes to bed at eight. I'll put her down, work for a few more hours, and no one will ever know the difference." She smiled broadly, excited and relieved by her plan. "How hard could it be?"

* * *

"How'd the hearing go, man?"

Justus looked up from the paperwork on his desk to see Brian standing in the doorway of his office. Glancing at his watch he saw it was five-thirty, nearly time to wrap it up here, go home and change and head over to Angela's to get Maya. He waved Brian inside, putting away the timesheets for now, and Brian sank into the chair opposite him. "Who's out front?" Traffic at the club picked up between four and six, when people came by to exercise after work, and he wouldn't feel comfortable chewing the fat back here with Brian without someone manning the employees.

"Ed," Brian told him. "How was the hearing?"

"Pretty good, I guess. The magistrate said Maya should stay with Angela for now, but I can have overnights. And she ordered a home study. She said Angela and I are in pretty much equal positions."

Brian, always loyal, scowled as if the magistrate had sent Justus to the gas chamber. "Yeah, but she doesn't know how involved you've been with Maya."

Justus shrugged, not terribly concerned at this stage of the game. "She'll find out soon enough, I guess."

Brian propped his elbow on the arm of his chair and ran his fingers through his hair. "Is Angela still being reasonable with you?"

"Oh, yeah." Angela was nothing if not fair, and that particular issue was the least of his concerns right now.

"I don't see how you think you're going to get something started with Angela when you're trying to take Maya away from her. And what about when it's over? Have you thought of that? You'll still have to deal with her for the rest of Maya's life."

Justus stared at him feeling vaguely troubled. He hadn't thought of that, actually, but now that he had he didn't much care for the idea of things ending between him and Angela.

Most likely their affair would run its course and die a natural death, but he couldn't quite picture that happening. He'd wanted her for so long he preferred to focus on having her, not letting her go.

"I'll cross that bridge when I come to it."

"Made any progress yet?"

Justus leaned back in his chair, propped his feet on his desk and scowled, reliving his heinous miscalculation of the other night. "No. In fact I shot myself in the foot the other day." Brian's eyes widened with exaggerated shock, which Justus ignored. "I told her how I felt—"

"And she didn't throw her panties in your lap?" Brian asked, laughing.

Justus felt the first stirrings of irritation, and his frown deepened. This was the sort of conversation he and Brian had had dozens—hundreds—of times over the years, but for some reason Brian's question was deeply offensive when applied to Angela. Janet and her ilk were one thing, but Angela belonged to another category completely, and he wouldn't have Brian talking about her like some slut.

"A little respect, man," he said, his voice laced with an edge he rarely used with Brian.

Brian started, his eyes rounding to the size of bowling balls. Suddenly a knowing little smirk turned up the edges of his mouth, blackening Justus's mood even further. "I see."

Justus resisted the urge to kick his butt for the amused, speculative gleam in his eyes. "No, you don't."

Brian just grinned.

Justus abruptly swung his feet down and jumped up, turning away so Brian couldn't see whatever he thought he saw on Justus's face. He jerked open the small closet and snatched his black down jacket from its hanger.

"My point is I miscalculated a little and now I have to back off for a while," he said over his shoulder.

Brian stared at him, no longer smiling. "But you're not giving up."

"I never give up."

Brian shook his head, bemused. "Don't I know it."

Justus slid his arms in his jacket and grabbed his keys. "You got things covered for tonight, man?"

"Yeah. No problem."

Brian stood and followed him to the front door. At a glance Justus saw that all was well with the club; the smoothie bar was crowded and people hustled up and down the steps and in and out of the locker rooms. His lifelong dream of owning his own gym had come true, and he owed it, in very large part, to Brian's support, financial and otherwise.

He held his hand out. "I owe you one, man," he said gruffly. He'd lost his biological brother; thank God he still had the other, unofficial one.

"Forget it." Brian took his hand, then hugged him. "It'll all even out in the end."

Justus pulled away, his emotions still a little too close to the surface these days. "Later." He put his hand on the knob, but before he could turn it, the heavy front door opened by itself. Startled, Justus stepped back and his father, wearing a camel wool topcoat over his suit, his thin face looking more dour than usual, walked in.

Justus stiffened, bracing himself.

Chapter 13

When Justus ushered him inside, Vincent sat and surveyed the small but tidy office, stalling for time while he tried to gather his thoughts. Justus's desk, which looked to be little more than an oak kitchen table, sat in front of a pair of over-sized windows through which plenty of light undoubtedly streamed during the day. Bookshelves and file cabinets lined one wall; on the other side of the room he saw a doorway leading into a private bathroom. A natural-colored sisal rug with a lovely navy tapestry border warmed the hardwood floors. The walls were a muted sage. All in all, Justus, or someone, had done quite a respectable job of fixing the place up—and not just the office, either. It felt warm and homey, or it would, if Justus would stop glowering at him.

He could remember this old Victorian house from when he was just a kid, so that would make it—what?—at least sixty years old? The façade had recently been painted, the floors refinished, and the rooms remodeled. Had Justus done all this? Most likely. One of the qualities he liked about his youngest son was his absolute focus and determination when he set his mind to something. When Justus made up his mind, he rarely changed it.

Which was why he knew his mission today was most likely futile.

Justus stared warily at him from behind his desk, studying him the way Bobby Fisher watched an opponent, waiting for the opening gambit. It had always been that way between them. He couldn't recall a time when they hadn't been locked in a battle of wills, ready to fight to the death for their respective positions, whether they were playing chess or discussing where Justus should go to college.

Vincent cleared his throat, intending to tell him the club looked like a great place and he had obviously worked very hard on it. But what came out was, "The club is . . . nice."

Justus's eyes narrowed. "Thanks."

The silence lengthened, with Justus unwilling to make even a token attempt to carry a portion of the conversation. So much for small talk, Vincent thought bitterly. His mind veered off to Vincent Jr. and he felt a violent stab of longing in his chest. He and Vincent Jr. could—and did—talk for hours on end. With his oldest son, the conversation had always flowed like milk and honey in the land of plenty. They'd never had these awkward pauses, these interminable moments where the air hummed with tension and barely leashed accusations. They'd understood each other, rarely, if ever, needing to bother to explain anything.

But with Justus, every conversation was rife with misunderstanding. More than once he'd felt like a deaf man, trying to communicate in sign language to his blind son.

And there was no translator in sight.

"I came to talk to you about Maya."

Justus stared levelly at him, his hands folded in his lap.

Vincent plowed ahead, knowing Justus would twist and distort whatever he said next, no matter how diplomatically he managed to say it. "I think Angela should raise her."

"I know," Justus said, shrugging disinterestedly.

"Don't you agree?" Vincent asked delicately.

"No."

Vincent felt the first flare of his temper. Ignoring it, he kept his voice low. "I'm not sure I understand why you think you'd be a better choice."

Justus's jaw tightened almost imperceptibly, the first sign of emotion he'd shown so far. "I'm not sure it really matters what you understand or don't understand—"

Vincent blinked aside the red haze of anger that began to cloud his vision.

"—but since we're having this polite, civilized conversation I'll go ahead and explain." Justus leaned forward, planting his hands on the desk. "I love Maya. I've been a damn good uncle to her. I take her everywhere. She's had more overnights with me than I can count. I'm making a little money and I have a nice apartment with a bedroom for her. V.J. trusted me with her, and he'd expect me to take care of her now." His unwavering gaze glittered with anger, but his voice remained calm. "Have I answered your question?"

Vincent put his hands on the arms of his chair and levered himself up, working hard to keep from grimacing; the last thing he wanted right now was for Justus to see how weak he'd become. Staring down at Justus, he said, "I think this is all a novelty for you, and when the newness wears off you'll realize raising a small child interferes with work and your sex life."

Justus's lips tightened into a sneer, but he said nothing.

"And I'd rather not have my granddaughter grow to depend on you, only to be uprooted in a few months when you get tired of her." He fished his cashmere-lined black leather gloves out of his pocket, smoothed them, then slid them on his fingers. A frigid wind blew outside, and he had no intentions of catching a chill when it would take him hours to get warm again. "So I'll be throwing my support behind Angela. I'll testify for her, or help her with a larger apartment or her legal fees, whatever she needs. But I intend to see her awarded the guardianship over Maya."

Justus's smile was cold, almost reptilian. "You could have saved yourself the trip down here, Vincent," he said in that same mocking little tone that had made Vincent want to lunge for his throat since Justus was ten years old. "I knew you wouldn't ever be on my side. You're as predictable as the sun rising in the east."

So it was war, then. Again.

Vincent sadly held his son's malevolent gaze for a moment longer, then turned to leave.

Angela hovered out of sight in the doorway of the guest bedroom and watched Maya play with her massive Barbie doll collection. The girl sat cross-legged on the floor, her back to the door, humming tonelessly to herself, a large clear plastic bin crammed to the top with Barbies and Barbie paraphernalia sitting next to her. She held a doll in her lap and Angela stared, amazed, as the same stubby little fingers that hadn't mastered the buttons on Maya's clothes quickly dressed Barbie with the dexterity of an orthopedic surgeon.

"Hey, Sweetie."

"Hey," Maya piped in her high, clear voice. She didn't look up from her work.

Angela crept into the room and faced Maya. They'd been home from preschool for about an hour—Justus was due any minute to pick Maya up for dinner—and Maya hadn't said two words the whole time. Angela was at a complete loss. She was secretly glad for a little peace and quiet at the end of a long day and a brief reprieve from Maya's unrelieved chattering, but the silence felt unnatural.

She sat on the floor and picked up the nearest doll, a naked specimen with electrified brown hair. "Whatcha doing?"

"Playing."

"How was school today?"

"Good." Maya reached for a tiny pink plastic brush and began to work on her doll's hair, a losing proposition judging by the snarled mess.

"Uncle Justus will be here soon. Are you ready?"

Maya nodded, turning to reach her hand inside the bin and rummage around for God knew what.

"I'll bet he'll take you anywhere you want to go!" Angela cried in her brightest, most animated voice, trying to generate some enthusiasm—some reaction of any sort—from Maya. "Where would you like to eat?"

Maya raised and lowered her shoulders once in a half-hearted shrug. Her hand emerged from the bin holding a red satin dress with sequins that would surely make Barbie look like the Happy Hooker.

The doorbell rang and Angela, relieved the cavalry had arrived, waited for Maya to jump up and race to the door like she always did. But Maya just sat there, changing Barbie's clothes.

Deeply troubled now, Angela got up and walked to the door, pausing, for some unknown reason, to check her reflection in the hall mirror. She smiled a little, liking what she saw. She'd chosen her outfit carefully a little while ago when she changed out of her work clothes. Some internal devil had prompted her to dig out her old, faded Levis, the ones that rode low on her curved hips. She'd also thrown on a new stretchy blue long-sleeved T-shirt that clung to her breasts and torso like shrink-wrap. Back before the accident, she'd bought the shirt, tried it on, decided it was too small, and earmarked it for return to the mall. But today she'd decided she'd keep it. So what if it was a little tight and, when worn with the hip-huggers, let a two-inch sliver of her belly—including her belly button—show? She ran on that stupid treadmill every day and faithfully attended Pilates class. Why not show off a little of her hard work?

No ponytail tonight. She'd combed her long bangs off to the side so they nearly covered one eye, and left the rest to hang, gently curled, over her shoulders. Her reflection in the mirror looked quite nice, if she did say so herself, and not at all like the regular Angela.

So Justus thought she wasn't his type, did he?

Well, they'd just see about that. She still had no intentions of becoming involved with him—not in any way. She couldn't take a risk like that—not now, not ever. Not with Justus. But still, he *was* attracted to her—hell, he was attracted to anyone with two X chromosomes—and she intended to prove it. And then she'd cram his words back down his stupid throat.

She swung the door open and backed inside to let him in. He'd leaned against the doorframe; in his black cable-knit sweater, black leather jacket and faded jeans he looked indecently handsome. Ignoring her body's violent response to him—the racing heart, the breathlessness, the pool of heat in her belly—was impossible, so she focused on disguising it.

"Justus!" She gave him her sweetest, most sisterly smile. "Right on time, as usual. Come in."

Justus's answering smile faded. For half a second, as his gaze flickered quickly and discreetly over her, she could have sworn she saw a glimmer of masculine interest—heat—in his eyes, and she thought, *Candy from a baby*. But then his gaze shot back to her face and he smiled a polite, dispassionate smile that was probably no different than the smile he gave the cashier at the grocery store.

"Hey, Duchess." He brushed by her and headed for the living room. "Maya ready? I'm starving."

Disappointment crashed over her, but she shoved it away. Obviously, where Justus was concerned she'd lost the last of her good sense. Goodness knew she had plenty of other, infinitely more important topics to dwell on than whether or not Justus found her attractive.

Recovering quickly, she shut the door and followed him. "Do you have a minute?" She perched on the edge of the sofa. "I need to talk to you."

"Yeah, sure." Without bothering to take his jacket off, he sat on the chair closest to her, stretching his legs out in front of him.

"Maya's been really quiet since I picked her up from school. I'm thinking I need to make an appointment with Dr. Brenner as soon as possible."

He frowned, staring off in the distance. "Good idea. I'll come with you when you go."

"Really?" she asked, startled.

"Of course. Did you think I wouldn't?"

"I—I guess I don't know what to think these days. About anything."

He grunted, slouching more deeply into his chair. His face darkened into that brooding look she recognized and hated to see. "You and me both."

Something inside her twisted painfully. In the last week she'd become attuned to his moods, a development she hated but couldn't do anything about. Without thinking she scooted from the sofa to sit on the ottoman directly in front of him. "What's wrong, Justus?"

His lips curled into a mocking little smile and his fingers tightened their grip on the arms of the chair until the tendons stood out. "What could be wrong?" She stared reproachfully at him until his gaze wavered and fell. Finally he sighed harshly. "It's nothing. Forget it."

Her instinct was to back off and let the man have a private

thought or two, if that was what he wanted. But she sensed his need, as if he wanted to tell her, but couldn't quite give himself permission to do so. Taking what was, for her, a huge risk—when had she ever cared so much about anyone else's feelings?—she reached out and covered one of his hands with hers. He immediately flipped his hand over and held hers in a warm, tight grip.

"We're friends," she murmured. "After the week we've been through, I didn't think there was anything we couldn't handle together."

A flare of some intense but indefinable emotion burned in his eyes; for a long time he didn't speak. Finally he said, "My loving father came to my club for the first time ever today. I thought finally he'd decided to show a little interest in my life." A muscle throbbed in his jaw. "But no. Not my father."

Angela winced from the bitterness in his voice. Of course she hadn't gone to the club, either, but now that she saw— again—how important it was to him, she'd go immediately. "Justus—" she began.

He ignored her. "No, he made a special trip just to tell me he thinks I'm useless and I'll give Maya back after a few months when I get sick of her and she interferes with my screwing around." He smiled that hateful, sardonic smile again. "Aren't you glad you asked?"

Anger blurred her vision and she blinked furiously. She'd thought her opinion of Vincent Robinson couldn't get much lower, but she'd been wrong. "That's ridiculous," she snapped, furious that hateful man had shaken Justus's self-confidence like this. "And I'm glad you're much too smart to believe your father's bull."

For a second he gaped at her in surprise, then jerked his hand free and jumped up to pace. "Is it bull?"

"Of course it is!" She hurried over to stand in front of him and put her hand on his arm; beneath her fingers she felt the pulse of his tight muscles. "Justus, your father is poisonous. Don't let him do this to you. Nothing he said is true." He stared disbelievingly and she squeezed his arm for emphasis. "Look at all you've accomplished with your life. You got your degree and became a trainer like you've wanted to be for years, built up your clientele, and then opened your own gym. Give yourself some credit—look what you've accomplished."

He froze, staring at her, an arrested expression on his face.

"And Maya! You're a wonderful uncle. She would be lucky to—" She broke off, realizing she was about to make an admission that could hurt her in court, although some instinct told her Justus would never use her own words against her that way. In her heart she knew the truth: Maya *was* lucky to have him and, if the court ordered it, Maya would be lucky to live with him. "Maya is lucky to have an uncle like you."

"My father doesn't think so."

She stepped closer, trying to reach him. She had so much faith in him. Why didn't he have any in himself? "Your father doesn't see what I see."

His eyes darkened; his jaw flexed; he stilled, waiting. "What do you see, Angela?"

They were now firmly in dangerous territory, and Angela knew it. Because at some point—she couldn't say when—her attraction to him, which should have been purely physical, had deepened. She saw his humor, his sexiness, his intelligence, his mischief, but of course she'd seen all that ten years ago when she met him. Now she could also see his strength, his determination, his *heart*. And those qualities were as attractive—more attractive, actually—as the others. She wanted to tell him she saw it all, but she wouldn't. Couldn't.

"I see a good man."

She held his surprised gaze, determined, if nothing else, to show her faith in him. Eternity passed. A thousand emotions skated across his face and she couldn't decipher any.

"I'm hungry."

Startled, Angela whirled to see Maya come down the hall with a now neatly dressed and coiffed Barbie. Reaching out to her niece, Angela was aware of Justus's unblinking gaze still on her face; he didn't even greet Maya. Feeling suddenly flustered, and grateful for the opportunity to divert her attention from Justus, she knelt. "Come here, Sweetie." Maya walked over and waited while Angela surveyed her critically. "You look pretty good. Clean face. Neat hair. I think you're ready for dinner. Did you say hi to Uncle Justus?"

Maya obediently walked over to Justus and gave him his leg a hug. Angela got up, tugged her jeans up over her hips, then turned to face them. Her face felt hot so she kept her eyes lowered—she couldn't risk letting Justus see what she was thinking. He stared at her, one hand absently patting Maya's back as she clung to him.

"You could . . . come with us," he said casually. "Or did you have other plans?"

"No." Spending more time with Justus seemed like a spectacularly bad idea. Agitated, she sifted her fingers through her bangs, not looking at him. "Well, I mean I don't have any other plans, but I can't. I need to do some work, and I wanted to start getting some of my stuff out of Maya's room. And you and Maya probably need to spend a little time alone together."

Justus nodded once, curtly. "Where's your jacket?" he asked Maya, focusing on the child for the first time. "We need—"

The doorbell rang, startling them. Sparing Justus a quizzical look—who would be stopping by without calling at six-thirty on a Friday night?—Angela hurried to the door, checked the peephole and gasped. Astonished, she swung the door open to let a grim-faced Ronnie in.

* * *

Most likely he'd just come from the hospital; his black dress pants and crisp white shirt told her he'd been working today. His thin, pursed lips told her he wanted to have a Serious Discussion, which she was not in the mood for. "What are you doing here?" She didn't move aside, keeping her hand on the knob in case she needed to slam the door in his face.

Ronnie gasped and stared, his eyes sliding over her hair, shirt, and jeans as if he suspected a pod person had taken over her body. She braced herself for a negative comment—she'd certainly never dressed like this when they'd dated—but to her surprise, when his eyes eventually flickered back to her face they registered appreciation. Interest.

"My God, you look great," he said, blurting the words out as if he couldn't help himself.

"I—thank you." She couldn't remember when Ronnie had last commented on—much less complimented her for—her appearance.

Blinking furiously, Ronnie seemed to recover. "I . . . didn't like the way we left things the other day. I didn't call first because I figured you'd tell me not to come."

"You were right."

Justus materialized at her side in the narrow foyer, put his hands on his hips, and surveyed the scene imperiously. Ronnie stiffened, then scowled. Justus glared disdainfully at him, apparently decided not to bother with a greeting, then turned to Angela. "You okay?"

"Yes," Angela said quickly, hoping to diffuse the situation before Justus flew off the handle—something she knew instinctively would *not* be good. He looked as if he would happily divest Ronnie of his teeth, one at a time, for any minor infraction. "Ronnie wants to talk to me."

Justus turned to Ronnie and deigned to speak through his

tight jaw. "She told you the other day she didn't want to talk to you. Looks like you're still having trouble listening."

Ronnie's sallow skin paled, but then he puffed up with outrage, managing to look like a yappy little terrier next to a panther. "I didn't realize you were Angela's spokesperson."

Justus made an irritated sound and jerked Angela behind him as if to shield her from some impending disaster. Grabbing the doorknob he told Ronnie, "Get out. Don't come back."

Angela touched his arm. Justus stilled, still glowering at Ronnie. "It's okay, Justus," she said. "I'll talk to him." She shot Ronnie a warning look. "For a *minute*."

Ronnie smiled slightly, obviously relieved.

Justus kept his hand on the knob but pivoted to stare, aghast, at her. "*What?*"

Angela raised a calming hand. "I think—"

"What the hell are you doing?" Justus cried. Still staring at Angela, his arm jerked and the door slammed like a thunderclap in Ronnie's startled face. Angela jumped and made an involuntary squeaking sound. Justus grabbed her upper arms and gave her a small shake. "Are you going back to this jackass?" He jabbed his thumb at the closed door.

"Of course not!" she cried, throwing him off. "I'm going to hear what he has to say, then he's going to leave!" Thoroughly agitated now, she tossed her hair over her shoulder. "Good grief! What's gotten into you? Why are you acting like a caveman again?"

"Aunt Ang-la?" Maya, wide-eyed, crept around the corner. "Who's there?"

Angela tried to relax her features a little before she scared the poor girl to death. "No one, Sweetie. Just a friend of mine." Turning back around, she shoved Justus, who guarded the door, legs braced, like a military policeman at Gitmo. "Get out of the way!" she barked.

Grumbling under his breath, a vein throbbing visibly in his temple, Justus reluctantly stepped away from the door. "Let's go, Maya." He stalked over to the hall closet, snatched Maya's little jacket off the hanger, then stalked back to the front door.

Angela opened it. Ronnie leaned against the wall opposite her door, arms crossed, apparently prepared to wait indefinitely. When he saw her, his mouth twisted down, but he didn't say anything. Justus brushed by her from behind, towing Maya along with him.

"I hope you know what you're doing," he muttered before disappearing down the hall.

Trying to compose herself, Angela held the door open for Ronnie. "Come on in."

Ronnie stepped inside and looked warily around, as if he expected Justus to magically spring out from behind some piece of furniture to kick his ass after all. He sat on the end of the sofa and stared up at her, his expression slightly accusatory. "I thought you said there was nothing going on with him."

Angela couldn't believe she'd ever dated anyone who was this big a hypocrite. "First of all, my personal life is no longer any of your business," she cried, sitting on the other end of the sofa. "And second, there *isn't* anything going on with me and Justus."

Ronnie's eyes narrowed. "Then why is he so possessive?"

"He's not possessive!" she snapped, shocked by the very suggestion. Justus had probably never been possessive before in his life. And anyway, if he was the possessive type, he'd made it abundantly clear he wouldn't waste the emotion on her. "He's protective."

"Yeah, right."

Angela had had about enough. Maya would be back before she knew it and she still hadn't eaten dinner, done any work, or started on Maya's room yet. "Why are you here, Ronnie?"

she asked, checking her watch. "I've got a lot of stuff to do before they come back. If you want me to pack up your toothbrush and your—"

"No!" He leaned forward, propping his elbows on his knees. "I want you to know how sorry I am about Carolyn. And how sorry I am that you have to deal with our breakup and her death at the same time. And if there's anything I can—"

"Don't worry," Angela said, her claws out now. "The good thing about my sister dying was that it put our little breakup right in perspective for me. I haven't given you a second thought." It was a lie, of course, but one she had to tell for her pride's sake.

Ronnie flinched as if she'd slapped him. "Don't, Angela," he said reproachfully. "We really had something—"

"Not much, apparently."

"Angela—"

"Why couldn't you have just told me you wanted out, Ronnie? At least then I would have had some good feelings left for you instead of *this*—" She stopped herself.

"You hate me," he said dejectedly, slumping back against the cushions.

They stared at each other for a tense moment, at a standoff. "No, I don't." It was true, she realized. She was sad over the failure of their relationship, of course, and sad she'd invested three years of her life in him, although that was much better than, say, marrying him and divorcing, as they surely would have. But she wasn't heartbroken—not really. She knew life would go on and Ronnie's loss wouldn't kill her. Funny, she hadn't really felt his loss, and she wondered now if she ever would.

"I wouldn't blame you if you did hate me."

She could almost feel sorry for him. He looked so sad— not at all like someone in the throes of a passionate new affair. And why wasn't he spending his Friday night with his new girlfriend? Finally Angela's curiosity got the better of her and she decided she may as well ask the question that had been plaguing her, since she didn't know when she'd have the chance again. "Why, Ronnie? What does she have that I don't?"

He flushed, looking embarrassed. His gaze darted away. "I don't think—" he began.

Suddenly she knew. "It's the sex, isn't it?"

Ronnie had the decency not to answer, hanging his head instead.

Of course it was the sex. Obviously he'd decided that three years of lukewarm sex was more than enough and had gone in search of—and found—greener pastures. Angela felt her cheeks burn with humiliation. She'd feared, in the darkest corner of her heart, that Ronnie would claim he'd taken one look at this new woman and fallen in love with her; that destiny brought them together; that he would move heaven and earth to marry her. But the truth was so much more painful. He didn't love the other woman, but he sure preferred her bed to Angela's.

She should have known.

Abruptly she got up. She studied her feet, unable to look Ronnie in the face. "I, uh." She cleared her throat. "I have things to do."

Ronnie also stood. "You're a wonderful woman, Angela," he said, his voice husky now. "I'm glad for all the time we spent together."

Sure, she thought dully. He admired her. Respected her. He just didn't want her.

Hurrying to the door, she opened it for him. He paused, putting his hand to her chin to try to tip her face up so she would look at him. She jerked away, looking instead at some fixed point over Ronnie's shoulder. "If you need anything . . ."

Finally she forced herself to meet his gaze. "I won't."

Ronnie dropped his hand, turned, and left.

As soon as he'd gone, Angela forgot all about dinner. She went to the cabinet under the kitchen sink, fished out her rubber gloves and orange cleanser, and marched into Maya's room.

Justus watched Maya play with her dessert, the same unappetizing concoction of soft-serve vanilla ice cream, hot fudge sauce, gummy worms, and M&Ms she always got when they came here to her favorite restaurant, that perpetually crowded Mecca of gluttony, Golden Corral. As always, they sat at the table closest to the dessert spread of miscellaneous cakes, pies, cookies, and brownies, which was about as close as Maya could get herself to the food without actually parking her booster chair in front of the buffet counter. They'd been here more times than he cared to count; Maya liked the freedom of being able to choose her own food, so he would trail behind her in line, balancing their plates, while she barked out orders about what she wanted. Generally she wound up with some sort of Jell-O salad or other, fried shrimp and fish nuggets, pizza, and a cheeseburger—more food than she would normally eat in a month. When he registered the obligatory protest that she hadn't chosen anything healthy, she grumbled and grudgingly let him put a small scoop of corn on the edge of her plate. Then, when she'd finished a few bites of everything, they'd return to the buffet for her little sundae. Usually they had a delightful time.

Tonight had been a complete bust.

"Aren't you going to finish your ice cream?" he asked, raising his voice over the crowd.

Maya listlessly stirred the soupy mess in her bowl. "I'm full."

"Are you getting sick? You barely ate." Justus pushed aside his own plate of broiled fish, salad, and baked potato. Reaching across the table he pressed his hand to her cool forehead. She scowled but did not move away. "You don't feel warm."

Maya fished a gummy worm out of the ice cream with her fingers and, dangling it over her face, lowered the dripping mess into her mouth.

"What are you doing?" he cried, groaning, wondering how he'd ever get her cleaned up enough for Angela to let her back into her pristine apartment. He picked up her sticky spoon and shoved it into her stickier hand. "What? Is your spoon on strike all the sudden? Why don't you use it?"

She put the spoon down. "I'm done."

He stared at her, wondering when he'd ever seen such a mess. The entire lower half of her face was covered with ice cream and hot fudge, as were her hands. "Look at you! I'm going to have to take you out back and hose you off!"

She giggled, the first sign of the old Maya he'd seen all night. Dipping his napkin in his ice water, he tried to clean her up a little. "How are you doing, Little Girl?" He took one small hand and wiped her fingers. "You haven't said much tonight."

Her little shoulders moved up and down once. "Good."

"How was school today?"

"Good."

"Did Emily hit anyone today, or was she being nice?"

"Nice."

Justus picked up a fresh napkin, dipped it, and went to work on her face. "Did you have cheese and crackers again for snack, or—"

"No, Sam brought cupcakes for his birthday."

"Oooh! Cupcakes!"

Maya yawned so widely Justus wondered if her lower jaw wouldn't unhinge. He wanted to ask her about how she felt and whether she missed her parents, which would, of course, be a really stupid question. Angela was right, though—Maya wasn't herself. They needed to see the child psychologist soon so they would have some idea of how to deal with her grief. He sighed. "You ready to go, Little Girl? You look tired." He reached for her coat on the chair next to his.

"I don't like that man!" she blurted abruptly, scrunching her face.

Justus was puzzled but glad she finally had something to say. "What man?"

"At Aunt Ang-la's house," she said impatiently.

Oh, *that* man. His stomach twisted back into its jealous knot. *Join the club*, he wanted to tell her. "That's not a very nice thing to say."

"I don't!"

"Have you, uh, seen him before?" he asked casually, aware he'd sunk to heretofore unseen depths by grilling a pre-schooler about Angela's personal life.

"No."

"Does he . . . does he ever call Aunt Angela?"

"No."

Relieved, he got to his feet and slid his arms into his own jacket. It was time to go. He needed to get back to Angela's and find out what, exactly, had happened with her and Ron.

Chapter 14

Angela smiled gamely when she opened the door, but Justus could see she was upset. And if he needed any further proof, he immediately smelled that stupid orange spray she used. She'd obviously worked herself up into a cleaning frenzy after Ron left, although Justus couldn't imagine what in the apartment—where every conceivable surface, including the floor, was so sanitary it was practically sterile—could possibly need to be cleaned. Renewed fury at that SOB twisted in his gut. How many times would he reappear and flatten Angela's fragile self-esteem?

"Hi, guys." Angela stooped to kiss Maya's cheek. Maya paused long enough to allow Angela to slip off her jacket, then fluttered off into the living room. "How was dinner?"

"Good." Watching her carefully, he took off his own jacket. He fully intended to help get Maya into bed—immediately— and then talk to her. Angela's smile faltered slightly when she saw he intended to stay a while, but then she recovered, took his jacket, and hung it and Maya's in the hall closet.

"Maya didn't eat much, though." He lowered his voice. "You're right. She's not okay."

Frowning, she led him into the living room and he took the

opportunity to stare at her, something he'd wanted to do earlier, but hadn't. For once she'd worn clothes that accentuated, rather than hid, her fantastic body, and keeping his eyes away was pretty much impossible. Her wide, toned shoulders tapered down to a narrow waist then flared out to lush hips and a butt that swayed provocatively, taunting him, with every step she took. She'd also let her hair down, softening her features and accentuating her sweet brown eyes.

What on earth had made her dress like this? Was it his little taunt about her not being his type? He hardly dared believe it. He almost regretted those stupid words; he'd already wanted her more than any other woman back when she dressed like a repressed librarian. Now he wanted her infinitely more than that.

"Maya!" Angela clapped her hands. Maya, who'd collapsed and stretched out full length on the sofa, groaned. "Time for bed! Let's go! Get your jammies!"

"Noo-ooo!"

Angela's shoulders went rigid and she put her hands on her hips. "Maya?" she said briskly.

Justus, standing safely out of sight behind Angela, rolled his eyes. He could feel her hackles rising and sensed an imminent power struggle from which Maya would undoubtedly emerge the victor. "Come on, Little Girl." He stepped around Angela and squatted in front of the sofa, his back to Maya. "If you come right now, without whining, I'll give you a piggy back ride."

Maya popped up, beaming, and jumped onto his back, throwing her arms so tightly around his neck she threatened to crush his windpipe. He stood and, holding her ankles, headed off down the hall. As he passed Angela she stiffened and pursed her lips, oozing disapproval from every pore. As usual, he couldn't resist needling her.

He leaned close, murmuring in her ear, "It's all in the technique, Duchess. You'll discover that one day."

Angela, clearly furious, humphed and twisted away, but not before he had the satisfaction of feeling her shiver as his breath feathered her ear.

After helping Maya with her pajamas and teeth, Justus ducked into the bathroom. When he came out he looked for Maya in the guest bedroom, but she wasn't there. Listening, he heard soft voices and followed them down the end of the hall to the one part of the apartment he'd never seen: Angela's bedroom. His heart quickened pleasantly.

He stepped into the doorway unnoticed and studied the room. Angela's enormous black wrought-iron bed, framed by a nightstand and a beautiful, hand-painted lamp on each side, was positioned between two windows with shades drawn. Glancing around he saw a gas fireplace with mantle, a couple of overstuffed chairs, bookshelves, and several arrangements of fresh roses in pretty little glass bowls. Impressionist prints dotted the walls; dressers and an entertainment armoire stood against opposite walls. Heavy, ornate silver frames with black-and-white family pictures covered every available surface. Off in one corner a closed six-panel door led, he presumed, to her bathroom. The room was beautiful—warm and inviting.

His gaze strayed back to, and remained, on the bed.

It was tall, the kind that came with a stool, although *he* would not need a stool to get into it. He was glad to see it was more than long enough to accommodate someone as tall as he. Crisp white sheets, a floral duvet, and several fluffy embroidered pillows made the bed infinitely inviting. He felt irresistibly drawn to it, like a bear to honey.

His curiosity about the room slaked slightly, it occurred to him that Maya, clutching her little dog, was in the bed and Angela sat, a picture book in hand, facing her on the edge reading to her. He stared at Maya, an irrational jealousy springing to life from nowhere and causing his entire being to fixate on his little niece.

Look at her! What the hell was she doing *there*, in Angela's bed, where he desperately wanted to be? He had the ridiculous urge to grab her little arm and throw her out of what he considered to be *his* rightful place.

A blinding realization hit him suddenly. Yes, he wanted to make love with Angela, and he was willing to fight for that right and, more difficult for him, be patient. But he wanted more—much more—than sex from her. He wanted to lounge in bed with her, to watch TV with her, to cook dinner, to tell her about his day and, infinitely more interesting, to hear about hers.

He wanted, in short, a place—a *prominent* place—in her life. And he would have it, too. Come hell or high water, he would have it.

If he had his way he'd announce his intentions—again— and just throw her over his shoulder and carry her off to bed, and to hell with her protests. She wanted him sexually and he could have her if he pushed the matter a little. As for the rest, he could wait her out and she'd come around eventually.

But he didn't want her coming around eventually. He wanted her hot and eager—as enthusiastic for his company as she would be about him sexually. And she wasn't ready for that. Thanks to that bastard Ron, he was now paying for another man's mistakes. Well, fine. He'd be patient and gain her trust. She deserved no less. And one day he would have it all.

Or die trying.

He cleared his throat. Startled, Angela looked up from her book. "Come on in," she called softly. "I didn't hear you. We're finished now. Maya can't keep her eyes open."

Sure enough, Maya's eyes had drifted closed and her breathing became rhythmic. Justus crept up to the bed and stood right next to Angela. Ignoring the sharp intake of her surprised breath, he leaned down and, pressing his hand to her shoulder as if for balance, kissed Maya's smooth cheek. Straightening, he kept his hand on Angela's back, fully expecting her to pull away, but she didn't.

"She . . . sleeps with you?" he asked around his dry mouth. "Is that a good idea?"

Angela ducked her head sheepishly. "Probably not, but it comforts her." She smoothed the sheet over Maya's shoulders. "And me."

To his horror, some terrifying, unidentifiable but undeniable emotion bloomed in his chest as he stood there with the two women in his life. It was way too much. Dropping his hand as if he'd touched an open flame, he turned and fled, dimly aware of Angela twisting around on the bed to stare after him with wide, curious eyes.

Reaching the relative safety of the kitchen, he planted his hands on the counter and bent double at the waist, trying to slow his suddenly harsh breathing and heartbeat. Was this a panic attack? He wouldn't be surprised. That was all he needed to close out the worst week of his life. After several deep breaths his heart returned to a steadier rhythm, although he realized his hands shook as he found a goblet and helped himself to a glass of Angela's rich Cabernet from an open bottle she'd set breathing on the counter. Throwing his head back he took several deep gulps.

A minute or two later, Angela came out of the bedroom. "Your father called earlier. I'm going to drop Maya there tomorrow while I go to work for a while and work on her room."

Justus grunted, barely hearing her.

"Are you okay?" she asked worriedly. "What's wrong?"

Her concern equally thrilled and repelled him. On the one hand he didn't want any responsibilities, expectations, or attachments, not to Maya, not to Angela, not to anyone. He hadn't had any since his mother died and didn't need any now. On the other hand he desperately wanted someone to worry about him, to wonder what was wrong. To care. The darkness that was always nearby, always hovering over his mood, heart, and soul, floated closer, beckoning. But for the first time in a long time something else was there, too—something he was afraid to believe in and wasn't certain he deserved: the light.

Indecision paralyzed him. "Nothing."

She stared suspiciously, obviously not believing him. For a second he thought she'd press the issue, but then she said, smiling, "I see you found the wine."

He barked with surprised laughter and, just like that, the gloom lifted. "I prefer Merlot, though. For future reference."

"I will try to bear that in mind." Coming to stand beside him, she poured her own glass and took a sip, making an appreciative sound. "I needed this."

"Me too." He put his glass down and turned to face her, leaning his hip against the counter. "What did Ron want?"

She shrugged and quickly turned away, going to the living room and sitting on the sofa with her legs curled under her. "Just to tell me how sorry he was and to offer his help."

He followed, sitting on the chair closest to her. "Then why are you so upset?"

Her startled gaze shot to his; she opened and shut her mouth. "I—I'm not—"

"Don't bother denying it, Angela. You've been cleaning again."

A nervous hand ran through her hair, sifting it. "I don't want to talk about it."

"Bullshit." She recoiled, her brows flying up in surprise. "You make me spill my guts about my father and now you think I'm gonna let you get away with this 'I don't want to talk about it' crap? Are you serious?"

For a few seconds she just stared at him, nostrils flaring, her eyes bright with tears. He wanted to catch her hand, pull her into his lap, and hold her, but he felt her determination not to cry and instinctively knew if he touched her she'd fall apart.

"It's personal," she said finally.

"Angela," he said, infusing his voice with that slight, mocking tone he knew she hated, "I can keep a secret and nothing you could possibly say would shock me."

She took a deep, steadying breath. "Ronnie left me because of sex."

Justus gaped at her, shocked.

"I thought maybe he'd fallen in love with her at first sight or wanted to marry her or thought she was his soul mate or something . . . *profound*," she said hurriedly as if she had to tell the whole story before her time ran out. "But I don't think he's in love. He just wanted to be free to have sex openly." Her chin quivered. "So I guess I'm not *your* type *or* Ronnie's type."

Justus stared, his mind spinning, trying to make sense of what he'd just heard. It was inconceivable that anyone—even someone as obviously idiotic as Ron—would ever dump Angela. How could any straight man keep his hands off her? *He* certainly couldn't if she was his. She was, by far, the most beautiful woman he'd ever seen, and he couldn't even think of a close runner-up. As exciting as her beauty was her passion, the way it shimmered around her, barely contained, waiting to explode. Didn't Ron see it? How could he resist it?

Suddenly everything came into focus, the way it did when he took pictures with his camera and adjusted the lens that last millimeter. That was just it: Ron didn't see it. He didn't see what Justus saw in her. And their sex life, obviously, had reflected it. That bastard had made Angela doubt herself. The irony was staggering: the sexiest woman he knew—the *only* woman he wanted to have sex with—didn't know she was sexy.

He wanted to kill Ron.

But beneath his anger he felt a savage satisfaction. So Angela didn't know much about passion? Didn't know how much pleasure her body could bring both of them? Well, good.

He would teach her.

"Angela," he said incredulously, "did it ever occur to you that *he* was the problem?"

Her surprised gasp answered him; she didn't speak, but seemed to wait breathlessly for him to explain what he meant.

The hardest thing he ever did was measure his words, sound nonchalant, as if the matter of Angela's sexiness, her sensuality, was, at most, only of passing interest to him. He looked away, afraid she'd see the heat in his eyes or, worse, that his gaze would slip to where it wanted to go—her dewy mouth or lush breasts.

"It's amazing to me," he said casually, "how many men think women are bad in bed, like it's the woman's fault." He took a deep breath, once again trying to even out his heart rate, aware of Angela, frozen and wide-eyed, staring at him. "A woman's body is a complicated instrument." He shrugged negligently. "You don't blame the Stradivarius if the violinist doesn't know how to play." Somehow he managed to turn his lips up into what he hoped was a wry smile. "A lot of men don't understand that if they figured out how to satisfy their woman completely—every time—their sex life would be a million times better. You might mention that to Ron."

The words hung in the air for an eternity and Angela gaped, dumbfounded at him. Keeping his face bland, as if they'd been discussing the Bengals' season, he picked up his wine and took a disinterested sip. When he put it back down he made a show of pushing back his sleeve and glancing at his watch.

"It's late," he said, desperate to get the hell out of here before the last of his self-control disappeared and he decided to show Angela exactly how sexy he thought she was. He jumped up and found his jacket, and staring down at her said, "Good night."

Angela seemed to awaken from some trance. Giving her head a violent shake, she jerked her face up to look at him with eyes that were unnaturally bright. "I—of course. I'll see you tomorrow." Leaping to her feet, she raced to the door, flung it open, and stood aside.

As he passed by, Justus decided kissing her tonight, even on the cheek, was a bad idea.

Angela, thoroughly winded, adjusted the treadmill's settings and slowed to a brisk walk to begin her cool down. After doing a couple hours work at the office, she'd raced over to the gym. She'd done her four miles and, probably due to her agitation over the conversation she'd had last night with Justus, had maintained her pace—eight and a half minutes per mile—the whole time. She picked up the white hand towel she'd flung over the control panel and wiped the sweat off her face and bare chest. Once again today she found herself dressing in clothes she thought might catch Justus's eye: a black-and-white-striped tank top and black shorts. But even though she'd been here at his club for half an hour or so she hadn't seen any sign of him which, of course, served her right for being so vain.

She loved the club. The main gym, where she was now, was sunny and open, the equipment all state-of-the-art. The women's bathroom, where she'd changed out of her work clothes, was spotless and smelled fresh. She planned to have lunch in the little café—she'd spied delicious European rolls, quiches, and soups—on her way out. Luxury cars packed the street and parking lot. Young, well-dressed professional types—disproportionately beautiful women, she noted sourly—streamed in and out and greeted each other warmly, as if they were the regular crowd. If they were, she could certainly understand why: Justus's club had a young, hip energy that surely made the clients feel they'd miss something exciting if they skipped a workout.

But of course she'd known Justus would create a place as exhilarating as he was, and that it would be a huge success.

"Angela!" cried a voice behind her.

Justus! Her heart rate, which had only just begun to slow down, kicked back up a notch. Snatching the headphones from her ears—she was sick of the blaring hip-hop she listened to while running, anyway—she kept walking but looked over her shoulder. To her vast disappointment she saw Justus's blond friend, Byron—no! Brian!—standing to the side of her treadmill, grinning as if he'd found his long lost sister. He wore navy warm-up pants and a light blue polo shirt with the club's logo.

"Hi, Brian. What a great club you have here!"

Brian's grin widened and she realized for the first time how handsome he was. Tall and muscular, like Justus, his tousled blond hair, vivid blue eyes, and dimples made him irresistible in a Brad Pitt sort of way. He and Justus had probably broken a lot of hearts.

"Do you like it?"

"It's wonderful. You should be very proud."

He leaned his arm on the rail of her treadmill. "Did you join?"

"Not yet. Justus gave me a one month trial."

He studied her closely. "He know you're here?"

"I haven't seen him. I was starting to think he wasn't here."

"There's another gym on the third floor. It's where he trains his clients. Saturday's his busy day—he's got appointments all day—"

"Oh," she said, trying to keep her disappointment from her face.

"—but I'll tell him you're here. He'd want to know." Brian watched her intently; she had the strange feeling he was a casting director evaluating her for some role in his movie.

The treadmill stopped and she hopped off, grabbing her water bottle. "Oh, don't bother him." She wiped the rails clean with her towel. "I'll probably talk to him later anyway."

"Oh, no!" he cried, as if she'd suggested a joint bank heist. "You're not getting me in trouble. Don't go anywhere." He strode off toward a second staircase she hadn't noticed before.

Angela wove her way through the row of treadmills and wandered to the huge arched doorway to wait, trying to control her inexplicable excitement. She caught sight of herself in the wall of mirrors and grimaced. Big surprise—she looked awful: flushed and sweaty, her hair ruffled from the headphones and coming out of her ponytail. Looking away—she hated it when people primped and preened in public—she smoothed her hair back, which was as effective as spraying air freshener on a landfill. Realizing she'd officially become one of those vain people she so hated who were obsessed with their looks, she gave up and dropped her hands.

Justus. There was no denying she was anxious to see him again, as if it had been eighteen months since she saw him, rather than eighteen hours. Even worse, she wanted to look her best. One little taunt from him and she'd turned into someone she no longer recognized—someone obsessed with a man she barely knew and what he thought of her. And with sex.

She couldn't stop thinking about what he'd said—that the problems with her and Ronnie's sex life had been *his* fault, not hers. The idea was novel and jarring—she couldn't quite wrap her mind around it. She felt as if she'd just heard, for the first time, that the earth was round, not flat. More insidious was his comparison of a woman's body to a Stradivarius, and the implication—unspoken but nonetheless hovering in the air and filling the room like oxygen—that Ronnie was a sausage-fingered clod who couldn't play, but Justus was Yitzhak Perlman.

God help her, she knew it was true; she didn't have a single doubt in her tingly body. Hadn't she known, when she danced with him at the wedding, that he was a prodigy at seventeen? That even then he knew more—much more—about sex than she did? And that had been ten long years ago. Surely by now he was a virtuoso—

"Angela?"

Startled, she looked up to see Janet standing right next to her, smiling the way she imagined a cat would smile before torturing and eating a mouse. She hadn't even seen her coming. She looked fresh and beautiful in an itty-bitty bra top and painted-on yoga pants. A sickening knot of jealousy clotted in Angela's stomach. This woman, and countless others, no doubt, knew firsthand what a great lover Justus was, something she would never discover. And this woman—who somehow managed to have perfect hair and makeup in a gym and could exercise without breaking a sweat, as well as simultaneously possess both a tall, willowy body *and* breasts the size of watermelons—was Justus's type. The type who could keep up with him in bed and surprise him with a few new moves while also unabashedly pursuing—and getting—her own pleasure. The type who unapologetically wallowed in her own sexuality.

The type that Angela would never—could never—be.

"Hello, Janet," she said coolly, moving away before Janet's claws came out.

"Wow!" Janet looked her over disdainfully. "That must have been some workout!"

Angela stiffened but refused to swallow the bait. "It was." She turned away.

Janet caught her arm, swinging her back around. Outraged, Angela snatched her arm back. Janet dropped her malevolent voice until it was low enough that any passersby wouldn't hear. "You don't really think you can hold him, do you?" she said with utter disbelief, as if Angela thought she could get to the moon on a tricycle.

Angela's face burned with humiliation. "*Excuse me?*"

Janet's sly grin widened. "Well, I mean, you are attractive, in a plain sort of way, and he feels sorry for the way your sister died and your boyfriend dumped you in public like that—"

Angela cried out with mortification.

"—but you're, what, fifteen years older than he is, aren't you?" Janet shrugged ruefully, as if she deeply regretted being forced to say something so indelicate. "So I just want you to know that in a week or two, when he gets bored with you, he'll come right back to me."

Something possessed Angela. She would not let this hateful woman demean her and have the last word. "Oh, honey," she said, adopting Janet's regretful tone and mocking little smile. Janet froze, her eyes widening as if the cat had discovered the mouse had an AK-47. "Don't fool yourself. If *you* were so good in bed, *I* wouldn't be here, now would I?"

Janet's jaw dropped.

"Ladies?" said a concerned voice to their right. "What's going on?"

Justus stood there. Ignoring Janet, his intent gaze locked with Angela's. She raised her chin, determined not to show how embarrassed she was, but he knew anyway. His face darkened; his jaw throbbed. Clearly furious, he looked to Janet.

She seemed to realize she'd made a huge mistake and smiled angelically. "Justuuus," she said sweetly. "We were just having a little girl talk. Do you have time to talk?"

Justus held out his hand. "Give me your card."

Janet's whole body jerked. "Wha—?"

"Give me your membership card," he said again in a low voice that screamed Janet did not want to force him to ask a third time. "I'll mail you a refund check. Find yourself another club."

Janet's face crumpled. Fishing around in her pocket— Angela had never dreamed yoga pants that tight could have a pocket—she extracted her blue membership card, shoved it into Justus's hand, and flounced off.

Justus immediately turned to Angela, worry etched on every line of his face. "What did she say to you?" he cried.

Chapter 15

Angela ducked her head, surreptitiously swiping at her eyes. Justus shuddered with anger. He could happily squeeze Janet's scrawny neck. What sort of venom had the jealous witch spewed in Angela's ear? "What happened?"

Angela raised her head, her smile falsely bright. "Nothing. Nice friend you have there."

"I'm sorry," he said helplessly, seething. If Janet just irreparably harmed his fragile relationship with Angela, he would kill her. "You know whatever she said is bull."

She managed a small, unconvincing smile. "It doesn't matter."

Without thinking, he reached out and wiped the wet, fragile skin under her left eye with his thumb. "She hates you." Janet was many things, but never stupid. She'd no doubt seen the writing on the wall—that he hadn't given her a second thought since he'd laid eyes on Angela.

Angela stiffened and stepped away, out of his reach. When she spoke again her voice dripped ice. "Yeah, well, you should put her out of her misery and tell her how you don't think I'm your type." She whirled and stalked down the steps to the first floor.

When she was out of earshot, Justus cursed viciously, then raced after her. "Angela!"

She paused at the bottom, but didn't deign to turn and look at him. He felt a clammy sweat under his arms and realized how nervous he was. Nothing in his life had ever felt as important as smoothing things over with Angela now. He floundered several steps above her, unable to move or to think of anything to say. "Please don't go. Please."

Dropping her head, she stared at her shoes for what seemed like decades. His heart thundered the whole time. Finally, when the silence became unbearable, she raised her head and gave him a sidelong smile. He froze, waiting.

"Who do I need to see around here about getting a tour? I'm thinking of joining now that the clientele has improved."

Delirious with relief, he threw back his head and laughed. After a startled minute she laughed too, and he thought he could die a happy man. Luckily, when Brian had told him Angela was here, Justus had him reschedule his next client so he would be free for this very purpose. Not the way to run a business, of course, but some things were more important than business.

Grabbing her hand, he towed her after him. "Good. That'll give me the chance to train you."

"Train me?" she said tartly, pulling her hand away. "I'm in very good shape, thank you."

Amusement and satisfaction bloomed in his chest. She *was* in good shape. When he'd come down the steps just now and seen her flushed and sweaty in that skimpy little outfit, he'd almost wet his pants. She was all gleaming brown skin, full breasts, wide hips, flat belly, big butt, and long legs. Angela was made for him—only him—even if she didn't know it yet. Her figure was ripe with all the individual features he loved, and the whole was a billion times more than the sum of the parts.

But she didn't need to know that.

Unsmiling, he turned and studied her shoulders with all the clinical detachment he could muster, which wasn't much. Keeping the taunt subtle but unmistakable, he said, "Well, look at your shoulders." He skimmed his fingers from the curve of one smooth shoulder, across her collarbone, to the other shoulder. Goose bumps appeared under her satin skin in his wake. "You could use a little more definition."

Angela gaped at him.

He trailed his fingers down her right shoulder in the barest of touches, stopping at her upper arm. She shivered and he felt more satisfaction. "And here." Ignoring the heat in his blood, he smiled down at her with the innocent smile that had always worked on his mother. "I can shape you up in no time. Okay? This way for the tour." He gripped her elbow.

For one arrested moment, Angela stared at him while turbulent emotions flickered through her unnaturally bright eyes. His gut tightened with need. She was hot for him; that simple, fluttering touch had her ready to melt. If he had any doubts, her shallow breath, almost a pant now, and the hard points of her nipples beneath her top removed them immediately.

He repressed a tremor of desire. What would she be like when he finally touched her the way he wanted to? His head spun with the possibilities. He couldn't believe stupid Ron had ever thought this woman was cold. If he wanted to, Justus imagined he could pull her into his office and, without too much trouble, take her now, against the wall or across the desk. But he'd decided long ago he wouldn't press her, and he'd meant it. His pride wouldn't let him.

Suddenly she looked down at her iPod, which was clipped to her shorts, shuttering her emotions from view. On the pretext of unclipping the iPod, she gently but firmly removed her arm from his grasp. "Let's go."

Justus swallowed his frustration for what seemed like the one-millionth time. He knew what she was doing. Obviously she felt the electricity—the heat—between them as strongly as he did, and, since she didn't want to act on it, couldn't stand him touching her. He got it. And he also got that, for her sake, he needed to go slowly. But the constant pretending—pretending they were just friends, pretending he wasn't attracted to her—would surely kill him. That and his constant, desperate, and overwhelming desire to touch her.

"Let's go to the bar first," he told her lightly. "I'll buy you a smoothie."

"Angela, dear, come in." Vincent, giving her his most charming smile, swung the front door open wider to allow her to walk past. The crisp fall air, cooler now that the sun was setting, felt good against his face before he shut the door. "I'm sorry I missed you earlier when you dropped Maya off. I'd like to talk to you for a minute before she comes down. She's upstairs with Lena." He waved her into the living room.

Angela did not smile back; she had, in fact, the resigned air of someone who had to get a root canal over with before she'd be allowed to continue with her day. Squaring her shoulders as if to steel herself for the ordeal ahead, she marched stiffly in front of him and, without removing her leather jacket, perched on the edge of the sofa as if she were being forced to sit on a pile of manure.

"What can I do for you, Vincent?" she asked tightly.

Vincent sighed. He'd hoped she'd cooled down a little after their last encounter, but apparently she hadn't. His gloom deepened. As much as he loved his beautiful home, late afternoons here were always difficult, especially as the fall went on. The days were so short now, and it seemed like the house was usually dark, shadowy, and chilly, no matter how many lamps he turned on or fires he burned. Soon Maya would go home and the house would be eerily silent. At times like this he felt like exactly what he was: an old man rattling around alone in a mausoleum.

He sat in the chair next to the sofa, determined to at least observe the social niceties. "Would you like some tea or a soda—"

"I'm fine."

Crossing his legs, he decided to just plow ahead. No point being delicate. "I'd like to help you get Maya's guardianship."

Angela's eyes narrowed. "I don't need your help."

He'd expected as much. Still, the girl obviously didn't know what a valuable friend he could be. Surely she wouldn't let her personal feelings get in the way of what was best for Maya. "Don't you know an olive branch when you see it, Angela?" he asked irritably, drumming his fingers on the arm of his chair.

"No, but I know a Trojan horse when I see one."

Intrigued, Vincent laughed; he really hadn't expected the girl to have this much spark. "You don't like me, do you?"

Emotions flashed across her face, as readable as the type that crawled across the bottom of the TV screen during the news. He saw her innate respect for her elders war with her virulent dislike of him, her desire not to make a scene in someone's home struggle with her need to tell the truth. In the end, the truth won out. "No."

To his surprise he felt a vast disappointment. He rather liked Angela and would have been pleased to think she had some soft feelings for him. And he had the feeling she could be a far more powerful ally than he could. He leaned forward, more interested in this conversation than he could remember being in anything else for a long time. "Why not?"

Uncrossing and recrossing her legs, clearly embarrassed, she said, "Mr. Robinson, I really don't think—"

"Tell me. It's because of Justus, isn't it?"

Speaking the name out loud seemed to inflame her and she

blew, spewing her anger the way a boiling teakettle spews steam. "I don't understand how a man can treat his son the way you treat Justus! Can't you even *pretend* to be a good father?"

He shrugged, bored again suddenly. This was familiar ground and he didn't feel like treading it again. "Why? He doesn't pretend to be a good son."

Her eyes bulged nearly out of her head, but she kept her voice low. "Because *you're* the parent! He's probably so sick of being treated like a second-class citizen and banging his head against a brick wall he won't even try to meet you halfway! But if you would try, so would he."

If only that were true. Sighing, he closed his eyes and leaned his head against the back of the tall chair. "I've tried."

"Try again."

"I'm too old and tired for this." He couldn't expect a young woman like Angela to understand the depths of his exhaustion. He was tired of seeing the disappointment and reproach in Justus's eyes. He was tired of Justus rebuffing him every time he invited him to the house for the holidays. He was tired of hearing the phone ring and knowing the caller could be virtually anyone in the world except his youngest son—he had a better chance of receiving a personal call from the President than he did from Justus. He was tired of dancing on eggshells, attempting the impossible task of thinking of something— anything—to say to which Justus would not disagree. Most of all he was tired of being exhausted.

"I don't have the energy for dealing with Justus. He's worn me out."

"You know what? I feel sorry for you."

Stung, he opened his eyes to glower at her. The one thing he wouldn't stand for was pity. "How dare you—"

Clearly agitated, she made a strangled sound and leapt to her feet to pace around. "I do. I feel sorry for you. Because you're wasting what's left of your life with hard feelings. And you don't even realize how much like you he is." She stalked toward the door, fishing around in her purse for her keys. "I'm leaving. Where's Maya?"

Vincent shot to his feet, ignoring the resulting lightheadedness and tightness in his chest. This girl had just poured a pound of salt on a wound that had festered for nearly thirty years. If Justus had ever shown even the tiniest tendency to be anything like him, they could have found some common ground and their entire relationship would have been different.

"My son is nothing like me!" he roared, clutching the chair for support. "That's the problem!"

Angela recoiled slightly in surprise, blinking at him as if she thought she couldn't have heard correctly. "My God, how can you be so blind?" Raising and lowering her hands, palms up, as if she didn't know where to begin, she stared at him for a long time. When she spoke again her voice dropped to a murmur. "He's smart and funny and mischievous, just like you are. He put himself through school on a scholarship, just like you did."

Something twisted inside his gut. He waited breathlessly for her to continue.

"He's started his own business, just like you did. You're both as stubborn as a thousand mules. You both work very hard." A slight smile flitted across her face. "You should take the time to go to his club and have him show you around. It's like he's given birth and you haven't even bothered to go see his baby. You won't believe the work he's done there."

He believed it, all right. Hadn't he seen it with his own eyes the other day and been too stubborn to compliment him on it? Shame, an emotion he hadn't felt in years, weighed down on his shoulders; he didn't bother trying to defend himself.

"And you both play chess, of course."

Vincent had gone to stare blindly out the window, but at

this his head whipped back around. His heart began to beat crazily, but for once it was a craziness born of excitement, not illness. "What did you say?" He couldn't seem to raise his voice to anything above a whisper. "How do you know he plays chess?"

"Because he's taught Maya to play," she said, waving her hand impatiently. "He's got a Wizard of Oz set they use, which you would know if you only—"

"Maya's too young to play chess."

Angela smiled a smug, satisfied smile, clearly pleased she'd taken her enemy by surprise. "Justus taught her."

Vincent froze, too stunned to think of any reply. His knees felt weak suddenly, but not because of his heart. She was right, he realized suddenly. Maybe the reason he and Justus didn't get along was because they were too much alike.

Angela marched up to stand right in his face and her pained, determined expression had him bracing for a blow. "If I were you and I'd just lost one son, I'd be down on my knees every night, praying for God to let me live long enough to work things out with the other one."

He stared, awed by her strength, courage, and passion. Clearly she would fight to the death for something—or someone— she believed in, which was why he felt so strongly she should raise Maya. Suddenly he realized exactly why Justus was so smitten with her, other than because of her beauty: she reminded him of his wife. She didn't look anything like her, of course, but they had the same steely spine, the same passion for the people they loved. God, how he missed Sharon. Well, he would be with her soon enough.

He smiled ruefully. "My son is a lucky man, Angela. Have you told him how you feel?"

An endless silence followed. Angela spluttered, opening and closing her mouth several times. Amused, Vincent watched her struggle. Maybe it hadn't occurred to her yet that she was in love with his son.

"I—we're good friends. That's all."

He grinned. "Angela," he said reproachfully, "don't kid a kidder."

She flushed to her ears. Still, as embarrassed as she obviously was, she tried to hide it. "The best defense is always a good offense, isn't it, Vincent?"

Before he could laugh his chest tightened in a precursor to the pain that was always with him these days and he stiffened, his smile fading. "I'm sick, Angela."

Her face darkened. "I know." She raised her hand, hesitated, then put it on his arm, squeezing it. "You should think about what I said."

"*You* should think about what *I* said," he told her, winking.

A reluctant grin turned up the edges of her mouth, and it felt like the sun dawning over the Arctic after months of darkness. "I'm leaving, Vincent." She hitched her purse up over her shoulder. "You'll have to find yourself someone else to torture for the rest of the day."

This time he did laugh, delighted with this girl. If he were young enough he'd more than give Justus a run for his money. "I'm going to keep working on you, Angela. One day you're going to like me," he told her, meaning it.

Her lips pursed around her reluctant grin. "I doubt it."

"I hate it," Maya said in the whine that so grated on Angela's nerves. She folded her arms across her chest, planted her feet wide, and poked her lips out, pouting.

Stunned, Angela gaped at her, turned to stare at the guest bedroom, which she'd completely made over per Maya's specifications, and tried to figure out what the girl could possibly hate. After finishing up at the gym early this afternoon, she had, in a frenzy of activity, gone shopping, then come back here and thrown a coat of lilac paint on the walls. She'd folded up her treadmill and wheeled it into her own bedroom, where it hopelessly crowded the space. She'd gotten rid of the old, adult linens, and replaced them with a beautiful floral duvet and pillows. She'd replaced the curtains with white tulle scarves she'd draped romantically over the rods, and then woven garlands of flowers through the tulle. She'd found a flower lamp and a white wicker rocker for Maya to sit in while looking at her books, and she'd found a huge, flower-shaped rug to warm the floor. She'd done all this before racing back over to Vincent's to pick Maya up.

She had, in short, spent a small fortune and worked her butt off to create a room any preschool princess would be proud to call her own. She'd expected Maya to, at the very least, burst into ecstatic applause and whirl deliriously around the room like the Tasmanian Devil. She'd expected some acknowledgement of the beautiful room she'd worked so hard on.

She had *not* expected sullen pouting.

Angela sank to the edge of the bed, determined not to take this personally. "But it's beautiful! Look at the pretty purple walls." She waved a hand. "Purple is your favorite color!"

Maya snorted. "I hate purple."

Angela scooted around and turned on the flower lamp. "Look at this lamp, Maya," she cried in her most syrupy voice. "It's shaped like a giant flower! Isn't that cool?"

Maya rolled her eyes and stomped a foot. "I hate flowers. I wanted a rainbow room."

Angela's face burned with anger. Enough was enough. It was late and she was tired and hungry. Her feet hurt and her back ached. She still had to cook dinner, bathe, and read to Maya before putting her to bed, then do about three more hours of work before she could think about going to bed herself.

She shot to her feet and decided the time had come to put her foot down. How on earth had Carolyn ever let this girl get so out of hand? Surely the little diva didn't think she'd run right out and redecorate the room again, did she?

"Maya," she began, unable to keep the sharp edge out of her voice, "you told me you wanted a purple room with flowers, so I made this into a purple room with flowers. I worked very hard in here all afternoon, and you should thank me." Maya crossed her hands over her chest and studied her for a long time, clearly weighing her options very carefully. Angela decided to help her along a little. "I'm waiting, Maya."

Maya's lips compressed into invisibility. Angela jammed her fists on her hips. A silent tension pulsed through the air, as if they were opposing coaches waiting for a referee's ruling during the Superbowl. Finally Maya made her move and Angela waited breathlessly.

Everything seemed to happen in slow motion. Her soft brown eyes blazing with a virulent three-and-a-half-year-old anger, Maya uncrossed her arms, raised one hand toward Angela, and very deliberately gave her the finger.

For one arrested second Angela wondered crazily if she was seeing straight. Realizing she was, she roared with fury and lunged for Maya. Maya's eyes widened into saucers. Seeming to realize she'd gone too far, she dropped her hand and took off, shrieking, down the hall.

Angela stepped over the threshold into Maya's room, which had, in the last couple of hours, begun to feel like a demilitarized zone teetering on the brink of renewed hostility. Maya, freshly bathed and jammied, sat cross-legged on the bed, glowering at her in the soft lighting of her rejected flower lamp. They watched each other in a seething silence for a moment.

"Maya," Angela said in her most imperious tone, "you may get off your bed and come into my room to call Uncle Justus and tell him goodnight."

"I don't want too," Maya said through lips that barely moved.

Angela threw her hands up, losing her battle to remain coolly detached and in control. "Of course you don't want to. You didn't like your new room, you didn't want the spaghetti I made for dinner even though you loved spaghetti the other night—"

"I love *Uncle Justus's* spaghetti!"

"Yeah, well, Uncle Justus *is not here*!" Angela screeched. Realizing she was dangerously out of control—in the last couple of hours she'd begun to understand why gerbil parents sometimes ate their young—she took a deep and, hopefully, soothing breath. "You didn't want to take your bath," she continued, counting off on her fingers, "you didn't want to brush your teeth, you didn't want to sit on the bed for your time out, and now you don't want to call Uncle Justus." She took another deep breath, the first one not having worked very well. "Why don't you just tell me what it is you *do* want to do?"

Maya flopped over backward on the bed, kicking her feet out from under her.

"Fine. Suit yourself. Stay on the bed." Ignoring Maya's groan, she whirled and stalked off down the hall. Before she could collapse on the sofa—she hadn't sat down in what seemed like forever—the phone rang.

Cursing, she snatched it up. "Hello," she snarled.

A long pause, then, "Duchess? You okay?"

"Justus!" Relief flowed through her. Never in her life could she recall being so glad to hear someone's voice. "Thank God it's you!" Lowering her voice, she shot a covert glance over her shoulder to make sure Maya hadn't somehow snaked a listening device down the hallway to eavesdrop. She sat on the sofa, sinking deep into its cushions. "Maya's driving me *crazy*!"

"Yeah? What'd you do to her?"

Having her hands full with more pressing matters, Angela decided to let Justus's obvious amusement over her misfortune slide this one time. "I worked my *butt* off all afternoon trying to put her room together and the little princess says she hates it!" she hissed in a loud whisper. "She's done nothing but disobey me all night! She didn't even want to call you just now!"

Another long silence ensued. Finally Justus said, "I thought you were going to hold off on that whole room thing, Angela. Until the magistrate decides where she should live."

Angela didn't like his reproachful tone. "I never said that. I promised Maya I'd decorate her room, and I kept my promise. Anyway, if the magistrate gives her to you, she'll still need a room to sleep in when she stays here."

She could feel Justus's reluctant agreement. "Well," he said gently, "did you ever think maybe she doesn't want a new room because she realizes if she has a room with you she really won't be going back to her old room?"

"Oh, God." The horrible, constricting pain she thought had receded slightly in the last couple of days tightened across her chest again. Of course Maya didn't want some new room. She wanted her old one—and she wanted her parents back. "You're right. Dr. Brenner warned me when I called him, that she'd act out." She smacked her hand against her head feeling equally frustrated and clueless. "I don't know what to do."

"I could come over . . ."

Yes, she wanted to cry. As much as she hated to admit it, even to herself, he could handle Maya in a way she couldn't. If he came he would have Maya giggling and singing *Kum Ba Ya* in no time, and peace would reign in the household once again. For Maya's sake she should invite him over. And maybe . . . for her own sake as well.

But if she did that, how on earth would she ever learn to handle Maya herself? What made her think she could be Maya's guardian when she couldn't even make it through one night alone with her? "No," she said, very reluctantly. "I'll work this out on my own. And"—she cringed at the thought—"it's Saturday night. I'm sure you have plans anyway."

He grunted unintelligibly.

"Well." Angela stood and stared dispassionately down the quiet hallway. There was no telling what mischief Maya had gotten into now; in another minute or two Angela would probably start smelling smoke. "I should go check on her."

"Okay," Justus said dully.

She hated to let him go—for more reasons than she cared to think about. "Wish me luck. She gave me the finger earlier, by the way."

Justus laughed. Now that a little time had passed, she had to admit the incident had been funny—well, slightly funny. She laughed too.

"Was it an appropriate use of the gesture?"

"Oh, yeah."

"I hope you didn't make too big a deal out of it. Some kid at preschool who has an older brother—it's always the ones with the older brothers—got all the other little kids started doing it. V.J.—" Angela felt him stiffen over the phone, then heard him take a sharp breath. He cleared his throat. "V.J. and Carolyn were having a terrible time with her the other week. They decided the best thing to do was ignore it. She doesn't even know what it means."

"Oh." The melancholy in his voice caused a deep ache in her chest because she couldn't bear the thought of him sad and alone. "You're not brooding, are you? I hate it when you brood."

He sighed harshly. "Brooding is what I do."

"You should stop."

"I'll try."

She heard the laugher in his voice. Relieved, she said, "I'll talk to you tomorrow?"

"Good night, Duchess."

Angela hung up and, squaring her shoulders, marched down the hall prepared to see a bonfire of new linen burning or maybe a magic marker mural on the freshly painted walls. The scene that greeted her was much more startling. Maya sat cross-legged in the wicker chair, a fleece throw tucked over her lap, upon which sat a small, open book. She had her head bent low, her face screwed up with concentration, almost as if she was actually reading. She did not notice Angela. Pointing a tiny finger at the page, Maya, with absolute focus and great effort, said, "Th . . . the c . . . the c-cat s-sat—"

Angela cried out with astonishment. Maya's head jerked up and the book slid from her lap. "Sweetie! You're reading!" Angela rushed to kneel by her chair. "You can read!"

Maya puffed up like a strutting peacock; a delighted, surprised smile split her face, as if she hadn't quite realized what, exactly, she was doing. "Yeah!"

"Let me help you." Angela scooped her up and, sitting in the chair, put Maya in her lap. Resettled, Maya helped her find her page in the book and they sat reading together for another fifteen minutes, Angela's heart swelling with a pride so powerful it took her breath away.

Later, after Maya was safely asleep and she'd finished about three hours of correspondence, research, and dictation for work, Angela, sitting at the kitchen table, finally looked up from the glowing light of her laptop and rubbed her bleary eyes. She was beyond exhaustion. Even so, she knew there was no point going to bed—at least not yet.

Because late at night, when her apartment grew quiet and

dark, uncontrollable thoughts roamed free, like the wild horses racing up and down the beaches at the Outer Banks. Not of work, or of how Maya had gotten the best of her that day, or of Ronnie and how much, to her surprise, she didn't miss him, or even of her dead sister, whom she missed more than she'd thought possible. No, in the dark hours of the night, only one thing came to her mind.

Justus.

What was he doing right now? Who was he with? Did he have a good day? What did he have for dinner? What was his favorite color? Did he ever think of her?

And there were more insidious thoughts—thoughts she would have gladly taken a mallet to her head to stop. Was he really over his attraction to her? Did he consider her a sister now? Had he already found someone else to replace Janet? Someone younger, prettier, taller, slimmer, more voluptuous, more uninhibited than Angela? Someone who could handle him in bed? Someone who, even now, could touch him to her heart's content? Someone who could rub the smooth brown satin of his skin, knead the hard, powerful muscles of his shoulders, arms, and butt? Who could press her lips to his—

Angela, her body burning with frustrated heat, cried out, propped her elbows on the table and dropped her head into her hands. Her breasts and sex throbbed with a painful hunger she'd never—*never*—felt before, even during her most intimate moments with Ronnie. For the first time she wished she'd gone to one of those sex parties her friends were always throwing and bought herself some device to relieve the constant ache for Justus she felt inside, high up between her thighs. It was just as well. No battery-operated toy could possibly substitute for having that six-foot-four-inch slab of hot, moving, breathing marble in her bed.

After a minute she looked up to check the red numbers on

the range's digital clock. Twelve-thirty. It was going to be a long night.

"Justus? Someone's here to see you. He didn't give his name."

Cursing, Justus threw down his pen and raised his head from the stack of invoices. Sunday mornings at the club were a little quieter than Saturdays, and he'd hoped to make a good start on his paperwork but that hope had died a swift and painful death. He'd gotten here at seven-thirty, only to find a small flood in the men's shower area. Once he'd fixed that—he was pretty handy with the wrench, if he did say so himself—he'd had to listen to the manager of the smoothie bar area whine about the unreliability of some of the high school kids he'd hired. He glanced at his watch: nine-fifteen. Great. He'd sat down at his desk a whopping five minutes ago. At this rate he'd have to take the paperwork home with him tonight—again—and look at it there.

"Well, what the hell does he want?" Justus barked at the speakerphone perched at the end of the desk from whence the receptionist's voice came. "And why can't Brian help him?"

"Brian had to go upstairs and help a client with the Smith machine."

"Fine. I'll be right out." He walked out of his office to the lobby, his mind shifting inevitably back to Angela and Maya. Much to his disappointment, Angela hadn't called him back last night—not that she'd said that she would, but he'd hoped—so he took that to mean that she and Maya had reached a truce of some sort. He hadn't called again this morning because he really didn't want to seem overeager, although that ship had probably already sailed.

He wanted to see them today, of course, but—

His steps slowed, then stopped, and his feet took root in the floor. Standing next to the front desk, not six feet away, was his father.

The old man stared uncomfortably at him, his hands shoved deep into the pants pockets of his navy warm-up suit. Justus gaped at him; on top of the surprise of seeing his father here—again—was the surprise of seeing him dressed in anything other than his perpetual dark suit and tie. It was as if Colin Powell had shown up in overalls and galoshes.

Vincent looked, in fact, as if he'd come to work out, but that, of course, was impossible. He smiled slightly. "Hello, Justus."

Justus stiffened, bracing himself for the inevitable unpleasantness. Automatically the muscles between his shoulder blades tightened into knots. The man really should not be allowed to move freely among the general public. At the very least he should be fitted with some sort of bell or alarm or other early warning device so Justus could have ten minutes warning before he appeared—then he could get his thoughts together and make some small effort to protect himself from his father's venom.

"What are you doing here?" he asked rudely, dimly aware of the receptionist's shocked, reproachful stare from behind the counter. "I'm pretty busy today."

Vincent's jaw tightened almost imperceptibly. "I just paid for a two-year membership to your club." He cleared his throat and paused as if he couldn't quite get the words out. "I . . . thought maybe you could show me around."

Justus couldn't believe it. He'd have been less surprised if Vincent had said he'd come to feed the dinosaurs. He opened and closed his mouth several times, blinking furiously, trying to make a modicum of sense out of what he'd just heard.

Turning his head slightly so his ear was better positioned to hear Vincent, he said, "*What did you say?*"

"I'd like a tour," Vincent told him, his voice firm now. "Of your club."

"Why?" Justus snapped suspiciously, thrusting his chin out, all out of patience now. He really didn't have time for this crap—his father's little mind games and manipulations. Didn't the old man have anything better to do today than come all the way down here to bother him? "Don't you have any ambulances to chase today?"

To his further astonishment, the corners of Vincent's lips turned up in what could almost pass for a smile, but of course it had been so long since Vincent really smiled in his presence he couldn't tell for sure. "I don't start chasing ambulances until after lunch on Sundays."

Justus snorted, at a complete loss for words.

Vincent turned and strolled to the archway leading to the crowded cafe, reaching up to lovingly stroke the highly polished oak woodwork. "You don't see workmanship like this anymore," he with approval. "Is this oak—"

Justus had had just about enough. He stalked to his father's side, out of range of the receptionist, and snarled, "What do you want, Vincent?"

Vincent answered patiently, without a hint of disapproval, disappointment or a hidden agenda. "I want to see what my son has built. . . . Please."

Without warning, V.J.'s angry, frustrated voice filled his head, as clearly as if he'd popped down from heaven for a minute to whisper in his ear. *How long are you gonna keep up this wounded son routine? No one lives forever! How many chances do you think you're gonna get?*

Completely undone, his heart contracting painfully, Justus looked away and shoved his fists in his pockets. When had his father ever asked him nicely for anything? Maybe he should give him a chance. Suddenly he felt that same roiling panic he'd felt the other night at Angela's apartment and wondered wildly if he wasn't cracking up at the age of twenty-seven. He sucked in a deep breath and risked a glance at Vincent, who pretended he didn't notice his turmoil and continued to look as innocent as morning dew.

"Well . . . okay."

Vincent nodded, clearly satisfied and pleased.

Justus pointed. "Well . . . this is the cafe. And smoothie bar."

"Smoothies!" Vincent cried with delight, as if he couldn't imagine anything more thrilling than a smoothie. "Do you have raspberry?"

Justus's body jerked; he felt like he'd seen a ghost. "Raspberry was V.J.'s favorite."

"Oh." Vincent's face fell. Hanging his head, he stared at his shoes. "I miss him."

Something in Justus's heart softened. He stared at Vincent and saw the slightly stooped shoulders, the drawn face, the head that was now entirely gray. For once he looked past the frustrated dictator who'd tried to run his life for as long as he could remember and saw instead the tired old man who'd just lost a son. "I know, Pop."

Vincent nodded once, brusquely, then slid onto a stool at the bar, lost in his thoughts. Justus sat next to him. "Had an interesting talk with Angela yesterday," Vincent said after a while, picking up a laminated menu and studying it.

Justus was all ears. He waited for the rest of the story, but Vincent remained utterly absorbed in his menu. "Raspberry, strawberry . . . ooh, *blueberry*," he murmured.

Finally Justus couldn't stand the suspense any longer. "What did she say?"

Vincent chuckled, still looking at the menu. "Only that I'm the worst father who ever walked the face of the earth and she doesn't like me." He shot Justus a bemused sidelong glance. "She's a very passionate woman, and she believes in you. I think she'd defend you to the death if she needed to." His hand circled his neck. "I'm lucky my head's still attached to my shoulders."

Justus stared at his father, too overcome with emotion to risk speaking. Somewhere in the last ten minutes—hell, in the last ten days—his world had stopped making sense. At one point all he'd wanted was to tell his father to go to hell. Then all he'd wanted was to be a trainer. Then all he'd wanted was to sleep with Angela.

Now all he wanted was Angela's love, her heart. Worse, he wanted to be worthy of it.

"She's a hell of a woman," Vincent said, looking back at the menu. "She reminds me of—" He trailed off into silence, but of course Justus knew what he'd wanted to say. "Well," Vincent said, staring at some distant point over the bar, "let's just say I knew another woman like her, once upon a time." He looked back at Justus, his eyes churning with intense emotions. "If I could get my hands on a woman like *that* again," he said pointedly, "I wouldn't let her go."

Justus couldn't answer.

Chapter 16

Three weeks later

Angela, dressed in a tailored black wool dress, hurried around the corner and down the hall to Maya's room, pausing only long enough to slip her remaining pump on her foot, hopping once or twice for balance. Straightening, she glanced at her watch: seven-fifteen. They'd never make it if they didn't leave soon. She had a pretrial conference in federal court for the Golden Valley case at nine, and she had to drop Maya at preschool before that. They'd eaten breakfast already, so as soon as she brushed the front of Maya's hair they'd be out the door in no time—

Angela stumbled to a halt outside Maya's door, aghast. Her heart thundered sickeningly as she calculated how much time she was about to lose. So many things were wrong with this picture she hardly knew where to look. Maya sat on the floor playing with her Barbies, dressed not in the lovely pink velour warm-up suit Angela had laid out for her, but in her red-and-green-plaid Christmas sweater and pink-striped jeans. She looked like a clown in training. Her socks were not on. Her shoes were not on. Her toys were not picked up. She had, clearly, done none of the things Angela asked her to do fifteen minutes ago.

The one thing Maya *had* decided to do was to unbraid her waist-length hair, which Angela had painstakingly braided last night. The wavy mass hung wild and free like a lion's mane gone haywire. Still that was not the worst of it. The worst of it was that Maya, maybe bored with styling only her dolls' hair, had decided to do her own—starting with a haircut. A telltale clump of gleaming black hair lay on the flower rug, as if someone had divested a panther of its tail. The corresponding bald—well, nearly bald—spot on Maya's head was, of course, right in front for the whole world to see, above her right eyebrow. Angela's orange-handled office scissors lay forgotten, off to one side. Huge globs of pale pink conditioning cream dotted Maya's hair, which explained the overwhelming and cloying scent of coconuts saturating the room. If Angela started washing Maya's hair this very second she was sure it would take a week to get the stuff completely out.

Angela cried out in horror. "What did you do?"

Maya smiled proudly. "I cut my hair. Like you did."

Angela cursed under her breath. What on God's green earth had possessed her to leave the bathroom door open the other day when she'd trimmed her bangs? She hurried in and, leaning over Maya, tried to scoop some of the product out of her hair without getting it on her wool dress.

"May-aaa," she muttered, "why'd you have to pick today to do your own hair?"

Maya scrunched up her face but resumed brushing the stupid doll's hair, further infuriating Angela. She snatched it away, ignored Maya's outraged yelp, and tossed it in the bin.

"I'm playing with that!" Maya cried.

Angela planted her hands on her hips. "Now is not the time for playing. I want you to march over to the bed, right now, and take off these ridiculous clothes you've got on and put on the outfit I picked out for you so I can do your hair."

Her hands flew protectively to her shirt. "I want to wear *this*!"

Surely Maya didn't think she'd let her leave the house in the Technicolor nightmare she wore. "I don't have time for this!" Angela checked her watch again and saw they'd already lost five minutes. She reached for Maya's shirt and tried to jerk it off over her head. "Take this off!"

Maya instantly locked her arms by her sides. "Nooo," she wailed. "Nooo-ooo!"

Grunting, Angela refused to let go of the shirt and wildly wondered what she should do now. Things had never gotten this bad during any of their other power struggles—she'd never spanked Maya before, but maybe now was the time to start. Over Maya's howls she heard pounding. Great. Now, on top of everything else, the neighbors were pissed off. Well, she'd deal with them later. Tightening her grip on Maya, it occurred to her that the pounding came from her front door. What on earth?

Growling with impatience, she turned Maya loose and ran to the door, checking the peephole. An attractive twenty-something blonde raised her hand to pound determinedly on the door again. Angela snatched the door open. "Can I help you?" she snapped, uncomfortably aware of the screeching racket Maya continued to make down the hall and how it must sound to this woman. With her luck, the woman would whip out a cell phone and call 241-KIDS on her.

The woman frowned, her vivid blue eyes darkening. "Angela Dennis?"

"Yes . . ." Angela said suspiciously. "And you are? . . . "

The woman's lips thinned. "Olivia Warren. I'm here for the home study."

* * *

It took several long, awkward seconds for Angela's frazzled brain to process the words. This . . . this . . . this child, who seemed barely out of diapers herself, was here to inspect her home to see if she was fit to raise Maya? Right now?

Angela managed a tight smile. "Ms. Warren," she said, raising her voice in the vain hopes of drowning out Maya, who had lapsed into loud, though fake, sobs, "Obviously I'm very anxious to meet with you, but this really isn't a very good—"

Ms. Warren, apparently having realized Angela had no intention of voluntarily inviting her inside the apartment, shouldered her way past, leaving Angela no choice but to shut the door and follow her. "You see, I've got court in a little while and I—"

Ms. Warren did a three-hundred-and-sixty-degree turn, surveying the apartment like a U.N. weapons inspector in Baghdad. Angela's heart sank; the place was a mess. Maya's little toys—Barbies and accessories, baby dolls and their stroller and high chair, miscellaneous picture books, coloring books and markers—lay strewn about her once pristine apartment as if someone had detonated a toy store. Over in the corner by the sofa lay a huge stack of old newspapers and law journals she hadn't had time to read. Clearly visible on the kitchen counter lay the dirty breakfast dishes she'd planned to soak before she left. Vaguely she remembered how she'd smugly told Justus that Carolyn never knew how to keep a house clean. Oh, the irony.

Ms. Warren raised her eyebrows. "You knew we'd make an unannounced visit . . . ?"

"Yes, but I—"

"Just ignore me," Ms. Warren said in what she clearly thought was the end of the matter. "Where's Maya?"

Angela opened then shut her mouth and, praying for the best, trudged down the hall, Ms. Warren trailing behind.

Maya's wailing had stopped, which could or could not be an ominous sign. If she was lucky, Maya had calmed down and resumed quietly playing with her dolls. If not, the sky was pretty much the limit in terms of mischief. In the last couple of weeks Maya had sketched her masterpiece in green magic marker on her freshly painted bedroom, forcing Angela to re-paint the walls all the way around the room. She'd also, on separate occasions, made a potion consisting entirely of Angela's expensive face creams and lotions, and pulled all of her neatly folded clothes out of the dresser, then shoved them under the bed so Angela wouldn't see what she'd done.

Holding her breath, Angela peeked in the room and saw, to her profound relief, Maya sitting on the floor pulling on—oh, for goodness sake!—orange socks. "Maya," she called sweetly, "this is Ms. Warren. She's come to talk to us and see your room."

Entering the room, Ms. Warren stooped down to Maya's level and held out her hand. "Hello, Maya," she said, smiling with obvious delight. Maya smiled shyly back and shook the woman's hand. "What a colorful outfit you're wearing! Who picked it out?"

Maya's chest puffed out like a helium balloon. "I did!"

"And who cut your hair?"

Maya's smile wavered. She shot a cautious glance at Angela. "I did."

"I see," Ms. Warren said gravely. Although the woman hadn't opened her briefcase or taken any notes thus far, Angela imagined her making mental slashes through the por-tions of Angela's file that dealt with her supervisory capa-bilities. Getting to her feet, she turned to Angela. "Don't mind me." She scooped Maya's books and fleece blanket off the rocking chair, put them on the unmade bed, and sat down. "Just pretend I'm not here."

Angela managed a sickly smile. She found the basket with

Maya's hair accessories, pulled out the heavy plastic comb with three-inch tines—the only comb she'd found capable of piercing Maya's long, wavy hair—and motioned to Maya. "Come on, Sweetie. We need to go. We're going to be late." Maya obligingly knelt in front of Angela, who sat on the edge of the bed. Angela took a deep breath, feeling as if she'd narrowly dodged a bullet. This wasn't so bad! Why had she been so worried about the home visit? Ms. Warren was obviously a very sensible woman—she wasn't out to get Angela!

Angela took a section of Maya's hair in her left hand and raised the comb with her right. She lowered the comb, but, before it could even make contact with Maya's head, Maya jerked away and shrieked like a pig being slaughtered with a dull ax. *"You're hurting me!"*

Angela winced.

Ms. Warren's sharp eyes narrowed.

Justus scurried around his third-floor gym like a hen with one chick, too excited to bother laughing at himself for being so silly. He checked his watch. Four twenty-seven. Angela would be here any second for her first training session. His heart sped up. Surveying the room, he decided it was a little too sunny—he didn't want to have to squint at Angela the whole time—so he slanted the blinds on the floor-to-ceiling windows, allowing only slashes of sunlight to peer through three sides of the room. The effect was that the huge, high-ceilinged room shrank to a cozier, more intimate size, which was, of course, the whole point.

The large blue exercise mat lay unfolded across the hard-wood floor. In a far corner sat the weight bench and free weights. He'd pulled out the BOSU and Swiss balls, along with the jump rope, just in case. On a small table sat his clipboard, along with water bottles and towels. Everything was perf—

Angry, stomping footsteps out in the hallway intruded on his thoughts. Vaguely alarmed, he wandered to the room's arched doorway in time to see Angela's head come into view as she climbed the stairs. He didn't need to look twice to see she was pissed. Her delicate brows had flattened over her eyes and her lips were pursed tightly together, giving her a thunderous expression. Interesting. She'd been fine when he talked to her last night, so something must have happened today. Or maybe she just really didn't want to be here alone with him. Maybe the unspoken tension between them was getting to be too much even for Angela the Ice Princess. Well, good. He'd had about enough of the games anyway.

As she continued up the steps he saw she wore the stupid ponytail and some sort of striped top with a partially zipped hooded sweat jacket over black yoga pants. Damn. He'd really hoped she'd wear the same kind of skimpy shorts she'd worn the other time she came to the gym, but no such luck. He should have known she'd cover as much of herself up as possible to keep him from touching her bare skin. He cast a fleeting glance over his shoulder at the thermostat on the far wall and wondered if there was time to crank it up to eighty—at least then she'd have to take off the jacket—but decided against it.

She reached the top and saw him. "Hi," she said sourly.

"What's wrong with you?"

She stalked past him, tossed her gym bag on the chair and turned to face him with a now bland face. "Nothing." She managed half a sickly smile. "Let's get started. I have to pick up Maya soon."

He put his hands on his hips. "Something's obviously wrong."

Her jaw tightened and she abruptly squatted to untie and

retie her shoe. "Yeah, well, I told you last night I don't really have time to be trained today."

"Yeah, well, you've already cancelled on me three times." Staring down at the top of her head, he infused his voice with a challenge. "I'm beginning to think you're avoiding me for some reason."

Her head whipped up and she stared at him with a virulent, flashing anger that made him wonder if she wouldn't spring out of her crouch to tackle him to the floor. "That's ridiculous."

"Is it?"

She leapt to her feet, her jaw flexing. "Let's get started." She didn't look at him.

"Fine. You can leave your jacket right here." He waved a hand at the chair.

Her eyes widened as if he'd told her to get ready for the strip search. Clutching the unzipped edges of her jacket together over her chest, she licked her lips worriedly. "Why?"

"I don't want you to get too hot."

Their gazes locked, the air heavy with tension. After a minute she smiled crookedly, telling him the innuendo wasn't lost on her. "Don't worry."

Irritated, he wheeled away and reached for the ribbed silver Swiss ball. "I thought we'd work on some core strength first. We'll do some lateral rolls." Sitting on the big ball, he simultaneously leaned back and slid forward, so the ball was between his shoulder blades. "See?" Tightening his abs and butt, he held his arms straight out to the sides, palms up, and rolled slowly across the ball, so the ball moved from one wrist to the other. "The main thing is to keep your abs and butt tight. And you don't want to go too fast. It's harder than it looks."

He'd been staring up at the white ceiling, his unfocused gaze on the fluorescent lights, but now he turned his head to look at her. To his enormous satisfaction, she was staring fixedly at his flexed bare thighs and calves. As he watched, her gaze traveled up over his body, lingering briefly on his face-up crotch in black shorts, then slid over his bare arms, which were still out to the sides. Her chest heaved with rapid, shallow breaths.

With every ounce of his being he ignored and willed away the reflexive tightening of his groin. "Angela?"

She jumped, flushing. Looking away again, she grabbed her ponytail and flipped it over her shoulder. "I can do that. No problem."

"Great." Standing, he rolled the ball to her. Cautiously sitting on it, she leaned back and assumed the starting position. "Good," he told her. She held her arms out, palms down. "Palms up." He leaned down and grabbed her smooth, warm wrists to flip them over. For one thrilling moment they were face to face, her wide gaze riveted on him, but she immediately jerked away, only to slide off the ball and land on her butt with a thump. The ball rolled off.

She leapt up, clearly embarrassed, and tugged the bottom of her jacket down. "I'm okay."

"I told you it was harder than it looks," he said, unable to keep the glee from his voice.

Shooting him a death glare, she marched off, got the ball, and marched back. "I can do it," she said tartly. "Just give me a minute. I've never used one of these things before."

She started again, this time keeping her palms up. "Good," he told her. "Now slowly roll to the right. You've got to ease up on the ball a little so it'll roll. That's where the ab strength comes in." Screwing up her face, she eased to her right, but immediately began to slip. Without thinking he bent and caught her hips to stabilize her, and she leapt away again, eyes flashing.

"Don't touch me!" she screeched. "I don't know how you expect me to do it when you keep touching me!"

Something inside him snapped and he knew they were both at their breaking points, if not just past them. How dare she tell him not to touch her when they both wanted him to? How long was she going to hold out? And how much more could he take?

"Don't touch you? Are you kidding me? We both know I just kept you from falling on your butt again!"

She skittered away, her body vibrating with nervous energy and adrenaline. "You're always"—she waved a hand as if she couldn't quite put his heinous misdeeds to words—"touching me and I'm not a very touchy person!"

"What the hell is wrong with you?" he roared.

"What's wrong? Well, let's see." Tapping her index finger against her lips, she tilted her head thoughtfully. "Let's start with the obvious: I didn't want to be here today. I'm too busy."

Bull. Well, not bull, of course, but that wasn't what was most wrong with her. He crossed his arms, studied his fingernails, and tried to look bored. "Yeah? Anything else?"

She shot him another look that should have incinerated him in his shoes. "They did the home study this morning—did I mention that? At seven-fifteen, when I was already running late for court and had just discovered that Maya hacked off a big hunk of her hair, some woman showed up and demanded to meet Maya and see my apartment, which, for the first time in my life, was a disaster."

"Oh."

"Yeah, *oh*." She blinked furiously and he wondered if she wouldn't cry. "So I was late for court on the biggest case of my career and when I got back to the office, my boss gently reminded me if I intend to make partner in January, I better get my butt in gear."

"Angela," he began, reaching for her without thinking.

"Don't!" she cried, backing away, throwing her hands up. "Don't . . . touch . . . me!"

He cursed viciously, all patience gone; that only seemed to set her off. "And don't pretend you care if I'm upset!" she shrieked. "Don't pretend this isn't exactly what you've been praying for! Now Maya will be yours, free and clear!" Her voice rose with hysteria. "You'll have everything you want!"

With an outraged cry he grabbed her by the shoulders and shook her once, hard; she gasped with surprise. Again his groin started to tighten with lust. He leaned down to stare directly in her wide, shocked eyes. "I can assure you," he said, his low voice sounding dangerous even to his own ears, "I don't have everything I want."

She jerked away or he let her go, he wasn't sure which. They glared at each other for a long moment while the air around them seethed. Finally Angela's gaze wavered and she looked away. Moving to the chair she shoved her gym bag off and collapsed.

"I'm so tired," she said, burying her head in her hands. "I don't recognize anything about my life any more."

Just like that his anger disappeared, replaced by a gnawing ache in his chest. He knew what it must cost her to make such an admission, to him of all people. Squatting between her legs, he pulled her into his arms. To his astonishment she came eagerly, locking her arms around his neck. He soaked her in, threading his fingers through her thick, satiny hair to cup her nape, feeling her breath against his neck, rubbing the soft cotton of her jacket while seeking the warmth of her back and shoulders.

"The only thing you need to recognize," he murmured, "is that you and Maya and I are a family now. And I will always be here for you—it doesn't matter who gets Maya and it doesn't matter whether you make partner or not. You can always count on me." He held her tighter. "My God, when will you realize—"

He stopped, too choked up to continue. What had he just said and, more important, what had he been about to say? He didn't have the faintest idea—he only knew he meant it, whatever it was.

Stiffening, she pulled far enough away to look at him with shocked eyes that surely matched his own. "Justus." Her eyes fluttered, the lids falling slightly as if she'd involuntarily succumbed to some spell, and then her gaze lowered to his lips. She licked her own and his groin tightened into a throbbing, painful knot. When finally she looked back up at his eyes, her own were unnaturally bright, her face flushed.

"I—I'm sorry," she said, her voice husky. "I didn't mean to take my awful day out on you."

"It's okay."

Flushing, she let her arms drop from his neck. Knowing he was teetering on the brink of a catastrophic loss of control, he quickly stood up and turned away before she noticed his arousal. Snatching his oversized fleece pullover off the table, he quickly slid it on. "I guess we're done for today?"

"Yeah." For a moment she stared as if she'd never seen him before, her gaze dropping again to his mouth. Abruptly she turned away on the pretext of picking up her bag. "What are we doing about Christmas, Justus?" she asked over her shoulder. "We need to do the shopping for Maya. And your father called to say he's having dinner at the house."

"I don't know." He shrugged dispassionately. It was hard to get worked up about the holidays when he knew so many places at the dining room table would be empty. "I guess I'd like to be there when Maya opens her presents, so—"

"You could spend the night."

Justus gaped at her.

She stood up. "We have space on the sofa," she said

quickly, flushing again, "and there's no telling what time she'll wake up, probably the crack of dawn, so why don't you—"

"I will," he said, not giving her the chance to change her mind. "Thanks."

She smiled happily, as if he'd just granted her fondest wish, and Justus felt his entire being clench with need for this woman. Desperation felt like his oldest buddy, and if Satan appeared right now he'd gladly sign on the dotted line for just one night with Angela. And she was almost ready. Every time they were together he could feel her softening, opening. There was no mistaking the way she'd looked at him a minute ago. He'd promised himself he wouldn't push her, and no one could say he hadn't done his level best to keep his word. But enough was enough. He was a man, not a saint. She was so close he could taste it, and if a small nudge or two would push her into his arms a little sooner, then he'd have to nudge.

His continued sanity required it.

The meat thermometer read one hundred and seventy degrees. Angela took her perfectly medium-rare roast tenderloin out of the oven, put it on top of the stove, covered it with a tent of aluminum foil, and surveyed the rest of her Christmas Eve feast with satisfaction. Rich brown gravy, flavored with butter-sautéed mushrooms and Madeira, simmered on the stove. Bright, crisp green beans flecked with pancetta steamed in their pot. In the oven her world-famous potatoes, mashed with sour cream, cream cheese, and chives—low fat was the least of her concerns during the holidays—browned nicely. She'd already iced the carrot cake with her favorite lemony cream cheese frosting. The dinner was, she decided, a culinary masterpiece.

She only hoped Justus thought so.

Maya twirled by in the living room, singing her off-key, off-lyric version of *Jingle Bells*, putting special emphasis on the part where "Batman smells." Angela smiled. Maya's nonstop bouncing and whirling throughout the apartment reminded her of a ball ricocheting around a pinball machine. Angela couldn't ever remember her being so excited before, but, as her guilty conscience reminded her, she'd never spent Christmas Eve with her. As she watched, Maya slowed then stopped in front of the fragrant fir tree they'd trimmed the other day, gingerly touching the white lights and her favorite ornaments. Then she skipped to the crackling fireplace and, staying well clear of the screen, touched the fresh garland, also laced with white lights and red-and-green-plaid satin ribbons, that framed it. Sneaking a glance over her shoulder at Angela—Angela quickly ducked her head and pretended she was too absorbed with wiping the counter to notice what Maya was doing—Maya furtively squeezed the bottom of the white-topped red stocking with her name on it, apparently making sure Santa hadn't made any early deliveries. Angela chuckled.

The brisk knock at the door startled them both. Maya whirled around to face Angela, making sure she'd heard. "Uncle Justus!" she screeched delightedly. "Uncle Justus!" She spun and raced to the door as fast as her little black patent-leather Mary Janes would carry her.

Angela's insides turned as squishy as her cranberry chutney. Inviting Justus to spend the night had seemed like a good idea at the time, but now she had no idea how she planned to keep her promise to herself, which was to ignore her overwhelming attraction to him at all costs. Her obsession had gotten exponentially worse ever since she'd caved in and kept her appointment for him to "train" her. She'd known it would be a disaster, and it was. Because now all she could think about was Justus's flawless brown skin, heavily muscled, well-defined bare legs, flexing thighs and calves, and, let's face it, bulging groin. She'd been lightheaded with desire that day and, big surprise, was lightheaded with desire now. Keeping her hands to herself seemed like an increasingly ridiculous idea, like vacationing in the North Pole. And spending the night in such close quarters with Justus—while keeping her distance, which she still firmly intended to do—promised to be an agonizing exercise in self-control. But she would do it. She had to do it.

She jerked the heavy white cotton apron off over her head, tossed it on the table, and quickly smoothed her hair. Even though she was every bit as excited as Maya, she managed to walk sedately to the door and unlock it for Maya to swing open. As usual, the girl launched herself at Justus, who, laughing, squatted down in time to scoop her up for a hug. Angela's pulse went haywire; he'd dressed entirely in black, from his leather jacket to his cashmere turtleneck and wool slacks. Never before had he seemed so dangerously attractive, so virile. Maybe somewhere, in the far reaches of the earth, there was a man more stunning than Justus Robinson, but she doubted it.

Over Maya's shoulder, his gaze immediately found hers and widened with obvious appreciation even as he let Maya go and stretched to his full height. She'd spent a ridiculously long time on her appearance, even for this new Angela who existed solely to catch Justus's eye; now, seeing his reaction, it had been worth it. Her hair was tousled and free, and she'd worn a red silk wrap blouse that plunged deeply in the front, black palazzo pants, and black stilettos. His gaze traveled slowly from her face down over her breasts, hips, and feet, absorbing every small detail of her appearance, before it returned to her face.

"Hi," he said hoarsely.

Her breathing turned rapid and shallow, as if she'd been plunked down in Denver, where the air was thinner. She smiled tremulously. "Hi."

"What's this?" Maya cried from the doorway. Justus didn't seem to hear, but continued to stare so intently at Angela her face and ears burned. "Oooh," Maya said breathlessly. Angela heard a rustling sound. "*Presents*."

Justus sprang to life, wheeling around in time to snatch the shopping bag full of brightly wrapped gifts out of her eager little hands. "Get outta there!" He smacked her hands away.

Maya hopped from one foot to the other. "Are those for me?"

Justus's brow wrinkled thoughtfully. "I don't know. Have you been good this year?"

"I'm always good!"

Angela coughed discreetly, a gesture entirely lost on Maya; Justus glanced over Maya's head at her, his grin widening. "Well, we'll see." He moved into the living room and knelt beneath the tree, which was already overloaded with gifts. "I think I'll just put them under the tree with the other presents."

"Okay." Maya supervised while he removed several large gifts from his bag and arranged them under the tree, then grabbed the hem of her dress and, holding it like she was a waltzing princess, whirled around for Justus to admire her. "Don't I look pretty?"

Angela had to laugh; Maya did look adorable. She wore a beautiful little dress with a black velvet bodice, cap sleeves, and a green-and-red-plaid taffeta skirt that tied in the back. Under her Mary Janes she wore white dress socks with lace trim. Angela had woven fat red grosgrain ribbons through her braids and had subdued with a barrette the sheared portion of her hair, which had an unfortunate tendency to stick straight up like grass.

Justus got to his feet and looked indulgently down at his niece. "You look *beautiful*. Like a princess."

Beaming, Maya pointed at Angela. "Doesn't Aunt Ang-la look beautiful too? Isn't her outfit pretty even if it isn't a dress like mine?"

Angela held her breath, too excited to be embarrassed about being the center of attention. Nor did she care that Maya had put Justus squarely on the spot and basic chivalry demanded he agree with Maya. Justus took forever to turn his head and follow the path of Maya's finger, as if he wasn't quite certain he should look at her at all. Finally his gaze locked with Angela's and she felt a stunning jolt of electricity surge through her body and pool in her breasts, belly, and loins. If the white light of a lightning strike had flashed through her apartment in that instant, she wouldn't have been surprised. Justus stared openly at Angela—hotly, hungrily, and openly.

She knew, suddenly. As clearly as she knew her own name she knew he wanted her. Still wanted her. Had always wanted her. And meant for her to know it. Her knees dissolved, and she clutched the chair for support.

"Uncle Justus?" Maya tugged impatiently on his hand.

"Yes, Maya," he said softly, never looking away from Angela, never blinking. "Aunt Angela is the most beautiful woman I've ever seen. I've always thought so. It doesn't matter what she wears."

Angela's sex tightened and throbbed to the point that she wondered, in a far corner of her brain, whether she'd be able, for the first time in her life, to bring herself to climax simply by tightening the muscles between her thighs. From a great distance she was aware of Maya looking curiously back and forth between them.

Frowning, Maya said, "But what about Mommy?"

A fleeting expression of sadness crossed Justus's face and he wrapped his arm around Maya without ever looking away from Angela. "Your mommy was beautiful, too, Little Girl," he murmured. "But there's something about Angela that . . ." He swallowed convulsively, his Adam's apple bobbing up and down, as if he couldn't get any more words out.

Suddenly Angela couldn't stand the heat—not the heat in his eyes nor that in her own feverish body. She hurried into the kitchen to put the sturdy countertop between her and Justus. She called over her shoulder, trying to keep her voice light. "You should go easy on the compliments, Uncle Justus." Reaching the stove, she snatched the lid off the gravy pan and stirred it with the wooden spoon, hardly aware of what she was doing; gravy sloshed over the sides and hissed on the burner. "Santa's watching."

"Santa knows I'm telling the truth," Justus said in her ear, his hot breath feathering her cheek. "Do you?"

Angela jumped a foot in the air. He'd come up right behind her and, putting one endless arm on the counter to either side of the range, neatly caged her. Somehow he managed not to touch her anywhere, although Angela knew if she backed up half an inch her entire body would press against his.

God, she wanted to back up.

"I—I hope you're hungry," she said ridiculously, trying to pretend she was not nervous, that she wasn't so breathless she was practically panting, and that it was perfectly normal for Justus to effectively seduce her up against the stove while dinner cooked and Maya watched.

To her agonized astonishment, she felt his fingers trail downward from the crown of her head and filter through her hair to her nape, which he caressed gently but firmly. She sighed helplessly, allowing her eyes to drift closed.

"I'm starving," he whispered for her ears only, his voice slightly muffled now, and she realized he'd pressed his nose to her freshly washed hair and was inhaling its floral fragrance.

Angela leapt away, thoroughly undone. "*Maya!*" she screeched loud enough to wake the dead. Maya, who'd apparently gotten bored with them and turned her attention back to the tree, jerked as if she'd been shot from a cannon. "Wash your hands! *Dinner!*"

Justus dropped his hands and stepped away a little, although he seemed to have forgotten what the socially acceptable distance was and remained firmly in her space. Reluctantly she raised her eyes to his, certain she'd see a knowing smirk because he'd so obviously unsettled her. But he stared, his jaw tight, his expression intense and, if she didn't know better, deeply troubled.

Chapter 17

After laying out a plate of carrot cake and a glass of milk for Santa, Maya went reluctantly to bed and Angela stayed with Justus late into the night, talking on the sofa, unable to leave him.

The living room had never seemed so cozy and intimate before, even though she'd lived here for years and decorated the apartment every holiday season. On the mantelpiece, cinnamon candles burned low, and in the corner the white lights on the tree sparkled and winked, but other than that only the floor lamp near the sofa provided any light. The world shrank down to her and Justus, here, now, in this room, together.

The way she wanted.

Justus snuck down the hall to make sure Maya was safely asleep, then came back and snatched up Santa's snack plate, taking a large bite of cake. "Mmmm." He sank onto the sofa beside her. "This is fantastic," he told her around his mouthful. "You're a great cook."

Angela paused and smiled with satisfaction, her goblet of Cabernet Sauvignon suspended halfway to her lips. She couldn't recall anyone ever eating her food more lustily than

Justus had tonight. "You ate like it was your last meal. Hasn't anyone fed you this week?"

"Not like that."

She sipped her wine appreciatively. "I don't know where you put it."

Justus finished off the cake—had he even bothered chewing?—then smeared a little icing around the plate for effect. "How's that look?" he asked, turning the plate this way and that.

"Like Santa was hungry. Don't forget the milk."

"Right." He grabbed the tall glass and downed the milk in what seemed like three swallows. "There." He carefully replaced the glass, then sank back against the cushions.

"Sooo . . ." she began carefully, well aware she was raising a touchy subject. "You're going to your father's for dinner tomorrow, right?"

Scowling, he said, "I suppose so."

"Try not to get so excited." His lips twisted down and she could sense one of his dark moods hovering over his head, waiting to settle down for a long stay. She touched his arm and he looked at her in surprise. "Why don't you go with an open mind? Maybe it'll be fun. Your father seemed like he might be willing to try to be . . . nicer."

Justus snorted. "That's the first time my father and the word 'nice' have ever been used together in a sentence." He leaned forward, balancing his elbows on his knees and studying his hands. "He mentioned that you and he . . . talked the other week."

Angela felt a twinge of apprehension. She'd never dreamed Vincent would talk to Justus, much less repeat anything she'd said. Had he told Justus his little theory about Angela caring for him? "Umm-hmmm," she said, taking a careful sip from her goblet.

Justus looked up at her, his sharp eyes focused on her face

as if he didn't want to miss so much as the blink of her eyes. "He said you gave him a hard time—about *me*."

"Oh." The effort to keep her face blank got to be too much for her, so she jumped up, grabbing her now empty glass. "More wine?" She went to the kitchen and poured herself another glass.

"No," Justus snapped, the first notes of exasperation creeping into his voice. "Did you?"

"Did I what?" She sponged up a drop of wine before it stained the counter.

"Give him a hard time."

Clearly he wasn't about to let it go, but she was equally determined not to tell him the details of the discussion. Forcing herself to meet his eyes, she smiled and shrugged. "Well, you know. There're a couple of chapters of Dr. Spock I think he missed."

Justus scowled and rolled his eyes, but said nothing. Angela, figuring it was safe, went back to her seat on the sofa and tucked her legs beneath her. "I want to ask you something, but not if it'll make you sad."

"Go ahead."

"Tell me about your mother."

His eyes lost their focus and he stared off in the distance. "My mother," he echoed softly, slumping back against the cushions and throwing his arm over his eyes. "God, I miss her. Especially now—at the holidays."

"What was she like?"

Justus dropped his arm. "She got pancreatic cancer when I was fifteen. She was dead in six weeks." Angela waited silently. "She was my biggest fan. She came to all my games. She made our Halloween costumes." Suddenly he grinned. "She beat my ass when I didn't listen."

Angela laughed, then decided to go ahead and push her luck some more. "Did she and your father have a good marriage?"

His smile vanished; his eyes went dark. "If by *good marriage* you mean she waited on him hand and foot and waited, night after night, for him to come home from the office at a decent hour, or to remember our games, or to go on vacation and not cancel it, or to eat dinner with us without leaving in the middle for a phone call, then, yes, they had a good marriage."

"Is that why you're so angry with your father?"

Justus slouched back again, staring at the ceiling. He sighed harshly. "What are the chances of you dropping this little interrogation and letting me enjoy Christmas Eve?"

"Not good."

Giving her a sharp, sidelong look, he said, "Just remember, Duchess. There are a few things I want to know about you, too. So you might want to keep a little concept I like to call *karma* in mind."

Angela nodded eagerly, figuring she'd cross that bridge when they came to it. "Fine."

He sighed again; his voice dropped. "Pops never liked me. Never."

"Justus—"

He held up a hand to stop her. "You know what? Don't bother. Okay? I know you want to say something comforting, like 'Oh, I'm sure your father loved you but couldn't express his feelings,' or 'Oh, I'm sure you were too young to really understand,' but don't bother. If we're going to talk about it, you need to listen. I was there. You weren't." To her surprise he seemed only resigned, not angry. "I'm sure he loved me, but he didn't *like* me. He didn't want me around. He didn't *get* me. And I didn't get him." He paused. "He and V.J. got each other."

"I'm sorry, Justus."

"Don't be," he said, shrugging impatiently. "I got over it a long time ago. Anyway, he was always a self-involved jerk, but I could take him or leave him, I guess. But when Mama died, he went into this poor widower routine. You know—sobbing at her funeral, mentioning her name every two seconds, her pictures all over the house, telling me and V.J. how much he loved her, how she was his whole life." His voice hardened; his jaw flexed. "Can you believe that crap? He broke her heart more times than I can count. He never paid her a damn bit of attention when she was alive, then when she died he pretended he'd been the greatest husband in the world. For sympathy." He shot to his feet, pacing away to stand at the sliding glass doors, pull back the blinds, and stare out. "And I'll never forgive him for that."

She sensed his withdrawal, which was the last thing she wanted. "Okay. That's enough of that topic. Since you answered my questions, I'll tell you something personal about *me*."

He turned from the doors and stared at her with open curiosity. "Let's hear it."

She placed her hand over her heart, as if her confession was almost too painful to make. "I wear a size nine shoe," she said solemnly. "I have big feet."

He gaped at her for an arrested second, then threw his head back to roar with laughter. "Oh, no." He came back to the sofa. "I'll ask the questions from now on."

"Go ahead," she said sourly, twisting to face him and rest her arm on the back of the sofa.

"What about your parents?"

That inevitable sadness crept over her heart and she propped her head on her hand, stalling. No amount of time, apparently, would make telling the story any easier. "My dad had a heart attack when I was ten. He was an architect. I kissed him good-bye when he dropped me off at school that morning—it was a Friday—and he promised he'd take us to Graeter's for ice cream after dinner. But when I got off the bus that afternoon there were a thousand cars at my house and I knew right away something terrible had happened."

Justus gently smoothed the hair away from the side of her face. "Sorry, Duchess."

She shrugged, looking away. "So I guess I'm a little sensitive about fathers with heart problems."

"What about your mother?"

"She died when I was a freshman in college. Colon cancer."

"You miss them."

Her throat constricted so painfully she doubted she'd be able to answer. "My—" She cleared her throat. "My whole family is together except for me."

He smiled faintly, absorbed with tracing the side of her face with his fingers. "Not your *whole* family, Angela."

Reaching for her wine gave her the excuse to pull away before she said or did something she didn't mean to do, although it was becoming harder to remember why she shouldn't be with Justus. "Are we going to talk about anything happy tonight?" She took a fortifying sip.

"Yeah, but not yet." He took a deep breath. "I want you to tell me about Ron."

"Ron?" she cried. "What more is there to tell?"

He stared intently at her, as if he expected her to tell him where to find the hidden treasure of the Knights Templar. "I don't know. You loved him, didn't you?"

For a minute she couldn't answer. Loved Ron? Had she? Once upon a time the answer would have been an automatic and enthusiastic *yes*, but those days felt like a millennium ago. They'd been together for so long and so much of her past was tied up with him, so many memories. Dinners, movies, weekends, vacations, cooking, making love, holidays. Shouldn't there now be a gaping hole in her life and heart where he used to be? There wasn't. When he'd dumped her, she'd been so worried about the holidays. Shouldn't her mind be focused on him this time of year? It wasn't—she hadn't thought of him until Justus brought him up.

She floundered helplessly, her mouth opening and closing. "He was perfect for me. I thought I'd marry him. I thought we'd get engaged today or tomorrow. A June wedding."

"You *loved* him," Justus insisted, his jaw rigid, apparently determined to wring the confession out of her.

Was it possible she'd loved only the idea of Ronnie? "I thought I did," she said faintly, aware of how faithless she must sound.

But to her surprise the storminess cleared from his expression and he looked away, like he was satisfied with her answer. After a minute he sprang to his feet and went to the kitchen. She stared after him as he swung open the refrigerator door and leaned inside. "Any more cake?"

By midnight they'd exhausted every conceivable topic of conversation, laid out all of Maya's gifts from Santa and stuffed her stocking. They'd even remembered to install batteries in the toys that needed it. It was time for bed, and Angela wanted to go. Just not alone.

"I should let you get some sleep. I'm not being a very good hostess." Standing, she smoothed her pants and pointed to a stack of linens and blankets on the chair. "There are towels and sheets and a blanket. This is a sleep sofa, but it's probably not big enough for you."

Justus stood slowly, shoved his hands in his pockets, and studied his shoes. "Great."

She went to the fireplace and reached for a candle. "Should I blow these out, or—"

"Leave them."

She smoothed her hair behind her ear with fidgety fingers. "And there's toothpaste in the bathroom, and shampoo—"

Finally he raised his gaze. "Then I have everything I need, don't I?"

She thought she heard the faintest trace of mockery in his tone, but his eyes were wide and innocent. "Well. Goodnight."

He grunted after her as she scurried from the room.

Angela flopped onto her back and kicked the covers off in frustration. She checked her nightstand clock for the ten millionth time: three-fifteen. Her body on fire for Justus, she hadn't slept a wink and had no prospects of doing so, either.

Why, oh why had she invited him to spend the night? What had made her think she had even the remotest possibility of sleeping when he was in the other room? After her own shower, she'd listened for him, acutely aware of everything he did even through her closed bedroom door. She'd heard the shower, water running, the toilet flush. And then—nothing. For three hours she'd heard nothing. Not the rustle of his sheets, not a snore. Nothing. Was he dead? Had he finally overdosed on carrot cake? How could he sleep so well when she couldn't sleep at all?

Maybe she would just check on him. He'd be asleep, she'd see with her own eyes that he was okay and not sleepless from wanting her, and she'd be able to go to sleep herself. End of insomnia. Without giving it any more conscious thought, she crept out of bed and down the hall in her bare feet, not bothering to throw her robe on over her white negligee. Peering around the corner into the living room she was astonished to see not only wasn't he sleeping on the sofa, he hadn't even made up the sofa—the linens, minus the towel and washcloth, lay exactly where she'd left them on the chair. Gasping, she wondered wildly whether he'd gone home, but he couldn't have because she'd have heard the door. From the corner of her eye she detected a slight movement and whirled to see him standing, his back to her, by the sliding glass doors with hands on his hips, his feet braced wide, the blinds opened enough now for him to gaze out.

He'd turned out the lamp, but the white glow from the Christmas tree and mantle garland let her see he wore only baggy flannel pajama bottoms of some indeterminate dark color. His naked back and arms, heavy with muscles, gleamed in the dim light. Endless broad shoulders only slightly narrower than the doors themselves, tapered to a narrow waist, forming a perfect vee. His butt flared, high and round, then gave way to powerful thighs. Bare feet peeked beneath the wide legs of his pajamas. Angela felt suddenly faint with lust; her breasts and sex swelled and ached insistently. His beauty and perfection were unearthly. He looked like Zeus, surveying the world of mere mortals from atop his perch on Mt. Olympus. Turning his head slightly, he stared over his shoulder, waiting for her to speak.

"I—I just came to get some water, and I—"

"No you didn't."

His voice, low and dangerous, yet seductive, struck terror in her heart. "No, really I—"

He made an aborted, irritated sound and even in the near dark she saw anger in his flashing eyes. "It's amazing to me," he said softly, "how you can be so brave when it comes to dealing with your sister's death and taking care of Maya and cutting my father down to size—"

Panic flared. "Justus—"

"—and such a lying little coward when it comes to dealing with me."

Pain—and fear—knifed through her chest. Nothing else hurt quite as much as the truth. For a long, challenging moment they stared at each other, but then she raised her chin and glared haughtily down her nose at him. "I don't know what you think you're talking about," she told him, "but I'm going back to bed."

Whirling, the silk of her nightgown swishing behind her, she made it all of two feet before he crossed the room in a flash of movement, blocking her from taking another step unless she wanted to walk directly into him. Staggering back several steps, she cried out.

"You're not going anywhere."

She began to tremble. So here was the wolf again. As much a part of Justus as the solicitous, supportive friend. She couldn't face him and would do anything to escape. Justus was right. She was a coward. If fleeing didn't work, maybe wheedling would.

"Please . . . don't do this . . . to me, Justus," she said through strange, panting little breaths. "Please let me go."

He stared dispassionately at her, his face as immovable as the pyramids. "Come here."

Angela stiffened, her feet attaching her to the floor like the roots of a banyan tree.

He held out a hand. "Come *here*," he commanded, leaving her no doubt she could do it voluntarily or not, but either way she would stand by his side.

Wobbly knees carried her to within three feet of him and then refused to go any farther. Her trembling blossomed into shaking, although whether from fear or desire she couldn't tell. When she stopped in front of him, his hot gaze roamed over her thin halter-style negligee, which was, she felt certain, transparent since she was backlit by the tree. His eyes lingered on the deep valley between her breasts and on her nipples, which were painfully aroused, as he could no doubt see. His breath turned harsh. Why hadn't she at least thrown on her robe? Better yet, why hadn't she stayed in her room, where it was safe?

His gaze, hungrier than before, flickered back to her face, and he abruptly held out his hand. "Give me your hand."

Paralysis had set in, but Angela managed to shake her head once. She could no more give him her hand than she could thrust it into the open jaws of a crocodile.

Justus growled with impatience. "Don't be ridiculous, Duchess. I can control myself. All I want is your hand. If I wanted more than that I'd already have you flat on your back—voluntarily—on the sofa right now, and we both know it."

"Oh, God," she whimpered, exhaling breathlessly.

He smiled slightly, his mouth, eyes, and voice softening. "Give me your hand."

Something came over her like a spell. She couldn't resist his seductive pull any more than a sailor could resist a siren. As if in a daze, she reached for him and the second she touched his smooth, warm palm she felt a jolt of energy as powerful as if a healer had laid hands on her. Strangely, she immediately felt the frustrated tension leak away from his body. He clasped her small hand between both of his and she watched, enthralled, as his eyes drifted closed. Raising it, he pressed her palm to his lips, where she felt the wet, warm tip of his tongue as he tasted her.

His face twisted as if he were in pain—or ecstasy. "Angela," he murmured, his voice raw and reverent. "*Angela.*"

Her whole body dissolved into a pulsing, hot liquid that flowed freely between her thighs. She tried half-heartedly to pull her hand away when what she really wanted to do was press her body full against his and beg him to touch her everywhere. "You shouldn't—"

He went rigid and his eyes flew open to glare at her with a virulence bordering on hatred. "Don't tell me not to touch you," he warned. "Not ever again. *Do you understand me?*"

"Yes," she whispered.

He relaxed again, pressing his mouth to the tender skin on her wrist now. Unbearable bolts of pleasure rocketed from her arm to her belly, then to her sex. He nipped her with his sharp teeth and she cried out, not certain how much longer her legs would support her. He stared at her, absorbing her every reaction with the intensity of an epidemiologist studying a new strain of the flu virus under his microscope.

"How long, Angela?" His lips nuzzled her wrist as he spoke. "How long are you going to make me wait for you?"

He loosened his grip and for one second her heart sank, fearing he'd let her go. But then he turned her hand and pressed it against the center of his smooth chest, where his heart hammered powerfully and uncontrollably. She gasped and he tightened his hand on top of hers, as if he feared she'd pull away.

"Another month? Another ten years? I can wait, but I just need to know how long. Please, Angela, *please*. Tell me."

Angela swayed on her feet. The agonized longing in his voice made her want to clap her hands over her ears and block out the sound. She was drowning fast, with no sign of rescue. His near nakedness, fresh, just-showered scent, masculinity, husky voice, primitive, savage hunger, and mastery over her—all those were bad enough. But this new, gentle, beseeching, vulnerable, *worshipful* Justus was irresistible.

"I'm scared," she whispered before she could stop herself.

"Why?" he cried, as if she'd given him the worst imaginable answer. "Tell me why."

A thousand insecurities streamed through her mind, none of which she could tell him: *Because you're so intense*; *because you seem to see right through me*; *because you're younger than me*; *because you're not the kind of man I ever imagined myself being with*; *because I don't think I can keep up with you in bed; because I think you'll get tired of me and move on to someone younger, prettier, and sexier.*

Because if I let you in you could destroy me and I would never recover.

"Because—because of Maya," she said, the first acceptable excuse she could think of.

He grabbed both of her hands, squeezed them, then pressed the palm of first one, then the other, to his mouth. "That's not it," he said flatly. "Tell me the truth."

Desperate now—of course he'd know she was lying!—she tried again to pull away; he frowned and tightened his grip. "Because it's too soon after Ron, and—"

His face twisted into a furious, obscene caricature of himself and she knew she'd gone too far by mentioning Ron and putting him between them. "I can make you forget Ron," he said roughly. "If you give me the chance."

He already had. Oh, God, he already had. "I don't—" She let out a bewildered laugh. "I don't understand you at all. You said I wasn't your type—"

"I lied."

"My *God.*" She snatched her hands away and clapped one hand to her forehead. "You'll say anything to get a woman into bed!"

His eyes narrowed. "I'll say anything to get *you* into bed," he said unapologetically.

"Yeah? And what about the woman *after* me?"

"I can't see that far in the future."

She started. Maybe he simply meant he couldn't predict the future, but she didn't think so. It sounded like he meant it would take him so long to get tired of her it was a non-issue. Could that possibly be true? Would it matter? A man like Justus loved women—*needed* women. He might think he could change, but he probably couldn't.

"You only want me so much," she said slowly, voicing one of her worst fears, "because you haven't had me yet."

"Wha—?" He stared disbelievingly—disgustedly, as if it was all he could do to force himself to even look at her. "Do you think I make the effort to be friends with every woman, the way I have with you?"

She threw her hands up in frustration. "I don't know! How would I know that?"

"Well, I don't," he snarled. "And I also don't take care of women the way I've taken care of you the last few weeks. And you sure as hell better believe I've never been this patient with a woman I wanted to sleep with."

"Why, Justus, I declare," she said, speaking in an exaggerated Southern accent and fluttering her hand over her heart, "you'll sweep me clean off my feet with all your sweet talk."

His eyes bulged like baseballs. "This is not a joke!" he roared.

"I know that!"

Facing off, they stared at each other, at an impasse. "I hope I live long enough to see the day when you realize this is *not just about sex*—" Breaking off, his breath harsh, he looked away and swiped his arm across his mouth. With his back to her, he put his hands on his hips and hung his head and for several charged seconds she just watched as his tense shoulders heaved up and down. After a while he collected himself and faced her again. The fight seemed to have gone out of his eyes. "And maybe one day you'll realize if you want anything worthwhile sometimes you have to take risks."

Suddenly he seemed to have had enough. He turned and shuffled to the sofa, collapsing heavily on it. He propped one elbow on the back and stared at the tree, refusing to look at her. "Go to bed," he said softly. "Maya'll be up soon."

"Justus—"

"Lock the door while you're at it."

Aroused, frustrated, confused, Angela could only gape at him. Realizing finally that he wouldn't say anything more to her tonight if his life depended on it, she turned and walked back to her room as gracefully as she could, which wasn't very.

She left the door unlocked.

Maya woke her by bouncing on her bed at six-thirty. Angela felt groggy, as if she'd had only ten minutes' sleep. Maya graciously allowed her about ten seconds to brush her teeth before she grabbed her hand and, laughing and chattering, tugged her to the living room to see if Santa came. Angela vaguely heard her delighted screeches as she surveyed the small toy store Santa had left under the tree: books, more Barbies and accessories, games, puzzles, stuffed animals, and dress-up clothes. She and Justus had, for obvious reasons, gone overboard with Maya's gifts this year, and Angela was very glad to see Maya so excited. But her attention was riveted on Justus.

He sat on the sofa, pretty much where she'd left him last night. Mercifully he'd thrown on a white T-shirt, not that that did anything to hide the rippling muscles in his back and chest or his granite biceps. Glancing at the pile of linens and blankets, she realized he was either as meticulous a folder as she was—doubtful—or he hadn't bothered with trying to sleep at all last night. Miraculously he looked fine, except for his eyes, which were a little bleary.

"Hey, Little Girl," he cried when he saw Maya. "Merry Christmas!"

"Merry Christmas," she sang over her shoulder, diving for the nearest present.

Justus grinned indulgently after her, then slowly looked to

Angela. She froze, lingering at the edge of the room. His gaze flickered over her navy velour robe as if it were invisible, and her sex and breasts tightened hopelessly in response. How silly of her to think something like a piece of clothing could protect her—in any way—from Justus and the power he had over her. She stiffened and waited for him to say something first.

His smile was equally rueful and sardonic. "Morning, Duchess. Sleep well?"

"No."

His eyes widened with surprise she'd admitted it. "Then I guess we're both in hell, huh?"

"Oooh, Twister!" Maya uncovered her game with a huge, flourishing rip of Santa wrapping paper, sparing Angela from having to answer Justus. Instead, she knelt beneath the tree to admire Maya's loot while Maya rummaged among the boxes.

"Uncle Justus! This one's for you!" She found a large square box and slid it across the carpet to him. "Open it! Open it!"

Justus stared at the box, which was wrapped with red paper and a thick red-and-green-plaid satin ribbon. His surprise was obvious, as if he'd stumbled upon Martians hiding under the tree. Blinking at Angela, he said, "This is for *me*?"

"Isn't that your name on the card?" she said, pointing and laughing.

Rather dubiously, Justus slid to the floor and picked up the box. "Wow. It's heavy."

Angela and Maya looked at each other and giggled conspiratorially. Maya clapped her hands. Justus looked at Maya, his eyes narrowing. "Is this from you, Little Girl?"

Maya looked to Angela. "It's from both of us," Angela said quickly.

Justus's smile widened into the boyish grin that always tied

Angela's belly in knots. He leaned down to whisper in Maya's ear. "Tell me what it is."

Maya shrieked with laughter. "No! It's a surprise!"

"You don't think I'm foolish enough to trust a three-year-old with a secret, do you?" Angela asked him smugly.

Justus humphed, then ripped into the package. Angela held her breath, more concerned with his reaction than she'd been with Maya's to her presents. Justus pushed the wrap aside, then gasped; his shocked gaze flew to Angela's, then returned to his present.

"My God, Angela!" he cried. "This is beautiful! You shouldn't have—it's too much."

"What is it?" Maya leaned over his shoulder to see.

"It's a chess set and board," Justus told her, sounding awed. "It's white-and-green onyx, Little Girl. That's a precious stone." Opening the box, he unwrapped a piece and gave it to Maya. "This is the black king—"

"But it's green."

"Well, yes." Justus laughed and took the piece back from her. "But the colored piece is always considered 'black' in chess."

"Oh." Maya turned to her pile of new stuffed animals, apparently having had more than enough of the whole chess discussion.

Angela wanted to dance with glee. He liked it! *He liked it!* It was an extravagant gift, of course, much more than she usually paid for a Christmas present, but when she'd seen it on some chess Web site—she'd spent hours on the Internet; who knew there were so many chess fanatics in the world?—she'd known Justus had to have it. And now, seeing his face, she knew she'd been right.

"Do you like it?" she asked him, grinning idiotically.

"Yeah," he said hoarsely. "I like it."

"I thought you would."

He rewrapped the king piece very carefully, as if it were a vial of nitroglycerin that would explode if he didn't handle it properly, then placed it back into the box. "You know," he said without looking at her, "I think Santa may have left something in your stocking."

Frowning, she looking at the mantle. "I don't have a stock—" The protest died away and she cried out with surprise. There, hanging next to Maya's regulation red flannel stocking with white trim and her name in glitter across the top, a creation too beautiful to be a mere stocking had appeared since last night. A dark, rich purple velvet, it was embroidered with silver-and-gold thread in an intricate diamond pattern and studded with glittering crystals.

"Oh, Justus, what a gorgeous stocking!"

One side of his mouth twisted up. "The stocking's not the present, you silly girl."

Maya, from the far side of the tree nearest the sliding glass doors, cried out, "Oooh! Easy Bake Oven!"

Sparing her only a quick glance, Angela sprang to her feet and rooted around in her stocking. She felt a small, hard box at the bottom and pulled it out; brightly wrapped in elegant green paper with an elaborately tied gold lace bow, it was obviously a jeweler's box of some kind, although too big to be a ring—now why on earth would that thought even cross her mind?

Looking up, Angela discovered Justus staring intently. "Open it."

Her fingers trembling with excitement, she did. Inside the black velvet box was a stunning brooch: three long feathers that curled at the tops—plumes—stood inside a gold crown; the feathers were made entirely of diamonds. Of course the gems weren't real—probably even Justus's father couldn't afford such a piece with real diamonds—but it was an exquisite, expensive reproduction nonetheless, and the most wonderful gift she'd ever received in her life. Angela gasped, staring disbelievingly at it.

"It's a—" Justus began.

"I know what it is," she said faintly. "It's a duchess's pin."

The beginnings of a smile softened the intensity of his expression, and the vast warmth in his eyes was unmistakable. "You know it?"

Gently she traced the pin with the tips of her fingers. "It's the Prince of Wales pin. The Duke of Windsor—King Edward—gave it to his duchess, Wallis Simpson. And after she died, Elizabeth Taylor bought it at auction."

"And now it's for *my* duchess."

Their gazes locked and held for an electric moment while Angela's heart pounded so furiously she began to feel lightheaded. With a rush of despair she realized one thing with sudden and utter clarity: somehow—completely against her will—she'd fallen hopelessly in love with this man.

Chapter 18

He had to find her, and soon.

A quick glance at his watch told him what his knotted gut already knew: it was almost midnight and his precious little bit of remaining time was fast running out. The New Year's Eve party hummed along at full speed, and Justus had been to enough of these gigs in his twenty-seven years to know how they worked: at midnight everyone broke out ridiculous hats, kissed, drank champagne, and sang. He had no intention of missing the kissing part. His frustration grew. With each tick of his watch he felt chances slipping away, opportunities evaporating; magic vibrated in the air tonight, and he fully intended to take advantage of it. If only he could find her. Craning his neck to look over the black-tie-clad crowd, he paused to consider the irony of his situation. Here it was, ten years later, and he was in the same ballroom—it looked almost exactly the same, with white tablecloths, low lighting, glittering candles, obscenely expensive centerpieces of holly, ivy, and berry laced with gold satin ribbons—looking for the same woman.

He devoutly hoped tonight would end more satisfactorily than that night had.

"Don't worry. She's here."

Startled, Justus turned to see his father's girlfriend Lena, champagne flute in hand, watching him with a little more amusement than was strictly necessary. As always, she looked very beautiful. Tonight she'd chosen a shimmery gown in some sort of a pale pink color. Smiling, he leaned down and kissed her soft cheek. "I have no idea what you're talking about."

Lena's smile widened. They stood side by side and stared out over the crowded dance floor. "Oh, I think you do. You remember Angela. She's here. And you and I both know she's the reason you've come to your father's big party for the first time in the last ten years."

Justus fought and lost his struggle not to flush like a twelve-year-old with his first crush. Still, he tried to keep cool and, recovering, stuck his hands in his pants pockets. "I take it you think something's going on with me and Angela."

"Isn't there?"

Grinning, he dropped his head to study his shoes. "Let's just cut through all the cat-and-mouse nonsense, Lena, and you can go ahead and tell me whatever it is you want to say."

She faced him, beaming as if she'd discovered a calorie-free chocolate alternative. Reaching up, she straightened his bow tie and smoothed his lapels. "Angela's a wonderful girl. You could do worse."

"Worse for what?"

Frowning, she said, "Worse for someone to get serious about, of course."

An automatic denial rose in his throat, but he clamped his mouth shut. Why pretend? Leaning down, he kissed her again on the cheek. "Did I tell you look beautiful?"

Lena giggled like a schoolgirl, making a show of primping her hair. "Ah, well."

"You're damn near perfect." He caught sight of his father

across the dance floor, waving his arms as he talked to a laughing couple. "Except for your taste in men, that is. Do yourself a favor, though. Just don't ever marry him."

He'd been joking—mostly joking—but Lena's face fell anyway. An awkward silence followed and Justus wished the floor would open up and swallow him.

"I'd marry your father in a minute if he ever asked me," Lena said quietly. "But he won't."

"Why not?" Justus demanded, stunned. This poor woman had devoted years of her life to Vincent, and he'd never asked her to marry him? How could Vincent waste her time like that?

Lena took a sip of champagne, then lowered the glass and studied the bubbles as if they contained the secret to happiness. "He's always said he'll only ever have one wife."

"But he loves you? . . ."

Her smile was sad but resigned. "Not like he loved her." Shrugging, she reached up to stroke his cheek. "I've made my peace with it. Anyway, why are we talking about this when Angela's out there somewhere, waiting for you?"

Troubled, Justus nodded and watched as she moved away to greet some other guests. Had his father really loved his mother, then, or was this just another one of his attempts to play the martyr? And why did he care one way or the other? It really didn't matter. Shaking his head, he went to the enclave where the musicians played in order to have a word with the pianist.

And then he'd find Angela.

"I still can't believe you wore that dress, Angela," Carmen said in a scandalized stage whisper. "You look amazing. None of the men in the room can take their eyes off you. Neither can I, for that matter."

Angela smiled nervously, tossed her hair—which she'd curled, waved, and tousled until she looked like some courtesan freshly emerged from her bed after an afternoon with her lover—and resisted the urge to fidget with the Swarovski crystal-covered spaghetti straps of her dress. She felt naked. When Vincent, in what was probably another one of his misguided attempts to win her favor, had invited her to his legendary black tie New Years' Eve party—the one she'd read about for years in the Life section of the *Enquirer*—she'd jumped at the chance. She hadn't had any other plans, and she certainly didn't want to spend the night on the sofa watching the ball drop in Times Square. So she'd sent Maya off to spend the night with the housekeeper at Vincent's and dragged Carmen along. Now it was almost midnight, and they'd wined and dined their way across the glittering ballroom, listening to a jazz combo and eating scallops, lamb chops, caviar, miscellaneous pastries, and other delicacies too numerous to count.

But as for the dress, well, that was a little harder to explain, especially to herself. Despite years of swearing she'd never set foot in the overpriced place, she'd immediately set off for Sak's downtown and found this dress that properly belonged on a goddess, or at least a Hollywood movie star, not a mere mortal like herself.

The bias-cut, floor-length satin gown was made of a simple, silvery gray silk and had a plunging neckline that was, she devoutly hoped, sexy without being slutty. The back of the dress was pretty much nonexistent. Nevertheless, in theory and, on the hanger, the dress was tasteful and lovely. On her body, however, it slid over her curves like running water. Worse, the bodice, such as it was, and straps seemed to have been designed for someone a little less . . . endowed than she was. She would have to remember not to raise her arm to wave to anyone tonight, or else this provocative dress would become a scandal of Jayne Mansfield proportions.

The thing was, she'd known all this about the dress within ten seconds of trying it on at Sak's. And she'd bought it anyway. Because she'd wanted Justus to see her in it. And in case the message wasn't clear enough, she'd taken her brooch and pinned it to the vee between her breasts, where he couldn't miss it.

"Do I look like a slut?"

"God, no!" Carmen cried. "You look gorgeous! You've got great shoulders, by the way. I could never carry off this dress. It's just not the kind of thing I ever thought you'd wear."

"Me, either," Angela muttered into her champagne glass as she took a sip. "I'm freezing my butt off."

"Hey, listen." Carmen hesitantly touched her arm, as if she wasn't quite sure how to tell her something important. "I hate to do this tonight, but I thought you'd want to know. Olivia Warren faxed over her preliminary report today."

"The case worker! What did she say?"

Carmen smiled gently and Angela's heart fell through the floor. "She said that while you and Justus both have great apartments and jobs and seem loving—"

"Blah, blah, blah," Angela interrupted impatiently. "Cut to the chase."

"She's concerned about your work hours and your ability to supervise Maya effectively. Also she knows you haven't exactly been close to Maya up till now."

You're the only aunt she has! You and she are the only family I have!

Angela felt ill suddenly. Closing her eyes to block out the crowd and the tables and the candles, she pressed her hand to her forehead. Carolyn's reproachful voice, however, was not so easy to get rid of. She opened her eyes to find Carmen, obviously worried, staring at her.

"So that's it, then? Maya goes to Justus?"

"No, that's not it." Carmen gripped Angela's forearms, and Angela gratefully covered her hands with her own. "We'll still have our day in court."

Have you ever thought about how much it would mean to me if my sister actually liked my daughter? Can't you do it for me?

"But the expert thinks I'm not the best choice for Maya." Angela pressed a hand to her stomach and tried not to get sick all over her beautiful dress before Justus even saw her in it.

"But that's not the only evidence we'll have, Angela. The child psychologist you hired for Maya could be very helpful, and didn't you tell me Vincent said he'd be willing—"

"No."

Carmen started unpleasantly. "Why not?"

Over Carmen's shoulder Angela saw Vincent, looking dapper in his tuxedo, walking toward them, and seeing him reminded her that this really wasn't the time or place for such a discussion. "Because," she said, keeping her voice low, "I don't want Vincent's help. I will never do anything to come between Justus and his father. So you can just forget about it."

Carmen's lips thinned, leaving Angela no doubt she was less than thrilled about her edict. "Fine," she snapped. "But you're not leaving me much to work with." Turning on her stiletto heels, she stalked off toward the pastry table just as Vincent arrived.

He raised an eyebrow. "Was it something I said?"

"She's angry with me."

"Oh." He looked her over with an admiring, though respectful, gaze. "You're beautiful."

The more time Angela spent with Vincent, the more she saw how much he and Justus had in common. They both, for instance, were handsome, vital, and interesting. But more than that, they had a virile sort of confidence that, probably more often than not, proved fatal to its female recipient.

"Thank you." She raised her champagne flute in a toast. "And you, once again, have thrown a wonderful party."

He inclined his head, accepting his due. "I'm glad you could come. And I want to thank you—you apparently got Justus to come, too. That's something that hasn't happened in an ice age." He raised his champagne to his smiling lips. "Maybe I should have you take a look at my stock portfolio. See what sort of magic you can work on *that*."

Vincent was teasing of course, and if she had any sense whatsoever she would just ignore him. But at the mention of Justus's name she was suddenly too excited to worry about playing games with his father. She and Carmen had been here for nearly two hours and they hadn't seen Justus; Angela had worried he'd changed his mind at the last moment and decided not to come.

"Justus is here?"

Vincent smiled that nasty little knowing smile she hated so much. "I saw him over talking to the pianist a minute ago. Why do you ask, dear? Are you anxious to see him?" She narrowed her eyes and prepared to blast him with a sharp retort, but before she could say anything, he said, "Don't worry, Angela. When he sees you in that dress, Justus will be here so fast it'll make your head spin." He put his glass on a nearby table, then took hers and did the same. "In the meantime, you can dance with an old man." With the gallantry of a knight helping his queen down from her horse, he took her elbow and led her to the crowded dance floor.

Angela followed along, ignoring her desperate impulse to look around for Justus. She didn't want to be rude or, worse, transparent. Placing one palm on Vincent's shoulder, she gave him her other hand and they moved to the music.

"It'll be midnight soon, Angela. Do you have any resolutions for the new year? Maybe . . . to make partner at your firm?"

"That would be nice."

He stared intently at her. "Can I give you a piece of advice?"

"Could I stop you?"

Chuckling, he said, "Hard work has its place, of course, but it's not everything. Family is more important—family is *everything*." He gave her hand a slight squeeze for emphasis. "I've been where you are, and if I had it to do over again, I would. I don't think anyone on their death bed has ever looked back and said, 'Gee, I wish I'd spent more time at the office.'"

"Is that your regret, Vincent? You didn't spend enough time with your family?"

His nostrils flared and for one astonished second she thought maybe he'd actually choke up right here on the dance floor. "I have so many regrets I wouldn't know where to begin." He blinked furiously and pulled himself together. Starting, he stared off over her shoulder. "And now here's someone who's looking for you."

Angela's pulse quickened and she knew, even before she turned within the circle of Vincent's arms and saw him, that Justus had arrived.

Justus approached slowly, his expression unreadable. Very discreetly his gaze flickered over her, from head to toe, before locking with hers. An appreciative, slightly mocking half-smile crossed his lips. "Hello, Duchess."

Suddenly breathless, the best she could manage was a squeaky, "Hi."

In his simple double-breasted tuxedo he was astonishingly

handsome. God had obviously loosed him for the sole purpose of wreaking havoc on women everywhere. On top of everything else—his brooding, hooded eyes, his tender lips, his size, his height, and his overwhelming masculinity—he wore a slightly more generous dash of cologne tonight. The spicy notes quickly fogged her brain with a haze of desire until she could hardly think.

Without looking away from her, Justus said, "Happy New Year, Vincent. Great party."

"Glad you could come," Vincent said archly, keeping his arm around her waist.

Justus took her elbow. "I'll take it from here, Pop."

Angela moved toward him, but Vincent's grip on her tightened. "We weren't finished with our dance yet."

Angela heard the amusement in Vincent's voice but, judging from the way Justus's jaw tightened, *he* didn't. "Oh, you're finished, Pop." Very firmly he wrapped his arm around her waist and pulled her to him, leaving Vincent no choice but to let her go or risk making a scene.

Vincent smiled smugly, having achieved his rather obvious goal of getting a rise out of Justus. "Well, you two enjoy what's left of the evening."

"Yeah," Justus said shortly, narrowing his eyes at his father. "We'll do that. And you don't want to neglect your other guests."

Laughing, Vincent turned and wove his way through the crowd.

Dropping his hand, seemingly oblivious to the fact they were talking but not dancing on the dance floor, Justus glared down at her. "What's that you're not wearing?"

Angela gave him her most innocent look. "Oh, this?" She raised a hank of the skirt between two fingers. "I like to call it a dress."

His brows lowered until they formed a single, forbidding black line over his eyes. "Did you borrow it from Janet?"

She laughed gaily, happier than she could remember being since . . . well, since forever. Touching the brooch, which was snuggled between her breasts, she said, "I picked the best dress to show off my beautiful pin."

Dropping his head, he stared openly—hungrily—at her cleavage, then hastily looked away, rubbing the back of his neck. "Trust me. No one's looking at the damn pin."

Stepping closer she pouted a little, acting disappointed. "You don't like my dress?"

Justus stared intently, his eyes warm now, all traces of irritation gone. Around them the other guests paused and clapped, and she realized for the first time that the music had stopped. "Angela," he said, his voice hoarse, "you're so beautiful it hurts to look at you."

Just then the pianist—a surprisingly young man with a clear, high tenor—struck up the chords that had haunted her for ten years and began to sing "A Kiss to Build a Dream On."

Angela gasped with surprise. Justus watched her, his sharp eyes never wavering from her face. "Do you like this song?" he murmured, opening his arms.

Gratefully she stepped close, wrapping one arm around his neck and taking his palm with the other hand. "Yes," she whispered, pressing her body, including her hips, full against his. Every tender curve and hollow of her body found a home against the granite ridges and angles of his. "It's my favorite."

Chapter 19

Justus shuddered and passion burned, white hot, in his eyes. Ever so subtly, as they swayed with the music, he thrust his hips against her soft, wet loins letting her feel his arousal. Angela managed not to cry out, but she couldn't suppress a tiny whimper. "*Justus.*"

Never looking away, he planted one hand, fingers splayed wide, on the small of her bare back, caressing gently. Her eyes fluttered closed; her knees went weak; she collapsed slightly against him, allowing her forehead to rest against the smooth, hot skin of his chin, his breath feathering her face. With agonizing slowness he trailed his fingers up her back, then sifted them under her hair. When he found her nape he massaged, gently but firmly, and Angela began to tremble.

"My God," she whispered. "You don't play fair."

"I'm not playing." Unsmiling, he pulled away enough to raise her hand to his lips. Paralyzed, she watched as he kissed her knuckles, tasting her with the scalding tip of his tongue. This time she didn't even bother trying to fight the moan that escaped her lips.

A sudden commotion around them drowned out the rest of the song. Angela was vaguely aware of people hastily passing around noisemakers and hats. Was it midnight? Who cared? Justus seemed not to notice, either.

The crowd began to chant, softly at first, then louder. "Ten . . . nine . . . eight . . . seven . . ."

"Did I tell you my resolution for the new year?" she asked, standing on her tiptoes to whisper in his ear and tightening her fingers around his neck.

"No," he said faintly.

"This year I'm going to take a few more risks."

His eyes widened with surprise.

". . . three . . . two . . . one—Happy New Year!" the crowd roared. All around them people threw themselves into each other's arms, hugging and kissing with abandon.

Angela lifted her chin, parting her lips. "Happy New Year, Justus."

For an arrested moment Justus just stared at her mouth. He seemed frozen with indecision. Maybe he knew, as well as she did, that a kiss on the lips between them could never be just a kiss. Finally he blinked and came to life. Slowly, painstakingly, he lowered his head and fitted his lips to hers for a kiss so tender she wanted to sob with the perfection of it. Drunk with desire, she brushed his lips with her own, opening to him, but he stiffened slightly and brought his hands up to keep her from coming any closer. After an agonized second he pulled away entirely, dropping his hands.

"Happy New Year, Angela." Turning, he moved to leave the dance floor.

He wasn't just going to leave her, was he? Like that? With no conscious thought her arm shot out and grabbed his hand. Startled, he looked down at their joined hands, then up at her face, a question in his eyes.

Even though she knew what she had to say—knew what he wanted to hear—her courage failed her. She couldn't get her dry lips to form the words and she floundered, opening and closing her mouth. His face darkened but he squeezed her hand supportively.

"I'm not going to make this easy for you," he told her, his voice low. "If you have something to say to me, just say it."

Afraid of his rejection, but petrified of his acceptance, Angela took a deep breath and chose: she couldn't wait any longer. Ten years and several-odd weeks had been much, much too long to wait. She loved him—completely, passionately, and crazily. In a way she'd never loved Ron and could never love anyone else. Telling him was out of the question, though. She could never give him any more power over her than he already had. Even so, she had to touch Justus tonight or die. She simply couldn't see any other choices. And if tomorrow he told her it had all been a giant mistake, or that she hadn't satisfied him, or left her and returned to Janet, well, she would deal with that tomorrow. For right now there was only tonight—this moment. She wouldn't waste it.

Stepping closer, her gaze locked with his, she said, "I need you, Justus. Come home with me. Make love to me."

Justus made a strangled sound; his eyes widened; his nostrils flared. She realized the harsh breathing she heard over the noise of the crowd singing *Auld Lang Syne* was his. For a second—but just a second—he again seemed frozen with indecision. But suddenly his hand clamped down around hers as if to prevent her from changing her mind and trying to get away. "Let's go," he told her.

By the time he drove to Angela's, Justus had worked himself up into a righteous fury. He stalked down the long hall to her door, pounded on it with a fist trembling with equal parts excitement and anger, and waited. Her cheery lighted

Christmas wreath, with its elaborate gold satin ribbon, berries, holly, and beaded gold garland, only fueled his fire. That was his Angela, always proper, always efficient. No doubt on January second, at twelve-oh-one A.M., she'd be out here taking down this wreath and putting up one for Valentine's Day.

The door swung open and there she was, the source of all his misery, standing there in the damn dress that had obviously been designed for the sole purpose of driving unsuspecting men, like him, out of their minds. Things had been bad enough when she dressed plainly. Now she'd started flaunting her incredible body—how *did* those tiny little straps support the weight of her amazing breasts?—and wearing clothes that left little, well, nothing, to his imagination. He had more than half a mind to grab the throw she kept on the arm of the sofa and toss it over her shoulders so his heart would stop pounding so hard and he could think.

Her eyes glittered with excitement, a pretty flush stained her face and neck a warm reddish brown and her chest heaved slightly, almost in a pant. A glorious smile bloomed across her face and sent a painful stab of longing right to his gut.

"Hi," she said breathlessly, as if she'd just run up twelve flights of steps. "I was afraid you'd changed your mind."

He stared at her dewy lips and tried to remember what he'd wanted to say. "No . . . I, uh . . . No."

Nodding, she let him in. He shoved his hands deep into his pants pockets, mostly to keep himself from reaching for her, and walked into the living room. He did not bother to sit down—he was way too agitated for that.

Her happy smile faded and she touched his arm. "What is it, Justus? Is something wrong?"

Stalling, he noticed for the first time the cozy, romantic scene—the crackling fire, the lit candles on the mantle, jazz—it sounded like Wynton Marsalis playing on the CD changer—and the bottle of champagne chilling in a pretty silver bucket on the counter. Knowing he was a goner no matter how this conversation unfolded, he broke out into a fine sweat. "I'm . . . not sure we should do this."

She recoiled as if he'd slapped her. "Why?" she asked, her voice filled with dread.

Swallowing convulsively, he tried to gather his thoughts. *Yes, Justus, by all means tell the woman why, after waiting ten years and several desperate weeks for her, you would reject her when she finally offers herself up on a silver platter. And while you're at it, why don't you explain how, in the car on the way over here, you suddenly decided to warn her about the magnitude of the commitment she was making? And feel free to mention how your pride made the ridiculous and insupportable decision not to have her at all if she was still hung up on Ron.*

He cleared his dry throat. "Because I'm not sure what's changed. You've been holding me off for weeks and then all of a sudden—"

"It's not all of a sudden."

"—you decide you're ready. What's changed? Was it the champagne? The dance?"

"No. I'd decided before I ever saw you tonight at the party that I—"

"But why?" He heard the frustration creep into his voice and forced himself to stay calm. "What changed your mind? What's different?"

A slight frown line appeared and immediately disappeared between her delicate brows—come and gone so quickly he'd have missed it if he'd blinked. But in that millisecond he glimpsed something dark, like fear or panic—as if something *had* changed, but she didn't dare tell him what. Whatever it was, she blinked it away and gave him a sensual, heavy-lidded smile instead.

"Justus." Her voice dropped an octave, taking on a seductive quality that slid right under his skin and caused him to swell despite his upset. She sidled closer. "I want you. You know that. I'm ready to make love to you."

His conflicted misery made him angry again. Who'd have thought his sweet Angela would play such dirty, effective tricks? "Stop trying to manage me!" he shouted. She flinched, then gaped. He wheeled away, propped his elbow on the mantle right on top of her stupid, fragrant garland, and fought a losing battle to remain rational. She was happy to admit she *wanted* him, but didn't trust him enough to tell him what was really going on. God, what a kick in the teeth; why didn't she just go ahead and spit in his face? Most women *wanted* him. Janet, Renee, Julie, and too many other women to count *wanted* him. He wanted Angela to want him, of course, but he needed her to care about him. To love him. To *trust* him, have faith in him.

"You want me?" Disgusted, he stalked back to lean down in her face, throw his arms wide, and taunt her. He looked her up and down with his most insulting leer. "You want me and . . . what? Your body's a little hot since Ron dumped you? You finally got horny enough to give in? Is that it?"

Angela went wild. With an outraged cry she shoved him, hard, on the chest as if she actually thought she could throw him out. He stood his ground, his heart thundering.

"You get out of here!" she shrieked, shoving him again. "Don't you ever talk to me like that!"

Something inside him snapped. How dare she play the insulted victim when she held all the cards over him—had always held all the cards? Quick as a flying bullet he lashed out and grabbed her roughly around her upper arms and shook her once. "Because if this is just about some itch you have, you can get someone else to scratch it!"

She cried out again, wrenching free but staying right in his face. Tears shimmered in her eyes, but she stubbornly lifted her chin. "Why are you doing this? You've said you wanted me—"

Disgusted, with himself as much as her, he pivoted away again, pounding one fist on the wall as he passed. What had happened to him? What was he doing? She wanted him, he wanted her, they'd waited long enough—everything should be coming up roses. But it wasn't. For the first time in his life having a woman's body wasn't enough—nowhere near enough. Frustrated, he bent double at the waist, propped his hands on his thighs and fought and lost his battle for control. Panting now, he jerked upright.

"I spilled my guts to you!" he roared, waving his arms. "Over and over again I spilled my guts to you! And now you finally say 'jump' and I'm supposed to say 'how high' without wanting to know why? Are you out of your mind?"

She froze, staring at him. In her wide eyes he saw her sudden comprehension and fear. God, why was she still so afraid? He couldn't understand it. Didn't she know she was everything to him? That he would do anything for her?

"What do you want?" she whispered.

His throat constricted, making it impossible for his lungs to draw air. For long seconds he couldn't form any coherent thought at all, much less get the words out. "I want to make sure you understand what I've been telling you: that this is about more than sex." His mouth twisted, and he felt the bile rise from his belly, as if his body violently rejected what his mouth was about to say. "So if your body is the only thing you're offering me, then let's just call it a night."

Hours seemed to pass as they stared at each other, both as

immovable as hundred-year oaks. Finally she blinked. Shaking her head with disbelief, she let out a strange, high-pitched little laugh. "No, it's not just about sex." An odd, wild light filled her glittering eyes, almost as if *she* was the one on the verge of losing control. "This is about me thinking about you every waking minute of every hour of *every single day!*"

His entire body jerked with shock and relief.

She whirled and paced away, the silly little train of her dress flowing behind her. "This is about me wondering where you are and who you're with and when you'll be with *me* again!"

"Angela—" he reached a hand out to her.

"No!" She threw both hands up in a don't-touch-me gesture. "This is what you want to hear, isn't it? Well, hear it! *Hear it!*" She looked as if she'd happily kill him for making her strip herself bare like this, but then suddenly the fight seemed to leave her. Pressing her hand to her heart, her face slowly softened. "Oh, God."

"Angela—"

Her eyes swam in tears, but she blinked them all back except one that splashed on her cheek. Swiping it away, she smiled a little. "And I can't"—she took a choppy breath—"live through another night without knowing what it feels like . . . to have you inside me." She ran her hand under her nose. "Happy now?"

God, he was. He felt completely drained, as if he'd just finished a triathlon. He'd gladly play in a thousand championship games rather than endure another scene like this one. What would he have done if she'd changed her mind? He couldn't bear the thought.

Suddenly lightheaded with relief he dropped his head forward and pressed his hands to his temples, but it didn't help. Exhausted, his legs gave way and he fell lightly to his knees in front of her, throwing his arms around her waist and burying his face in the silky sheath of her belly.

"Justus." Her arms clamped around his neck like manacles. "*Justus.*"

The need in her voice almost matched his own. He inhaled deeply, breathing in her skin's floral fragrance—lilies, he thought—and, underneath that, her body's musk. His body roared to life. He couldn't control his frantic hands. They slid down from her waist to cup and knead her delicious, round, satin-covered butt, which was every bit as firm as he'd expected it to be. Angela trembled so violently he thought she might vibrate right out of his arms. Drunk now that he had her willingly—eagerly—he clenched his hands on her wide hips and nuzzled her sex until she writhed uncontrollably. Raising his head, he saw her standing above him, eyes closed, head back, breasts thrust forward, lips parted—the sexiest sight he'd ever seen. Her uninhibited sensuality stunned him. If this was what she was like when he'd barely touched her, he could hardly wait to see what she did when she came. His groin, squeezed painfully inside his trousers, screamed for release.

"Angela."

He waited until she dazedly lifted her head and looked down at him with unfocused eyes, her hair shifting and falling over her shoulders. One final warning seemed like a good idea. He'd give her this one last chance to change her mind, because once she was his he'd never let her go. Never. "I want everything."

A seductive smile flitted across her lips. Tossing her hair, staring him in the eye with an unspoken but unmistakable challenge, she deliberately unwound his hands from her hips and pressed them to her soft, heavy breasts, where her aroused nipples felt like cherries under his palms. He heard a weird, strangled sound and realized vaguely he was the one who'd made it.

Letting her head fall back again, she said, "Take it. Whatever you want . . . it's yours."

Chapter 20

Her words unleashed something inside both of them, and they lunged for each other, hard and fast. Crying out, unable to believe she'd just given him carte blanche to touch her—to do whatever he wanted—Justus roughly grabbed her face, angled it, and closed his mouth over hers. He kissed her hungrily, savagely, his tongue thrusting deep. When he nipped her bottom lip she bit him back, driving them both wild. Breaking away, he dragged his hands over her cheeks and into her hair, pulling her head back to expose her neck.

"*Angela.*"

With a low growl he buried his lips and tongue in the hollow between her collarbones, then ran his mouth up the side of her neck to her ear, scraping his teeth along her tender flesh as he went. His hands pulled her hair, hurting her, but it was a joyous pain she would never get enough of. She laughed and cried while her clumsy, trembling fingers slid his heavy silk tuxedo jacket over his massive shoulders and down his arms. Somehow she worked free the buttons on his shirt and pushed that off too. He jerked his T-shirt off over his head by himself, too impatient to wait for her to do it.

Pausing to admire his naked chest and arms right now was

out of the question—he immediately yanked her back into his brutal embrace, kissing her and roaming his hands over her bare back—so she frenetically rubbed the tight, corded muscles that apparently covered every inch of him. His skin was as smooth and warm as bath water, and she broke their kiss to press her face into the strong, satiny column of his neck, smell his spicy scent, and *absorb* him. When she touched her tongue to his hot, slightly salty flesh, a deep groan told her he approved. Grabbing her butt he stroked her hard, up and down, up and down, grinding her against his raging erection. Every drop of blood in her body flooded her already full loins, and if he hadn't been holding her so tightly she would surely have fallen to the floor with dizziness.

Whimpering with need, she scratched his back hard enough to leave welts. "Hurry," she said, panting. "*Hurry.*"

Reaching between them, he pressed his hands to her breasts, stroking and molding them with no regard for her expensive dress. She didn't care. His hands roved over her bodice, then went to the sides and back, searching.

"Tell me where the zipper is before I rip your pretty dress," he growled in her ear, biting her lobe.

"I—it's—" Breathing was hard enough without having to explain that the zipper was cleverly and invisibly sewn into the side of the dress, up under her arm. "I can't—"

"Forget it." Stooping slightly, he slowly slid his hands under her dress and up the insides of her legs to her underwear, which he quickly divested her of. As she stepped out of her panties, the dress slithered back down to her toes. Standing again, he held her black lace panties high for a brief inspection.

"String bikinis?" His eyes glittered and one side of his mouth twisted up in what could have been amusement. "You're full of surprises, aren't you?" She didn't really understand words by then, and he didn't bother waiting for an answer.

Squatting this time, he started at the bottom again, sliding the silk over the exquisitely sensitive skin behind her knees to her waist. Once there he stood, held the dress up with one hand, and slid the other hand down over her butt and between her legs, stroking her from behind. The room swam in and out of focus until Angela finally gave up and let her head fall back and her eyes drift closed.

He stopped. She opened her eyes and whimpered a protest until he stooped again and rubbed her—slowly, slowly—from the front with his long, shapely fingers. She moaned loudly. For several seconds he stared, as if hypnotized, at the black triangle between her legs, which only made her wetter. Angela held her breath. Finally he cursed and, kneeling, pressed a hot, wet, sucking kiss to her core and she keened, mindless with pleasure. Her knees finally gave way and she started to collapse, but his strong arms held her up. Surging to his feet, holding the hem of her dress up around her waist, he put his hands on her butt, lifted her, took a couple of steps, then sat her on a cool, smooth surface.

Dazed, she looked down and realized disinterestedly she was sitting on the portion of the counter separating the kitchen from the living room; aliens could have invaded the apartment in that moment and she wouldn't have noticed or cared. He fumbled with the front of his pants, opening them, and she reached for the bulging front of his heather gray boxer briefs. The second she touched his hard length, he removed her hand and brought it to his lips for a kiss.

"Next time," he said apologetically.

The insistent throbbing in her sex increased. "Please, Justus," she begged, squirming and spreading her legs wide for him. "I need you inside me. Now. *Please. Pleee-ease.*"

In a flash of movement he ripped open a small package with his teeth, sheathed himself, and pulled her to the edge of the counter. Angela, having lost all track of time or place or anything else other than her need to make Justus a part of her body, felt grateful he'd remembered. With one violent stroke he came inside, burying himself to the hilt, stretching and filling her to the breaking point. The tightness and friction in her throbbing sex increased until the pleasure was excruciating. Crying again with joy, Angela wrapped her arms around his neck and her legs—with her strappy stilettos still on her feet—around his waist, giving him more access.

"Oh, *God*, Angela," he cried. "Angela, *Angela*." Pulling him close she felt the urgent trembling in his arms and the slick sweat covering his forehead. "God, I've waited for this."

She'd fully expected—braced for—wild pounding, but he froze, panting and staring her in the face. He seemed prepared to wait—what was he waiting for?—all night. His stillness, perversely, drove her insane and she writhed shamelessly against him.

"Please," she begged. "Please don't tease me. Please don't do this to me."

"Do what?" His wild, hot, intense gaze held hers and she wondered if he realized he owned her now—her body was, and would always be, a toy he possessed and could play with at will. She would never walk away from this kind of pleasure. "What is it you need, Angela? I'll do anything for you. *Anything*."

"Please move, Jus—"

"Like this?" With agonizing slowness he eased out of her, almost to the tip. "Is that what you want?"

"Yes," she mewled. "Yes, yes, *yes*."

He inched back inside and she came. Wave after wave of violent spasms rocked her, threatening to tear her body in half and she, who had never before in bed made a noise louder than a polite cough, cried out loud enough for the neighbors down the street to hear.

Suddenly he laid her back and climbed on top of her, stretching her out so they both lay, full length, on the counter. He slid his hands under her hips to hold her butt and she tightened her legs around his waist. An explosive wet crash told her someone had kicked the champagne bucket to the floor, but she didn't care. Justus pounded her ruthlessly, the sensations in her sex all the more acute because the countertop, unlike a bed, had no give.

"Angela, Angela," he chanted, whispering, his eyes closed, his face strained and wet. To her surprise the waves built and crashed over her again, so strong now she felt as if her womb had been ripped from her body. She arched backward, pressing her sweaty body closer to him, her mouth open in a silent, astonished scream.

With a hoarse shout and a final powerful thrust, he came, shuddering so intensely she thought they'd both drop to the floor in a tangle of slippery arms and legs. She clung to him, raking her nails across his back. At last he stilled, collapsing on top of her.

After a minute, when she'd started to catch her breath, she began to smile, then laugh. Embarrassed, she threw her hand over her eyes, but couldn't stop laughing. Justus, still panting, tiredly raised his head.

"Is something funny?"

She moved her hand to find him smiling down at her. "I'm pretty sure this isn't an authorized use for a countertop."

He shrugged, his grin widening. "It should be."

"Yeah?" Deliriously happy, she slapped him lightly on the arm. "Well, who's going to clean up that ice and wipe down these counters?" She pointed to the dented ice bucket, miraculously intact champagne bottle, and what looked like a small iceberg worth of cubes sprayed across the tile floor.

Laughing now, he slid to his feet, adjusting his pants. "I will." He scooped her into his arms as if she weighed less than Maya, and swung her around toward the bedroom. "Later."

By the time Justus returned from the bathroom, Angela had remembered the precise location of her zipper, successfully unzipped and removed her dress, and burrowed into bed, luxuriating in the soft sheets. She hadn't bothered with a nightgown and devoutly hoped she wouldn't need one. Over on the corner table she'd turned on a small lamp.

Justus opened the bathroom door and for one second, before he clicked the light off, she had a tantalizing glimpse of his magnificent body, which was all sharp angles and long, hard planes. Heavy, ridged muscles defined his hairless chest and belly; his taut, powerful thighs and endless legs reminded her of the trunk of a young oak. Staring at him, she ridiculously felt her sex tighten again, as if she hadn't just experienced the two most intense orgasms of her life.

He hurried to the bed and dove inside, immediately pulling her up against him so they were face to face. His arms and legs wrapped tightly around her.

Laughing, she said, "Feel free to make yourself right at home."

A wide, delighted grin split his face. "You don't know how much I've wanted to get into this bed." He let her go long enough to adjust the pillows under his head. "It always looked so cozy. That time I saw Maya in it I wanted to throw her little butt out."

"Jealous of a child, were you?"

"Damn right. Let's get one thing straight right now: this is *my* side of the bed, okay?"

"But Maya—" she began weakly.

"*My* side." His jaw tightened into that stubborn, determined line she knew from past experience did not bode well for her. "I don't want to fight anyone for it."

And he would fight for it, she realized. He looked like a knight prepared to defend the castle from the barbarian hordes. "But it comforts us." She felt sheepish, admitting her vulnerability. But he may as well know nights were the times when Carolyn came to her—haunted her. "And I—lately I don't like sleeping alone."

"You won't be."

His unwavering intent to stay in her bed—when Ronnie couldn't jump out of it fast enough—thrilled her as nothing else ever had. Still, a certain amount of decorum was appropriate with a young child.

"Justus," she chided gently. "We have to set a good example. We're not married, so we shouldn't be sleeping together when Maya's here. Don't you agree?"

His unforgiving frown told her he didn't. He opened his mouth to argue—she half hoped he would—then apparently changed his mind and shut it again. One side of his mouth twisted up into something that was more grimace than smile. "We'll talk about it later."

That was the best she'd get from him tonight, and she knew it. "Anyway," she said, tightening her legs around his and pressing her hips closer to him, "don't we have more important things to say and do tonight?"

He stared at her with wide, unblinking eyes. Very gently he stroked her cheek, then smoothed the hair away from her face. "I knew," he told her, his voice barely a whisper. "When we danced at the wedding I knew it would be like this between us. *I knew it.*"

Tracing her thumb against his tender lips, she realized she was not too proud to fish for compliments. "And how is it between us?"

"Mind blowing," he said so quietly she had to read his lips to understand. "Unbelievable."

She had the feeling he wasn't too happy about it—and if so, she couldn't blame him. Their lives would certainly be a lot less complicated without each other. "I knew it, too." She closed her eyes, not certain she wanted to see the look on his face when she made her confession. "I wanted you. I was so freaked out about it—wanting a seventeen-year-old kid—but I did."

"I know, Duchess." His hand slid around to her nape, pulling her in for a kiss. Tilting his head to deepen the angle, he surprised her by merely brushing his lips against hers. She mewled, protesting, as her loins flooded—again. "I really like your New Year's resolution, by the way."

"Let's hope so." She ran her palm over the hard curves of his upper arm, enjoying the flex and play of his muscles. "Do you have one?"

"Umm-hmmm." His attention riveted on the white sheet, which he stealthily pulled down and away from her breasts. "It's to get to know you much better."

"Interesting."

The sheet slid past her waist, revealing the curve of her hip and butt. He heaved a ragged sigh. "You're so beautiful, Angela." His hand squeezed her hip, as if to measure its width. His gaze, troubled now, shot back to her face. "I can't believe how lucky I am."

Her heart twisted painfully because whenever he showed her this vulnerable side she fell a little bit more under his spell. He looked anxious and unsure, as if he did not, in fact, think he deserved her. Ridiculous. She wanted to scream she was the lucky one, but she didn't dare—he already had far too much power over her.

"I'm so glad you're with me," she said instead.

That seemed to please him. Grinning, he said, "I hope I wasn't too rough." He gave her another feather-light kiss, flicking her lips with the tip of his tongue. "I usually have a little more finesse." He rolled her onto her back, stroking his hand slowly over her breasts.

On fire, she bowed into him. He took the hint, lowered his head to one breast and sucked her, hard, into his mouth. "Oh, I know," she said, groaning and cupping his head so he wouldn't stop. "You totally ruined the experience for me. Where can I lodge a complaint?"

Still suckling, he bit down, scraping the nipple with his teeth. Her entire body jerked with violent pleasure and she wondered, astounded, if this virtuoso would make her come just by doing this. He slid up, giving her another teasing little kiss on the lips.

"Sorry." His hand slid up her leg to the inside of her thigh, then higher. "Can I have another chance to get it right?"

"Yes." She began to squirm. "Yes. Yes." Levering up on her elbows, she caught his mouth with her own, thrusting her tongue deep. Justus cried out, grabbed her hips and rolled on top of her, nudging her thighs apart with his knee.

Angela detected a movement out of the corner of her eye and looked up from the thick file to see Carmen standing in the doorway. She'd thought she'd be the only poor dope here in the eerily silent office on New Year's Day when the rest of humanity was at home, eating nachos and drinking beer in front of a football game, but she should have known Carmen would also put in an appearance.

"Come on in," she said, waving her inside.

Carmen, smiling delightedly, hustled into the office, closing the door behind her. Angela's heart sank; one look at Carmen's face told her the only reason she'd made the long trek down the hall from her own office—and maybe the only reason she'd come to the office today at all—was to hear about what happened with Justus last night.

"So?" Carmen plopped into a chair, crossed her legs and leaned her elbows on the desk. "What happened with Justus last night? And don't leave out any details."

Angela grabbed her pen and blindly flipped pages, keeping her head down. "Oh, you know." She shoved the heavy file aside and picked up another, smaller one. "We talked."

"Did you *sleep* with him?"

Angela shot to her feet and bolted to the file cabinet, jerking open the top drawer. "I don't really want to—"

Carmen twisted in her chair to stare after her. "You did!"

Angela shoved the file in the drawer—she'd probably hopelessly misfiled it, but she'd worry about that later—and slammed the drawer shut. "I don't want to talk about it." She went back to her desk and took her seat.

"How was it?" Carmen persisted.

Resistance, Angela knew from long experience, was futile. Leaning against the tall back of her chair, she closed her eyes and sighed, her body flooding with warmth. "I can't begin to describe how amazing it was."

She couldn't. Even if she wanted to share the most deliciously intimate experience of her life—which she didn't—what words could possibly make Carmen understand how Justus had made her feel? She'd lost track of how many times he'd made love to her, and each time was more incredible than the one before; they'd barely slept and she hadn't cared. He was a confident, masterful lover, so skilled it seemed like he'd surely been put on earth for that purpose alone. No one else could possibly know a woman's body—her body—like he did. When he'd finally left this morning, only his promise he'd be back for dinner with her and Maya tonight had enabled her to let him go. Her day here at work had been endless; no matter how she concentrated, she couldn't make the hours go fast enough. She was, in short, in very bad shape.

"Oh, my God!"

Angela opened her eyes to see Carmen staring at her, a look of dawning horror on her face. "You're in love with him!" Angela, shocked she'd been so obvious about her feelings, tried to sputter a denial, but Carmen just shook her head. "Justus is a player, honey, and we both know it! He's not a man you build dreams around! He's a man you *sleep* with. That's it. Otherwise he'll break your heart."

Angela, now too miserable to speak, didn't bother answering. Here, in a succinct fifty words or less, Carmen had just described, and confirmed, her worst fears: Justus would get tired of her; Justus would find someone younger/prettier/sexier; even if they did develop a relationship of some kind, it would never lead to anything because Justus wasn't the marrying type. There was no worst-case scenario Carmen could throw at her that she hadn't already thought of herself. Still, she hated the fact that Carmen thought she was so stupid.

She smiled coolly. "I know he's not someone to get serious about. And I won't. Anyway"—Justus's words popped into her mind—"he's not exactly my type, is he?" She managed a small, artificial laugh. "I can't see myself married to someone who wasn't a professional, anyway. Justus and I have nothing in common other than sex and Maya. Don't worry. I get it."

"Well . . ." Carmen watched her dubiously. "I just don't want you to get hurt again so soon after Ronnie."

"Don't worry," Angela said tightly. "So what are you doing—" A light tap on the door interrupted. "Come in."

Larry poked his silver head into the office. Angela caught a glimpse of his starched white oxford shirt and dark dress pants; it went without saying a man like Larry didn't own any jeans, much less wear them to the office, holiday or no.

"Happy New Year!" he sang. "I thought I was the only one here, but I should have known my two hardest working associates would be here, too."

Angela and Carmen murmured greetings.

Turning his sharp eyes to Angela, Larry said, "Isn't the final pretrial hearing on the Golden Valley case tomorrow?"

Angela smiled brightly, as if she couldn't imagine what would ever please her more than working on Golden Valley. "That's right. Nine sharp." She waved a hand at the thick file. "That's why I'm here."

"Everything under control? No more surprise visits from case workers?"

Angela sometimes thought Larry should come with subtitles to explain what he really meant, as opposed to merely what he said. In this case, the subtitle would say something like, "I sure hope you don't screw anything else up because it'll ruin your partnership chances for good."

Nodding, she gave the only acceptable answer. "Everything's under control."

"Wonderful." Larry beamed. "Well, you two ladies should finish and go on home. Enjoy the rest of the day." He ducked out, shutting the door again.

Angela and Carmen looked at each other, rolling their eyes. Since it was now five-thirty, there was precious little of the day left to enjoy. Carmen stood to go, then paused, staring worriedly at her. "You'll think about what I said?"

Angela smiled again, a brilliant, false smile that hurt her cheeks. "Believe me," she said, swallowing hard around the growing constriction in her throat, "I know exactly where I stand with Justus."

Inside the cozy warmth of his library, where a fire crackled in the fireplace and mugs of hot chocolate cooled on the side table, Vincent sat deep in his brown leather wingback chair and squared off with Maya over the chessboard—they'd used the Napoleon set. Her little face, which rested on her arms, which in turn rested on the edge of the mahogany game table, was screwed up with absolute concentration. For the past half hour he'd pretended he had roughly the mental acumen of a three-year-old chimpanzee, resulting in Maya thoroughly beating him. Studying the board, he saw she could put him in check in two more moves, but her attention had begun to wander in the last few minutes.

She looked up. "I resign, Grandpa."

He threw a hand over his heart. "You resign? How can you resign when you're about to beat me fair and square?"

"I'm ti-erd," she complained, rubbing her eyes.

"Well, you played a good game, Maya." He held his hands out. "Come here, Little Girl."

Maya scrambled down from her chair and scurried around the table to him. He pulled her to his lap, covered her small head with his hand and stroked her wavy hair. "That's what Uncle Justus calls me," she told him.

Vincent froze, his hand suspended mid-stroke, too surprised to speak for a moment.

You don't even realize how much like you he is. My God, how can you be so blind?

He wanted to forget what Angela had said in her fit of anger—one of her fits of anger—at him, but her insidious words would not leave his brain. Eventually curiosity about the son he barely knew got the better of him. "Really? What do you do when you're with Uncle Justus?"

"I dunno."

"Do you play chess with him?"

"Yeah." She giggled. "But he always loses, just like you."

Smoothing her hair again, he said, "Do you ever go anywhere with him?"

Her head bobbed enthusiastically up and down. "Yeah. To the mall and the playground. And *Golden Corral*."

Vincent shuddered inwardly. He'd once seen a commercial about that place, where people sidled up to some communal buffet line like farm animals at chow time. Well, leave it to Justus to yield to Maya's baser impulses. And yet . . .

"Do you ever spend the night at his apartment with him?"

More head bobbing. "Yeah. On Friday. Not every Friday, but a lot of Fridays." As an afterthought she added, "He makes *pancakes*."

She made it sound as miraculous as spinning thread into gold. Maya loved Justus, he realized with surprise. Of course he'd known she loved him, but this was different. Maya adored Justus; he doubted whether Maya was this excited about spending time here with him, and he had a swimming pool. More surprising was the fact that Justus was obviously a conscientious and devoted uncle—and apparently had been long before the accident. He'd have been less surprised if Justus announced he was planning to undergo a sex-change operation.

Just then the door swung open and Justus, smiling broadly,

strode into the room. "Happy New Year, Little Girl," he cried. "What's up, Pops?"

Vincent gaped, almost not recognizing his own son. Well, he recognized him, of course, nothing about his physical appearance had changed since last night, not even a haircut. But he looked entirely different, as if there'd been some subtle but fundamental change that left him forever altered. Vincent tried to figure out what it was. Justus's step seemed lighter, his face brighter. His smile, in fact, wasn't the begrudging smile he dredged up whenever he came here. It seemed to be freely given, to emanate from some more profound place than just his mouth.

Justus seemed, in short, happy.

He realized Justus was staring quizzically at him, and hastily cleared his throat. "Maya, here, just beat me in chess."

Justus grabbed her and swung her, squealing, high in the air. "Is that true, Little Girl?"

"Yes!" She kicked her legs as if she meant to swim across the Atlantic. "Put me down!"

Justus planted several wet kisses on one of her plump cheeks before he obligingly swung her down. "Go get your little bag. Aunt Angela is waiting for us." He swatted her gently on the behind and sent her racing on her way.

At the name, everything clicked into place. Angela was responsible for Justus's newfound happiness. He should have known. Actually, he'd known there was an attraction between them, but he hadn't expected this: his son, the inveterate womanizer, the man who used and discarded women like paper towels, was in love for the first time in his life. And if he knew anything about it, this would be Justus's only time in love. Some of his astonishment must have shown on his face, because Justus ducked his head, a little sheepishly, and turned to stand before the fire. "Did she behave herself?" he asked, sounding like any father he'd ever heard.

"Of course."

"Good." Justus grabbed the fireplace poker and leaned over the screen to jab at the logs even though the flames were already high; he seemed reluctant to face him.

"I was surprised to see you at the party last night," Vincent said experimentally, keeping his voice as disinterested as he could manage. "Didn't seem like you stayed long, though."

Justus, his back still to him, shrugged. "Well, you know. I'm not really a night owl."

"Well." Tired, suddenly, his mind swimming with all the new things he'd learned about his son today, Vincent heaved himself heavily to his feet, wrapping his wool cardigan more tightly around himself to ward off the chill that followed him pretty much wherever he went these days. "Let's go see what's keeping Maya."

Justus faced him, a faint wrinkle of concern marring his smooth forehead. "You okay?"

"Of course," Vincent lied.

Angela took her sweet time about opening her apartment door for Justus and Maya, which only fired his blood to see her. Twice he'd called her at the office and left voicemails, which she hadn't returned, further agitating him. Was she okay? Was she avoiding him? He didn't know when it'd happened that he started measuring time in Angela increments: thirty seconds until he'd see her; two hours until he could call her and see how her day was going; three hours until Maya went to bed and they could make love again. The only time that passed quickly was the time he actually spent with her. By the time she flung the door open and let them in, he was ready to look for a battering ram. Maybe he should ask for a key. He'd never done anything so possessive before, but pretty much every aspect of his relationship with her was a first.

Her gaze went right to him and he saw her color was high, her eyes feverishly bright, and her breathing fast. A guarded, though obviously pleased, smile curled the edges of her mouth. She wore a soft black turtleneck sweater and jeans; he fervently wished she were nude. He forgot her stern lecture about how they should behave in front of Maya and reached for her, but then Maya cried, "Hi, Aunt Ang-la!" and rushed forward, forcing Angela to stoop and hug her. Frustrated, he turned and shut the door.

"Hi, Sweetie!" Angela took Maya's little pink backpack from her, put it on the floor by the door, and kissed her on the cheek. "Did you have a good day with Grandpa?"

Maya unzipped her coat, jerked it off, and shoved it at Angela, chattering a mile a minute. "Yeah! Last night I got to have popcorn and I watched—"

Justus stepped forward. "Maya." He used the brisk voice that came so much easier to Angela than to him; Maya started, her eyes widening with surprise. "Don't leave your bag in the middle of the floor like that. You know Aunt Angela doesn't like a mess."

As one, Angela and Maya, wearing identical quizzical expressions, looked at Maya's backpack against the door, where it couldn't possibly offend anyone, even Angela, then at each other. Justus clapped his hands. "Take it to your room. Let's go. March."

Grumbling, Maya snatched up the bag and slunk down the hall toward her room. The second she disappeared around the corner, Justus grabbed Angela, who let out a startled peep, and pulled her to him, wrapping her close. Like last night, he was rougher than he meant to be, but she didn't seem to mind.

She immediately sighed contentedly, tightened her arms around him, and pressed her face into the hollow between his chin and neck. He inhaled deeply, soaking her in—lilies, fresh shampoo, and Angela. For the first time today he felt like he could really breathe.

"I missed you," he whispered.

"I missed you, too."

"I called you today," he said casually. "Did you get my messages?"

She hesitated. "Yeah, sorry. I was . . . really busy, and I just wanted to finish up and get out of there, so I—"

"It's okay," he said, but it wasn't. Something in her voice told him she was lying—she hadn't wanted to call back. Why? Some awful feeling—like despair—twisted in his heart. Did she regret last night? He loosened his grip just enough so he could look down into her face and her warm, though still-guarded eyes and tender lips undid him. Lowering his head, he covered her mouth with his own, tasting her with the enthusiasm of a child with his first bowl of ice cream. When she opened for him like a daylily in the sun, he pushed away his insecurities. He was here with her now and she still wanted him—that was all that mattered. Breaking away, he kissed her forehead, eyes, and cheeks, letting his hands roam under her sweater to her warm, sweet-smelling skin.

"Missed you." Forgetting himself a little, he kneaded her breasts through the heavy satin of her bra, then dropped his hands to her butt and pressed her, hard, against his raging erection. "Missed you, missed you, missed you."

"*Justus.*"

She had a way of saying his voice—half agonized whisper, half sob—that drove him insane. He quickly turned and backed her up against the wall taking her mouth hungrily, with no real idea what they could possibly do with Maya down the hall. Her hips began to undulate against him, and he wondered dazedly whether Maya would notice if they disappeared into Angela's bedroom for a few minutes. He could put in a video for her, and—

"What's for dinner?"

They leapt apart as if someone had turned a fire hose on them, turning in time to see Maya run back up the hall. Angela had the presence of mind to stand in front of him to block him from Maya's view. "I'm hungry."

Angela tugged the bottom of her sweater down, took Maya's hand, and led her to the kitchen. "Barbequed chicken." Grabbing the oven mitts, she opened the oven and took out a white casserole dish. Only her swollen lips and slightly trembling hands marked her as a woman who had been seconds away from making love. Justus, who couldn't pull himself together so easily, had to sneak into the bathroom and hide for long minutes until he became decent again.

Chapter 21

Angela yawned as she moved through her already darkened apartment, clicking out lights as she went. She hated these still, black hours of the night where she felt like the only living person on earth, and her cozy apartment felt like a cavern. At the kitchen table she gathered up her miscellaneous legal pads filled with notes on top of notes for the hearing tomorrow, and shoved them into her chronically overstuffed briefcase. Tonight she'd worked about three hours on the case after she put Maya to bed—not too bad. There was more to do, of course, but given her almost complete lack of sleep last night—and the fact she'd spent all day today, a holiday, at the office—three hours was the best she could do. She put the briefcase and her laptop near her purse, where they'd all be ready to go first thing in the morning. Her hearing started at nine and, barring any further surprise appearances from the overzealous case worker, she'd be on time.

Walking into the kitchen to get a final glass of water, she swung her arms in wide arcs, trying to work out some of the kinks between her shoulders. Hunching for hours over her paperwork wasn't good for her muscles, but then neither was the sexual tension that burned between her thighs. Whatever the reason, she was way too agitated to go to bed just yet.

Her evening with Justus had been very unsatisfying. Oh, sure, she'd been glad to see him and just breathe the same air for a while. But with Maya's constant chattering, and her sharp, curious little eyes watching them all evening, she'd had no chance to share a complete sentence with Justus, much less to lure him into her bedroom. When it was time for him to leave, he'd given her a perfectly respectable, G-rated kiss on the cheek and gone without protest, a fact she found horribly disquieting, especially after the hello kiss he'd given her. Ultimately his visit had been more frustrating than anything else, and after he'd left she'd grumpily bundled Maya off to bed, taken a cold shower, and thrown on her soft cotton sheep pajamas, figuring if she couldn't have sex, she may as well be comfortable.

She'd just double-checked the bolt on the door and started back down the hall to her bedroom, water glass in hand, when she heard a soft knock. Startled, she waited; a few seconds later she heard it again. Putting her glass back on the counter, she went to the door and checked the peephole. And saw Justus.

Her heart went haywire. Flinging the door open she cried, "Wha—?"

She saw the hot, determined gleam in his eyes and the knot of desire low in her belly tightened in response. "You didn't think I was gone for the night, did you?"

"Maya—" she began half-heartedly, but he'd already sidled past her and gone to the living room, where he took off his leather jacket and tossed it on one of the chairs.

"Maya's asleep," he said flatly, his voice low. "And I'll be gone before she wakes up."

She could barely hear him over the roar of her pulse pounding in her ears. The ache in her sex started to throb, demanding attention. God, she was so weak where he was concerned. All he had to do was walk into the room—exist—and her resolve melted away, like an ice sculpture in the sun. Still, she was ready to fight, determined to set a few limits—how else would she keep a little distance between them and stop him from breaking her heart when he got tired of her?

Her hands found her hips and she stared at him, frowning. His face twisted into an obstinate glower, which she ignored. "I think the best thing," she said in the no-nonsense courtroom voice she liked to think made judges and juries sit up and pay attention, "is to set up a few ground rules, and I—"

"Shut up, Angela."

For an arrested, outraged moment, she could only stare at him, her jaw flapping uselessly. Surely she'd heard wrong. *"What did you say to me?"*

His eyes narrowed into dangerous, almost reptilian slits that had her shrinking into her skin. He stalked over to stand in her face and she took two hasty steps backward before she realized what she was doing and stood her ground. To her complete astonishment and dismay, he reached for the bottom of his fleece pullover and in one smooth motion swept it and his T-shirt off over his head to reveal the sculpted perfection of his arms and torso. He tossed his clothes to the floor. Immediately a wave of heat from his huge body swept over her, flattening her outraged protest like an atomic explosion flattens everything in its path. Choking with desire, she could make only a weird, strangled sound.

He came closer again. "I'm not seventeen years old anymore, Duchess, and I'm sick of your stupid little rules. 'Don't put your feet there, don't get water on the floor, don't touch me, don't let Maya see,'" he mimicked in a high-pitched voice that made her palm itch to smack him across his smart mouth. He kicked off his shoes and socks. "I think even you'll have to agree I've been pretty patient, but enough's enough.

You have a rule for every part of your perfect little life, and I'm sick of it."

"*How dare you—*"

Slipping his hands under the waistband of his sweatpants, he slid them down and off his long legs, then stood to reveal the thing she most feared at the moment and couldn't resist: his full, insistent arousal. She whimpered; her knees began to tremble; a thin trickle of sweat slid down her chest and into the valley between her breasts.

"So from now on," he said, his voice deceptively soft now, "we'll do things my way. Luckily I only have one rule. Want to hear it?"

She didn't. Too paralyzed to even shake her head, she waited.

Justus stepped forward again until a bare inch separated them. Panting now, her loins flooded, she stared at his strong throat, the only safe place her eyes could find, determined not to look either higher or lower. With an impatient grunt he tapped the bottom of her chin, forcing her gaze up to his eyes. Looking into them, she saw an iron will and determination ten thousand times stronger than her own and knew she was lost. Completely lost.

"Here it is: you and I will be together. That's it. I know it's not fancy, but I like it, don't you? It has a nice ring to it and I think it's pretty easy to remember. You and I will be together."

Her head spun. She began to sputter, with no real idea what she'd say other than to express outrage at being told to shut up and then bossed around in her own apartment, but he waved a hand, silencing her.

"You'll have to get used to it, I guess," he continued reasonably, as if they were discussing the summer humidity in Cincinnati. "Maya will have to get used to it. Anyone else who has a problem with it will have to get used to it." He paused, giving her the chance to object even as his glittering eyes told her there'd be hell to pay if she did. "Now," he said, angling his mouth over hers so his lips were less than a whisper away. "Do you want to argue or do you want to make love?" Reaching his hands behind her, he cupped her butt and jerked her close, grinding against her.

"Go to hell, Justus," she snarled.

Before he could react, Angela pressed her hips closer, reached up, dug her nails into the back of his neck, and pulled his face down for her aggressive, biting kiss. He shuddered violently, holding her tighter, and she reveled in the sudden shift of power.

Tearing her lips away, she looked up into his stunned, hot eyes. "I want to make love."

Completely inflamed, Justus gaped at Angela. Her little hot-and-cold routine had him teetering on the brink of madness, and it could go either way. He couldn't shake the feeling she thought of him as just a visitor in her life—a welcome visitor, but a visitor nonetheless—to whom she refused to become attached. Why was she so determined not to let him get close? Oh, sure—with a little duress she gave him the use of her body, and for that he was profoundly, everlastingly grateful. But she refused to let him *in*, and *in* was where he so desperately needed to be. Yeah, she'd needed and relied on him after the accident, back when they were friends and their relationship had no explicit sexual dimension, and that was all well and good. But did she need him as the man in her life? Did she *trust* him? He needed to know she couldn't do without him any more than he could do without her—that she couldn't do without him physically or, more importantly, emotionally. But if the physical was all she would give him, he would take it—for now.

And he would punish her for it.

Eagerly he fused his mouth with hers, swung her up into his arms, and practically ran to her bedroom. Once inside, he kicked the door shut and raised his head. "I better not find Maya on my side of the bed."

"No," she said, shaking her head frantically. "Hurry, Justus." For good measure, to make sure she drove him completely wild, she tugged his earlobe with her sharp little teeth.

Crying out, he dumped her on the bed and tumbled down on top of her. On her back, she immediately opened her arms and legs to him. "Come here," she begged. Levering herself up on her elbows, she sat up long enough to rip her pajama top over her head—were those *sheep*?—revealing the ripe brown globes of her incredible breasts. He nuzzled first one, then the other, biting a little since she seemed to like that so much last night.

Angela went crazy, moaning and thrashing so hard beneath him he could hardly hold on. His erection lengthened and throbbed, crossing over into painful territory. He wanted—needed—to drive himself into her, full length, and love her, hard and fast, until his back or hips gave out. But not yet. He wanted her wilder than this first, and he would ignore what he needed for as long as it took. Trembling with determination and desire, he broke out into a sweat.

Abandoning her breasts, he slid lower, jerked her bottoms and panties off over her hips, buried his face in her flat belly, and shoved his tongue into her navel. Sure enough, she lost all control, throwing her arms over her head, writhing and arching into him. He slid even lower, pressing his mouth to the meaty part of her inner thigh; unable to resist, drunk on the scent of her intimate musk, he opened his mouth wide, sucking and biting her tender flesh. Angela sobbed.

Experimentally, he grazed the tip of one finger against her sex and she froze, her ragged breath and whimpering the only sounds in the universe. Brushing her with his fingers, he discovered, to his immense satisfaction, she was sopping wet. He stroked for a minute, gliding his fingers in her hot dew, then thrust his fingers inside, catching her by surprise. Crying out, she climaxed violently, her tight inner muscles massaging him.

A drop of sweat trickled down his nose and onto the sheet. He was close—dangerously close—to the limits of his endurance. The ache in his sex screamed for release, but it wasn't his turn. Not just yet. She'd come, but he wasn't satisfied or finished punishing her.

"Is that the best you can do, Duchess?" he asked rhetorically. He raised his head, looked up her torso and past her breasts to see her weakly move her head. He couldn't tell if it was a nod or a shake. Her eyes were closed and she didn't even try to answer him; he wondered if she could.

Returning to his work he found her hard nub and rolled it between his fingers, then lowered his head to stroke with his tongue. Angela revived enough to begin to mewl and cry again. When he scraped her a little with his teeth she leapt off the bed, crying out his name.

As much as he would have liked to prolong the exquisite pleasure he knew he was giving her, enough was enough; he'd tortured her—and himself—all he could for now. Moving swiftly, he jerked open her nightstand drawer, pulled out a condom, and put it on. Rousing herself, Angela eagerly opened her legs and reached for him. Climbing over her he thrust home, blindly driving deeper and deeper into her hot, wet, throbbing body. Angela's eyes fell closed and she bucked beneath him until the pleasure threatened to kill him.

"Justus," she whispered hoarsely. "Oh, God, what are you doing to me?" Her long legs tightened around his waist, letting him plunge even further into her tight flesh. To his astonishment she came again, her pulsing body squeezing him like a fist. He couldn't handle it. Shouting her name—maybe she'd been right about them making love where Maya couldn't hear—he came so forcefully he almost passed out.

When he'd stopped shaking he rolled onto his side and, still joined, held her tightly. He felt better now, but not good. He owned her body, but so what? He'd owned the body of every woman he'd ever slept with, and besting that punk Ron in bed was obviously no great feat. Did she love him yet? Was she really his now? He doubted it to the depths of his soul. Despair constricted his throat because he knew when morning came and he had to let her out of bed, she'd push him away again.

Angela, wearing her favorite power suit, a navy boucle with fitted jacket and slim skirt, along with her heels, marched into the sunny kitchen hustling a bleary-eyed Maya in front of her like an Australian cattle dog with her herd. Despite her near total lack of sleep, she wasn't tired. After Justus left at about five-thirty, she'd done her four miles on the treadmill, ignoring the delicious soreness between her thighs. As a result, she felt rejuvenated, as cheery and bright as the January sun reflected off her pale yellow walls; she was ready to conquer the world and defend Golden Valley to the death.

She took a quick glance at the range clock: seven-thirty. They were in great shape. She'd had the brilliant idea of letting Maya pick out her clothes last night, thus cutting about ten minutes off their morning routine. Maya's little backpack sat on the table next to her briefcase and purse. Somehow she'd managed to brush and rebraid Maya's hair without bloodshed. Heaving a great sigh of satisfaction, as if she'd just finished the Boston Marathon in record time, she surveyed her handiwork: a smoothly running household. She'd planned for every contingency and wouldn't possibly be late for court at nine.

Wouldn't Carolyn—and her boss—be proud of her now?

They just needed to eat a quick breakfast, then be on their way. Plunking Maya up onto one of the bar stools, she said, "What would you like for breakfast?"

Maya shrugged, yawning. "I dunno."

Angela set the kettle on for her own tea and oatmeal, then turned back to Maya, her hands on her hips. "Frozen waffles?"

"No."

"No, *thanks*?" Angela raised an eyebrow, waiting.

Maya's jaw tightened into a sullen pout. "No, thanks."

"Oatmeal?"

Maya slumped over on the counter, resting her chin on her arms so that only her huge dark eyes were visible. She shook her head.

Angela felt the first stirrings of irritation. "Cereal? Cinnamon toast?"

Maya didn't answer, her attention now riveted by the salt shaker and pepper mill. She sprinkled a few grains of salt on the counter, wet her finger, then licked it. Angela took the shaker away and quickly wiped up the salt with her sponge, running her hand over the spot again to make sure it wasn't gritty.

"That's not a toy!"

Maya didn't answer, but stared fixedly at some distant point straight across the counter.

Angela glanced at the clock: seven thirty-four. There was still plenty of time. "Maya!" Maya's gaze shifted reluctantly to Angela. "Do you want cinnamon toast or cereal?"

Maya shook her head again. Frustrated and vaguely alarmed, Angela crossed her arms over her chest, but before she could say anything else, the kettle whistled. Grabbing a bowl from the cabinet, she quickly fixed her apple cinnamon oatmeal and tea. Maya watched the whole time. Just as she was about to take a bite—for some reason she was starved this morning—Maya raised her head and said, "I want oatmeal."

Angela lowered her spoon. Leave it to Maya to wait until the very second she was about to enjoy her own hot food before she made up her little mind. She put her bowl on the counter with a loud thunk, cocked her head, and put her hand to her ear. "Did you say something? I don't understand when people talk to me and they don't use nice words."

"I said I want oatmeal," Maya said through clenched teeth. "*Please.*"

"Fine." Angela slid the bowl across the counter to her. "You can have mine." Maya raised the spoon and stuck out her tongue to test the oatmeal's temperature. "You're welcome," Angela added.

"Thanks," Maya said sullenly.

While she fixed herself another bowl, Maya sniffed and tongued the oatmeal without ever actually taking a bite. Finally she shoved the bowl away and crossed her own arms over her chest. "It's too hot," she whined.

Angela shoveled two quick bites of oatmeal in her mouth and darted a glance at the clock: seven forty-five. Okay. Now they were into the yellow zone. Not time to panic yet, but time to get serious about getting out the door. "What? Do you want me to put an ice cube in, or—"

"I don't want it."

Angela had had it up to here with the little princess and the daily breakfast ordeal. Why couldn't she just eat a bowl of cold cereal like every other American child? Why did they have to have this delicate negotiation, like they were engineering a plan for Palestinian statehood? Why did she have to waste time *and* perfectly good food?

"Maya Robinson! I stood here and made that oatmeal for you, and I expect—"

"I don't want it!"

Angela finished her own oatmeal in two more gulps while she fumed and plotted. Normally, she'd take her mother's approach and tell the little diva her behind would stay on the stool until the oatmeal was all gone and she didn't care how long it took. Unfortunately, she didn't have time for that this morning. They needed to leave and Maya needed to eat something—anything—before they did. She could not send a child to school on an empty stomach. "Well, fine," she snapped. "What do you want?"

Maya flopped against the back of her stool, staring at the ceiling. "I dunno."

Something inside Angela snapped. "Maya Robinson!" she shrieked, waving her arms. Maya jumped. "I am going to fix you a peanut butter and jelly sandwich—on wheat bread— and I want you to eat *every single bite*! Do you hear me?"

Nodding, Maya began to cry silently. To Angela's everlasting dismay, they were not the crocodile tears she'd come to know and hate—they were genuine, heartbroken three-and-a-half-year-old tears. It crossed her mind to apologize, but she was still too pissed off to successfully manage a sincere apology—besides, they were almost out of time. Cursing under her breath—she felt like she'd kicked Bambi—Angela whirled to the fridge and grabbed the jelly. As quickly as she could she made a sloppy sandwich, threw it on a napkin, and slid it across the counter to Maya. Maya swiped her hand across both of her eyes, sat up straight and, picking up the sandwich, took a big bite.

Satisfied, Angela turned to soak the oatmeal bowls in soapy water; generally she'd wash them before she left but, again, thanks to Maya, she didn't have that luxury this morning. Running to the hall closet, she got their jackets so they'd be ready. Jackets, backpack, briefcase—what was she forgetting? Oh, keys. Hurrying back to the kitchen, she swiped them off the wall hook and put them in her pocket. Calmer now, she took a quick gulp of tea, scalding her mouth in the process. Dumping it out—there was no time to wait for it to cool down, anyway—she rinsed the mug. Now she'd just start the dishwasher, and—

Behind her, Maya made a broken wheezing sound unlike any human noise Angela had ever heard. She whirled, sending the mug crashing to the floor in her terror. Maya was now unrecognizable. Angry red welts the size of grapes covered her cheeks, forehead, and chin; her lips were swollen, her eyes panicked and wild. Angela watched, disbelieving, as Maya struggled to draw a breath, her little hands clawing at her throat as if she meant to tear open her airway. Another harsh wheezing sound escaped her, as if air was being dragged, kicking and screaming, to her lungs. Angela's adrenalin surged and she lunged for the wall phone, slipping on the floor and falling flat on her face in the process. Yelping, she leapt to her feet and grabbed the phone.

"It's okay, Maya." She tried to keep her voice calm, an impossible task, as she dialed the numbers 9-1-1. "Everything's going to be fine."

But Maya kept scratching at her throat, her mouth convulsively opening and closing like the death throes of a fish out of water.

Chapter 22

Justus peered through the doorway of the small, windowed room in the emergency section of the hospital and stared at Angela and Maya, his head still spinning with the medical jargon the nurse had just given him. The poor woman, in her cheery blue-and-white puppy smock over white pants and sensible green clogs, had explained everything very calmly and encouragingly, but his hearing had pretty much shut down after the words "acute respiratory problem." She'd also mentioned peanut allergies, oxygen saturation levels, and epinephrine, but none of it meant a thing to him.

Was she trying to explain Maya had almost died this morning?

It didn't seem possible. She was resting quietly—was she asleep?—on the bed, her silly little dog tucked under the covers with her. Basically she looked exactly the same as she did every night at bedtime, except for the telltale oxygen mask on her face and some little plastic thing clipped to her index finger. Angela sat beside her in a chair, her elbow resting on the bed rail, staring as if she meant to personally count and verify every breath Maya took. Her eyes looked huge and haunted in her drawn face, and she seemed to have aged ten years since he saw her several hours ago.

"Angela?"

Angela started, then jumped to her feet, putting her finger to her lips for him to be quiet. He rushed forward and pulled her into his arms, desperate to comfort and be comforted. But she stiffened, submitting rather than participating in the hug. Vaguely disturbed, he looked to Maya and realized she was, indeed, asleep. What he could see of her face looked a little red and swollen, but other than that she seemed fine. Taking Angela's hand he led her to the doorway, where they hovered.

"She's okay now," Angela whispered. "When I called 911 they had me give her some Benadryl—thank God I still had some from when she had that cold the other week—and then when the paramedics came they gave her a shot of epinephrine. With the oxygen, she's been breathing okay. They'll check her oxygen levels again in a little while, and if they're good they'll let us take her home."

This clinical recitation of the facts was all well and good, but he still couldn't make himself understand what'd happened. "She's . . . allergic to peanuts?"

"Yes."

"Yeah, but . . ." He struggled to think. "Hasn't she had peanut butter before? All little kids eat peanut butter."

"This is how it happens, I guess," she said, shrugging. "The doctor thought maybe that time you saw that rash on her face was the beginning of it. She'd had a peanut butter and jelly sandwich then, too."

"Oh," he said faintly. "So what, exactly, happened?"

"She took a bite of her sandwich, got hives, her mouth swelled, and she couldn't breathe," Angela said dispassionately, as if she was reciting entries in the phone book.

Justus's sense of unease grew. Angela was so disconnected, so cool—not at all like someone who'd had a major scare thrown into them. Was this what they called shock? He touched her shoulder. "You must have been terrified, baby. Are *you* okay?"

She moved away. "I'm fine." The annoyance in her voice was unmistakable. "The important thing is Maya's fine and she'll have a full recovery. We'll have to learn about her new diet, of course. But everything's fine."

If she said "fine" one more time he felt like he'd put his fist through the nearest wall. Anyone who'd just witnessed the near death of a child she loved could not, by definition, be *fine*. But of course he should have known it would take more than a crisis for Angela to open up and lean on him a little. He shoved his fists in his pockets to stop himself from reaching for her again and making matters worse.

"Well, what happened with your big hearing this morning? Did you reschedule?"

Her gaze lowered to the floor and her voice dropped, as if she couldn't bear to say what had happened aloud. "I forgot about the hearing. I didn't think to call until after they'd stabilized her, and I didn't think to bring my cell phone with me in the ambulance." She rubbed her palm back and forth across her forehead. "The client was furious. So was my boss."

He grabbed her hands—to hell with her not wanting him to touch her. "Angela." She tried to pull away, her gaze still on the floor, but he refused to let her go. "Your boss will understand when you finish explaining. Everything will work out. You'll see."

With a great jerk she heaved herself free and scurried to the other side of the bed, wrapping her arms around herself as if she needed some sort of protection from him. "It doesn't matter," she said tonelessly. "Maya's the only thing that matters."

No! Justus wanted to scream. *You matter, too.* But he kept his mouth shut.

* * *

Vincent surged into her apartment as if he'd used a batter-ing ram to weaken a gate and had finally broken through to the keep. Dressed in a black cashmere topcoat over his suit, his tufted white brows low over his eyes and his entire body quivering with indignation, he was obviously beside himself. It felt weird seeing him here, at her humble abode, rather than in his own mansion, almost as if the President had hopped in his limo and shown up for a visit instead of invit-ing her to the White House. The mountain had definitely come to Muhammad.

"Where is she?" he demanded.

Angela shut the door behind him, simultaneously feeling her temples throb and her last finger hold on sanity slip away. It was six-thirty and she was exhausted. Shadows stretched and lengthened through the living room and her sofa invited her to sit down and relax for a minute or two—something she hadn't done all day—but first she had to deal with Vincent. She'd survived Justus's sympathetic concern when he should have been furious she'd almost killed Maya, but she didn't know if she could also survive an interrogation from Vincent.

"Please keep your voice down," she told him. "I just put her in bed. She's pretty tired."

Vincent snatched off his coat and scarf and thrust them at her. Nostrils flaring, he said, "What happened?"

Anger simmered as she laid his things on the sofa. There was no mistaking his tone, which clearly said she'd better tell him exactly what happened and she'd darn well better make it good. Pressing her palm to her head, she closed her eyes and tried unsuccessfully to find a calm, respectful place from which she could speak with Maya's grandfather and Justus's father. She opened her eyes.

"I fed her a peanut butter and jelly sandwich. She had a bad reaction to the peanut butter. I called 911. We went to the hospital. They treated her, and we came home."

Sneering, he all but laughed at her, as if this was the single biggest load of bull he'd ever heard. "How could you feed her *peanut butter?*" He made it sound like she'd force-fed her a plate of scrambled dragon's eggs. "How could you not know she was allergic to *peanut butter?*"

"I didn't know she was allergic to peanut butter. Did you?"

That shut him up in a hurry. He gaped at her for an arrested moment, his mouth opening and closing, before wheeling away and sitting on one of the bar stools. Collapsing his head in his hands, he sat quietly for several minutes. Suddenly he looked not like a formidable opponent, but the tired old man he was.

"I'm sorry."

"It's okay." Angela hung her head, too ashamed to look him in the eye. Why didn't lightning strike her dead on the spot? She should be apologizing to him, not the other way around. And if Vincent weren't so upset, his lawyer's instincts would surely kick in, and he'd nail her to the wall. Because even though she hadn't known Maya was allergic to peanuts, the real issue here was whether she should have known. And the answer to that question was an unequivocal yes.

Today, when she'd sat staring at Maya's disfigured, sleeping red face, she'd faced the ugly truth about herself. What kind of aunt was she? She thought sadly back to the day after the accident. She was the kind of aunt who fed a small child a peanut butter sandwich and then didn't notice the child's face was covered with hives. The kind who refused to get medical treatment for the child because it was inconvenient. The kind who screamed at the child, then didn't apologize. The kind who was more concerned about her career than she was about the child's needs. The kind who, prior to the accident, hadn't even bothered to get to know her niece. Worst of all, she was the kind of aunt who tried to atone by adopting the child when it was painfully obvious to anyone with half a functioning brain she wasn't the best person for the job.

Peanut butter, for God's sake! Every idiot who'd ever watched half an hour of prime time TV knew what the symptoms of a peanut allergy were! It wasn't as if Maya was allergic to something exotic!

A wail of hysteria, deep in her chest, broke free and threatened to explode out of her mouth. Only with great difficulty did she tamp it back down. Her knees shaking with the effort, she collapsed on the sofa, slumping her head in her hands.

"Where's Justus?" Vincent asked tiredly.

Raising her head, she said, "He dropped us off, then went to the pharmacy to get Maya's prescription filled. She'll need an EpiPen with her everywhere she goes. And I guess we should see about getting her one of those medical ID bracelets."

Vincent nodded approvingly. "You're a good aunt, Angela. She's lucky to have you."

Shame had her hanging her head again—shame and guilt. If the one didn't kill her, the other surely would.

When Angela opened the door for him after he got back from the pharmacy, Justus was not happy to see his father embedded at the kitchen table eating take-out pizza. In fact, his father's presence was a direct and material breach of the unwritten armistice they'd developed over the years, namely that they stayed out of each other's way. It was petty of him, sure, to feel having his father here somehow contaminated the one little corner of heaven on earth he'd managed to eke out for himself, but that was how he felt. Still, Vincent was probably as concerned as the rest of them about Maya's condition, so he would try to be polite.

"Hey, Vincent," he murmured.

Vincent, in his shirtsleeves, dabbed at his mouth with a white paper napkin. "Justus."

Bemused, Justus stared at his father for a minute. He couldn't remember ever seeing the man eat something as lowly as pizza before; watching him finish his slice was as strange as watching a tiger eat a salad. Justus walked past Angela, brushing a quick kiss on her cheek as he went by; he'd meant what he told her last night about them being together, so his father may as well know, and adjust, to their relationship right now. Vincent's sharp, speculative gaze narrowed. Angela hastily stepped away, her lids lowered, and, after shutting the door behind him, resumed her spot at the table.

Irritated, Justus jerked off his jacket and tossed it on top of a chair. The box of pizza—smelled like pepperoni—lay on the table, along with an open bottle and glasses of Merlot. "She's still asleep," Angela told him, picking up a fresh paper plate and tossing several slices on it. "I didn't bother waking her up for dinner. I think rest is more important than food right now, don't you? Are you hungry? Have some pizza."

He took the plate and sat, taken aback by her chattering. Clearly she was not herself. It crossed his mind to ask how she was doing, but he didn't think he could tolerate another recitation of how fine she was without vomiting.

"Did you talk to anyone at the office again?" he asked instead.

"Larry wants to speak with me first thing in the morning."

Vincent cleared his throat. "Is everything . . . okay?" he asked delicately.

Angela whirled away, shrugging impatiently. At the sink she wet her sponge, then marched back to the table and vigorously wiped it even though they were still eating. "I was so upset about Maya this morning I forgot to call in to the office." Although her head was down, Justus could still see her jaws pulse. "I missed a final pretrial hearing."

"Oh." Vincent frowned thoughtfully, pursing his lips. "Larry's a golf buddy of mine," he told her. "If you think it would help I could call and—"

"No." Straightening, Angela rolled her eyes and shook her head, and if Justus didn't know better he'd almost swear there was some affection for Vincent in her tired smile. "I know you don't believe it, Vincent," she said, patting his hand condescendingly, "but there are some things in life even you can't control."

Uh-oh. Justus braced himself; better women than Angela had received a tongue lashing for less impertinence than this. But to his astonishment, the old man just laughed. "That doesn't seem possible, dear."

Justus's irritation grew. What the hell was going on here? When had Angela and his father gotten so buddy-buddy— and why? He didn't like it one little bit. Even though he was starving, he pushed his pizza, mostly uneaten, away.

"Justus?" Angela's brow knit with worry. "I've never seen you push food away."

Well, at least she'd remembered he was still here. He opened his mouth to tell her he'd eat later, but before he could say anything, his father said, "It's me he objects to, not the food."

Vincent's tragic, resigned tone—*woe is me, my irrational son hates me!*—rubbed Justus the wrong way. Itching for a fight, he crossed his arms over his chest, leaned his elbows on the table and leveled his father with his most intimidating glare. "Don't start, Vincent."

Angela materialized on his side of the table, sponge still in hand. The warning smile she directed at him—him!—sent a chill down his spine. "No one will be starting anything," she said pleasantly, her voice interlaced with steel. "Not tonight. Not in my house."

Justus slouched, sulking, against the back of his chair. Angela made him feel like an immature seven-year-old for picking a fight with his father, a trick no one had managed since his mother died. He glanced at Vincent, half expecting to see the old man smirking at him. But Vincent just stared, and if Justus had to name his expression he'd call it . . . sad. Not reproachful. Not disappointed. Not angry. Just sad. Suddenly he felt small and petty. Worse, he felt an emotion he'd never felt before, no matter how badly he treated his father: shame.

Just then they heard a sound from the bedroom, as if Maya had stretched and yawned. Without another word, Angela dropped the sponge in the sink and ran down the hall, her heels clicking a staccato beat.

Justus picked up a slice of pizza and, refusing to meet his father's gaze, took a big bite.

"I was just trying to think when we last sat down to a meal together, other than Christmas Day," Vincent said softly.

Justus froze, keeping his eyes lowered. "Been a while," he said out of the side of his mouth.

"Well." Vincent sat quietly for a minute, then wiped his mouth again. Finally he got up and threw his plate away. "I guess I'll kiss Maya goodnight and go on home. But maybe you should stick around and make sure our ladies are all right."

Justus bristled at the word *our*. Well, here it was, at last: the portion of the conversation where Vincent told him what to do. Next would come some sort of recitation about how disappointed he was in him, followed by the inevitable name-calling.

"I know you don't believe it," he snapped, leaping to his feet, "but I know what Maya and Angela need and I'm perfectly capable of taking care of both of them."

To his astonishment, Vincent didn't lash back at him. Instead he smiled, a warm half-smile that would almost fool a casual observer into thinking it was full of fatherly pride.

Justus stilled. "I know you are," Vincent said. "Why else do you think I asked you?"

Angela poked her head into Maya's room—if she wasn't really awake she certainly didn't want to disturb her—and saw Maya sitting up in bed, yawning and rubbing her eyes with her fists. Wearing a purple-striped flannel nightgown, her floppy dog by her side, she looked exactly the same as she had every other night she'd spent here; maybe numbness had set in, but Angela couldn't believe Maya had been seriously ill just a few hours ago. The light from her small nightstand lamp was not bright enough for Angela to get a good look at her face, but the hives had been almost all gone when they left the hospital.

"Hi, Sweetie." She crept into the room and sat on the edge of the bed. "How are you feeling?"

"Good." Maya's tone was dismissive, as if she couldn't understand why Angela kept asking her. Her brow furrowed. "Aunt Ang-la?"

"Yes, Maya?" She smoothed Maya's rumpled hair away from her face.

Maya's wide eyes seemed to take up three-fourths of her face and she hunched over a little, like a scared, shell-less turtle. "Are you mad at me?"

Her sweet voice was so small, as if she was at the other end of a long tunnel. Angela's heart twisted painfully. "No!" Jerking Maya into her arms, she pressed her head to her bosom. Maya gratefully snuggled closer, her short arms clutching Angela's sides, and there was more heartbreak. "I'm so sorry I yelled at you this morning. Please forgive me."

"I didn't listen," Maya said, her voice muffled against Angela's blouse.

"I still shouldn't have yelled at you."

"It's okay." Maya pulled away to look up at her. "Aunt Ang-la?"

"Yes, Sweetie."

"Can I have some juice?"

Angela had to smile. Maya was not, apparently, too sick to take advantage of the situation. Pressing her hands together as if she was praying, Maya held her breath and stared hopefully at her. "Maya," Angela said reproachfully. Health crisis or no, she just couldn't let go of the rules entirely. "You know my position on sugary drinks."

Maya had apparently thought of that already. "I know. But if I eat all my dinner . . ."

The child was obviously a born lawyer. "Well," Angela said, pursing her lips as if giving the matter careful consideration, "I guess this one time won't hurt anything."

"Yay!" Clapping her hands, Maya scrambled out of bed, pausing to bend down and slide her Barbie ballet house slippers on her feet. "But, Aunt Ang-la?" Her expression turned grave.

"Yes, Maya?"

"No peanut butter, okay?" She made a face. "I don't like peanut butter."

"Justus, really. I'm fine. You should go on home and get some sleep. I really don't want to take the chance of Maya seeing us together. I'd be surprised if she slept through the whole night, and if she comes into my room—"

It was after eleven and a maze of shadows crossed Angela's dark living room. For about half an hour he'd sat on the sofa and flipped channels while Angela settled Maya in for the night. He was looking forward to the moment when he could just hold Angela and soothe her—keep her safe. He'd satisfied himself that Maya was okay—well enough to demand a second helping of rainbow sherbet and extra bubbles in her bath, anyway—but Angela was another matter altogether.

"I can sleep on the sofa," he said, clicking off the TV. So much for wrapping her in his arms. Streaks of tension shot, like lightning strikes, up his lower back to his neck and shoulders, where they settled. His entire body, come to think of it, felt like it had been dipped—twice—in plaster of Paris. Worse, he was slowly but surely losing his grip on his temper, the way a climber dangling over the edge of a cliff feels his fingers slip away, one by one.

Angela leaned against the archway, her arms folded across her chest in what she probably thought was a relaxed posture. She didn't fool him; so much adrenalin blanketed her she was practically phosphorescent. Come to think of it, she looked about as relaxed as the queen presiding over the opening of Parliament. Raising one shaky hand, she dropped her head enough to worry the side of her hair, messing it up. Deep hollows had carved themselves underneath her eyes, giving her a haunted, hunted look.

She tried to smile. "I'm really fine. I appreciate what you're trying to do, but you should just go home and get a good night's sleep in your own bed."

He'd had just about enough of this crap. Justus stood up slowly and tossed the remote onto the sofa with a little more force than he'd meant, and it bounced once and fell to the floor. "Really?" He crossed his own arms over his chest and planted his feet wide. "Do you really think I can go home and sleep well tonight? You don't think much of me, do you?"

Angela flinched, as if he'd sneezed right in her face. "Excuse me?"

Again his temper surged, trying to run free like the horses straining at the gate at the Kentucky Derby. His heart pumped so violently he could feel his blood pulsing in his throat. "Did it ever occur to you, Duchess—"

She gaped, wincing at the nastiness in his voice.

"—that maybe we need *each other* tonight?" Sharp pricks of pain stabbed his palms and he looked down to discover, much to his surprise, he'd clenched his fists so tightly he'd almost cut himself with his nails. "That maybe I need you tonight as much as you need me?"

He must have hit a nerve because for the first time her defiantly independent gaze wavered. Misery—or was it terror?—streaked across her face. For a few seconds she wrung her hands repeatedly, as if she'd put lotion on them, but then her jaw tightened and she tossed her head.

"I don't know what you're talking about," she said coolly. "I keep telling you I'm fine."

At the word, something inside him snapped with the finality and clarity of a pulled wishbone. Stalking toward her, he didn't stop until we was right in her face. Angela didn't move and he thought he saw the shimmer of tears in her eyes.

"If you're fine only hours after you watched your niece almost die," he taunted softly, determined to force a reaction out of her no matter how he had to do it, "then you must be a heartless bitch—"

Angela quietly made a mangled, broken sound.

"—but I know you better than that."

A low, moaning wail gave him enough notice to leap forward and catch her just as she crumpled, distraught in a way he'd never seen even during the darkest hours after the car accident. They sank to the scratchy carpet together and Justus cradled her between his legs, leaning back against the chair and pressing her head to his chest. She was too upset to bother protesting. A volcano of tortured sobs erupted from her chest, wracking her strong body so violently it was all he could do to hold on. Soon his shirt was wet with her hot tears.

"Shhh." He rocked her gently, willing her to stop crying

before she killed him; already his throat and chest were so constricted he could barely breathe. "Shhh. It's okay."

"I-I almost killed her—"

"No, you didn't."

"—and she was grabbing at her throat and trying to get some air and she stared at me the whole time because she was begging me to help her, but there was nothing I could do for her—"

"No."

"—and do you want to know the funny part?" Wrenching away, she twisted to face him. He didn't recognize this wrecked Angela; eye makeup ran in twin black channels from her puffy, wild eyes down her cheeks; her nose ran; her lips quivered. Suddenly she threw back her head and laughed maniacally, scaring him. "Do—do you want to know the funny part?"

"No." He tightened his grip on her.

"The funny part is she shouldn't have been asking me for help because I'm the one who poisoned her in the first place. Why would she think I could help her when I almost killed her?"

"No!" Her laughter shredded his nerves like scissors through tissue paper; he shook her sharply and she stopped. Her wide, wet gaze caught his and held, beseeching him silently to deliver her from this pain. "It wasn't your fault, Angela! You didn't know she was allergic to peanuts! None of us—"

She dropped her head so he couldn't see her face, but her heaving shoulders told him she was crying—or laughing—again. After a minute she looked up again, her eyes wetter and more swollen than ever. Swiping her hand under her nose, she whispered. "But I should have known, Justus. That's the whole point. *I should have known.*"

"How?" he cried helplessly. "How could any of us have known?"

"That day I fed her peanut butter and jelly and she got hives on her face, remember?"

Justus gasped as the memory came back to him—Maya with angry red marks on her face. Suddenly he saw where Angela was going with this. "You can't blame yourself for that," he began, gripping her shoulders. "That wasn't your—"

She smiled tiredly. "Why shouldn't I blame myself, Justus? You have good child instincts. You wanted to take her to the doctor. Remember? And I talked you out of it."

"Angela!" He heard the rising desperation in his voice and tried to tamp it back down. "You can't blame yourself for that. That's the kind of judgment call every parent makes."

"Really?" One fine brow arched toward her hairline. *"You* didn't." She paused, looking away. "Carolyn wouldn't have."

Dread uncoiled in his belly and slithered up his spine. He felt like Angela was dangling on the edge of some terrible precipice and he couldn't pull her back. Deciding to take another tack, he smoothed her hair away from her face, kissing her temple. "I don't blame you. Neither would Carolyn. Don't do this to yourself."

"You want to know what Carolyn told me the last time I spoke to her?" she asked faintly. "I've never told you."

His sense of impending doom sharpened; if his heart beat any harder or faster it would surely implode. Inch by inch he felt her slipping away, his grip on her loosening. Something told him if she said what she wanted to say, she—they— would be lost. "It doesn't matter—"

Angela smiled gently, as if she hated to disillusion him but couldn't help it—he imagined a mother telling her child Santa really didn't exist would look exactly the same way. "She said I was a terrible aunt. That I was self-absorbed and selfish and only cared about my career. That I didn't know anything about Maya."

Justus blinked in shock. He just couldn't imagine sweet, quiet Carolyn saying something so cruel. He had an easier time imagining Mister Rogers telling little kids to go to hell. "Angela," he began, "I'm sure she was just upset and didn't really—"

Angela stared at him with an unearthly calm, her eyes now clear and dry. "She meant it. And she was right—I didn't spend time with Maya. I didn't try to get to know her." Though she'd stopped crying, she made a choked, hiccupping sound. "I didn't even like her."

Justus wanted to clap his hands over his ears to protect them from such blasphemy, but he didn't. "But that was then!" he cried, squeezing her arms again. She dropped her head, apparently too ashamed to look him in the eye. Putting his hand under her chin, he jerked her head up. "Look at me, Angela!" Reluctantly she raised her gaze to his. "That was then. But when Carolyn died you stepped up to the plate. You took Maya in. You gave her a room and a home. Everything has changed."

She gaped at him as if he'd told her chocolate came from dogs. "No it hasn't! This morning I was rushing around, yelling at her to hurry up because she was making me late for court." Swallowing convulsively—he had the feeling she needed to force down the bile in her throat—she said, "I'm not sure anything much has changed at all. Except that I do love her." Her chin crumpled and trembled. "So much." Ducking her head, she swiped her eyes.

"See? That's a big deal, Angela! You've changed!"

"I've changed enough to know I want what's best for her."

The new resignation in her voice somehow scared him worse than everything she'd said up to this point. Bracing for the worst, his jaw rigid with fear, Justus said, "What do you mean?"

Angela shrugged dispassionately; her face looked entirely devoid of emotion, as if she'd used up her day's supply of energy and was now running on fumes. "I mean I was so busy trying to prove my dead sister wrong I didn't bother thinking about what was best for Maya. Until now." She took a deep breath. "I mean Maya belongs with you."

Chapter 23

Lawrence Whittington, watching Angela with vast disappointment, the way the principal watches a truant, laced his fingers together and rested his hands on the blotter atop his spotless and nearly empty desk, a massive mahogany monstrosity so large she'd often wondered if he'd needed a crane to lift it up to his corner office here on the nineteenth floor. Only a couple of family photos and two slim files sat on the desk; Larry seemed to spend most of his days wining and dining the firm's corporate clients and managing the office's myriad personnel issues rather than actually practicing law. On every wall space hung expensively framed abstract paintings in colors so vibrant and garish they looked like a 64-count box of Crayolas had projectile vomited. Although she'd seen the office and paintings many times before, Angela had never felt comfortable here. After today she certainly never would.

A slight shift of his weight caused the exquisite cordovan leather of his tall chair to squeak softly. "Angela," he said, appropriately somber as he got ready to deliver the death blow to her career, "I think you'll agree that with all you've got going on in your life right now, this is not a good time for you to be worried about partnership."

Angela watched him steadily without bothering to answer. What could she say? While the pre-accident Angela—or even the Angela of yesterday morning—would have argued, cajoled and, if need be, fought over her future with the firm, today's Angela, the one who'd seen her precious niece almost die on her watch, didn't care all that much that she was, in all likelihood, about to be fired.

"Of course."

He tapped his forefingers to his thoughtfully pursed lips. "Still . . . we are very fond of you here. When you're on your game you're a hell of a lawyer, and we'd hate to lose you."

Angela waited, resisting the urge to squirm, and wished Larry would just get the whole business over with. He'd probably give her a three-month window to transition all her cases to other lawyers in the office, so she needed to start putting together summaries, and of course she'd need to update her resume, and check in with the bar association to see what jobs were availab—

"So we'd like to offer you another position with the firm."

For the first time Angela felt a flare of interest in this conversation. She had to eat, after all, and she really didn't want to start from ground zero somewhere else. Scooting forward, she said, "What is it?"

Reclining in his chair, Larry cupped his hands behind his head. "One of our partners in the D.C. office is retiring to Florida. We'd like you to replace him. As you know, the satellite office is smaller, so the workload is lighter. In three years we'd reconsider you for partner."

Angela's heart sank. Being sent to the D.C. office was the career equivalent of being banished to St. Helena. Worse, Larry's claim that the workload was lighter there was bull— the workload was actually heavier because there were fewer lawyers to do it. So she would, in effect, be doing more work at a worse office without the long overdue pay hike she'd receive if she made partner.

And what about Maya? How could she possibly move so far away from her? It would be bad enough when Maya went to live with Justus—how could she bear to move five hundred miles away, where she'd only be able to see her on holidays and odd weekends?

And Justus. God, how could she ever leave Justus? She couldn't.

Smiling politely, she said, "That's quite an offer, Larry. I don't know what to say."

Larry waved a manicured hand, his onyx cufflink winking at her from its nest in the crisp white fold of his shirt. "Sleep on it for a few nights, Angela," he said benevolently, the czar giving the peasant a few extra grains of rye. "Think it over. There's no rush."

Angela nodded, but her mind was made up. She'd sleep on it to make it look good—no need to burn all her bridges behind her—and in the morning she'd tell Larry that although she greatly appreciated his generous offer, she couldn't possibly move so far away.

In the meantime she'd work on her resume.

Justus followed his father into his library, took his usual seat in the chair opposite the desk, and watched while Vincent sank, somewhat gingerly, into his chair. Weak afternoon sunlight tried—unsuccessfully, for the most part—to stream into the room via the wood blinds; the roaring fire and well-placed, softly lit lamps were the only things rescuing the room from outright gloom. Justus considered it a sign of how bad he had it for Angela that he'd come here, to the lion's den, to ask for help. He'd always hated this formal room, where the walls themselves seemed to stare reproachfully at him and require him to think only Serious Thoughts. When he was little and he and V.J. played the board game Clue, Mrs. Plum and the others always met their ghastly fates in libraries that looked, in Justus's mind at least, just like this. Well, the setting didn't matter. If he had to follow his father down into hell to get his help, he would.

An insidious little idea had burrowed its way into his brain the way a rabbit tunnels through the ground. Once there, the idea had taken hold, but if he was being honest with himself—and why not?—he had to admit he really didn't want to dislodge it. And as long as he was being honest he should also admit that although the idea solved a pressing problem, it would have come to him, sooner or later, even if there hadn't been a problem.

Vincent folded his hands in his lap and tried to control his amused smirk. Finally he gave up and grinned gleefully. "I didn't know hell had frozen over today."

"Check the papers." Justus shifted uncomfortably in his chair, as if finding the exact right position would save him from the embarrassment of what he was about to do.

"So." Vincent eyed him steadily. "What can I do for you?"

"I need two favors."

Vincent's eyes widened in obvious shock. "I—I'll do whatever I can," he said, as if he was afraid Justus would change his mind and leave if he didn't answer quickly.

Justus held up a hand, slowing things down a little. "Before you go promising things you won't be able to deliver on, I also need to tell you I don't want you asking a lot of questions."

Vincent blinked twice. "Of course."

"Well, okay." Justus rubbed the back of his neck, which was shot through with tension. "Can Maya stay here tonight? I can bring her over right after sch—"

"Of course."

Well, that wasn't so hard, was it? Except of course that was the easier of the two favors—when had a doting grandfather ever said no to having his grandchild spend the night? Vincent watched him patiently, and Justus broke out into a fine sweat across his forehead. His fidgety hands rubbed up and down his thighs several times, making that strange, high-pitched whistle as they skimmed over the nylon of his athletic pants. Realizing what he was doing, he took a deep breath and blew it out his mouth. "And I need Mom's ruby ring."

Vincent's eyes widened infinitesimally; one side of his mouth turned up a fraction of an inch. "Is it time?" he asked softly, leaning forward a little over the desk.

Justus thought of Angela, and his heart swelled like a sponge taking on water. Was it time to burn his little black book—all twelve volumes of it? Was it time for him to come home at a decent hour and do the dishes after dinner? Was it time to put someone else's needs before his? Was it time to embrace fiscal responsibility? Was it time to be a father and to bring other children into the world at the soonest possible time?

With Angela by his side? "Hell, yeah," he told Vincent. "It's time."

Vincent's eyes warmed and misted, and he gave a sharp nod of satisfaction. Planting his palms on his desk, he pressed himself to his feet and turned to the wall behind him. He swung open the hinged painting—another hunt scene—to reveal a large wall safe. With deft fingers, he entered the combination and threw open the gleaming steel door. A black velvet box appeared in his gnarled hand, and he quickly shut the safe and put the picture back in its place. Sitting down again he hesitated, his unfocused gaze staring off in the distance. Finally he brought the box to his lips.

"This is hard," he whispered. "I haven't seen it in a long time."

Justus heard the tears in his voice, but for once his father's show of emotion over his mother didn't infuriate him. He felt, instead, an infinite sadness and a strange bewilderment. Had Vincent really loved her, then? For so many years Justus had thought otherwise, but now he wasn't so sure. Comforting words wouldn't come, so he sat quietly, waiting.

Blinking furiously, Vincent came to life. "Well." He opened the box and held it for Justus to see under the green glass of his banker's lamp.

Justus's breath caught and his heart twisted violently. Vincent was right: this was hard. There was something deeply unsettling about seeing his mother's ruby ring without also seeing his mother. He'd gotten used to seeing Carolyn wear Mom's diamond anniversary ring over the years, but this was somehow different. Tears pooled in his eyes and he furiously blinked them back. After a minute his vision cleared and he looked objectively at the ruby-and-diamond ring that would surely cover the entire bottom third of Angela's finger.

Even though he was no expert on jewelry, Justus could see what a work of art it was. The shape reminded him of the way a child draws a flower, with a large central oval ringed by eight loop-de-loop circles for the petals. But saying the ring looked like a flower was like saying the ocean looked like many drops of water. If forced at gunpoint Justus couldn't begin to describe its magic—the flaming, bloody red of the ruby, the simultaneous icy clarity and rainbow brilliance of the diamonds.

Normally Justus would roll his eyes with disgust, snort, and do all but spit on such an outrageous display of conspicuous consumption. What woman, in good conscience, could wear this . . . this mineral when she could sell it and buy a lovely four bedroom, two-and-a-half-bath house for some deserving needy family instead? But staring at the ring now, his mind on the woman who'd wear it, he could only think one thing. *It isn't good enough for her*.

"I bought this for your mother after I settled my second big case," Vincent told him. Leaning back in his chair, he propped his feet on the desk and crossed his ankles. "I paid off the mortgage with the first settlement." He chuckled at some distant memory. "She about died when she saw it. Cried and said it was too much and we needed to save for college." Turning, he winked at Justus. "But that ring stayed on her finger until the day she died."

Justus remembered. The fiery ring had perfectly complemented his mother's understated elegance. Sometimes, as much as he hated to admit it, he had trouble seeing her beloved, loving face, but he could always remember her delicate hands with the flashing ring. What other kid's mother wore a ruby while she rolled out a piecrust—or Play-Doh? "I know."

Lost in his thoughts, Vincent studied the ring, turning it this way and that under the lamp. Justus studied his father. The harsh light was not flattering; Vincent's eyes looked hollow, his skin waxy and his jaw gaunt, almost skeletal. His face sagged, as if the weight of his memories, good and bad, was too much for him. "Ah, well." With the delicacy and precision of a technician disarming a bomb, he closed the box, pressing both halves together so they didn't snap. "It'll be nice to see it on a woman's hand again."

He held the box out to Justus, but when Justus reached across the desk for it, Vincent's arm drew back, as if he couldn't quite bear to part with it. He touched the box to his lips again. Staring off in the distance, he said faintly, "I wish—" His voice cracked like a preteen boy's, and he broke off.

Justus shifted awkwardly in his chair, too fascinated to look away. In his entire life he couldn't ever remember his father voluntarily sharing his vulnerable, emotional side with him.

Nostrils flaring, Vincent took several deep breaths and finished his thought. "I wish I'd known I didn't have forever to be with her." Getting quickly to his feet, he walked around the desk and past Justus's chair, pressing the box into Justus's hand as he went. "Give it to Angela with my blessings. Now if you'll excuse—"

"I'm not sure . . ."

Pausing, Vincent turned and quirked one tufted white brow, genuine concern written all over his face. "Not sure about what, Son?"

Slumping back in his chair, Justus stared up at the beamed ceiling and wondered what stupid impulse had made him open his big mouth. He was not, to say the least, in the habit of confiding in Vincent. But he may as well admit it, to himself if no one else: he was petrified. He, Justus Robinson, who'd slung more women's panties over his shoulder than almost anyone he knew, was terrified that, once he finally got up the nerve to ask her, Angela would reject him. What a kick in the teeth. He would almost laugh at the irony if he weren't so damn scared.

As a betting man he had to put his odds at about fifty-fifty, if that. Sure, she was fond of him. Sure, they had phenomenal sex. But she'd never claimed to love him, and he knew a woman like Angela would probably never marry someone if she didn't love him.

Even if she did love him, he certainly wasn't anything like Ron, the idiot she'd thought she'd marry. He wasn't a doctor, lawyer, or accountant, and he never would be. If she wanted to spend her evenings sitting around discussing the law and politics and other matters of Great Interest, then she was sorely out of luck with him.

And of course he was younger than she was—seven years

younger. She'd never really mentioned that fact, but what if she thought he was too immature for her? What the hell would he do then? He couldn't very well age himself like they did to the children on the soaps.

"Justus?" Vincent said softly. "Are you okay?"

No, he really wasn't okay. He was afraid—more afraid than he'd been of losing Maya to Angela, more afraid than he was of financial failure with the club. Staring up into his father's sympathetic face, he revealed his worst vulnerability: "I'm not sure she'll say yes."

"Ah." Vincent nodded sagely, as if Justus's fear didn't surprise him at all and he agreed only the most foolish of men would be unafraid at a time like this. Stepping closer he clapped Justus on the shoulder, the first time Justus could remember Vincent voluntarily touching him in more than ten years. "You can trust me on this, Justus." He squeezed Justus's shoulder. "You may have to ask her more than once, but she'll say yes. Don't you worry."

Dropping his hand, Vincent slipped quietly out of the room, leaving Justus to stew in his own juices.

Angela, still in her red wool coatdress from work, sat brooding on the steps of the wide curved staircase in Carolyn's house, her back against the wall. She'd flicked on the kitchen light, a couple of lamps in the living room, and the lamp on the foyer table, but the house was otherwise dark. Much to her surprise, though, it didn't feel creepy. She felt oddly comforted, as if Carolyn was closer here, which was, of course, the reason she'd come. Maybe if she sat quietly enough, listened hard enough, and concentrated enough, Carolyn would give her some sign she was doing the right thing by giving Maya to Justus. After a few minutes of absolute silence, though—she didn't even hear the drip of water in the sink or the on/off cycle of the furnace—she concluded she was wasting her time. She was just about to stand and give her back a little relief from the carpeted stairs, when she heard a car pull into the driveway. Within seconds a key turned in the door and she watched as Justus let himself inside.

Sitting up straighter, she smiled slightly, her heart picking up its beat. Ten years and all these weeks later, she still hadn't gotten over the breathless excitement she always felt whenever he walked into the room. His black sweater, dark jeans, and black leather jacket kicked up his virility several notches; the moody intensity in his eyes deepened the usual air of danger that wrapped around him like his skin. If he was surprised to see her sitting on the steps in a deserted house in the near dark he didn't show it.

"Hi." He pocketed the keys and leaned back against the door. "Looks like I found your hiding place."

"Am I hiding? We need to get the house ready to list for sale, and I—"

One heavy brow slid toward his hairline in open challenge. "You're not going to waste my time and deny it, are you?"

That shut her up. Unable to meet the weight of his gaze, she looked to the living room, the polished hardwood floor, her lap—anywhere but in his speculative, intense eyes. Smoothing her dress over her knees, she finally said, "How was your day?"

"Okay, I guess." His hands slid into the pockets of his jeans. "I called the school about thirty times to check on Maya."

"Yeah." She smiled grimly. "So did I. Where is she?"

"My dad's. I wanted to talk to you."

"Oh."

She watched warily as he came closer, sat on the step at her feet and leaned against the rails. A crowded, claustrophobic feeling made her wrap her arms around her legs, as close to the fetal position as she could get. The hard glitter in his eyes told her she'd irritated him.

"I'm not going to bite, you know."

Her heart thudded uncomfortably in her chest, probably realizing before the rest of her that the remainder of this conversation wouldn't be pleasant. "I know. But I don't want you to try to talk me out of what I've decided. And I don't want to fight with you."

His jaw tightened down, reminding her of a catapult seconds before the rope is cut. Closing his eyes, he tipped his head back until it also rested against the railing. "What happened at the meeting with your boss?" he asked quietly.

She impatiently shrugged her tense shoulders. They had forest fires to put out and didn't need to be bothered with the smoldering trash can of her career. "He didn't fire me outright. He offered me a transfer to the D.C. office."

Justus's head jerked upright and his eyes flew open. "You're not leaving?"

He may have tacked a question mark on the end of his sentence for form's sake, but she knew—and hated—a command when she heard one. Anyway, they had far more important things to discuss. She waved a hand. "I told him I'd think about it."

His brows sank over his wide, shocked eyes, as if he'd just seen her steal a car and wasn't quite sure what to do about it. Leaning forward, she touched his arm.

"Justus, we have more important things to talk about. We need to figure out how to tell Maya she's going to live with you, and—"

"No." His angry, adamant voice cracked through the air like a sonic boom. "We're not us and them anymore, Angela. We're us. We can work this out another way."

She saw no reason for and couldn't understand his determined optimism. "How?" she cried irritably. "We can't both adopt her, and I can't see any other way—"

"I can." For the first time his gaze wavered. He swallowed hard and a deep flush crept over his cheeks. The silence stretched. "I know a perfect solution," he finally said softly, as if the idea was less revolutionary if he snuck up on it. Drawing a deep breath, he spoke again, firmly this time. "You can marry me."

Chapter 24

Angela heard his words but they didn't penetrate her understanding any more than a thrown pebble penetrates a frozen lake. If she hadn't been so shocked she might have accused him of making a very bad joke, but one look at his strained, waiting face told her he didn't think marriage was a laughing matter any more than she did.

Her heart nearly jackrabbited out of her chest. Its foolish, girlish recesses had waited all her life for this moment, her first—and only—marriage proposal, but the details were all wrong. She'd pictured a candlelit ballroom or a beach at sunset, not her dead sister's house. She'd pictured an older man—handsome, sure, with a suit and tie and an MBA, JD, or other string of letters after his name. She'd pictured declarations of undying love and repeated mentions of eternity and forever as she giddily shrieked *yes*. She had not pictured a devastating young womanizer in jeans. And yet . . . her confused, beleaguered heart also did the most thrilling somersaults at the thought of marrying Justus.

Maybe the first thing she should do was make sure she'd heard correctly. Clearing her dry throat, she said, "You—you want to marry me?"

He swallowed audibly. A brittle tension surrounded him, and she had the strange thought that one wrong move or misstep, one poorly chosen word from her would shatter something deep within him. What? His temper? His ego? She needed to tread very carefully here.

"Yes," he said quietly.

Her silly heart rose and soared free, like a kite breaking away from its string, while her head screamed no, she could never do it, he didn't really mean it anyway. That treacherous, girlish part of her whispered maybe he did mean it, maybe they could make it work, maybe they did belong together, but she didn't want to consider it, much less believe it. A question rose to her lips, one she knew she should leave unasked, but the lawyer in her couldn't drop it.

"Because of Maya?"

He stared silently at her, a thousand unrecognizable emotions scrolling across his face. She felt him weighing and filtering his words, throwing some away and choosing others. "Yes," he said finally. "Partially."

A small piece of her heart—well, not so small, really—withered, turned to black, and died, like a frostbitten finger. Bile rose from deep within her constricted throat, threatening to choke her. What a foolish, foolish woman she was—too stupid to live. Why else would Justus want to marry her? Because he'd fallen passionately in love with her? Like Ronnie? What a laugh! How many times would she have to learn this one painful lesson? How many times would she have to be slammed over the head with the same information before it finally sank into her thick skull? Men simply did not fall in love with her. Nor did they want to marry her—not for the traditional reasons, anyway. It just didn't happen. Period.

Struggling to keep her face from crumpling like a ball of used aluminum foil, she rose tiredly to her feet and walked to the bottom of the steps, making sure not to touch him in any way. She paced back and forth in the foyer, her heels tapping forcefully on the blond hardwood floors like a hammer. "That's no reason to get married, Justus."

"It's a great reason to get married."

"It would never work."

Still sitting, he twisted around to watch her. "We could make it work."

Their gazes locked and held with a thrilling jolt that sent a surge of adrenalin through her. Turning quickly away—his determined eyes stared so intently she felt as if he were dissecting her innermost thoughts—she struggled to keep her composure even though she could barely breathe. Her claustrophobic feeling intensified a million times. Reaching up a hand to rub her forehead, she realized distantly that it was shaking.

"Why should you make such a sacrifice for Maya?"

"It's no sacrifice."

"Don't say that!"

They both jumped at the rising hysteria in her voice. Justus froze. She rubbed her forehead again, realized she was doing it, and crossed her arms tightly over her chest. The air in the foyer was thick now, stifling. Like trying to breathe fudge. The powerful urge to throw open some windows to let in the cold night air or, better yet, just fling open the door and run away into the night was almost undeniable. Fighting hard to get a grip on herself, she managed half a strangled breath, terrified she was on the verge of careening completely out of control.

"Don't say that," she said again, calmly now. "You've told me before you don't want to get married—"

"I do now." He surged to his feet, took two long strides, and stopped right in front of her—way too close. When she took a hasty step back he clamped his hands on her upper arms, rooting her in place. Stooping down, he stared at her with glittering, determined eyes. "*I do now.*"

Her heart twisted as if a pair of invisible hands had wrung it like a wet towel. Again she felt hysteria struggling to run free, but she would not—*would not*—give in to it. Looking away, she laughed and said, "There's more to marriage than great sex and making a home for Maya."

The flare of anger in his eyes and hardening of his jaw told her she had irrevocably swum into dangerous, shark-infested waters. He would never physically hurt her, of course, but instinctively she understood life, as she currently knew it, was entirely in his hands and in mortal jeopardy.

"I know that," he said, his voice low and measured.

She snorted. "Yeah? We have nothing in common other than Maya. What about *that*?"

His mouth twisted. "That's not true. But even if it were, I wouldn't care."

God, he looked like he meant it. She struggled to break away—the air was so close in here now she wanted to tear her clothes off her body—but succeeded only in getting him to tighten his fingers until they dug painfully into her arms.

"This is so ridiculous!" she cried, incredulous, to the ceiling. Was anyone up there getting this? Did God think this whole marry-me routine was as funny as she did? "What about children?"

Without one second's hesitation, as if he'd already thought about it, he said, "We'll have them as soon as possible. At least two." His voice dropped to a husky whisper. "If I had my way we'd start on that tonight."

A sudden surge of blinding rage made her strong. With one great wrench she flung her arms free, sending him staggering back a step. Why was Justus doing this to her? Why was he putting her through this agony of pretending to want what she wanted?

"You're a liar!" she shrieked. "You're such a liar! I guess next you're going to claim you'll be faithful to me even if this little marriage of convenience lasts sixty years!"

He looked her right in the eye and didn't blink. "I will."

Shaking her head so violently she could almost feel her brain slamming into her skull, she cried out with fury and threw her arms wide. "I'm seven years older than you, Justus! Did you think about that? And—"

"Yes."

"—what happens in a few years when I'm forty-seven and you're only forty, and some hot little half-dressed twenty-five-year-old wants you to train her?" She made quotation marks with her fingers. "Huh? What about that?"

Justus stilled, staring disbelievingly at her, his thick brows sunk so low over his eyes she wondered how he could still see. The harsh silence that followed only made her seem all the more manic in contrast.

"I thought," he said so quietly she had to strain to hear him, "you knew me a little better than that by now. Maybe I was wrong."

The vaguely insulted note in his voice deflated her anger and almost made her feel ashamed for doubting him and introducing mistrust into their relationship. Her defiant gaze wavered and fell. But then a picture of Janet flashed through her mind, strengthening her determination to trust her instincts. Turning, she walked very slowly back to the steps and sank down again before her legs gave out from under her. She propped her elbows on her knees and dropped her head in her hands, pressing her palms to her temples.

Raising her head to lock gazes with him, she asked tiredly, "Have you ever been faithful before?"

He blinked furiously but didn't answer. Of course. They both knew the truth—why on earth had she bothered to ask?

"I've never been in a committed relationship before, Angela."

"Yeah, well, why don't you give one a test run before you start talking marriage?"

"That's what I've been doing."

She couldn't think of any response to that. Deadlocked, they stared at each other. Angela desperately tried to read his expression, to figure out why he was doing this—what he could possibly hope to gain—but the only thing she saw on his face was determination. He moved to the foot of the steps, his fists shoved deep in his pockets.

"I thought you wanted to get married."

The taunt was subtle but unmistakable and though his face was bland and sheep-like in its innocence, she knew the wolf was still there somewhere. She had the feeling he wanted to provoke some sort of admission out of her—about marriage, of course, but about some other, still unidentified thing, too—and wouldn't stop until he did. There was no point denying she wanted marriage; she would never tell such a colossal lie. But, foolish as she was, she still held out hope that one day she'd get a legitimate proposal—one given freely, without duress. Not like this. Never like this.

"I do. To the right man, when the time is—"

She could have bitten off her tongue even before she saw the pain—naked and raw—flash across his face. Just as quickly his broad shoulders squared off and his lip curled into a nasty, sarcastic sneer.

"Well," he said mildly, "since you were so desperate to marry Ron you'd have hopped the next plane to Vegas if he'd bothered to ask you, which of course he didn't—"

She flinched as if he'd called her a whore.

"—and since you can't seem to come up with excuses fast

enough, I can only conclude you're just not woman enough to tell me I'm not the right man."

If he'd taken a sword and impaled her with it, burying it up to the hilt in her heart, he couldn't have injured her more. Tears of humiliation blinded her and her lower lip trembled, but her remaining ounce of dignity forced her to stare him down.

"I may be desperate," she told him quietly, "but I'm not desperate enough to marry a man who doesn't love me."

His mouth fell open into a gape. He stared intently, as if he meant to see into her thoughts by sheer force of will. He took two steps closer, stopped, then wheeled away to pace the foyer in long, restless strides. Finally he approached again, palms up, beseeching.

"Is that what this is about?" he cried incredulously, as if he'd made a miraculous discovery along the lines of gravity or electricity. "*Love*?"

Her pride still gravely wounded, she could only nod. Dropping her head, she swiped at her eyes. "Among other things, yes."

Justus stilled. "Do you still love Ron?"

Sensing the direction the conversation could take, she watched him warily. Deep in her belly a knot of dread—and fear—pulsed to life. She opened her mouth, but her voice took several long seconds to activate. "No."

His eyes widened fractionally, but other than that he stood frozen. No, not entirely frozen—she saw the rapid rise and fall of his chest as he breathed. "Do you . . . love me?"

The fear in her belly exploded, sending shards of doubt and panic to every corner of her body. Her erratic heart began to skip every other beat and then lapsed into a frenetic rhythm that should have sent her to the hospital in full cardiac arrest.

Did she love him? Was he kidding?

Was it possible he didn't read her feelings on her face every time she looked at him? And did he think she went wild in bed like that for any man who happened to pass through? Of course she loved him. She loved his mischief, his kindness, and his compassion. She loved his strength and determination; whenever she thought about how he'd put himself through school and built his club, her heart swelled with unspeakable pride. She loved him beyond all reason—enough to give herself to him even though she was positive he would one day break her heart. The only thing scarier than the prospect of not having Justus in her life was the thought of dying.

And yet . . . she'd thought she loved Ron, too, hadn't she?

Staring into his strained, hopeful face, her fear wouldn't let her bridge the chasm between them, no matter how great the potential rewards. "I don't know."

His shoulders slumped and the hopeful light in his eyes died. Nodding, as if she'd only confirmed what he'd suspected all along, he turned, made his way slowly to the door and put his hand on the knob. The strangest stab of disappointment, almost as great as her fear, shot through her.

But then he leaned his head on the door for a second—as if he was praying or gathering his strength—and turned back to face her. Rushing forward, he sank to his knees in front of her on the steps, grabbed her hands and, ignoring her cry of surprise, pulled them to his chest where she felt his powerful heart pound as hard as hers.

"Well, here's what I know, Angela." At the sound of his raw, husky voice she wanted to cover her ears; worse, she wanted to close her eyes so she wouldn't see what looked like bottomless vulnerability on his face. "I know we belong together. I've known since I was seventeen there could never be another woman like you in my life—"

Angela shrank away in rising horror. How could he do this to her? How could he plant this insidious little seed in her mind—a life with him, Maya and their own children, living happily ever after—when they both knew, or should know, that it could never be? It was obvious he would play whatever dirty little tricks he thought were necessary to build the best life for Maya—and he was a master at dirty tricks, wasn't he? Wasn't it also obvious a man like Justus could never settle down and be happy with just one woman? And even if he could, it would never be with her! Ronnie, as milquetoast as Wonder Bread, hadn't been satisfied with her.

How could Justus?

"No," she said faintly, hoping to shut him up before he said any more untrue, unforgettable, and unbelievable endearments that would taunt her the rest of her lonely life.

"—and I can't raise Maya without you, and I wouldn't ever want another woman to be pregnant with my child—"

"Don't," she whispered, agonized by the thought of what would never be: her belly swollen, Justus's beautiful child inside. She was profoundly aware this could well be her last chance at motherhood.

A faint smile softened his intensity and his eyes shone with some inner light she couldn't possibly have put there. "I know I love you, Angela."

Just like that, her heart broke. Her throat knotted with unshed tears, threatening to choke her. There it was: the one thing in the world she wanted more desperately than anything else—the one thing she could never believe—had just been used as the ultimate weapon against her. Did he really think she was stupid enough to fall for this eleventh hour confession? What a manipulator he was—the consummate charmer. And just like she'd always known he would, he'd broken her heart.

"Oh, Justus," she said nastily, "I didn't think even you would stoop this low to get what you want."

Shock replaced the warmth in his eyes, followed quickly by what looked like anguish, then, finally, anger. His cheeks and the tip of his nose reddened; his nostrils flared. He backed carefully away from her, like a hunter who'd startled a lioness enjoying her kill and hoped to escape in one piece. Standing up to his full height he stared at her with open hatred, the vengeful hostility in his face a million times worse than she'd ever seen when he looked at his father. She realized immediately, with despair, that their relationship, whatever it had been, was over. Though she didn't understand, she knew she'd said something irrevocable, and if she apologized every day for the rest of her life he'd still never forgive her.

His malevolent, unflinching gaze locked with hers and she braced herself. "That's the second time today you've made it perfectly clear how little you think of me, Angela." He smiled crookedly. "Don't worry. I finally get it. I won't bother you again—there's too many other fish in the sea." Turning, he leaned casually against the wall, crossed his legs at the ankles and slid his hands into his pockets. "I used to think Ron was stupid for letting you go." His eyes glinted, hard and cruel. "Now I wonder how he ever lasted three years with a block of ice like you and made it out with his balls intact."

Angela flinched and made a startled, aborted sound.

Justus stared at her. "I oughta buy him a drink."

Angela's heart, merely broken until now, splintered into a thousand shards. Putting one hand on the banister for desperately needed support, she stood as gracefully as she could, climbed down the steps and picked up her purse and coat with her head held high. As she walked out the door, shutting it gently behind her, Justus's flashing gaze followed her.

Outside, the black night surrounded her. Shaking violently,

she gratefully took several deep gulps of cold air. She'd just fished her keys out of her purse when she heard a roar of rage, followed by a single, violent pounding sound, from inside the house. Ignoring it, she walked with wobbly legs to her car, got in, started it, and dialed her cell phone by the glowing blue interior lights.

"Larry Whittington," said the booming voice on the other end.

Pressing her knees together to stop shaking, she spoke in her bright, professional phone voice. "Larry, it's Angela. I've decided to accept your offer. I can move within the month."

"Wonderful!" Larry cried. "I'll talk to you about the details tomorrow."

Angela hung up, put the car into reverse, and pulled into the street.

She sobbed all the way home.

"Can I talk to you alone for a minute before we tell her, Justus?"

Shutting his apartment door behind Angela with his left hand, Justus turned to look at the woman who had so cavalierly rejected his love last night. She had the nerve to look awful—worse, actually, than he remembered her looking in the days following the accident. Huge, dark circles rimmed her puffy eyes, which looked all the more dramatic because she'd pulled her hair back in a ponytail so tight it threatened to pull her hair out by the roots. Dressed in jeans and a knit top, it didn't seem at all possible this one miserable-looking woman, holding her purse and jacket in a death grip, was capable of taking his heart and cruelly smashing it against the rocks.

But she was.

He couldn't get over the irony. He, a man who'd broken more hearts than he could possibly ever count, had fallen in love with, and had his heart broken by, a woman desperate to get married, but not desperate enough to marry him. Maybe he should call Janet and tell her about his comeuppance just so she could laugh her head off.

Realizing Angela was staring at him, waiting for an answer, he shrugged dispassionately. "If you want."

Her alarmed gaze locked on his Ace-bandaged right hand, then shot to his face. "What happened to you?" she cried as if he'd shown up with an ax buried in his skull.

Well, that was Angela for you. Practically laughing in his face when he bared his soul to her on the one hand, practically crying when she saw his little wound on the other. Queen of the mixed-message. He wasn't about to give her something else to laugh about by telling her he'd stupidly punched the wall after she walked out last night.

Flexing his swollen fingers, he felt stabbing jolts of pain shoot over the back of his hand and up his arm—a refreshing change from the emotional pain this little witch had heaped on him. Was his hand broken? He didn't know and couldn't care less. Narrowing his eyes, he glared at her and wished he could tear her limb from limb for toying with his emotions when he knew she didn't give a damn about him.

"You've gotta be kidding me. Save the act, okay?"

Teary wide eyes stared reproachfully at him and her chin quivered. Blinking furiously, she turned, laid her belongings on the hall chair and moved into the living room. Clearing her throat, she said, "Where is Maya?"

"In my bedroom watching TV." Luckily he'd gotten her from Lena this morning while his father was still in the shower. He wasn't ready yet to face Vincent and tell him he'd failed so miserably in his mission.

She gestured to the sofa. "Can we sit down?"

Having not slept a wink last night, he was beyond exhaustion. If he sat down now, there was every possibility he'd be unable to get up again. He turned his back to her, pacing away toward the window. "Sit if you want."

Pushing aside the curtain he saw what he already knew: it was a glorious winter day, the afternoon sky such a brilliant blue he had to squint against it. Canada geese splashed and honked on the small man-made lake. Didn't they know Angela had ruined his life last night?

Maybe later he'd bundle Maya up and take her to the park. They'd both need some fresh air and time—a lot of time—to decompress before this day was over.

The squeak of leather behind him told him Angela had decided to have a seat. Propping his elbow over his head against the glass, he waited. It was rude, of course, not to sit down or at least face her, but he couldn't make himself look at her. Balling his fist he welcomed the pain again, using it to clear his head.

She cleared her throat. "I've . . . decided to go ahead and move to Washington."

He couldn't summon one iota of surprise. Grunting, he said, "Of course you did."

As he should've known, the one thing that could make the whole situation worse had happened. Maybe he should just be grateful she hadn't announced she was relocating to Washington *and* marrying Ron. The only real surprise was that the crushing pain in his chest hadn't killed him; for half a second he actually wished he were dead—at least then he wouldn't have to look at her again, or hear her voice, or smell her.

"So—" she hesitated. "Maya can come visit me for a month over the summer, and for holidays, and we can go to the Smithsonian—"

Dumbfounded, he turned to gape at her, so revolted he wanted to throw her out of his apartment. Did she actually believe any of that crap would make one bit of difference to Maya? At the look on his face, Angela froze, her voice trailing off.

"Yeah," he said. "I'm sure that'll make all the difference to Maya. After you break your promise about being a family, just tell her you'll see her in six months when school's out. If you mention you'll take her to some museum with airplanes and dinosaurs, I'm sure she'll understand completely."

Angela's gaze wavered and fell and she dropped her head, mollifying him somewhat. He held a hand out toward his bedroom. "Let's go," he barked. "Dr. Brenner said we just needed to tell her straight out. I want to get this over with."

Like a mastodon trapped in a tar pit, Angela slowly got to her feet and plodded ahead of him into his bedroom, where Maya sat, cross-legged on the end of the bed, remote in hand, staring at the TV.

"Hey, Sweetie!" Angela sat next to her, pulling her into a hug. Maya smiled delightedly, a stab directly to Justus's heart because after this little conversation he didn't know when he'd see that glorious smile again. He sat on Maya's other side and clicked off the TV.

Angela smoothed Maya's hair with fidgety hands, obviously stalling for time. "How was Grandpa's last night?"

"Good. We had hot dogs and French fries for dinner. With strawberry ice cream."

Angela recoiled as if Maya'd said they'd eaten a stray puppy. If Justus hadn't been so upset he would have laughed at the absurdity. Angela just couldn't help herself. "Any veggies?"

Maya nodded, smiling proudly. "I told Gran'pa I needed some carrot sticks."

Angela kissed her forehead and hugged her again. "Good girl." Over the top of Maya's head Angela caught Justus's gaze and stared beseechingly at him, but he narrowed his eyes. If she thought he was going to help her break Maya's heart she damn well better think again.

"Sweetie," she began tentatively, again smoothing Maya's braids, "Uncle Justus and I have been talking about what's best for you, and we have something to tell you."

Maya sat up a little straighter, as if she sensed something important was at hand and wanted to take it as seriously as they did. "Okay."

Angela swallowed hard. "Well. . . you know how I always have to work late at night and go to work early and I hardly ever get to see you. So we thought maybe it would be best if"—she shuddered—"you came here to live with Uncle Justus."

Everyone froze while the words hung in the air like a noxious cloud of mustard gas.

"But—" Maya blinked furiously and Justus saw her little mind working, struggling to understand the inexplicable. He wanted to tell her not to waste her time. "I live with you now."

Angela nodded, her lips pressed tightly together around a strained smile. "I know. But from now on you'll stay here with Uncle Justus. He's going to fix up his extra room for you."

Maya's head jerked violently around to glance at Justus, her braids swinging and hitting her in the face. He tried to smile encouragingly, but it felt more like a grimace. Her brow wrinkled with bewilderment, as if she couldn't quite believe this little farce. She looked back at Angela. "What about my purple room?"

"I'm sure Uncle Justus would be happy to paint your new room any color you like."

"But you said I could live with you." A plaintive note crept into Maya's voice.

Tears filled Angela's eyes, and she didn't bother hiding them. "I'm not sure I've done such a good job taking care of you, Sweetie."

Maya's eyes widened with sudden comprehension. "Yes, you have! And I won't eat any more peanut butter. I promise!" She smiled hugely, obviously thrilled she'd discovered a workable solution to their problem.

"I know you won't, Maya." Angela's voice sounded thick—choked—with emotion. "But you still need to live with Uncle Justus."

A heavy, pregnant silence fell. Knowing Maya had finally reached the end of her short rope, Justus braced himself. Sure enough, Maya's entire body went rigid, as if she'd been hit with Harry Potter's *petrificus* spell. Her face twisted into a spiteful three-and-a-half-year-old's scowl.

"You said!" she screeched, her fists balling on either side of her folded legs. "You said we'd be a family now! *You said!*"

Tears spilled openly down Angela's face. "I'm sorry, Maya."

Justus had had enough. Pulling Maya back against him, he kissed the top of her head and stared malevolently at Angela. "You've done your damage. You can go now."

Nodding numbly, Angela surged to her feet and looked blindly around, as if she couldn't remember where the door was and needed someone to guide her. Maya, apparently realizing Angela actually meant to go and actually meant to leave her there, broke away from his arms, leapt off the bed, threw herself at Angela's legs, and shrieked like she was being hacked to pieces with a machete.

"*You said! You said!*"

Obviously alarmed, Angela bent at the waist and tried to

comfort her. "Shhh, don't cry, Sweetie." She ineffectually patted and rubbed her back and shoulders. "It's okay." Maya threw back her head and howled like a dying animal, her face and Angela's jeans already wet with tears. Angela tried to step away but Maya didn't let go, forcing Angela to wobble precariously.

Cursing viciously, Justus knelt and gently but firmly, ignoring the pain to his hand, peeled Maya's strong little arms away from Angela. His precious angel was a wreck: her face was a snotty wet mess, and her whole body shook with sobs. This was exactly the kind of breakdown he'd feared she'd have after her parents died—maybe she'd just finally reached her limit and couldn't be strong any more. He wondered distantly if she'd make herself sick enough to vomit. When finally he had her in his arms, he stood, struggling to hold her as she thrashed and flailed. One arm caught him squarely across the nose and sparks of pain had him seeing stars.

Angela dropped her head into her hands and sobbed openly, her cries nearly as loud as Maya's. He wanted to jerk her hands down and scream at her, to rub her face in the scene: *Look what you've done!* He didn't. Instead, balancing a now limp Maya over his shoulder, he used his other hand to grab Angela's upper arm, forcibly march her to the bedroom door and shove her out into the hall.

"Get out." He had a brief glimpse of her distraught, wet, unrecognizable ruin of a face before he slammed the door so hard the windows rattled.

Carrying Maya back to the bed, he sank onto it, resting against the headboard, and cradled her. She was insensible, shaking and crying worse than he'd ever seen. Rocking her, he murmured for what seemed like decades. "Shhh, Little Girl. I've got you. I've got you."

"Unnnhh, unnnhh, unnnhh," she said, shuddering, gasping, and sobbing.

He had no idea how long he rocked her, but finally, when long shadows drifted over his bed, she went slack and he realized she'd fallen asleep. Only then did he rest her head on the pillow, cover her with the blanket, go into the bathroom, shut the door, put the lid down on the toilet, collapse, bury his head in his hands, and sob like a baby himself.

Chapter 25

Vincent, wearing his navy warm-up suit, stepped into the club, noting the juice bar overflowed with people just like the small parking lot overflowed with cars. Nine-thirty on a weekday morning, when the early crowd had come and left for work already, and well before the lunch crowd, and the place was still packed with clients. He felt a surge of satisfaction and fatherly pride. Justus's club was clearly a huge success, and his hardheaded son had built it from the ground up without a lick of help from him.

He'd expected as much.

Sure, he'd hoped Justus would be a lawyer and join the firm like Vincent Jr. had, and he'd tried everything short of armed robbery and murder to bend his stubborn son to his will. It hadn't worked, of course. It never did with Justus. But he'd always known Justus would be successful at whatever he chose even if it was—he gave a mental sigh—a fitness club.

He walked to the front desk, but before he could ask the receptionist where Justus was, Brian appeared from around the corner and saw him. "Mr. Robinson!" he cried, a delighted smile on his face. Taking Vincent's hand, he pumped it warmly. "Good to see you."

Vincent clapped him on the back. There had been times, over the years, when Brian felt like more of a son to him than Justus, and he realized he missed him. "How are you, son?"

"I'm fine. But Justus isn't so good."

Vincent's heart fell even though Brian had only confirmed his suspicions. It'd been ten days since Justus came and got the ring, and the silence since then had grown ominous. Neither he nor Angela returned his calls, which he took to mean they'd both disappeared into the Witness Protection Program or things had gone badly and they'd retreated to their respective corners to nurse their wounds.

Nodding as if he knew all about it, he said, "That's why I'm here."

Brian pointed him to an elevator hidden beneath the curve of the stairs. "He's up on the third floor. I think he's between clients. You can go on up."

When the elevator slid open with a ding, Vincent stepped off and took a minute to get his bearings. Beautiful, sunny, open room. High ceilings. Blue mat on the floor. Desk, chair, table. Miscellaneous equipment, including a huge silver ball that looked like it belonged in some kid's yard. He detected movement out of the corner of his eye and, turning, saw Justus furiously doing one-armed pull-ups with his left hand on some exercise contraption—a Smith machine, wasn't it?— over by the window. Up and down he flew, grimacing with every one, his feet never touching the floor, his arm muscles bulging so violently Vincent wondered if he wouldn't rip the seams of his short-sleeved white polo shirt. He must have done twenty or thirty within a minute, and God only knew how long he'd been at it. His paternal instincts, long dormant where Justus was concerned, awakened and kicked into overdrive, tying his gut into knots.

Eventually Justus tired himself out and dropped to the

floor, panting, his face dripping with sweat. He didn't glance his way nor did he appear to hear Vincent even though Vincent was not particularly quiet as he crossed the hardwood floors and mat to where he stood. Justus's morose, exhausted expression did not match the bright warmth of this lovely space or the pulsating energy of the clients downstairs; Vincent felt like he'd entered a funeral home.

"Hello, Son."

Justus started and turned, giving Vincent a brief glimpse of a young face so lost and forlorn he was immediately catapulted back to that black time after Sharon first died and he'd wondered if grief wouldn't kill them all. But then Justus collected himself enough to shutter his expression and give him a surly stare instead.

"What's up, Pops?"

The bottomless pain in Justus's eyes—underneath the bravado—told Vincent things were much worse than he'd thought. "I . . . came to exercise. I thought I'd say hello."

"Oh," Justus grunted. He found a white towel in a chair, shook it out, and used it to wipe a minute smudge on the window, then wiped his own face with it. "Now's not really a great time. I've got a client coming soon, and all."

"Oh." Vincent rubbed the back of his neck and tried for a nonchalant, nonjudgmental tone. "I've been wondering what happened with Angela."

Justus's face tightened. Shoving a hand deep in the pocket of his black warm-up pants, he pulled out the ring box and gave it to him. "Let's just say I won't be needing this."

Vincent's heart sank. He'd been carrying the ring around? In his pocket? For God's sake, how bad did this boy have it? "What happened, Justus?"

"I proposed. She said no."

"But why?"

Justus shrugged, as if he'd gotten over it long ago and couldn't understand Vincent's continued interest in the topic. "You'll have to ask her." He stalked off toward the elevator. "I really need to get back to work, so if you don't mind—"

Vincent reached out and caught Justus's arm as he went past. Justus jerked away, looking equally surprised and irritated. Vincent's growing alarm made him forget about his intention to keep his tone bland and non-combative; his voice rose an octave. "What about Maya?"

Justus's hands found his hips and his feet widened into the fighting stance Vincent knew so well. A muscle throbbed visibly in his temple. "Angela's letting me keep her. She's moving to the D.C. office of her firm." Again he turned away toward the elevator. "Now, if that's all—"

"That's not all!" Vincent's voice boomed through the air like a shot fired from a cannon. Justus immediately went rigid, making him regret his loss of control. But what was he supposed to do with the inmates running the asylum? He put one fist on his hip and pointed at Justus with the other hand. "I want you to tell me how this happened," he said, vaguely aware he must look and sound like Yul Brynner in outtakes from *The Ten Commandments*. "And then I want you to tell me how you're going to fix this mess!"

"Fix it?" Furious, his face twisted beyond all recognition, Justus threw his arms wide, lashing out at some unseen enemy. "What the hell do you expect me to do? You think I have magic slippers I can click together three times and make this whole thing go away?"

Vincent's bewilderment battled with his fury. What on earth could be so bad? They loved each other, ergo they should get married. What was complicated about that? "What did you say to her?"

"I told her I wanted to get married—to be a family—and she practically spat in my face!"

Vincent had a brief flare of comprehension. He smacked his forehead, unable to keep the exasperation out of his voice. "For God's sake, Son! You can't propose and make it sound like a corporate merger! Haven't you learned anything? You've got to tell her you love her and—"

Justus lunged forward a couple of steps, as if he wanted to go for his throat, and Vincent resisted the blind instinct to dive for cover. "I did tell her I love her!" Justus roared, his eyes bulging like a gecko's. "I did everything but kiss her feet! What more do you want?"

Flabbergasted, Vincent could only stare, his mouth flapping like a flag in the breeze. He was totally at a loss. Never in a million years had he dreamed Angela would turn Justus down outright—not with the way she looked at him. Taking a moment to regroup, he paced away, rubbing his forehead. He turned back to see Justus watching him, his jaw rigid enough to cut diamonds. "I don't understand, Justus," he said quietly. "I know she loves you."

"Yeah?" Justus snorted. "Well, you should mention it to her because I don't think she's up on current events. She told me to my face I'm not the right man. I guess she thinks I'm not good enough for her."

"Not good enough? That's ridiculous!"

Justus stared incredulously. "Wow. I thought for sure you'd understand how Angela felt since I was never good enough for you, either."

Hanging his head, Vincent exhaled a long, choppy breath. What could he say? "I guess we never understood each other very well, did we, Son?"

A pulse ticked in Justus's temple. "No."

"I intend to work on that."

Justus looked away, shrugging impatiently.

Folding his hands together, Vincent absently tapped his forefingers against his lips and paced in a loose circle while he thought of a plan. "Well," he said finally, "you've just got to go back and try again. Tell her—"

"*What*?" Justus recoiled as if he'd said Justus needed to try sword swallowing again. "Try to keep up, will you? It's over." He flapped a hand. "She's going to D.C., Maya and I are staying here. I wish her well. I hope she has a great life."

Vincent couldn't stop his horrified gasp. "You can't be serious! You can't let that woman go—you'll regret it the rest of your life!"

Justus's shoulders went up and down again in an insolent shrug. "I gave it my best shot. I'm not going to beg anyone to marry me. Forget it."

A glare of anger clouded Vincent's vision as he stared into his son's proud, stubborn face. How dare he throw his chance at happiness away like this? Didn't he realize what he was giving up? Didn't he know how lucky he was to have found the woman of his dreams?

"How can you just throw Angela away?" he shouted. "Why, if I was lucky enough to have one more day with your mother—"

Justus went wild, lunging forward to jab two fingers in Vincent's face. "I told you never to mention my mother to me again," he screamed, spittle flying from his grotesquely contorted mouth. "You never gave a damn about her and you made her life a living hell until the day—"

Without conscious thought, Vincent raised his arm and backhanded Justus across the mouth, the first time in his life he could ever remember touching him in anger. Justus's head whipped around as the loud crack hung in the air and he froze, his blinking eyes wide with astonishment.

Vincent stared at him for long seconds, too choked up to speak, his body shaking uncontrollably. "I *worshipped* your mother," he said, his voice cracking on every other syllable. "She was—is—the first thing I think of in the morning and the last thing I think of at night."

Justus's eyes narrowed skeptically, but he wisely kept his mouth shut.

Vincent dragged in a breath and struggled to reduce the most profound thing in his life to a few sentences. "Every dime I made, I made for her. Every day I went into work I did it so she'd be proud of me. From the second I laid eyes on her, I never looked at another woman."

His constricted throat tightened to the point of pain; tears blurred his vision; his nostrils flared. Justus must have felt something of his emotion because his face softened and he stared curiously at him, his head tilted to one side.

"The mistake I made," Vincent said, walking slowly to the chair by the window and sinking into it, "was thinking she would always be here. Thinking the money was more important to her than I was." He smiled ruefully. "If I could have one more hour with your mother I'd give back every cent I ever made and go back to the flea-bit apartment we lived in when I was in law school." Swiping at his eyes, he looked up at Justus, who'd come to stand in front of him. "Don't make my mistakes. Don't have my regrets."

The stunned, round O-shape of Justus's slightly open mouth reminded Vincent of when Justus, age six, finally tried peas for the first time and discovered they weren't so bad, after all. It seemed too much to hope that Justus had changed his opinion of him—especially after all these years—but to his astonishment, Justus put a hand on his shoulder and squeezed it, as if to reassure him and relieve a little of his tension.

"Pop," he said, his voice gravelly and resigned, "I'd give thirty years off my life if I could change Angela's mind." He dropped his hand and turned away. "But I know I can't."

This time Vincent let him get on the elevator without stopping him. As the doors slid closed on Justus's heartbroken face, Vincent vowed—to himself, to V.J., and to Sharon—that even though Justus had given up on Angela, *he* never would.

He drove straight from the club to Angela's office downtown, even though he was dressed way too casually. In the hushed reception area he saw Larry Whittington's taste was still hit or miss—an elaborate but tasteful fresh flower arrangement sat on the receptionist's desk, and ugly but undoubtedly expensive original modern art lined the walls. When the receptionist peered up at him, he gave her his most charming smile, which she returned.

"I'm here to see Angela Dennis. My name is Vincent Robinson."

She adjusted her earpiece and reached to push a button on the complicated phone that looked like the control panel for a Boeing 747. "I'll call and tell her you're—"

"Ah . . ." Raising one finger to stop her, he chuckled conspiratorially and tried to look harmless. "I want to surprise her. She's not expecting me."

That, of course, was the understatement of the year. Angela seemed to have divorced herself from Justus and all things Robinson; at this point she'd probably be happier to see the Imperial Wizard of the Ku Klux Klan than she would to see him. Being no dummy, he wasn't going to let her hide behind this little gatekeeper and avoid him by pretending she was on her way to court or a meeting.

The poor woman's brow furrowed. "I'm not sure she's in her office—"

Vincent pointedly glanced over his shoulder at the empty chairs in the waiting area, then smiled again. "It's not busy now. No one will miss you for a second if you walk me back."

Pursing her lips, she smiled as if she knew when she was beaten. "This way." She led him down the hall, past various conference rooms and secretarial cubicles, to an office with a nice river view. "Here she is." Poking her head in the door, she said, "Angela, Mr. Robinson is here to see you."

Slipping in behind the woman, Vincent saw Angela doing something behind her desk, on top of which sat a large cardboard box. Her eyes looked flat and tired, her face tight and drawn. At the mention of his name, she paused in the act of putting something in the box and raised her head, an odd mixture of excitement and shock on her face. But when she saw it was him—she'd probably thought he was Justus—her face fell a little. Recovering quickly, she gave him a reserved smile as the receptionist left.

"Hello, Vincent," she said tartly. "I didn't realize we had an appointment today."

Stepping around some boxes on the floor, he crossed to her desk, picked up the phone, and listened for the dial tone. Her eyes narrowed to irritated slits. "No appointment, dear," he said, putting the phone back on the cradle. "I just thought I'd better come check your phone since it doesn't seem to be able to make any outgoing calls these days." He perched his hip on the side of her desk. "No need to call the phone company, though. It's working fine now."

She didn't smile but her eyes glinted with amusement as she grabbed a framed photo from the edge of her desk, placed it in the center of a large stack of newsprint, and began to carefully wrap it. "Can I help you with something?"

"You can tell me why you refused to marry my son."

As if she didn't want him to see her face, she dropped her head until only her gleaming brown hair was visible. Continuing to wrap the picture with military precision, she said, "We have no business getting married, Vincent, not that it's any of your business."

Leaning down and over, he tilted his face up to hers so she couldn't look away. "Why not? That's what people do when they're in love."

She jerked back and glared, then looked away. Finally finished wrapping the photo, she shoved it in the box. He heard a loud crack; she scowled. "We're not in love."

"Really? You could've fooled me."

Her accusatory, murderous gaze shot to his. "Did he send you here?"

Raising both eyebrows, he gave her his most imperious look. "No one sends me anywhere, dear. And my son doesn't need messengers."

After a minute her gaze wavered and fell. Turning, she snatched up another photo and began her laborious wrapping process anew. "Justus doesn't really want to marry me. He just proposed so he could give Maya a good home. I'm sure he felt forced into it."

The image was so ridiculous he gave a surprised snort, then threw back his head and roared with laughter. Eventually he had to take off his glasses, help himself to a tissue from the box on her desk, and dab at the tears in his eyes. Angela's arms crossed over her chest; she turned away to present him with a profile that looked like it belonged on Mt. Rushmore.

"Angela," he said when he'd caught his breath, "I've been trying most of my adult life to force Justus to do things he didn't want to do, and I don't think I've succeeded one time.

I couldn't make him wear shoes when he was one and didn't want to, or eat his veggies, or practice piano, or go to Yale." He stared at her wide, startled eyes. "You can bet your last dollar no one's forcing him to get married."

Her smooth brow furrowed. "He's doing it for Maya," she insisted.

"Oh." Reaching into his pocket, he pulled out the ring box and put it on Angela's desk. She gasped, then went rigid. "If that's true, I wonder why he came to get this from me."

She backed up a step, as if he'd laid a lit stick of dynamite on her desk. "What's that?"

"My wife's ring." He slid it across the desk to her. "Don't you want to see it?"

Her hands went up as if she was being held at gunpoint. "No."

Vincent decided the time for fun and games was over. Her attention seemed riveted on the ring box. Standing, he put his hand under her chin, tipped it up and stared, unsmiling, at her. "I'm disappointed in you, Angela. I never thought you were a coward."

"*Coward*?" she spluttered, jerking her head away. "How dare you—"

"Yes, a coward. Too scared to take a chance on Justus and too foolish to realize you're throwing happiness away with both hands. I feel sorry for you." Stunned speechless, she gaped at him, and he decided to take advantage of the silence. "Maybe you think Justus is a poor risk." He shrugged. "Maybe you're right. But you should know I knew another young man just like him once, and when he fell in love he devoted his whole life to his wife. He never thought twice about the dozens of women who came before her, and never looked at another woman after her."

Her stricken gaze held his. He saw her lips move, but no sound came out. *Who*?

"Me, dear." Hesitating, he let the words sink in. "Me." After a minute he cupped her chin again, stepped in to kiss her astonished face and moved out of her office, retracing his steps down the long hallway.

He left the ring with her.

Angela, dressed in a gray cotton warm-up suit with hooded jacket and white tank top, surveyed her apartment that night, stacking and rearranging her meticulously taped and labeled boxes. Her house was no longer a home. She'd reduced it to cardboard and packing tape, ready for moving and shipping the day after tomorrow. Only a plate, cup, and silverware remained out in the kitchen, her bedding and toiletries in the master bedroom. Packing Maya's room had been unbearable. She'd tackled that first, telling herself the whole time she'd recreate the room exactly in her new apartment in Washington. Hadn't she once thought she'd never be able to love another woman's child like her own? What a foolish, foolish woman she'd been. She'd happily give her right arm if Maya would appear this second and call her "Aunt Ang-la."

Sinking onto her sofa, she propped her feet on her ottoman and tried unsuccessfully not to think about how quiet and empty the apartment was without Maya, or how hollow she felt without Justus. Vincent certainly hadn't helped when he'd shown up unannounced today and muddied the waters. Why did he do it? Vincent was a master manipulator, of course, but what was he trying to do this time? Was he that committed to keeping her in Maya's life? Or . . . could it have something to do with Justus? Had he done it because he wanted Justus to be happy—did he think she could make Justus happy? And what about his comment—

A sharp knock at the door startled her out of her thoughts. She wasn't expecting anyone and thought about ignoring it— it would be just her luck if it was Vincent, coming back to give her volume two of his lecture. But whoever it was knocked again, more insistently this time, so she heaved herself tiredly to her feet, walked to the foyer, and checked the peephole.

Gasping, she swung the door open and let Ronnie in.

Chapter 26

Ronnie! She hadn't thought about him in weeks and wasn't particularly interested in seeing him now, although she was a little curious about why he'd come. He looked the same as ever—brown leather jacket, navy sweater and jeans, his curly black hair a little on the long side, his brown eyes wide and nervous behind his glasses—but her first nonsensical thought was how dull and washed out he seemed, how plain compared to Justus. Not because he was fair-skinned and Justus dark, but because of their personalities. Justus was vivid and intense, as stunning and bright as a rainbow, but Ronnie was muted grays and blacks. Justus was as layered and complex as Van Gogh's *Starry Night*; Ronnie, she now realized, was a stick figure.

What on earth could he want?

"Hi," she said warily. "What are you doing here?"

Dropping his head, he rubbed his hand across the back of his neck. A deep flush colored his face. "I want to talk to you—if you have some time."

She stepped aside by way of answer, closing the door after him and following him inside. When he got to the living room and saw all the boxes he froze, like he'd hit some invisible force field and couldn't take another step without risking electrocution. His head whipped around, and he stared at her in utter disbelief.

"What's going on?" he cried. "Where are you going?"

"I'm moving to the D.C. office of my firm."

His mouth fell open in horror, as if she'd told him she'd sublet a nice little apartment in Baghdad. "You're leaving?" He threw his arms wide; his voice rose steadily. "Just like that?"

For a minute she was too taken aback to answer. His obvious upset made no sense—he acted like her move was a personal affront to him and his ancestors. What the hell did he care if she lived in Cincinnati, or D.C., or Anchorage? She leaned her hip on the back of the chair, crossed her arms, and stared steadily at him. "What do you care where I live?"

He floundered, his mouth opening and closing without sound, like he'd escaped from a poorly dubbed *Godzilla* movie. "Ahhh, Angela."

Shoving his hands deep into his pockets, he stared at his shoes. Finally he looked up again, a strange new light shining in his eyes. She had the ridiculous idea he was going to tell her he wanted her back, and alarm tightened her chest. She couldn't deal with this—whatever it was—right now. Not tonight.

Holding up a hand to stop him before he said something to make them both uncomfortable, she said, "Ronnie—"

Suddenly he found his tongue. "I want you back. I keep thinking about how beautiful you looked the last couple of times I saw you. I must have been out of my mind to break up with you." The words rushed out in an unstoppable stream, like water from a broken sewer line. "I miss you. I made the worst mistake of my life when I cheated on you. I want to see if we can work things out." She watched in slow motion as he reached into his jacket pocket, pulled out a tiny jeweler's box in Tiffany robin's egg blue, and sank to his knees. Her mouth and the box hinged open simultaneously. "Will you marry me, Angela?"

Stupefied, Angela stared into the box and saw a stunning, round diamond in the classic platinum setting—her dream ring. Lightheadedness made the world swim in and out of focus. Perching on the edge of the chair suddenly required too much effort, so she slid down into its seat, slapped her hand against her forehead, and focused on taking one breath after the other so she wouldn't be forced into the humiliation of putting her head between her legs.

"Why are you doing this?" she asked breathlessly.

Scooting around on his knees to face her, Ronnie sat back on his haunches. His face vibrated with a passion she hadn't seen the whole three years they'd been together and couldn't believe she was seeing now. "Nothing is the same without you. I miss you. Forgive me."

"What about your little girlfriend?" She felt more baffled than bitter. What had happened to his lust for the other woman? Had it burned out so quickly? Or had the flame dimmed once he had the chance to be with her openly?

He waved a hand as if he wanted to dismiss all that past foolishness; he reminded her of a teenager who didn't like to be reminded he'd once been a bed-wetter. "That's over. Been over."

Was it supposed to matter that he'd broken her heart over something that turned out to be nothing? She stared, disbelieving. So that was it, then. Ronnie left her, played with someone else, then came back to her. "Oh, I see," she said tonelessly. "And what about the next time?"

"There won't be a next time. Can you give us another chance, Angela? We can have a June wedding and start trying to have kids right away—"

Angela's body jerked with surprise. Deep in his heart,

beneath the Ralph Lauren clothes and plain white cotton briefs, Ronnie was, it turned out, a street fighter. She'd never known.

"—and you could be pregnant by the end of the year." He pressed the box into her hand, as if he knew a thirty-four-year-old unmarried woman couldn't possibly resist a proposal from a man with a diamond from Tiffany. "Please, Angela." Taking her hand, he turned and raised it to his mouth for a lingering kiss with his cool lips, his mustache tickling her skin.

Angela raised the box, stared incredulously at the amazing ring, and tried to gather her thoughts.

Justus finished washing the last of the dinner dishes, dried his hands on the towel, flicked out the kitchen light, and walked down the hall to his bedroom. Maya, in her pink nightgown, floppy dog in hand, lay in the enormous bed, propped against the navy pillows. Her glazed, transfixed eyes told him she'd lapsed into The Zone and probably wouldn't hear him, much less answer, but he tried anyway. "Whatcha watching, Little Girl?" He sat on the edge of the bed.

"*Arthur*," she said, never looking away from the TV.

"*Arthur*?" He twisted around and saw she was right. "What about *SpongeBob*?"

"*SpongeBob* has no educational value whatsoever."

Justus snorted. The child, clearly, had been brainwashed by someone with a twisted, evil mind. "Well, it's almost eight o'clock, but you can stay up another few minutes and watch—"

She looked directly at him for the first time, her head moving back and forth in a firm no. "I need eleven hours of sleep so I won't be cranky."

Staring, aghast, at her, Justus wondered morosely why he missed Angela so much when Maya channeled her for him every time she opened her little mouth. He could not, in good conscience, let this child go to bed uncorrupted in some small way.

"Well," he said hopefully, "how about some juice before you go to bed?"

She glowered as if he'd tried to sell her a vial of crack. "No more sugar. I already brushed my teeth. See?" Opening her mouth in a wide grimace, she showed him what looked like ninety-six sparkling teeth.

"Oh." Defeated, Justus scooped her and her puppy up and walked down the hall to the guest bedroom. The place was still a mess, with golf clubs, a treadmill, and various free weights shoved against the wall to make room for her twin bed. He hadn't had the time to buy bedding for her, so he'd been forced to make due with black king-sized sheets from his bed.

"Sorry about the room, Little Girl." He swung her down and under the covers. "Maybe tomorrow or the next day we can go to the store and you can pick out some sheets you like."

Her mouth tightened and tiny shoulders went up and down against the black sheets.

Frustrated, he started to press the issue and try to get some sort of reaction from her—something that told him she was still a child who could take childish delight in small things like going to the mall, but something stopped him. As depressed as he was himself, he really had no business trying to cheer someone else up.

"Well, let's say your prayers."

He waited for her to put her hands together and close her eyes, but she stared stonily and rolled over to face the wall— the first open snub she'd ever given him. "God doesn't listen."

Why had he thought his heart couldn't break any worse than it had in the last few days? He wanted to argue the point, but he couldn't for the life of him think of a single example to prove her wrong. Finally he just dropped his head, murmured a quick prayer over her, kissed her cheek and slipped out, shutting her door behind him.

He roamed aimlessly around the living room, straightening books and newspapers on the coffee table. A beer sounded good, but not good enough to make the walk to the kitchen and get one. But he couldn't sit down, either. Angela, damn her, had done this to him—made him so agitated he couldn't sit, stand, or sleep, so detached from life he couldn't eat, drink, or care. God, how he hated her.

God, how he missed her.

He'd just decided to take his shower, get in bed, and watch ESPN all night, when he heard a light knock on the door, as if whoever it was knew a small child had just gone to bed and didn't want to disturb her. Intrigued, he passed through the foyer and opened the door. When he saw who it was, his knees almost buckled out from under him and his heart went haywire.

Angela stared at Justus and struggled to breathe through a throat that had evidently forgotten how the procedure worked. She tried not to stare too hungrily at him, but that was also impossible. Her mind went as blank as a sheet of notebook paper on the first day of school. Hopefully what she needed to say would reveal itself momentarily, but it didn't look good. Part of her problem was she'd finished talking to Ronnie then come right here—pausing only to brush her hair—so she hadn't had time to think about what she was doing or what she planned to say. She'd only known she had to come.

Justus gaped at her as if he'd witnessed her materializing out of thin air. He looked tired, she noticed right away, but his right hand, still poised on the doorknob, was no longer bandaged. His intent gaze swept over her from head to foot and then lingered on her face. He did not speak.

"Hi," she said weakly, her voice a croak.

"Hi."

Well, he hadn't slammed the door in her face or threatened to call the police to get rid of her, so she considered herself way ahead of the game. Still, he didn't look any too happy to see her. Mostly he looked . . . shocked.

She cleared her throat and prayed for a little more courage. "Can I come in?"

He blinked once, his gaze still riveted to her face. After a long pause he said, "Sure," but stayed where he was, blocking the door. Finally it seemed to dawn on him he needed to move out of the way and he hastily stepped back, swinging the door wide for her.

"I'm sorry I didn't call." As she walked past she paused right next to him in the narrow hallway, as he had done once before to her, and stared up into his face. He stiffened and she thought his shallow breathing sped up a little, but she couldn't tell for sure. "It couldn't wait until tomorrow." By tacit agreement they hadn't talked since the night she turned down his proposal, communicating only through voicemail. They'd agreed she'd come by tomorrow to say good-bye to Maya before she left town, but what she had to say wouldn't keep until then.

Nodding, he moved quickly away. When they got to the living room he turned to watch her, waiting. Tension hung heavy in the air, like ripe peaches dangling from a tree. Fear turned her hands to ice.

She took a deep breath. "I wanted to tell you what happened to me today."

His strained face tightened even further; he nodded sharply, once.

Licking her dry lips, she said, "Ronnie showed up at my apartment with a ring—"

Justus made a quiet, strangled sound.

"—and asked me to marry him."

She stared intently, willing him to say something—to react—but he just stared back with hard, glittering eyes. She'd hoped—ridiculously, as it turned out—for a jealous rage or outburst—something to tell her he still cared. Maybe he didn't. Her stomach plummeted sickeningly at the thought. If he'd washed his hands of her she could hardly blame him.

The only telltale signs of emotion she could detect were the insistent throbbing of his jaw and two bright patches of color high over his cheeks. His shoulders looked so tense she was surprised she didn't hear his muscles snapping like giant rubber bands.

Finally a crooked smile twisted his mouth. "Well, don't keep me in suspense."

"I told him no."

His eyes narrowed, and he cocked his head as if he wasn't sure he'd heard right. "*What*?"

"You heard me."

A silence mushroomed between them. He seemed to grow more agitated by the second until finally his whole body shimmied like Mickey Mouse in those old black-and-white cartoons. "Why?" One heavy, mocking eyebrow arched toward his hairline, and one side of his mouth rounded in a sneer. "Isn't this your whole little dream come true? Isn't this what you've been waiting your entire life for? A proposal from your Golden Boy?"

She flinched, but told him the truth. "Yes."

"Then why?" Wheeling away as if he'd been launched from a catapult, he stalked from one end of the living room to the other, then came to tower over her, waiting impatiently—angrily. He flung his arms wide. "Why?"

This was good, wasn't it? He wouldn't be so angry if he didn't care anything for her, would he? "Because I don't love him," she said quietly. "I realized today I never did."

Her words only seemed to further enrage him. "Wow." Cords thrummed in his neck. "The sidewalks are just littered with men you don't love, aren't they—"

"No—"

"*Aren't they*?" he roared, spittle flying from his mouth.

Angela felt like a young sapling bent double by the force of the wind. Never in her life had she been more scared, even though she knew he'd never hurt her. She wanted desperately to roll into a ball to protect herself from his fury, but she didn't. She held her ground, ignoring the violent, erratic thump of her heart.

"No," she said evenly. "Just Ronnie."

He paced in a loose circle, back and forth in front of her. Eventually he stopped, planted his legs wide, and jammed his fists on his hips. She heard him suck in a sharp, tortured breath. He seemed to be slowly falling apart; his chin trembled and his lips contorted as if an animal had died in his mouth and he needed to spit it out.

"Well." He kept his head turned away as if he couldn't stand the sight of her. "You'd better tell me what you mean because I don't have any idea what you're talking about."

"Justus," she whispered, nearly panting with fear, "can we sit down? Please?" She dared to creep forward and touch his hand but he snatched it away as if he was afraid he'd lose a finger. Glowering, he begrudgingly took two steps and sat on the edge of the sofa. She gratefully sank down right next to him.

He scooted away a little, another knife to her bleeding heart. Leaning his elbows on his knees, he stared at his hands. "Was there something you wanted to explain to me?" he

asked conversationally. Only the slight tremble in his inter-
twined fingers showed any emotion.

"Yes." Pressing a hand to her belly, she tried to calm her
roiling nerves and harness her thoughts. "When I saw Ronnie
today—when he proposed—the whole time I kept thinking I
didn't know what I'd ever seen in him. I didn't know why I
ever thought I loved him."

With Justus's head bent low over his thighs, all she could
see was the top of his head. She stared at him, desperately
looking for some sign of a reaction, but all she could see was
a slight stiffening of his broad shoulders. Well, at least he
hadn't laughed.

"And I kept thinking how different he was from you—"

Justus's hands balled into fists, but he didn't raise his head.
"Because he's a doctor and wears suits and I don't, you
mean."

The lack of self-confidence in his voice made her sick to
her stomach. "No!" she cried. "Because you're strong and
honest, and he's not. You're loyal and he's not. When you set
your mind to something—when you do something—you give
every part of yourself, and he doesn't."

Slowly he raised his head to stare at her with eyes that
flared with disbelief and, underneath that, reluctant hope. His
mouth dropped open into a round O-shape. She edged a little
closer to him on the sofa but couldn't find the courage to
touch him again.

"Seeing Ronnie brought me to my senses—I wouldn't have
Ronnie now, or anyone like him, for all the tea in China." She
paused, praying for more courage.

He went still, his wide-eyed gaze riveted to her face. "What
are you saying, Duchess?" he whispered so quietly she had to
read his lips to understand.

The loving use of the nickname, when she'd thought she'd

never be lucky enough to hear it again, undid her. Tears filled her eyes and quickly spilled over. "I'm saying I love you—"

"Oh, God."

"—and I'm sorry I was too much of a coward to tell you before."

He made a strange sound that was half laugh, half choke. Snatching up her icy hand, he pressed a hard kiss to her palm with trembling lips.

With her free hand she cupped his smooth jaw, enjoying the sudden hot flare in his eyes. "I need to be with you, Justus." She scooted closer until their knees touched. "There's no way I can move to D.C.—I don't know what I thought I was doing. I would never make it without you. We don't have to get married, but I just—"

"Now you're talking nonsense."

Reaching out, he grabbed her hips and hauled her onto his lap so her legs stretched out along the sofa, clamped his arms around her and buried his face in her neck. She cried out in surprise and joy, melding herself to the hard, strong body she'd missed so much. He inhaled deeply, as if he needed to revive himself by breathing her fragrance, his hot breath burning her skin.

"Do you believe I love you, Angela?" He pulled enough away to look up into her face. "Do you trust me enough to know I'd never hurt you like he did?"

Tears splashed down her cheeks and she didn't bother wiping them away. Life as she knew it—and the life she wanted—hung in the balance, but she still couldn't make herself give him the answer he needed. "I want to. But I can't believe I'd ever be that lucky."

His lips compressed and disappeared; she'd failed his test. He grabbed her upper arms and shook her. "Believe it." He stared into her eyes as if he meant to beat her into submission by force of his will. "*Believe it.*"

Something in her heart budded and quickly blossomed. When he looked at her like that—as if he was the lucky one for holding such a goddess in his arms—she felt ridiculous for questioning his feelings. "Maybe if you told me again—?"

"I love you." Planting his hands on the sides of her face, he kissed her forehead, eyes, and cheeks. "Love you, love you, *love you.*"

By the time his lips found her mouth she'd forgotten all about tears and doubts. Moaning into the kiss, she opened, surrendering everything—body and soul this time, not just body—to Justus. "Oh, God, I need you." Her hands tore at his polo shirt, ripping it off over his head so she could get to his warm, smooth skin. She tongued his throat and dragged her nails up and over his back and shoulders, wrenching a groan from deep in his chest. "Please make love to me, Justus. I need you now."

His need was as primitive and uncontrollable as hers. He deepened the kiss, thrusting, nipping and sucking until the faint but unmistakable coppery taste of blood filled her mouth. His hands slid under her tank top, burning the skin of her back to cinders. With a swift upward sweep he took off her tank and hoodie and his eager mouth immediately found the valley between her breasts and dove in. Laughing triumphantly, she threw her head back and arched forward, offering herself to him, but he stopped.

Raising his head, he slowly drew away, and stared dazedly at her. "Wait."

She didn't want to wait. Grabbing his hand, she flattened it against her breast. Justus's glittering eyes unfocused, and he rubbed his palm roughly over her nipple until she whimpered shamelessly. His mouth caught hers for another frantic kiss, but then he shoved her away again, this time abruptly pushing her off his lap and standing up. "I said *wait.*"

Shuddering with the effort to control her desire, Angela

smoothed her wild hair, crossed her arms over her chest, and tried to focus. "What is it?"

He paced away around the coffee table then turned to face her, giving her a tantalizing view of a bulging erection. Her mouth went dry. "We're not making love until I make sure we're on the same page—"

"We are!"

"—and we're both clear about what we're doing." He patted his pants pockets, front and back, then frowned. "Damn it! I gave it back to my father."

Angela shifted impatiently and wondered, with her lust-clouded brain, what could possibly be so important. She rose up on her knees, stretched out her arms, beckoning him, and managed half a seductive smile. "Come here."

"No," he said flatly. "I wanted to give you that ring."

She finally realized what he was talking about. "Oh." She got up, ran to the foyer on wobbly legs, grabbed her purse from the table, ran back and unceremoniously dumped it out on the coffee table. Her wallet, compact, and several lipsticks went flying; sunglasses and pens skittered across the table and fell to the floor. Angela found the jewelry box, snatched it up with a trembling hand and thrust it at Justus. "Here."

Justus took it and shot her a bewildered look. "Do you keep a supply on hand, or . . . ?"

"It's your mother's ring. Your father left it with me today."

His eyes narrowed into suspicious slits. "Do I need to know?"

Angela couldn't control her impatience. The deep, pleasurable ache between her thighs tightened and threatened to become painful. "Justus." Her voice dropped to a husky murmur she barely recognized as her own. Sidling up to him, she slid her hands across the hard, bare slabs of his chest, then down to rub over his heavy, engorged length. Immediately he went rigid and choked in a harsh breath. "Is there any way we can speed this up?" she whispered, her lips brushing his ear as she spoke. "I'm soaking wet."

His jaw dropped. He stared, aghast, at her for a few charged seconds, then nimbly dropped to one knee. "Angela, will you marry me?"

"Yes."

"Good." In one fell swoop he took the ring out of the box, shoved it onto her finger—she noticed only that it was big and seemed to fit—threw her over his shoulder in a fireman's carry, and surged to his feet. Dangling precariously, she shrieked and clung to his hard, round butt, enjoying the play of his muscles beneath her fingers. He took her into his dark bedroom and laid her gently on the bed, which was approximately the size of a tennis court.

Before she knew what was happening, he'd slid her warm-up pants, bra, and panties off. Then he moved away and a quick swishing sound told her he'd ditched his own pants as well. Clamping his hands on her hips, he dragged her to the edge of the bed so her legs hung over the side—she loved it when he played the caveman and slung her around like a sack of wheat!—then slid away and took a position somewhere near her feet. "Spread your legs for me."

"Oh, God," she moaned and then did as she was told. He settled her calves over his shoulders and did not bother with teasing her this time, instead zeroing in on the hard little nub that was the center of her existence and scraping it gently with his teeth. Throwing her arms over her head she arched, writhed, and mewled, climaxing almost immediately, hurtling through time and space, where the only things that existed were Justus, the endless, wracking pleasure he gave her, and her own cries.

Justus lingered, nuzzling her sex and kissing her thighs. Finally he surged up over her and took her mouth in a deep, frenzied kiss. "I missed you." The raw pain in his voice revived her a little; reaching up to cup his face she realized with a distant surprise that his cheeks were wet. Was he crying? "Don't ever do that to me again, Angela," he warned softly. "You almost killed me. I felt dead without you."

"Shhh. Don't say that."

Catching her hands in one of his, he slammed them up over her head, pinning them to the bed and holding her in place. With his free hand he took his penis and rubbed it insistently against her tender, aching sex; she cried out, desperate for him to take her.

"I swore I'd never forgive you." He stroked and circled her sex. "I wanted to punish you for hurting me like that."

"Justus, *please*," she begged, pumping her hips against him. "Please. I need you now. *Right now*." Leaning over her, he teased her with a light kiss. Angela strained to reach him, to catch his elusive lips, but he levered up on his elbow and stayed out of reach. Her body, no longer recognizable as her own, thrashed and whimpered brazenly. Having just experienced a climax that by rights should have torn her body in two, she'd expected her body's raging fever to burn off a little. It hadn't. If anything, it burned even brighter.

"Please come inside. *Please*."

He stroked over her again; she encouragingly widened her legs and angled her hips, but still he made her wait. She heard the satisfaction, and the strain, in his voice. "Don't you think I should punish you—just a little, Duchess?"

She was his to do with as he wished, and she may as well admit it. On this night, in the complete darkness, there was only the sound of his voice and the feeling of his heavy body, now growing damp with sweat, pressing her down against the cool bed. In the dark she could say anything and he wouldn't see her vulnerability, her need, or her tears as she cried. The dark would protect her if she admitted what she'd hidden in the deepest corners of her heart.

"I need you, Justus. Don't punish me." Tears ran down her

temples to wet the sheet. She heard the sharp hiss of his breath and felt his absolute stillness as he waited. "It was punishment enough not to see you every day—and to see how much you hated me. I was dead, too. I can't live without you. I don't want to live without you. Not ever."

Justus went wild, releasing her hands, grabbing her face and rewarding her for her courage and honesty with a long, deep, wet kiss. She clung, twining her arms around him like wisteria around a trellis. Breaking free, he flipped onto his back, bringing her on top of him. She straddled him eagerly and poised herself over him. "Tell me."

"I love you, Justus." She lowered herself, inch by inch, onto him. He stretched and filled her; the exquisite tightness of her body clamped around his made them both moan. "I love you."

His hands found her hips, anchoring her in place as he slowly began to move, grinding her against him. "Show me."

She did. Clutching the headboard for leverage, she rode him while his hips bucked so violently beneath her she thought they might both tumble off the bed. Leaning back the other way, she held his ankles, circling her hips until her pleasure burst open, sending spasms of satisfaction to every corner of her body. Justus rolled her again, coming on top of her and pounding so furiously her head banged the headboard. She wrapped her legs tight around him, absorbing every thrust until finally he threw his head back and shouted her name over and over.

Collapsing exhausted onto the bed, he gathered her against him and cradled her in his arms. The last thing she heard as she drifted off to sleep was his voice, still husky with emotion. "I've always loved you, Duchess. And I always will."

Angela came awake slowly. Cracking her eyes open the tiniest slits, she saw sunlight glowing behind Justus's heavy taupe Roman shades and realized it was morning. Justus's body, emitting heat like a radiator, was molded tightly to her from behind, his arms linked around her waist in a death grip. She was astonished she'd been able to sleep so well pressed together like this, but she had. Her body was deliciously sore, her limbs heavy. She smiled drowsily, stretching a little. He shifted and nuzzled her nape.

"How do you like the ring?"

The ring! With all the excitement she'd forgotten entirely about it. Snatching her hand out from under the covers, she held it up for inspection and gasped. "Oh, my God!" The most glorious ring she'd ever seen—ruby and diamonds—swallowed most of her finger. As she angled her hand this way and that, sunlight hit it, shooting rainbows to the walls and ceiling. "Have you been stealing from Elizabeth Taylor?"

He smiled against her neck. "I take it you don't want a plain diamond instead."

She threw her right hand over her left to protect it, and clutched both hands to her chest. "Don't you touch this ring!" When he made no move to take the ring away, she cautiously uncovered her hand and studied it again. "Ohhh, Justus. This is the most beautiful thing I've ever seen. I'm not sure I should wear it. Maybe it should stay in a safe, or—"

He took her hand and kissed it. "It's staying right here. It needs to be worn. You're acting like you've never seen it before. Didn't you look at it when my father gave it to you?"

"No. I didn't want to see it."

Just then a muffled thump down the hall reminded them they weren't entirely alone. Dropping her hand, she jerked away from Justus and whipped around to face him. "Maya!" Frantically smoothing her hair, she cried, "We can't let her see us like this!"

Justus stared, unsmiling, at her. "Oh, yes we can. We're getting married. We share a bed. She'll get used to it."

Angela snatched the sheet up. "Not like this! We don't even have clothes on!"

Frowning, Justus slid leisurely out of bed, opened a drawer, and pulled out some pajama bottoms. "Well, you can use my robe in the bathroom. But I'm going to tell her you're here. Hurry up."

With a nervous shriek, Angela scurried into the bathroom. She'd barely shut the door when she heard the flap of linens, as if Justus had thrown the duvet over the bed, and Justus's voice. "Hey, Little Girl," he said brightly. "Did you sleep good?"

"Yeah. Can I have some Sugar Smacks?"

Angela heard Justus chuckle as she slid on his navy silk robe. "I thought you told me yesterday sugary cereals weren't a healthy breakfast."

Angela almost laughed aloud. She'd thought Maya never listened to a thing she said, but maybe a couple of things here and there had accidentally sunk into her little brain.

"Well," Maya said thoughtfully. "This one time won't hurt."

Angela hurriedly turned on the water to brush her teeth. As she expected, Maya's sharp ears heard every sound she made. "Who's in there, Uncle Justus?"

Justus paused. "I have some really exciting news for you, Little Girl."

Maya clapped her hands and Angela heard the squeak of bedsprings as she bounced up and down. "What is it?"

"I'm getting married."

"Yay!" More clapping. "Can I be the flower girl?"

"I'm sure that can be arranged."

Angela rinsed her mouth and hurriedly brushed her hair. "Who is it?"

Angela took a deep breath, opened the door, and stepped out into the bedroom. "Me."

Maya sat on the duvet, her back against the pillows; Justus sat on the edge of the bed at her feet. When Maya heard the door, her head swiveled around and she gaped at Angela as if she'd seen Santa Claus in the flesh. For an arrested moment Angela waited breathlessly, not daring to blink, but then Maya scowled and Angela's heart sank. Of course she'd be angry at her, and Angela could hardly blame her.

"Hi, Sweetie."

"Hi," Maya said sullenly.

Aware of Justus's encouraging smile, Angela gingerly crept to the bed and sat on the other side. "I see you're really mad at me."

Maya's eyes lowered and her lips poked out into a pout. She fidgeted with the covers, smoothing the duvet, but said nothing.

"I don't blame you."

Maya's fingers stilled.

Angela's heart beat so furiously she had a hard time catching her breath. "I'm sorry I broke my promise to you. I was wondering if you might give me another chance."

Maya's suspicious gaze flicked back up to hers, but she didn't answer. Angela resisted the urge to smooth her hair or kiss her—now was clearly not the time. "Maybe you can just give it a day or two," she suggested. "See if you feel like forgiving me. Would that be okay?"

Justus stirred. "I think that sounds fair, Maya. What do you think?"

"Okay," Maya said through tightly compressed lips.

"Great!" Angela smiled with far more enthusiasm than she felt at the moment, then stood and moved around the bed toward the door. "Well, I don't know about you, but I'm starved." She turned to Justus and said blandly, "Do you have any cereal? I really feel like some Sugar Smacks or something."

Maya gasped while Justus struggled not to smile. "You don't eat Sugar Smacks!"

"Oh, sure I do," Angela said casually. "Every now and then I just have to have some."

Maya catapulted off the bed. "I'll show you!"

Sudden tears clogged Angela's throat and blinded her. She was desperately trying to blink them back when she felt Justus put a light, supportive hand to the small of her back. Her heart swelled and engulfed her chest.

She swiped discretely at her eyes and smiled down at Maya. "Let's go."

Epilogue

Justus leaned against the railing and stared across the white sand and out to sea, where the pink sun hovered on the horizon. The soft evening breeze provided a refreshing change from the day's heat, although today hadn't been nearly as hot as he'd feared. Across the terrace, on the other side of the round tables covered with fluttering white cloths, floating candles, and bright tropical floral arrangements, stood his wife laughing with Maya, Lena, Carmen, Brian, and some other guests. Maya, a halo of fragrant red-and-white flowers ringing her head, twirled happily in her pink floral gown until her long skirt flared out like a bell, no doubt to give the guests the full benefit of the dress. But Justus only had eyes for his wife.

Angela, at his request, wore her hair free and wavy, a huge white flower tucked behind one ear. The spaghetti straps of her filmy white wedding dress kept slipping off her gleaming brown shoulders, tempting him. That sight, combined with the way the light wind blew the panels of her skirt away from her long legs, made quite a lethal combination. He was having a terrible time keeping his hands to himself, so he'd slipped across the terrace to appreciate her from afar. In a few minutes he supposed they would cut the stupid cake and then he could have his bride all to himself for the rest of the night.

"She's beautiful, isn't she?"

Startled, Justus turned to see Vincent, wearing a tan linen suit much like his own, arrive at his side carrying some fruity island cocktail that looked like a milkshake. He'd followed his gaze to stare at Angela.

"You got that right," Justus told him. He waited for that sinking feeling, the wordless tightening of all his nerves he always felt when he talked to his father, but it never came. Maybe it wouldn't. "Thanks for bringing us to Anguilla. Everything was beautiful."

Vincent shrugged carelessly, but a bright flush colored his cheeks and a slight smile turned up the corners of his mouth. "Yeah, well. I figured that was the only way I'd be invited."

Justus laughed. "Nah. Angela would have snuck you an invitation. She seems to like you for some reason."

Vincent grinned delightedly, but then he stared off at a sailboat on the horizon and his smile faded. "I wish he were here. I miss him."

Justus's chest tightened. His mind had never veered very far from V.J. and Carolyn since they'd arrived the other day. "He's with us."

Vincent pressed his lips tightly together and nodded. "I know. I'm glad we scattered their ashes here. Angela was right about that." His nostrils flared repeatedly. "V.J. would have been pleased."

"Yeah." Justus clapped his hand on his father's back. "Well, this was where they had their honeymoon."

"Yeah." Vincent cleared his throat. "I thought . . . maybe we could play a little chess when you get back home."

Startled and ridiculously pleased, Justus grinned. "If you're up for it. I've learned a few tricks since the last time we played."

"I'll just bet." Smiling, Vincent sipped his drink and then nodded in Angela's direction. "I think you'd better go."

Justus turned to see her beckon him with her hand; she was now standing on the edge of the dance floor. Over on the edge of the terrace a pianist began to play the familiar chords of "A Kiss to Build a Dream On." Joy swelled his chest until he felt as light and airy as the fragrant breeze. He dropped his hand from his father and started eagerly for his wife.

"Yeah," he said. "They're playing our song."

Dear Readers,

Thank you for picking up this copy of *Risk* and spending some time with Justus, Angela, and Maya. I fell in love with these characters, and I hope you did, too.

What did you think of Justus? Do you like your romance heroes a little bit arrogant, strong, funny, moody, protective, and *really* sexy? I sure do. I thought it would be fun to make Justus a wild card . . . to throw him into a scene and see what outrageous thing he'd do. He didn't disappoint me.

As for Angela, well, I admit I know a little bit—okay, a *lot*—about tightly wound control-freak lawyers who like things neat. I used to be one, but my kids cured me years ago.

Speaking of kids . . . do you know any little girls like Maya? I do, but I'm not naming names. Let's just say I have *intimate* knowledge of the complicated love affair a person can have with a child; I know about the breakfast struggle, the TV struggle, the hair struggle, and, oh yeah, the clothes struggle. Fortunately, I also know how fun children are, how sweet freshly bathed children smell, and how precious they look when they're *finally* tucked in bed for the night.

If you have time, please stop by my Web site. You can find it at *www.AnnChristopher.com*. I'd love to hear from you.

Well, I'm off to work on another story. I've got an idea for a hero who's going to make Justus look like a choir boy . . .

Happy reading!

Ann

Grab These Other
Dafina Novels
(trade paperback editions)

Grab These Other
Dafina Novels
(mass market editions)

Some Sunday
0-7582-0026-9

by Margaret Johnson-Hodge
$6.99US/$9.99CAN

Forever
0-7582-0353-5

by Timmothy B. McCann
$6.99US/$9.99CAN

Soulmates Dissipate
0-7582-0020-X

by Mary B. Morrison
$6.99US/$9.99CAN

High Hand
1-57566-684-7

by Gary Phillips
$5.99US/$7.99CAN

Shooter's Point
1-57566-745-2

by Gary Phillips
$5.99US/$7.99CAN

Casting the First Stone
0-7582-0179-6

by Kimberla Lawson Roby
$6.99US/$9.99CAN

Here and Now
0-7582-0064-1

by Kimberla Lawson Roby
$6.99US/$9.99CAN

Lookin' for Luv
0-7582-0118-4

by Carl Weber
$6.99US/$8.99CAN

Available Wherever Books Are Sold!

Visit our website at **www.kensingtonbooks.com**

Look For These Other
Dafina Novels

If I Could
0-7582-0131-1

by Donna Hill
$6.99US/**$9.99**CAN

Thunderland
0-7582-0247-4

by Brandon Massey
$6.99US/**$9.99**CAN

June In Winter
0-7582-0375-6

by Pat Phillips
$6.99US/**$9.99**CAN

Yo Yo Love
0-7582-0239-3

by Daaimah S. Poole
$6.99US/**$9.99**CAN

When Twilight Comes
0-7582-0033-1

by Gwynne Forster
$6.99US/**$9.99**CAN

It's A Thin Line
0-7582-0354-3

by Kimberla Lawson Roby
$6.99US/**$9.99**CAN

Perfect Timing
0-7582-0029-3

by Brenda Jackson
$6.99US/**$9.99**CAN

Never Again Once More
0-7582-0021-8

by Mary B. Morrison
$6.99US/**$8.99**CAN

Available Wherever Books Are Sold!

Check out our website at www.kensingtonbooks.com.

Check Out These Other
Dafina Novels